"Relax," Nicholas murmured, and kissed her throat again, then traveled back to her lips. Waves of hot pleasure coursed through her as his hands wandered over her hips and back again, his fingers spreading around her back, then moving up over her ribs until they reached the swell of her breast. Georgia shivered as he caressed them as lightly as a feather.

"Nicholas!" she gasped against his mouth.

"What?" he asked with a lazy smile, "You don't like it?"

"No, I think I do . . . I . . . I was just surprised."

"Oh, Georgia, Georgia, we have some educating to do," he said, as he pulled the sheet down to her waist.

Georgia had so much to learn—on this night of love that stretched so long before her. . . .

"A WONDERFUL LOVE STORY . . . KATHERINE KINGSLEY HANDLES A POWERFUL THEME DEFTLY."
—Maggie Osborne,
author of *Emerald Rain*

No Greater Love

Katherine Kingsley

AN ONYX BOOK

ONYX
Published by the Penguin Group
Penguin Books USA Inc., 375 Hudson Street,
New York, New York 10014, U.S.A.
Penguin Books Ltd, 27 Wrights Lane,
London W8 5TZ, England
Penguin Books Australia Ltd, Ringwood,
Victoria, Australia
Penguin Books Canada Ltd, 10 Alcorn Avenue,
Toronto, Ontario, Canada M4V 3B2
Penguin Books (N.Z.) Ltd, 182-190 Wairau Road,
Auckland 10, New Zealand

Penguin Books Ltd, Registered Offices:
Harmondsworth, Middlesex, England

First published by Onyx,
an imprint of New American Library,
a division of Penguin Books USA Inc.

First Printing, April, 1992
10 9 8 7 6 5 4 3 2 1

To my goddaughter, Georgia Jay,
whose magic inspired this book.
And to all the men in my life
who nurtured me, humored me,
and endlessly listened
during its writing.

Greater love hath no man than this,
that a man lay down his life for his friends.

John, 15:13

Prologue

March 26, 1819

"Nicholas! Nicholas, where are you? Nicholas! Answer me!"

His mother's voice, raised in panic, just reached him over the pounding of the waves, the terrible sound of splintering wood, the cry of men's voices, the high wailing of the wind.

He tried to call out to her, but his words were cut off by a blast of salt water. His arms clung desperately to the rope webbing as another wave came roaring over him. But this time the wave was stronger than his ten-year-old arms, and it ripped him from the railing, violently throwing him through the air. Something sharp met with his thigh and he felt a hot stab of pain, and then suddenly the cold water of the pitching sea. It came up into his nostrils, his mouth, his eyes, threw him about like just one more piece of flotsam wrenched from the sinking ship.

"Mama! Papa!" he gasped, frantically trying to keep his head above water, to breathe in precious air, to look around him for something, anything to grab onto. But there was nothing save for the huge waves, the distant rocks, and the sight of the ship tipping crazily at an angle and slowly disappearing beneath the water.

There was nothing after that but the endless struggle to stay afloat, his limbs impossibly heavy, his lungs burning. And there was the fear. God, there was the fear. He was so frightened that he wanted to give up right there and then and let the water take him, just to extinguish the fear. But something kept him going. Some stupid wish to live, to see his mother and father again, maybe even his dog, if he ever made it home.

And then something caught at his legs and wrapped

around them, pulling him down . . . down, until the water covered his head with blackness and choked him.

"No! No! Oh, God, please, no!"

Nicholas shot up in bed, his body covered with cold sweat despite the heat of the night. He was shaking from head to foot, his heart pounding like an entire timpani section. The young girl in the bed beside him was watching him with enormous black eyes, looking as frightened as he was feeling.

"Damn," Nicholas muttered. He never let them stay the night, just in case this very thing happened. He must have fallen asleep after their last very heated exchange.

"Go," he said in Hindi. "Leave me. Go now. My man will pay you."

She pulled on her wrapper and scurried away without protest, and Nicholas took a deep shaky breath, then threw aside the thin linen sheet and went over to the window, leaning his head out. There wasn't much chance of finding a breeze, but after the dream he always had an irrational desire to fill his lungs with air.

Twenty-nine years old, and he was still having nightmares. He'd hoped he'd outgrow them, but they continued to come like clockwork. He had learned early on to avoid sleep as much as possible. As a child he'd sneaked out of the house and walked or ridden for hours on end. He still did. Now he had sex to distract him, and there was always work, which often kept him busy till the early hours, but he couldn't avoid sleep entirely, and in the end the dream would come. Not every night, sometimes not even every week, but eventually it came, and he drowned all over again, as if once hadn't been enough.

It was typical of his life that what had drowned him had in the end saved him, for the fishermen had pulled him out of the water, probably to save the nets, and saving his life only as an afterthought. He discovered later that in the hours he'd been in the water, he'd been swept around the coast, far away from the site of the shipwreck. He'd also discovered later that he'd been the only survivor. When he was judged fit, after nearly dying again, this time from blood poisoning after the gash in his leg had turned septic, he'd been sent home to England.

Nicholas sighed heavily. Well, it hadn't exactly been

home, although Ravenswalk was as near to his beloved house as one could get. Nothing could quite compare to Raven's Close, despite the grandeur of Ravenswalk itself. Nothing could really touch the beauty of the gardens his mother had created, nor equal the quiet loveliness of the house. A house that should have been filled with laughter and happiness, with a family that belonged to it, instead had stood empty for almost twenty years. For the ten years after the shipwreck, he had waited impatiently for the day that he could finally claim the Close as his own. Now, thanks to Jacqueline and her foul lies, he didn't even have that hope anymore. Or maybe he did. Maybe he did.

His eyes flickered over to his desk, where his uncle's crumpled letter gleamed in the candlelight, the first communication of any kind in nearly ten years. He walked over to the desk and unpicked the ball, his eyes scanning the brief contents again.

Come home, Nicholas. Things are wrong and must be put right. Please, Nicholas, come home.

The handwriting was spidery and shaky, very unlike the usually precise earl. His uncle didn't elaborate, either, also unlike him. Just: come home.

Nicholas rubbed his eyes. What the hell was that supposed to mean? Was it a royal command, and if so, why? Was his uncle asking for forgiveness? Had he suddenly decided after all this time that Nicholas was innocent? Or maybe he was unwell and didn't want to die without doing the forgiving himself. After all, Nicholas was his brother's only child, and his uncle was a big believer in family obligation.

"Damnation!" Nicholas said with annoyance. "Why should I go home to accept forgiveness for something I didn't do?"

But the fact of the matter was that he did want forgiveness, very much. It had been hell living without any family at all, not out of choice, but because he'd been cast out. He'd missed seeing young Cyril go through his childhood; he had, in fact, missed his crusty old uncle, damn him anyway. The only thing the man was really guilty of was poor judgment—that and not trusting Nicholas' word. Was he really going to hold that against him?

Nicholas scowled and threw the letter back down on the writing table. Going home would be very nice, if he had some kind of assurance that Jacqueline had been tossed out on her ear or had died of the pox. No—better yet—if he knew that she had been horribly disfigured by the pox. Oh, yes. That would indeed be justice.

He grinned, thinking of a badly scarred Jacqueline, condemned to wearing a veil for the rest of her life, knowing no man would want to look upon her or touch her ever again. But sadly, the latest word as of last December had it that she was as alive and lovely as ever and up to her old tricks. His grin faded as a rush of anger took the place of amusement.

He'd be damned if he let Jacqueline keep him from Raven's Close any longer. She'd had too many things her own way. And maybe he could find a way to make her life as miserable as she'd made his.

Yes, going home might be very nice indeed. It would take some time to get there, as travel by land from India was nearly impossible, but that couldn't be helped. Oh, what the hell. He might have to cross a few bodies of water, but it would be worth it in the end.

Raven's Close. His heart lightened at the very thought. Nicholas sat down at his desk and began looking through his papers, beginning the task of sorting out his affairs.

1

Georgia clutched her reticule in her lap, watching in a daze as the scenery passed by. She felt as if she'd just been traded at Tattersall's like so much horseflesh, without so much as a by-your-leave. She was scarcely in a position to argue, and she supposed she should be delighted to be taken into the employ of Lady Raven, whose reputation hailed her as a lady of the highest fashion. But Lady Raven also had a reputation of being difficult and demanding, at least within the trade. Georgia had heard harassed milliners and fellow modistes complaining bitterly about her temper, her stinginess, and her impossible demands. That was more than enough to give Georgia pause.

She didn't mind upheaval; she'd seen enough of that in her twenty-two years. But she did wish that she knew what had caused Lady Herton to suddenly let her go. She'd thought they'd gotten along quite well. Georgia frowned, catching her lip between her teeth. It would be terrible if Lady Herton had discovered her husband's late-night forays, which might explain why she'd made the extraordinary statement she had. "Pretty dresses do not mean as much to me, Mrs. Wells, as high moral standards." On the other hand, Lady Herton was a bit of a loose screw, and could just as easily have meant that her dress allowance would be better spent on the church.

Georgia sighed bitterly. If only people would consult her before they started playing the Almighty. She had never once been given the opportunity to make a decision about her life, as if she had no stake in it at all. She couldn't fault her father for dying: he could hardly have helped that. And she supposed it had been the logical thing to send her to the vicar and his wife when it had been her mother's turn to die. But to marry her to Baggie without consulting her on the matter was a bit much. And Baggie might have at least consulted her before he drove the farm into debt with his foolish schemes. He certainly might have consulted her before he decided to fall asleep on the highway in perfect position to be run over by the mail coach, leaving her with nothing but the clothes on her back.

The carriage made a wide turn through a pair of imposing stone gates and carried on down a long driveway. Georgia's heart turned over with nervous anticipation, but she reminded herself that her *maman* had taught her to make the best of a bad situation and to count one's blessings whenever possible. If she could find any blessing in this situation, she supposed it was that she was out of the city, which had half-suffocated her. She also no longer had to tolerate old Lord Herton tottering up to the attic in his cups, looking for a bit of comfort, as he'd put it. It wasn't easy having to push an old drunken gentleman with rheumatism half-down the stairs every Saturday night, but what was she to do, when he'd had the key to her door?

Her eyes widened as Ravenswalk came into sight. It was magnificent—no, it was spectacular. It was certainly quite the most beautiful thing she'd ever seen. Georgia's heart had never quickened at the sight of a pile of stone before, but it quickened now. Oh, she had liked Baggie's farm and had enjoyed having a house of her own, but this was entirely different. This house was enormous, baroque in style, faintly reminiscent of the pictures she'd seen of Versailles. The stone glowed like the sunshine itself, the lawns and gardens encircling it like the setting of a fine jewel.

She swallowed hard. Her mother had described houses like these in her wonderful stories about lords and ladies, and Georgia had thought those houses had come alive in her mind, but compared to the reality of Ravenswalk itself, her imaginings had been lifeless. Ravenswalk was a beautiful piece of art.

She thought she might be very happy here, after all, just to live surrounded by such beauty.

Three days later she changed her mind.

"So," Lady Raven said, looking Georgia up and down as if she were holding an audience with a scullery maid, "you are Mrs. Wells." She threw her gloves down on a table and walked around Georgia in a slow circle. "You made the dress you are wearing now?"

"Yes, my lady," Georgia said, thinking that this had to be one of the coldest faces she'd ever seen. Lady Raven was almost beautiful, but something in her face just missed. The structure of her bones was sound, the cheeks high, the nose thin and a trifle too long. She was younger than Georgia had anticipated, not more than thirty-two or three at most. Her hair was a light brown, her eyes slightly darker and set deeply in her head, but not unattractively so. She looked vaguely familiar, but Georgia couldn't think where she might have seen her. Perhaps it had been at Madame LaSalle's. They had been correct, the modistes. Lady Raven's figure was superb. She was tall and slender, her carriage regal, her neck long, her breasts well-proportioned to her height. Everything about her was correct. One sensed power about her, and confidence in that power. But Georgia couldn't help but feel as if she were looking into a mask. There was no real warmth on her face, but worse, her eyes were hard and calculating.

"It is inappropriate attire for your position. I have seen your work, Mrs. Wells. It will have to be better—much better—if you are to please me. I have only taken you on as a favor to Lady Herton."

"I shall try, my lady."

"Very well. You are very young. I had expected an older woman. You cannot be more than twenty. Where did you learn your skills?"

"I learned most of what I know from my mother before she died, my lady. I also spent a year in London working with Madame LaSalle before I began with Lady Herton. I am actually twenty-two, and so I have had time to gain experience at my craft . . ." She stopped because Lady Raven seemed slightly distracted. "Is there anything else, my lady?"

"Yes. I expect you to keep to yourself. There will be

no fraternizing with the staff, nor with the guests. You understand your position?''

"Yes, my lady," Georgia replied, thinking that it sounded as if she were about to be confined to a dungeon.

"You may use the grounds when there are not guests in attendance, and when you have finished work. Exercise is important for the health. I will not tolerate any trespassing into the main areas of the house unless you are summoned to my quarters. You may take your meals in your own quarters. The house steward will issue your orders to you, which you are to follow to the letter. I am sure we will march along famously if you heed these simple rules.''

"Yes, my lady." Georgia's heart dropped further with each pronouncement, with each second that went by in Lady Raven's company.

"You will do something about your hair. I cannot tolerate unruly curls, and you must look respectable. A cap would be appropriate, and I would have you dress in black or gray. I do not require a uniform. How long have you been widowed?''

"Two years, my lady."

"Very good. You surely must have appropriate clothes from your mourning. They will be suitable and will spare the expense. I would like to see you every morning at eleven, unless I order otherwise. I entertain frequently and so my wardrobe needs constant review and repair. We shall soon become accustomed to each other, I am sure. Thank you, Mrs. Wells. That will be all until tomorrow morning. I am sure you will soon settle into Ravenswalk.''

She gave Georgia a chilly smile and swept off, her back ramrod straight, her carriage impeccably graceful.

Georgia found her own spine stiffening. She swallowed hard against the lump that had formed in her throat. Gone was the magic that Ravenswalk had inspired in her, gone was the mist of fantasy she'd wrapped herself in for the last few days, fantasy she was so very good at producing. Gone was everything but the harsh realization that she was possibly in the most difficult situation she'd found herself in yet.

Lady Raven swept from her bedroom into her dressing room. She had a habit of sweeping, Georgia thought, her eyes burning from the long night of work. The daylight made her eyes water, but she did her best not to squint.

"Good morning, Mrs. Wells. I trust you have completed my evening dress?"

"Yes, my lady. Would you care to put it on so that I might make any appropriate alterations? It is hanging on the hook behind the screen." She was in a foul mood, Georgia thought with dismay. She could tell just by looking at her, for she had learned the signs long ago. In truth, she had been in a foul mood for a good week now, no doubt the result of her last amorous interlude not going her way. Georgia really didn't feel like suffering the consequences, but suffer them she would, no doubt.

Lady Raven vanished behind the screen, and just as quickly reappeared. "What is the meaning of this?" she demanded, the dress dangling from her outstretched hand, the delicate material crushed between her fingers. "This is not what I requested, Mrs. Wells. I told you in the most precise terms yesterday morning that I wished for *plaits,* did I not?"

"Yes, my lady, but there was not enough material available at such short notice. I thought the fullness of the skirt behind would please you, and the satin trimming—"

"Do not make excuses to me, my girl! I will not stand for it. The dress is unacceptable. You will take this absurdity back to your room, and you will make it right by six this evening."

"But, Lady Raven—"

"I will not hear another word. If you would like to be shown the door, then I am sure it is no problem of mine, although I caution you that I will give you no reference. Slovenly work is not tolerated amongst my acquaintances, Mrs. Wells, nor is impertinence. It is most certainly not tolerated here." She carelessly tossed the dress onto the back of a chair. "Bella? Bella, where are you?" she called, dismissing Georgia with an imperious wave of her hand. "Bella, why is my bath not ready?"

Bella, Lady Raven's personal maid, for whom Georgia

felt exceedingly sorry, came rushing through the door. "I'm so sorry, my lady. The water is still heating. There has been some upset downstairs, given that Lily's mother died last night, and she is late returning."

"Dismiss her," said Lady Raven. "I will not permit such laxness."

Bella's mouth opened and then shut. She knew better than to argue and lose her own job. They all did, Georgia thought, her fingers itching to slap Lady Raven's cold, self-absorbed face. They were all to pay because Lord Periweld hadn't succumbed to her ladyship's dubious charms and warmed her bed? Poor Lily. Her family depended on her wages since her father had been taken by the pox.

"What are you still doing here, Mrs. Wells?" Lady Raven turned the full force of her gaze on Georgia. "Have you not work to do?"

"Yes, my lady" Georgia stood very straight, trying very hard not to let her anger come through in any way. "I needed to know your preference, my lady. As I have no more white satin, my lady, and it is impossible to acquire any more before this evening, I thought you might consider a double row of silk flowers on the hem. I am sure if I begin now, that I can have the dress completed by six this evening."

Lady Raven considered. "Oh, very well, then. Leave me. What are you waiting for? Leave me now, I said! Bella, if my bathwater is not here within five minutes, you shall be gone from Ravenswalk as well. I suggest you do something about the situation."

Georgia collected the crumpled dress and quietly left, thinking that if she'd ever had murder in her heart, she had it now.

She wanted to cry when, ten minutes later, she saw poor Lily leaving, a small bundle of her possessions clasped to her chest, her head bowed, but her shoulders shaking with what must have been weeping. Georgia shook her head, feeling that Lady Raven surely had to be one of the most cruel, most dreadful women ever to have been put on the face of the earth. She inspired no loyalty from her staff, only fear and loathing. One could be summarily dismissed for nothing more than to be found holding friendly conversation with another member of the staff.

Georgia determined to send a portion of her wages that month to Lily. She rubbed her eyes, not because they held tears—she was far beyond that—but because she could hardly see straight after nearly two days without sleep. There were times that she thought Lady Raven spent most of her waking hours deliberately finding ways to torment the people who worked for her. Life at Ravenswalk almost made life with Baggie Wells seem like an idyllic dream.

The days went on. And on and on and on in one long, unceasing progression, with no hope for an end. If Georgia could have manufactured her own version of hell, this would be it. Every wicked soul would be sent directly to Ravenswalk to live under Lady Raven's charge for all eternity. There would be no hope for a reprieve, no forgiveness, just an unending procession of days and nights punctuated by Lady Raven's demands. Sleep? Who knew what sleep was? Food? Only when there was time. But fresh air was something she refused to give up. She made time for that, no matter what. And even that did not afford her privacy, for Cyril always seemed to be about, one way or another. He didn't converse much, nor wish to, but he was there. She tried to feel sorry for him, for in his own way he suffered almost as much under Lady Raven as the rest of them, even if he was Lord Raven's son and heir.

The first time she'd come across him he'd been sitting cross-legged in the forest, his eyes trained on the ground, his hands busily shredding what appeared to be a bloodied piece of cloth of some kind.

"Hello," she'd said, and he'd almost jumped out of his skin.

He shoved the cloth into his pocket. "Who . . . who are you?" he asked.

"I'm Georgia Wells, Lady Raven's new seamstress. Who are you?"

"Viscount B-Brabourne, Lady R-Raven's stepson." His eyes held a flicker of irony.

"Oh! I'm sorry—I hadn't realized. No one told me— that is, I hadn't realized you were from the house."

"Never mind. I suppose I should l-leave anyway."

"Oh, you don't have to do that," she said. "It's I who interrupted you."

He colored and looked down at the ground. "When d-did you arrive?"

"A week ago. Your stepmother had me sent down from London."

"Oh. She didn't s-say anything to me, but then I s-suppose she didn't c-consider it important."

Georgia's heart instantly went out to him. To have such a stutter at his age must be humiliating. She put him at about fifteen or so. He was taller than she, she imagined, but he hadn't yet filled out to the breadth of manhood. He was a handsome boy, with hair that was so dark as to be almost black, his arched eyebrows equally dark, and his eyes were a light gray, a striking contrast to his dark coloring. But there was something in his eyes as he watched her that was timid and skittish, like a frightened animal.

He suddenly jumped to his feet. "I . . . I must g-go now. I'm n-not supposed to c-consort with the s-servants. If you'll excuse m-me, I must r-return to the house. My t-tutor is no doubt in a s-state of extreme agitation." He left her without another word, and Georgia looked after him, her brow drawn down in perplexity.

After that she often found him near Raven's Close, a favorite spot of her own, separated as it was from the stifled atmosphere of Ravenswalk. Here was a sad house, a house that had been deserted, left to wither and die like a neglected child. Maybe that was what drew him there. He was a neglected child himself. And then there was his terrible stutter, which no doubt made him acutely uncomfortable around people. But despite her sympathy for his situation, she could not like him. He was an exceedingly difficult boy, inclined to moodiness and sulks, and he had a tendency to be extremely overbearing—not surprising, she supposed, given that he was a viscount. She wondered why he bothered speaking to her at all. And yet he seemed to seek her out, although he delighted in reminding her that she was a servant. Which she was.

Georgia's fingers were stiff with fatigue, but she bent her head back to her work and carefully pushed the needle through the velvet fabric, concentrating on finishing the fitted bodice. She would have been just as happy to poke the needle through Lady Raven's eye.

"Cyril, I will not tolerate an interrogation," Jacqueline said, and impatiently tapped his shoulder with her fan. "I haven't the time for this nonsense. Now, go and find something else to do with yourself."

"I w-won't," Cyril said stubbornly "I know what you're p-planning tonight, don't think you h-have me fooled. It's D-Dillon, isn't it? I saw how you were l-looking at him at d-dinner the other night. And he's . . . he's not the f-first, is he?"

"Cyril! You are being absurd! And stop that ridiculous stammering. Anyone would think you were an idiot. Now, stand aside; I must be on my way or I shall be late. Why don't you apply yourself to your books instead of concocting ridiculous tales? Mr. Fern has not been very positive about your studies, and it displeases me. This is the fourth tutor in two years, and the last, Cyril." She started out her bedroom door.

"It's n-no good t-trying to change the subject. You are t-taking D-Dillon as a l-lover."

Jacqueline stopped in her tracks and turned, giving Cyril a cold look. "Whether I choose to take him as a lover or not, Cyril, is absolutely none of your affair. I will not abide your speaking to me in such a way. I would not like to have to punish you, Cyril, but I shall if needs be."

Cyril hunched a shoulder and looked down at the floor.

"Now, enough of this. I would thank you never to bring up the subject again, for it is too foolish, my pet. Perhaps you and I need to take a nice long walk, spend the afternoon together. I have been busy of late, with all the guests we have had, and I know that you have felt neglected, but I will make it up to you, I promise, for I don't like you to feel lonely. So be a good boy and let me go, and sometime this week we'll find time for that walk."

She swept out of the room and down the stairs, calling for the carriage.

Cyril went out onto the landing and watched as she left. And then he went back into his stepmother's room and slumped into the chair at the dressing table, running his finger through a pile of spilt powder. The room smelled of her strong perfume, and he ran his tongue over his dry bottom lip, his eyes flickering over the table. He picked up a pair of nail scissors and very deliberately stabbed them into the heel of his hand, puncturing the flesh. The blood welled up and he watched it for a minute, then took his hand and rubbed it on the glass table-top, smearing the polished surface with a wide red streak.

Pulling his handkerchief out, he wrapped his hand with it, then looked in the mirror. His gray eyes appeared perfectly calm to him. He smoothed down his dark locks, his fingers shaking, but he forced them to be still too. And then he left the room, softly closing the door behind him.

Georgia heard a light tap come at her door, and she put her sewing down and went to answer it, hoping it was the maid with some more candles.

"Cyril!" she said with a mixture of surprise and wariness as she opened the door to find his lanky shape filling the frame. "Whatever are you doing up here? And at this hour—you must know it's not proper for you to come to my bedroom?"

"I kn-know that. Don't w-worry. No one s-saw me."

"That's a blessing. I'd be dismissed in an instant if anyone had."

"My step . . . stepmother is away for the evening and m-most of the s-servants are in b-bed. I didn't think it would d-do any harm."

"Cyril, what is it? You look upset about something."

He moved into her room, looking around him casually, as if it were perfectly natural for him to be paying her a midnight visit. "I'm n-not upset in the l-least. I am p-perfectly well. I was unable to s-sleep, and s-since you've been l-locked away for the last f-fortnight, I thought you might l-like some c-company. I know how l-lonely it can b-be here."

"Oh. Well, that's very considerate of you, Cyril, but I'm busy with your stepmother's wardrobe." Georgia couldn't think how to remove him from her room without being rude, or worse, hurtful. Cyril's feelings were exceptionally sensitive, and his face was more pale than usual. That there was something bothering him was unmistakable. "All right, sit down," she said impulsively, unable to deny him when he was so clearly in need of comfort. "But only for a few minutes. I really must finish this piece."

Cyril pulled out the chair and threw himself in it.

"Goodness," she said, noticing the stained bandage on his hand for the first time. "What did you do to yourself?"

"Nothing. A p-piece of glass. T-tell me about your l-life before R-Ravenswalk."

Georgia tried to think where this demand had come from. He'd never before shown any interest in her life. "Well," she said cheerfully, "I grew up in a small village in Cumberland. My father died when I was small, and my mother and I lived alone together until she died."

"D-did she t-take a l-lover?" he said abruptly.

"A lover?" Georgia colored, nonplussed. "What an extraordinary question, Cyril. I don't think it's quite appropriate for you to—"

"I only w-wondered. Most m-married women take l-lovers, whether their husbands are alive or d-dead." He squeezed his injured hand hard and a fresh red stain appeared on the bandage. He looked down at it with apparent fascination.

"I'm afraid I'm only a simple village girl, Cyril," Georgia said, frowning, her eyes fixed on his hand. "I haven't the sophistication to know about such things."

He shifted in his chair. "Oh. I thought y-you would know, as y-you were m-married. I s-suppose it's just the aristocracy, then. No one m-marries for l-love, only for c-convenience. It is f-fashionable to be unfaithful, d-didn't you know?"

"I'd like to know to whom you've been speaking about such things." She bent her head over her stitching to hide her embarrassment. "I scarcely think Mr. Fern has been instructing you in such matters."

Cyril's mouth tightened slightly. "Mr. F-Fern? No. I have n-no one to s-speak to about such m-matters but you, Georgia."

"And I'm not likely to speak to you of such things, Cyril," Georgia said bluntly.

"Oh. What a p-pity. I was hoping you might be a b-bit more forthcoming." He shrugged. "I am not the c-callow youth you might think, Georgia. I thought we might p-provide each other c-companionship. It would n-not be an unusual arrangement."

Georgia suddenly understood, and she felt a dark stain spread from her chest to her cheeks. "Cyril, I cannot believe you would even suggest such a thing! If we are to remain friends, then I must ask you to observe the proprieties. Do you understand? This really is not acceptable. I must ask you to leave at once."

Cyril's face went deathly white. "As you w-wish. I shall not c-come again. You are only a s-silly s-servant anyway. I will amuse m-myself elsewhere."

He did not give her a chance to say another word, he left so swiftly. Georgia sank down on her chair as soon as the door had closed behind him, resting her forehead in her hand. She knew that Cyril was young and probably just trying out his fledgling wings, but he had upset her, and she had upset him, she knew, for she was certain that his rudeness covered a deep sense of rejection and humiliation.

She spent the next hour piecing the blasted bodice to the dress and cursing herself for not having handled the situation better. Ravenswalk was nothing but a succession of obstacles to be circumvented as best as possible. One way or another, only disaster lay ahead, and when it struck, her life would be worthless, for Lady Raven would see to it that she never worked again. If only there was a way out. But there wasn't.

Georgia fell into bed, just barely managing to pull the covers up around her, and her eyes closed in exhaustion.

2

Nicholas opened his eyes and Binkley's face swam into his view, although he seemed to have acquired a second pair of eyes directly below the first. "What is it, man?" he muttered, foggily wondering why his mouth felt like the inside of a sewer. He tried valiantly to orient. "Where am I? God, who am I?"

"You are Mr. Nicholas Daventry, and you are safely installed at the White Stag in Dover, sir. It is the twenty-first of November in the year 1819. We have journeyed from India, where you have an enterprising business in free trade. You are in transit to your family home in Sussex—"

"I know all of that, you fool. How long have I been in this accursed inn?"

"Only four hours, sir. I took the liberty of arranging for two seamen to transport you from the ship. I must know your wishes for transport tomorrow, sir, or perhaps you will be feeling unwell and will wish to rest for an extra day?"

"How much did it take?" Nicholas said, trying to sit up and instantly deciding it was a poor idea.

"The full bottle of brandy and then a half again, sir."

"We'll stay the extra day. Did I disgrace myself?"

"Other than insulting an elderly matron—'broad-beamed,' I believe you called her, sir—on disembarkation, and trying to land a fist on the nose of one of your bearers, no, sir. Oh, and I felt it was only in good taste to pay extra for the state of the cabin. I'm afraid your stomach did not take well to the combination of drink and nerves, sir."

"A small price to pay. It's a damn shame England had to be an island surrounded by large bodies of water."

"Yes, sir. Speaking of which, there is a large carafe of water next to your left elbow. I would suggest you partake heavily of it."

"Thank you, Binkley. I will do so as soon as I regain the ability to put myself upright. Good-bye, Binkley. Good-bye and good night. I don't want to see you again until twenty-four hours have passed."

Binkley bowed. "Certainly, sir. I shall see to it that light trays of food are regularly delivered to you tomorrow to aid with the absorption of the spirits."

Nicholas, who was not accustomed to drinking heavily, but who'd had the occasional foolishness to do so and had suffered the consequences, groaned at the very thought of food and the day to come, and then mercifully passed out again.

The next day and night did not bear thinking about. He was sufficiently recovered to rise the second morning, bathe and be dressed, and shakily climb into the hired carriage.

"Progress, Binkley," he commanded, then fell asleep again.

Late that afternoon they pulled up near the gates of Ravenswalk, and Nicholas alighted, finally feeling like himself, although he was nervous and distracted. He had no intention of arriving with a fuss; he'd far rather quietly walk in the front door without the benefit of footmen and all the rest of it to herald him. But first he had another matter to attend to. He desperately wanted to see Raven's Close. It represented all the good things of the old day, before everything had changed so damned irrevocably.

"Stay here, Binkley," he commanded as he jumped off the step. "You may go to the Cock and Bull if I am not back by midnight, and if I have not appeared at all within twenty-four hours, then you had best come after me. It is possible that I misinterpreted my uncle's letter and he intends to have me shot at sunrise."

"Very good, sir." Binkley settled back against the box, and Nicholas loped off toward the gates. He turned right halfway down the driveway and took the old familiar path through the woods, reconnecting with the Close's own drive, now closed off. It was like a walk through his childhood. How many times had he taken the shortcut to

Ravenswalk, his dog at his heel, or at the heel of his horse? And then in later years it had been the other way around, going from Ravenswalk to look upon his old home. Perhaps at some time in the future his children would be taking the shortcut to visit Cyril, once again linking the two families.

Nicholas hated to admit it to himself, but he was sentimental. He had a burning desire not just to have his house, but also to have a family of his own to fill it. The invitation to return home had meant a great deal more to him than he'd originally cared to acknowledge, but as the months of traveling had worn on, he'd realized how staunchly he had denied the pain of being an outcast, pretending indifference. What he felt now was anything but indifference: his whole being vibrated with a contained excitement.

The sight that met his eyes caused him to come to a dead halt. The leap his heart made was not caused by joy, but rather by shock. Raven's Close was a ruin.

Weeds grew up all around it. The windows were too filthy for him to be able to see inside, and covered in cobwebs, but there was a hole in one near the front, and with a sick feeling in his stomach he made his way through the weeds and peered inside. It was just as he thought: it was a disaster on the inside as well. There was no furniture to be seen, and it appeared as if there must be at least one hole in the roof, given the stains on the walls and the general rotted state of things.

The door was locked, but it made no difference: at the moment he really didn't have the heart to go inside. He felt as if a dream had been shattered, a tiny kernel of dream that he'd held in the back of his heart for twenty long years. Nicholas sank to the ground, facing the wreck of his beautiful house, the wreck of his hopes for a family, his hopes for somehow putting the past right.

His uncle couldn't possibly care about him if he'd allowed this to happen. Nicholas' inheritance. It was a joke. A big ugly joke. Maybe his uncle had summoned him home so he could slap him one final time. "Things are wrong and must be put right"? To hell with it.

He put his head on his arms and he wept.

* * *

Georgia saw him as she came out of the clearing, her basket full of the roots she'd been collecting. His dark head was bent, and it was clear that he was upset. She could feel it almost tangibly across the twenty feet that separated them. It wasn't the first time that she'd come across Cyril in a fit of despair, but she felt slightly responsible, for she knew she had upset him greatly the night before. The least she could do was to try to make it better. She put the basket down and walked over to him, lightly touching his shoulder. "Cyril? Can we be friends again? It's not as bad as all that, is it?"

His head jerked up and she saw that his gray eyes were wet. But the terrible thing was that they weren't Cyril's eyes. They were near enough, as were the ebony hair and the arched eyebrows. The resemblance to Cyril was startling indeed, but it definitely wasn't he.

She took a step backward, her hand going to her chest. "I . . . I beg your pardon. I'm sorry . . ." She swallowed hard.

In one quick agile movement he was on his feet, and Georgia swallowed again, this time in awe. Standing as he was, it was more than apparent that he wasn't Cyril. His shoulders were broad and muscular, his waist and hips narrow, his legs powerful. Whereas Cyril was attractive enough in his own way, this man was magnificent. "Oh," she said in a small voice, realizing she was staring.

"Who in the blazes are you?" he asked, clearly shaken.

"I'm Georgia—Georgia Wells. I'm not . . . What I mean to say is, I'm Lady Raven's dressmaker. I truly am sorry, sir. I hadn't meant to intrude, but you look so like Lord Brabourne, you see, that I thought surely it was he."

"And do you often find Lord Brabourne sitting in a desolate heap and weeping?"

"Sometimes. That's another reason I thought he was you."

The gentlemen frowned. "I find that disturbing, seeing that Lord Brabourne is nearly seventeen years old and should not be given to such unfortunate habits."

28

"No, sir. He probably shouldn't. But he is, and it seems it must run in the family."

He raised one of those extraordinary eyebrows. "Oh?" he asked in that rich, deep voice.

"Oh." She colored. "What I meant to say is that you must be related. You do resemble a number of the family members in the portraits I've seen. The title is apt."

"Are you always given to making such personal comments, Miss Wells?"

"Mrs. Wells. I'm sorry." She was still in shock.

"That you're married? How unfortunate you should feel so." His eyes showed a flash of humor.

Georgia looked at him more closely. Humor was not in great supply at Ravenswalk, and she discovered that she'd missed it more than she'd realized. "Who *are* you?" she asked, suddenly relaxing.

"Nicholas Daventry. I'm Raven's nephew. I've been away for some time now, so I doubt you've heard me mentioned."

Georgia looked at him thoughtfully. "I see," she finally said, then glanced around his shoulder at the house behind him, for his shoulder was too high to look over it. "I think I understand."

"Just what do you think you understand, Mrs. Wells?"

"It was the condition of the Close, wasn't it, that was upsetting you? I know. It upsets me too. I love houses, you see, and it hurts to see it unloved and uncared-for. Houses are like people. They need to be loved, lived in. I come here often, just to sit and think. I've become very fond of the Close—it's a bit like an orphan, and as I was an orphan myself, I suppose I feel we have something in common. Someone needs to care."

He blinked, and then before Georgia knew what was happening, she found herself being pulled into his arms and kissed. It wasn't at all like the kisses Baggie had forced on her, which had been clammy and wet and suffocating, nor like Lord Herton's kiss, dry as parchment, the one time he'd caught her by surprise. This was quite a different sort of thing, but nevertheless it deeply alarmed her, and she took a deep breath and pushed him away, hard.

"You presume greatly, sir," she said, trying to stop

29

the shaking that had come over her, and wondering why the words sounded so silly.

He ran a hand through his hair, agitated, and took a step backward. "My apologies," he said. "That was unforgivable. I'm afraid I was overcome by a momentary pang of some hopeless emotion. I trust you won't send your husband after me, crying for pistols at dawn."

Georgia shook her head. "He's already dead."

"Already . . . Madam, do you have any sensibilities?"

"Oh, yes, many, although sensibilities aren't allowed at Ravenswalk, so I suppose I'm out of practice."

Nicholas cocked his head and scrutinized her with a keen eye. "Perhaps," he said slowly, "you wouldn't mind telling me a bit of what life is like at Ravenswalk at the moment. I used to live there, you see."

"Well," she said, relieved that he seemed unlikely to pursue her any further, "I suppose I could, if just for the conversation. I haven't really had any conversation with anyone for the last eight months, at least not any that has been gratifying." She dropped to the ground, thinking that she couldn't possibly conduct the conversation craning her head up to his height.

"Hmm," he replied, dropping down next to her and pulling one long leg up. He rested his forearm on his knee and regarded her pensively. "That sounds rather dismal."

"Lady Raven doesn't like fraternization among the staff, and we're all terrified of being discovered talking to each other, I think. Dismissal is like Madame Guillotine—fast, furious, and bloody."

Nicholas nodded. "I'm not surprised. Tell me, how is my uncle?"

"I don't know; I've never met him. He keeps to his rooms. I have heard he is unwell, although I have never seen the doctor arrive. But again, no one will discuss him, and Cyril will not speak of it. I think perhaps this is why your cousin is often upset. It's difficult when one's parent is ill—there is so much uncertainty and fear."

"Yes, I can imagine. Cyril was always a deeply sensitive child. It was very hard for him when his mother died. He was only six, poor lad. Lady Raven, as you've no doubt gathered, is not a particularly warm person. She made a poor substitute for a mother.''

Georgia bit her lip. ''I wouldn't say that she's made any kind of mother at all. If anything, Cyril seems intimidated by her. But then, most people are. She's that kind of person, don't you think?''

Nicholas smiled sourly. ''Maybe to most people. She doesn't intimidate me in the least.'' He absently pulled up a handful of overgrown grass and the roots came with it. His eyes fell to his hand and he tossed the grass away. ''How do you feel about her?''

''Feel, Mr. Daventry? I'm in her employ. I'm not allowed to have feelings.''

''Not even in the privacy of your bedroom, Mrs. Wells? Most people do have feelings in the privacy of their bedrooms.''

''Very well. In the privacy of my bedroom—my turret I should say—I dislike Lady Raven acutely. There.''

Nicholas laughed. ''Was that so bad? If truth be told, I dislike Lady Raven acutely myself. You might as well tell me the rest. I'm not likely to go running to her with your inner thoughts, and it would help me to have a clearer picture, given I've been away for ten years.''

''Ten years?'' Georgia said, wondering where he'd been and what he'd been doing. It was odd his name hadn't come up, although who would have brought it up in that strange house was beyond her. ''That is a long time, Mr. Daventry. But I must confess, I feel it would be unwise of me to say anything further. I cannot afford to lose my job; Lady Raven would see to it that I never found another.''

Nicholas considered this. ''That in itself says everything. Tell me, how did you come to accept a position at Ravenswalk?''

Georgia gave a shrug of her shoulder. ''I didn't exactly. I don't think I would have if I'd been given a choice. But in one day I found myself dismissed by my previous employer, and informed that I was to go to work for Lady Raven. As I wasn't consulted, and I really had no other alternative, I found myself here.'' Her eyes darkened, and she looked down so that Nicholas wouldn't see the

31

bitter, bleak expression in them that said everything about his family.

But apparently she hadn't looked down quickly enough, for he touched her chin lightly with his finger and pulled her face up to meet his eyes. "That bad?" he asked quietly, and she nodded miserably.

"I'm sorry. Now that I've returned, perhaps I can do something to help."

"Oh, no! Please, Mr. Daventry, I beg of you, leave it alone. If Lady Raven should take against me, my name would be worth nothing! She has a great deal of influence, and without my work I should starve." Her eyes started with tears, and she turned her head and quickly wiped them away. "Please," she said in a whisper. "I should never have spoken at all. It was foolishness. . . ."

"But true. I value truth, Mrs. Wells, above everything, and you have been truthful with me. I shall not jeopardize you in any way, I promise. You have made it much easier for me to walk back through that door in a way you cannot understand. I'll leave you now, for I shouldn't delay the inevitable any longer. I imagine I'll see you again."

Georgia bowed her head, thinking that was about as likely as Lady Raven growing a beard. She managed to smile at him. "I hope your homecoming is a happy one," she said, rising and brushing off her skirts.

"Not bloody likely," Nicholas muttered, also standing, "but it's bound to be interesting. And, ah—I really am sorry about the kiss. I have a tendency to act on impulse, and it seemed the right thing at the moment. It was your tender feelings for my house that did it."

"*Your* house? This is your house?"

"Yes. Well, almost. In theory. It's complicated. I was distressed to discover what it's come to, and I suppose I was touched that you felt the same way. Anyway, it's not the first time that I've regretted an impulse—not for my sake this time, but rather for yours."

"I quite understand. Don't trouble yourself any further over the matter. Good-bye, Mr. Daventry." Georgia collected her basket and started back to Ravenswalk.

* * *

Nicholas squared his shoulders and banged the heavy brass door knocker, his heart feeling just as heavy, and echoing as loudly in his chest. He almost wished now that he hadn't seen the state of the Close: he would have felt a great deal more benevolent toward his uncle had his illusions still been in place. But then, illusions were dangerous, and he needed every bit of ammunition at hand.

The man who opened the door was a stranger to him, but his eyebrows went shooting up when he saw Nicholas. It took very little to persuade the man to have him announced.

Nicholas waited in the hall, his eyes scanning every detail. The house had been improved, a great deal of money lavished upon it, that much was immediately evident. What was also evident was that there were items in the hall that had once resided at the Close, and that alone was enough to make Nicholas' blood boil.

His head jerked around at the sound of a dress rustling across the marble floor, and he slowly turned. Jacqueline hadn't changed much at all, the ten years honing her face into something approaching real beauty, in fact. There was more confidence in her carriage, as well. She no longer looked like a belligerent new countess, recently elevated from a humdrum existence as widow of a wealthy tradesman. She looked as if she'd been a countess all of her life.

The bodice of her dress was cleverly cut, covering but not disguising the full swell of her breasts, the skirt flaring out just enough, but not so much that the curve of hip was hidden. He knew what the material hid well enough, the memory burned into his mind for all time. He had not thought that his physical reaction to the sight of her would be so extreme, but it was, not unlike being kicked in the gut by a horse, and a vicious horse at that.

"So. Jacqueline," he said, his voice colder than ice.

"Nicholas," she replied stiffly, her lips appearing bloodless. Indeed, her entire face was ashen, and he could immediately tell that she was as unnerved as he was. But he had the advantage of surprise and he took it.

"My, my. How you haven't changed." He took a step

forward, and she retreated a step, but it was only fractional, a momentary lapse.

"What are you doing here?" she said, raising her chin slightly. "You know you are not welcome. I suggest you leave immediately, before I have the footman throw you out."

Her chest was rising and falling in a quick unnatural rhythm, and Nicholas smiled grimly. "How unfortunate for you, dear Jacqueline. I have no interest in your welcome, and I doubt the footman would be very successful in his efforts. I also have no intention of leaving, not before I've seen my uncle." He'd expected her to recoil, and so didn't understand the small, tightly folded smile she gave him.

"Very well, Nicholas. I will not deny you your wish. You may see your uncle. And then you will leave, for as you shall discover, you will have no choice in the matter." She started up the stairs, and Nicholas followed after, the sound of merry voices fading away as they walked down the corridor to his uncle's rooms.

He was tense, wondering how his uncle might greet him, not pleased that the first meeting had to be under Jacqueline's eye, in her presence, but he was in no position to argue. He was prepared to see his uncle indisposed, given what Georgia Wells had told him, but nothing prepared him for the sight that met him when he walked into his uncle's bedchamber.

Nothing could prepare anyone for the sight of a man once strong and forceful, now helpless. He lay in his bed, the covers pulled up to his chest, his arms lying neatly by his sides. His body appeared wasted and lifeless, and dribble fell from his mouth to his chin. His face was twisted and frozen, his eyes the only thing that seemed alive, although they looked cloudy, unclear.

Nicholas dropped to his knees beside the bed, his heart turning over. He took his uncle's limp hand between his own.

"Uncle William? Uncle William, it's Nicholas. Can you hear me?" He thought his heart might break. All of his anger, his resentment, melted away as he was confronted with the terrible devastation of the man who had acted as his surrogate father for ten years. In the following years of Nicholas' exile, those feelings had never vanished, even though they might have been well-disguised beneath careless nonchalance. Beneath that there had been bitter resentment. And apparently, beneath all of that, there had been a deep and abiding love. Whatever his uncle might have done, it hardly mattered now, not in the face of this.

"Uncle William, I'm home," he said gently. "I'm so sorry. We'll make it right somehow." He thought he saw a flicker of comprehension in his uncle's eyes, and he squeezed his dry hand. "We'll put the past behind us. I'll look after you now, just as you once looked after me."

"You most certainly will not," Jacqueline said from behind him, and he turned, having forgotten for a foolish, unguarded moment that she was there. "There is a manservant to see to his needs, and no one can do anything for him beyond that."

"Simple companionship might help, Jacqueline. Have you thought of that?"

"Your companionship, my dear Nicholas, would only upset him. Your uncle does not want you, and I do not want you. Neither of us has forgotten. You will leave now, I think." Her eyes had narrowed, catlike.

"Oh, but I think not," Nicholas said, rising. "I will stay, whether it pleases you or not. However, I think it might be wiser to step outside to discuss these matters." He turned and left the room, waiting for Jacqueline outside.

"So," he said as soon as she had shut the door behind her, "I imagine you've been quite content with the situation. How long ago did this condition overtake my uncle?"

"I cannot see why it is any concern of yours. You were cast off, and not a thing you can do or say is going to change that! I find it extraordinary that you have such spleen as to expect to return and be welcomed. Your uncle despises you, Nicholas. He despises you, do you hear me? I will not have you upsetting him in his delicate condition."

"You couldn't care less about my uncle's delicate condition, my dear Jacqueline, nor do you care about my uncle at all. So why don't we drop this absurd pretense and get down to facts? We both know the truth of the matter, although I have no stomach to discuss it. Instead, I would like the name of my uncle's man of business.''

"I am that person," Jacqueline said, demurely folding her hands across her skirt, but she could barely disguise her triumph. "What is it you would like to know?"

Nicholas gave her an incredulous stare. "Surely he wouldn't have been that stupid."

"He was not stupid in the least. If anyone has been stupid, it has been you, Nicholas. Now, tell me just what it is you want to know, for I am sure I can answer whatever questions you have."

"I would like Raven's Close handed over to me," Nicholas said between clenched teeth, barely managing to retain control. "It is long past time that I claim it, and it has been run into sorry shape, no doubt thanks to you. I would like to restore it to its former condition, and the sooner that I am given the deed, the better."

Jacqueline's vindictive smile broadened. "How unfortunate," she said. "You must realize that your position is not a secure one."

"My position, step-aunt, is that I am owed Raven's Close. It was an agreement between my uncle and myself that I should inherit it at the age of twenty-one. It's nearly ten years overdue."

"But things have changed, Nicholas," Jacqueline said, her eyes now so narrowed that Nicholas could only barely see the lower portion of her irises. "You see, when you were sent away, your uncle decided that your debauchery would either run its course or it would mark you for life. As you know, your uncle has full discretionary powers as to the conditions under which you might inherit. He changed those conditions shortly after you left."

Nicholas stood very, very still. Her voice contained such suppressed venom that he felt in danger of moving, as if she might literally strike with poisoned fangs, like the vipers in India that he had seen kill more than once.

"Yes?" he asked, his throat tight. "And just how do they stand now?"

"Under the new terms, you must be married by your thirtieth birthday or the property reverts permanently to

Ravenswalk, which is your uncle's full right. I hardly see you marrying within three weeks, Nicholas. Such a pity. So please remove yourself. As I have said repeatedly, you are not welcome here.''

"It's a shame you see it that way. But I intend to have what's owed me, and I intend to undo the damage done.''

Jacqueline gave an unladylike snort. "With what funds? Really, Nicholas. I cannot think so. Your uncle thought little enough of the property that it was not worth wasting the money on.''

"Yes, I've noticed already that you've seen fit to rob it, Jacqueline. I suppose I'm not surprised. You always did have a taste for attractive things. But don't count your chickens, as they say. It's clear you've had run of the henhouse for far too long.'' He turned and walked quickly from the room, hoping the uproar of his mind was not evident.

He let himself out of the house immediately, seeking air. It was not unlike his reaction to his nightmares, this need to gasp for breath. He had been dealt a series of blows, not the least of which was the grave physical condition of his uncle. The fact that he would lose the Close for all time if he wasn't married by the eighteenth of next month only hit him as an aftershock. He walked the ten minutes to the Close, grateful for the light of the moon, and he sat upon the stump of a fallen oak, contemplating his options. There didn't seem to be any.

"Dear Lord above,'' he finally whispered after another two hours had gone by and he had come up with nothing. He was desperate. He was about as desperate as he had ever been in his life. "Please,'' he said, raising his eyes to the star-clustered sky. "Please help me with this. There has to be a way. Surely there has to be a way?''

And then like a blinding flash of inspiration, a solemn, very beautiful face appeared before his eyes. He started at the very idea, then after a few moments of thought, relaxed into it. Well, why not? Why the hell not? "Thank you,'' he said, grinning at the stars. "Thanks very much.'' He rose to his feet, feeling a great deal better and set on his way.

* * *

Nicholas took his chances on the turret, reasoning that it would be the one over the servants' quarters. As a boy he'd been adept at escaping the confines of Ravenswalk, and it didn't take too much work to scale the backside of the building. He crept across the flat roof and peered in through the long window. Sure enough, Georgia Wells was soundly sleeping in the iron-posted bed. A table heaped with materials set off in one corner, and a dressmaker's form stood near it, covered with a half-completed gown of some sort.

He knocked at the window, and she rolled over, flinging her arm over her head. He knocked again, louder, and she sat up, then pushed back the covers and slid out of the bed, coming over to the window, her eyes three-quarters closed and bleary. He stepped back against the coping and threw a pebble onto the roof, and Georgia unlatched the window and threw it open, peering out.

"Good evening, Mrs. Wells," Nicholas said, moving into her direct line of vision. "A beautiful night, is it not?" He stepped over the low sill into the room.

"Oh, no," Georgia said, her hands going out in front of her automatically. "Please, you must go away immediately."

Nicholas took her wrists firmly and put them down by her side. "You misunderstand. I apologize to wake you at this hour and in this fashion, but what I have to say will not wait. I have an offer to make you, and there is a serious time constraint involved in your reply. I assure you this has nothing to do with a seduction."

She merely gazed at him, still fogged by sleep. "No? What, then?"

"Marriage, actually."

"Marriage? You must be mad. Or perhaps walking in your sleep. Or perhaps I'm walking in mine. Yes—that must be it. In which case I'll bid you good night, sir. Be a good dream and go away." She turned and began to grope for her bed, and he realized with amusement that she really must think she was dreaming.

"Mrs. Wells, I assure you I'm not mad, nor walking in my sleep. Nor are you walking in yours." He reached out, placing firm hands upon her shoulders, and he turned her around to face him. "Now, please wake up. I need to talk to you, and I'm not leaving until I do." He gave her a gentle shake.

A frown came over her face. "Oh, dear . . . you're not a dream."

"I'm afraid not."

"But you came in through the window! How did you do that?"

"I climbed. I thought it more discreet than using the stairs."

Georgia glanced down at her nightdress with dismay. "This won't do at all, Mr. Daventry. You really must leave at once. I cannot think why people always seem to feel they can make themselves free of my bedroom just because I'm a servant. I work very hard you know, and I need my sleep."

Nicholas had the absurd desire to laugh. She looked sweet and owlish and, oh yes, every bit as attractive as he remembered. He could see that her hair was the color of dark gold, now that it wasn't covered by that ghastly cap. Her face was rosy with sleep, her blue eyes heavy with what might almost be misconstrued as promise. He took a long, deep breath, consciously banishing such thoughts for the moment. He didn't need his brain to be clouded by lust while he was conducting a business arrangement.

"Mrs. Wells, will you marry me?"

"Why would I ever do a foolish thing like that?" She sat down on her bed and yawned, and he was slightly hurt that she didn't even seem flattered, much less interested.

"Well, because I discovered tonight that I desperately need a wife. As I told you earlier, Raven's Close should be mine, but if I'm to inherit it before my thirtieth birthday, which falls in roughly three weeks from now, I must be married."

"I quite understand your need for a wife, given those circumstances, Mr. Daventry. But there must be handfuls of other available women who would be delighted to be your wife."

"I know of no other available women in England, having only just arrived on these shores. You'll do beautifully."

"No I won't. You can't possibly marry a seamstress, Mr. Daventry. Surely there must be someone else more suitable?"

"I don't see anything wrong with you in the least. Are you thinking that you are a threat to my respectability? I assure you, I have very little of that, and in any case, I'm probably more of a threat to yours."

"Oh, no. I'm not worried about any of that in the least. How could I be? I simply don't see the advantages for you."

The conversation was not going at all as Nicholas had anticipated. If anything, he'd expected her to see the advantages for herself first. "They seem obvious," he said, slightly off-balance. "I honestly can't think of anyone else on the spur of the moment. You have fond feelings for my house, if not for me, and you told me earlier today that you're miserable here. It's a way out, is it not? If you marry me, Lady Raven will have no more influence over your life. I really haven't the time to find a wife in the usual sort of way, Mrs. Wells, not if I'm to keep what is rightfully mine. You'd be doing both of us a favor. Do you think you might at least *consider* marrying me?"

Georgia pulled her feet up inside her nightdress and regarded Nicholas pensively. "You know nothing about me," she said.

"You know nothing about me," he countered. "But I imagine we can learn the basic facts in a relatively short amount of time."

"Basic facts are hardly a basis for marriage."

"All right, then," he said, desperately snatching at straws. "Think of the Close. There is the fact that it needs a great deal of work, and you say you care about it. If it's not given to me, then Lady Raven keeps it, and allows it to crumble even further. My uncle seems to be totally incompetent. Actually, to be blunt, he's not functioning at all, poor soul. His wife has taken over all of his affairs, and that's a dangerous thing in itself. But if I can at least get the Close out of her hands, I can try to restore it. But I need your help."

"My help?" Georgia said doubtfully, but with a thread of hope in her voice. "You think I can help?"

Nicholas saw he had struck some sort of chord in her.

It appeared that Georgia Wells had a deep desire to help people. "You can certainly help me," he said, working on this theorem, "and that's a beginning. Look at it this way: if I'm not married, I can't help a blessed soul, myself included. If, on the other hand, you are willing to help me out of this mess, then perhaps I can help my uncle, and possibly Cyril as well, who sounds as if he needs it, from what you told me. I'm afraid all I have to offer in return is a broken-down house and a parcel of difficult relatives. What do you think?"

Georgia thought this over. "It is an awkward situation, isn't it? I can see that you are in a very difficult spot."

"Yes, and so are you. Marriages have been made for far less reason than that."

Georgia nodded. "That is certainly true."

"I realize this is sudden, and that we only met today, bu I'm afraid there just isn't the time to go about it in another way."

"No, I quite understand."

"Do you? That's good. So will you please marry me, Mrs. Wells?"

"Well . . ."

"Well?" he repeated anxiously.

"Well, I suppose I have nowhere else to go and nothing more important to do," Georgia said uncertainly. "I do hate my position here, and it's true that I have no way out of it other than your offer."

"Yes, and you will give me the satisfaction of being able to rescue you, as well as the satisfaction of infuriating Lady Raven. She will no doubt be beside herself."

Georgia laughed. "The situation does smack of Rapunzel, doesn't it? Lady Raven certainly makes a fine witch. Infuriating her is almost reason enough in itself. I don't know . . . I suppose it's not such a bad offer." She tapped the corner or her mouth. "There's the problem with the house, and having Lady Raven as a relative is not tempting. If only you had a decent fortune."

"If only I had a decent fortune?" Nicholas said, choking on the words.

"Yes. It's a pity, but there you are. On the other hand," she continued with a mischievous smile, "your teeth appear strong, your physique is fine enough, and you do have all your hair. It could have been worse—you might have been a corpulent, bald prince coming to the rescue.''

''Thank you very much, madam,'' Nicholas said, amused. ''And I also have no objection to your physique, your teeth, nor your breath, for that matter. May we come to terms?''

Georgia rested her cheek on her knee for a moment, then looked up and met his eyes, and he saw that the laughter had gone out of them. ''It's madness, you do realize?''

''It's an arrangement,'' he replied reasonably. ''Most marriages are arrangements. You and I might suit, who knows? We'll certainly suit far better together than apart, given our individual circumstances at the moment.''

''So you said. May I think about it?''

''I'd rather you didn't. It's not the sort of thing that bears thinking about.''

A little smile crept back on her face. ''I suppose I should be grateful to be consulted at all.'' She took a deep breath. ''All right, then, Mr. Daventry. I'll marry you, although I confess that I feel rather peculiar about it. But if I can help you claim and restore Raven's Close, then it only makes sense.''

''Bless you, Mrs. Wells. I can't help but feel you're heaven-sent.''

''I shouldn't think anything nearly so dangerous, Mr. Daventry. Will you please leave the same eccentric way you came?''

''Never fear, I shall descend the wall in the best of style. Do let's try to keep our agreement from Lady Raven, at least until Sunday, when the first banns will be cried. All hell is bound to break loose. She is determined to see the Close go to wrack and ruin.''

''Do you know, Mr. Daventry, I think it might be much wiser for you to obtain a special license, if at all possible. If Lady Raven is going to be as miffed as you think, she might try to find a way to stop you; and I wouldn't put much past her, including murdering me. I wouldn't be much good to you dead.''

Nicholas laughed. ''Now, that's thinking, my girl. I hadn't thought of a special license, but it strikes me as being extremely sensible. The sooner the better, then. Here's what I'll do. I'll leave first thing in the morning and make the arrangements. Then, once I've chased down the archbishop and acquired a license, I'll come back and send for you from the village. I don't think I ought to set foot back here until the deed is done. Lady Raven can learn about the marriage after the fact."

"Very well. I'll await word." Georgia gracefully showed him to the window as if they were concluding a formal meeting in the drawing room, but the nightdress fluttering about her ankles played havoc with the image. "Good night, Mr. Daventry." She held out her hand.

Nicholas graciously bowed over it, then climbed back over the sill and carefully made his way down the side of the building, all the while wondering what he had gone and done. But when he went to find Binkley and the carriage, he found that he was smiling.

3

Georgia read Nicholas' message one last time, then folded it and put it in the pocket of her cloak. She looked down at her trembling hands, then twisted off Baggie's wedding ring and put it in her pocket along with the note. She'd dispose of the ring in a bush somewhere. In about an hour, another ring would be sitting on her finger, put there by a man she knew not at all. And then she would belong to him.

She stared out the window. She couldn't help but wonder if she was completely insane. After he'd left, and the full implications had sunk in, she had run to the window, intending to call him back and tell him she'd changed her mind.

And then her hand had fallen away from the latch.

It was either marriage to Nicholas Daventry or continued, unending enslavement to Lady Raven. What was a little pain in comparison to that? And at least for once in her life someone had actually asked her what she wanted.

She looked around the turret room one last time, and then she straightened her shoulders, picked up her small valise, and crept down the stairs and out the back way to marry her desperate prince with his ruin of a castle.

The carriage was waiting outside the locked gates of the Close, exactly where Nicholas had said it would be, and both he and a stout older gentleman were standing next to it. The older gentleman wore no expression at all, but Nicholas looked anxious, she thought as she approached. She doubted he could possibly be as anxious as she was, but she tried very hard to school her face into an expression of calm. Apparently she was unsuccessful, for as he turned, hearing the crunch of her footsteps on the light blanket of snow, his eyebrows rose.

"Good day, Mr. Daventry," she said, cursing the shake in her voice.

"Good day, Georgia," Nicholas said with what she imagined was supposed to be a reassuring smile. "I am delighted you decided to come after all, but please, do try not to look at me like that, or the vicar might think I'm forcing you to a fate worse than death. I shall not murder you, you know, only marry you. You haven't had a change of heart, have you?"

"No," she said firmly, pulling herself up very straight. "I haven't. I gave you my word, and I do not go back on such things. I thought you might change your mind, if anything."

"After scaling Ravenswalk to claim your hand? Not a chance. Please, allow me to introduce you to my superior man, Binkley. I should be lost without him. Binkley, Mrs. Wells."

Binkley bowed. "Mrs. Wells. May I profess myself overjoyed to make your acquaintance. You are most obliging to take on my master in wedlock."

Georgia couldn't help smiling. There was something very solid and respectable about Binkley, and she liked him immediately. "Thank you, Binkley," she said. "I am sure your master is most obliging to take me on as well. Given that we know each other not at all, the experience is bound to be invigorating."

"Indeed, ma'am. But then, it has been my experience that life with Mr. Daventry is always invigorating. May I help you into the carriage?"

Georgia gathered her skirts and accepted his arm, glancing over at Nicholas as he moved in next to her. "You didn't tell me there was a Binkley included in the marriage."

"Consider him my wedding gift to you. Believe me, you will be grateful for Binkley soon enough. He can solve any number of domestic and nondomestic crises. On top of that, he has a mind like a razor and a much more highly developed sense of propriety than I, so he keeps me firmly in my place."

Georgia fell silent, suddenly feeling horribly shy. It

struck her for the first time that they would be setting up house together, that failing death or complete estrangement, they would be part of one another's lives from here on out. She shifted on the seat.

"Nervous?" Nicholas asked.

"Yes. I'm sorry, Mr. Daventry, but I cannot help myself; this morning I was Lady Raven's modiste. This afternoon I am about to become the wife of a man I've only ever met twice before, and then under fairly odd circumstances. I am not normally given to a nervous condition, I assure you, but you must admit the situation lends itself to such a reaction."

"I do understand," he said gently. "I'm a bit nervous myself, if truth be told. Marriage is a big undertaking. That is why I wanted to be married here, in the village church, where I used to go to services. We might not be well-acquainted, but this is our wedding, and I'd like it to feel right."

She nodded, and twisted her hands together in her lap.

"Good. And, ah . . . Georgia?"

"Yes?" she said, glancing over at him.

"Do you think you could call me Nicholas? It would make the situation more comfortable."

"Certainly," she said, clearing her throat and trying to sound sensible. "You must tell me what you would like and what you wouldn't like, and I shall do my best to accommodate you, Nicholas."

He leaned a little away from her and looked at her hard. "Accommodate me? Georgia, let me make it very clear that I do not wish to be accommodated. We are entering into a partnership together. It would be nice if you would approach your position from that angle. I would be happy if you would help me, occasionally gratify me, at times even humor me, but you are not to be a servant to me." His brow drew down. "You have been married before. Surely you understand?"

Georgia nodded again, feeling more miserable than ever. She understood perfectly. Nicholas just had a pretty way of putting it.

"Forgive me," he said quietly. "I've been insensitive. Perhaps it will help if we look at this as a fresh start for us both, an adventure we are undertaking together."

She looked over at him and managed a slight smile. "You must forgive me as well. You are being uncommonly kind, and I am behaving in a most foolish fashion. You are quite correct. We are both embarking on an adventure, and I shall try to keep that in mind."

"Good. And here we are, Georgia." He alighted and helped her down from the carriage, and then he tucked her hand into the crook of his elbow and took her into the church to be married.

It was dark and cool inside and Georgia noticed that there was a comfortable smell of old wood and beeswax. The vicar was perfectly pleasant, delighted to see Nicholas again, whom apparently he'd christened, and he professed himself delighted to marry them.

"It's no trouble at all, Nicholas, my boy. What a lovely woman you have chose as your bride. I am so pleased you decided to come back to your old parish to be married. Now, if you'll just stand here, Mrs. Wells and you here, Nicholas, and your man behind you—and Mrs. Petersby, over there, thank you. Now, shall we begin?"

Georgia thought she was going to be sick. She remembered this far too clearly from the last time, only then the vicar's face had been cold and disapproving, and the other faces had held barely disguised sniggers. But she had been innocent then, had not understood what the sniggers meant.

"Wilt thou, Georgina Eugenie, have this man to thy wedded husband? . . ."

Georgia glanced over and up at Nicholas as the words droned on. He couldn't have been more different from Baggie. The diffused light of the sun fell through the stained glass onto his cheek and the shoulder nearest her. She could only see the straight bridge of his nose, the definition of his cheekbone, the side of his mouth, and the smooth angle of his jawline, ending in a well-shaped ear, behind which his black hair curled.

Nicholas suddenly turned his head and met her eyes, and he smiled. She dropped her eyes abruptly, coloring.

No, there was no external resemblance to Baggie, none whatsoever. Baggie had stood at the altar in his best clothes, eye level to her, and he had never once taken those eyes off her. But he hadn't smiled. He hadn't smiled once. Now she knew what he had been thinking about.

"With this ring I thee wed. With my body I thee worship . . ." Nicholas said, slipping the gold ring onto her finger. She looked down at it. It was heavier than Baggie's had been, and the gold was deep and rich. Worship? It was a peculiar way to put it.

She stiffened as Nicholas lifted her chin and bent down and lightly kissed her. He kissed her in a far more circumspect fashion than he had in the weeds outside Raven's Close, his warm lips just brushing hers, and it really wasn't so bad after all. After receiving the congratulations of the vicar, the vicar's cleaning lady, and Binkley, he took her back to the Cock and Bull and told her to wait for him.

"I'll be back, Georgia. I'm going to Ravenswalk to claim the Close, and I think this is something I'd best do alone."

Georgia merely nodded, wishing him out the door as fast as possible. As soon as he'd gone, she went straight back outside and walked as quickly as possible down the village lane toward the open country. She needed a good quantity of fresh air and exercise to blow the troubles out of her brain, proprieties be damned.

She was not aware that Binkley had taken note of her flight and kept a discreet distance behind.

Jacqueline stood in the middle of the library, quivering with fury. "What do you mean, you are married?" She spat each word out separately. "I do not believe it. It is a sham! It is not legal! Show me proof!"

Nicholas tossed the marriage lines onto the desk. "Read. It's quite fresh, Jacqueline."

She snatched it up, her eyes running rapidly over the page, and then it dropped from her hand, and she looked up, looking as if she'd just been slapped. The color had gone from her face, leaving it white, with two violent spots of red flaming on her cheeks. "No. It is not possible. Not Georgia Wells. No. No!"

"Yes. Georgia." Nicholas crossed his arms over his chest. "Georgia Wells, now Georgia Daventry. Say goodbye to your modiste, Jacqueline, and say good-bye to

Raven's Close. I'd like the deed and the keys, not that keys are really necessary. The door would most likely fall in if I leaned on it." He scooped his marriage certificate up off the floor. "If you please? There's no point delaying. Accept it. All of your scheming has failed."

Jacqueline, who looked as ill as he'd ever seen her, pulled herself up. "I don't know how you managed this, Nicholas, although I wouldn't put anything past the scheming little baggage, nor you, for that matter. But I promise, you will regret this. I swear that I will make you regret this."

"Swear what you will, Jacqueline. It makes no difference to me. You make no difference to me—not any longer. You can't touch me now, can you, and I would lay money that that fact is tearing you up inside. So why don't you scurry along and get me my things?"

Jacqueline drew in a long, hissing breath. "Don't push me, Nicholas. You have no idea what I am capable of doing. You have no idea at all."

"You're probably right, Jacqueline. I'd hate to contemplate the true depths to which you're willing to sink. And since today is my wedding day, and I'd like to get back to my wife, I'm not going waste any more time in your highly questionable presence. My key, please."

She swept past him, and he laughed softly to see the speed at which she went. He had gotten to her. He had definitely gotten to her, and it pleased him. It was about time that something pleased him when it came to Jacqueline de Give.

He was just about to untie his horse from the mounting post when a young man came around the corner, and reflexively he glanced up. The young man stopped abruptly, and Nicholas stared, his mouth curving into a wild smile. Talk about spitting images—here was one, indeed. He might have been looking at himself fifteen years ago. "Good God. Cyril?" He quickly moved toward him, his hand outstretched. "What a pleasure it is to see you again! It is Nicholas—your cousin Nicholas? Surely you haven't forgotten me?"

"Wh-what are you d-doing here?" Cyril not only didn't take his hand, he took a wary step away, and Nicholas dropped his hand to his side, surprised.

"I've come home, Cyril. Did your stepmother not tell you? Ah—yes, I can see she did not. I'm going to be moving into the Close."

"The Close? B-but . . . but you c-can't!" Cyril looked shocked as much as anything else.

"Can't I? Why not?"

"B-because-b-because you c-can't. My father t-tossed you out on your ear. You c-cannot come home."

"But here I am," Nicholas said gently. "Here I am, and here is the key," he said, holding it up to Cyril's view. "My wife and I move in tonight. I'm sorry if the news doesn't please you, but I have waited a very long time for this. I've also waited a long time to see you again. I had hoped you would be happy that I'd returned. I confess to surprise at your dismay."

Cyril reddened. "I am s-surprised at your cheek. You d-don't belong here."

"Well. You're entitled to your feelings. I don't know what you've been told about the falling-out your father and I had, but it's clear to me that a black picture was painted. Look here, Cyril, you're the only cousin I have. I would hope we could be friends as we once were. I know you were very young when I left, but surely you cannot have forgotten everything we did together?"

Cyril poked at the ground with the toe of his boot, and Nicholas frowned. "Very well, Cyril. Why don't you take some time to think about it? You know where you can find me. Please feel welcome at any time. Good day."

He untied his horse and swung up into the saddle. "I'm sorry about your father, by the by, It's a terrible shame. I hope he'll recover."

Cyril went even redder, then ducked his head and turned his back, disappearing inside the house. Nicholas looked after him, trying not to be hurt by Cyril's reaction. Cyril had been only a young lad, he reasoned, when Nicholas had been forced to leave, and God knew what stories he'd been told. Maybe it would take a little time to win him over but he had plenty of that, not that he had any intention of begging. Let his actions speak for themselves. But the stutter the boy had developed surprised him, for he had always believed that speech was firmly established at an early age, and Cyril had never had any difficulty in that direction. He would ask Georgia. Maybe she would have some insight into the situation.

He urged his horse toward the Close. He had a feeling he was going to need privacy on his first full exposure to the ruin it had become.

An hour later he returned to the inn and ordered a large tankard of ale. Then he called for Binkley.

"Raven's Close is marginally prepared for inhabitance, sir," Binkley announced, returning from his mission. "It is not an attractive sight for a wedding night, but there will be a meal, the back bedrooms are readied, and there is moderate warmth. Mrs. Daventry's room has been prepared as you desired. I have also lit a fire in the next-door bedroom as you requested, although there was not enough furniture available to make it pleasing."

"Thank you, Binkley. Let me just go and collect Mrs. Daventry, and then you may take us over. You have provided the extra touches, I assume? I want this night to be as pleasant as possible."

"Yes, sir. The wine has been decanted. The candles are lit. In the dark one cannot see quite how unfortunate the conditions are. One could hope that Mrs. Daventry might in the morning see it all through a happy haze—"

"Binkley! You shock me."

"Begging your pardon, sir, but extreme measures are called for. Your own happy haze will also be required, sir, in order to absorb the conditions fully tomorrow. The upper story will need complete restoration. The roof, from what I could ascertain, is barely holding."

"Hmm. That bad. Never mind, Binkley. We shall prevail. You are a brave man indeed to take us on like this."

"You need me, sir," Binkley said pragmatically. "I shall await your pleasure outside." He left, his habitually measured pace unruffled by the recent turn of events. But then, nothing had ever ruffled Binkley that Nicholas had seen in their eight-year career together. He thought it might very well take an earthquake to shake a single hair on Binkley's solid head.

Georgia stood in front of Raven's Close, giving it a long, hard look. It looked no better than it ever had. The five pointed gables that fronted the three wings were missing great chucks of tile, the gaps showing white against the gray slate. Poor house, she thought. But at least it would finally have inhabitants to fill it, and eventually it would all be put to rights. It served as a welcome reminder of why she had married Nicholas Daventry. Together they would bring the house back to life.

Nicholas came over to her and took her hands between his own. "Georgia, you're cold as ice. Are you sure you don't want to change your mind and put up at the Cock and Bull until we have made the house more livable?"

"I do not, Nicholas, as I told you earlier when you asked. This is to be our home and we might as well begin straightaway to make it so."

"But on your wedding night?"

"What difference does it make?" she said, coloring.

"You haven't yet seen inside. But so be it. I admire your courage and I have to admit I'd rather be here myself, despite the discomfort. You had better come in. And steel yourself."

He opened the front door and led her through. "Oh, Nicholas . . ." Georgia slowly looked about, her eyes taking in the water stains, the plaster falling off the ceilings, the bare floors and walls. Her heart fell, and it hurt not only for the house but also for him.

There was a strong smell of damp, and she could immediately see that some of the floorboards had rotted. Those were the first impressions to strike her. They picked their way carefully across the hall and Nicholas calmly showed her the sitting room and library. Both were in sorry shape, but she was relieved to see that the books had not sustained too much obvious damage. The lower leakage seemed to be contained to the front portion of the house.

"We'll leave the upstairs for later. It's an even bigger disaster," he said, leading her back through the central wing.

They passed through the kitchen, where Binkley was hard at work despite the very primitive conditions, and entered the dining room. Nicholas ran a finger over the back of one of the mahogany chairs that sat at a long formal table.

"I imagine that my step-aunt left the dining room more or less intact because she had no use for the table at Ravenswalk," he remarked casually enough. "Aside from the sitting room, which for some unknown reason she decided to leave with the sofa and armchairs this is probably where we'll be living."

"Oh, dear. We do have some work to do," she said when he had finished.

"Yes, we do. I've already ordered the first of the materials, and they should be here within a day or two." He walked across the bare floor to the long window that looked over a ruined tangle.

"Nicholas? What is it?" she asked bewildered by the suddenly fierce expression on his face, when he had been so composed only moments before.

He turned to face her. "That was once a garden," he said, his tone carefully measured. "A beautiful, wonderful garden. It overflowed with flowers of every sort, different flowers for every season. My mother spent much of her time out there, carefully tending her plants. Even after she died the gardeners kept it exactly as she had created it. I would come over from Ravenswalk and sit in it, and feel closer to her. And then . . . never mind. I hadn't realized that it, too, was dead."

"Nicholas—" Georgia started to say, but he cut her off.

"Damn her," he said between clenched teeth. "Damn her!"

"I'm sorry," she said softly.

Nicholas pushed a hand through his hair. "No—I'm sorry. I didn't mean to lose my temper. I can't start letting this get under my skin now. The only thing to do is to look toward the future and restore what we can. So. Shall we have our supper?"

He pulled out a chair for her, and she sat, feeling quite odd to be treated like a fine lady. In the past, it had always been she who had done the cooking, the waiting. But she couldn't help reveling in the feeling of luxury. It didn't matter in the least to her that the house in which they dined was falling apart around them, or that the man sitting next to her did not love her, let alone know her. She certainly couldn't think about what he would soon be doing to her. She was determined to enjoy the food and conversation. Had she concentrated on all the unpleasant things that life held, she would have starved from lack of appetite long before.

Binkley had managed an extraordinary meal, given the state of things. He had somewhere found a smoked fish, and had prepared a roast of beef, with boiled potatoes and a selection of winter vegetables. He laid this modest wedding feast on the table, poured the wine around, then bowed and retreated to the kitchen.

"Binkley's a wonder, Nicholas. Wherever did you find him?" Georgia said, looking at the platters of food, terribly impressed. Her mother had instilled in her an appreciation for fine cooking, and as she'd been taught the art, she knew that what Binkley had produced was no mean feat.

"Actually, he found me. In a bazaar in India. That's where I've been living until now. In any case, I was attempting to buy some cloth for a suit of clothes, completely lost as to how to go about it and making a terrible hash of the matter. Binkley appeared as if by magic, took over the negotiations, led me to a reputable tailor, and ever thereafter took me in hand. His previous employer had recently married, and Binkley did not approve of his choice of bride."

"Oh," said Georgia. "I hope I pass muster. I would hate for you to lose Binkley on my account."

"The circumstances were quite different. As I understood it, the new bride was an old harridan who was inclined to interfere with Binkley's way of doing things. He no longer felt appreciated. So he adopted me."

Georgia smiled. "I see. You were very lucky. He took me in hand today too. I was feeling quite lost and frightened, but there was Binkley, treating me as if I were the finest of ladies on my way to St. Paul's to be married."

"I'm glad. He does that for me too. When I fall he picks me up, brushes me off, and sends me on my way."

"You don't seem to me to be the sort of person who falls very often, Nicholas Daventry."

"Don't I? Ah, but there you are mistaken." He stood and fetched the decanter.

Georgia watched the play of firelight on his face,

watched it catch in the ebony strands of hair, saw the shift of muscle beneath his coat as he leaned over to fill her glass. And then there were his hands . . . they were so long and elegant and graceful. She hadn't seen hands so beautiful since her mother's. They had been gentle, healing hands, but just as adept at threading a needle or working in the kitchen creating masterpieces out of nothing but scraps. And how often had her mother held her and stroked her hair off her forehead as she wove wonderful tales of places long ago and far away?

Georgia shook off the memories, watching Nicholas as he filled his own glass and placed the decanter down.

He looked over at her as he resumed his seat. "What is it, Georgia? You seem in another world."

"Nothing. It's nothing. I *was* in another world, I suppose. I'm sorry to say that daydreaming is a bad habit of mine. Nicholas, will you tell me about Raven's Close? How did it come to be yours?"

"It was the original family house before Ravenswalk was built. What you see of the Close now was largely built in the seventeenth century, added on to the original structure."

"Yes, I had thought so. But I don't understand about the deed, all these provisions."

"Ah, well, the actual ownership is a strange thing. You see, the property is entailed to Ravenswalk and can never be sold. My father had the house for his lifetime, as I now will have it for mine. But the present earl decides the manner in which it is to be passed on. I imagine it's a built-in protection against the occasional wastrel that tends to crop up in a family. In my case, because I was only ten when my father died, the Close immediately reverted to the Raven trust, until such a time as my uncle decided that I was ready to take it on."

"Why did he wait for so long, then, and make a provision of your being married by your thirtieth birthday? And why did he let it fall into such a state?"

Nicholas rubbed his neck. "We had a disagreement. It was rather a nasty one, and I left. I thought that when I came home, he would honor the original agreement—that I was to have had it when I was twenty-one. I also assumed that he'd keep the house up. God only knows why he didn't. I see Jacqueline's hand in that."

"Jacqueline?"

"Lady Raven, as you know her."

"Oh, yes, of course—I didn't know. Isn't it odd? She's that sort of person who strikes me as not having any Christian name—it's almost too human."

"Oh, she's human enough. A half-caste of the devil, perhaps, but otherwise human enough."

"Nicholas, do you think that perhaps we might not speak of her tonight? I cannot feel comfortable, having only just left, and . . ."

"And you are quite right. She does not bear mentioning. What shall we talk about, then?" He watched her over the rim of his glass, something amused lurking in the back of his eyes.

"You," she said, leaning back in her chair. "I want to hear about you and Raven's Close. I want to hear how it used to be."

And so he told her. He told her about his first memories of Raven's Close, about his mother and his father, and how cheerful life had been. He told her about his dog, and his pony, and later, his horse, and how proud and grown up he'd felt to be given him on his eighth birthday. He told her about his uncle's first wife, Laura, and how kind and gentle she'd been, of how she and his mother would sit together for hours on end, talking and laughing. He made it all sound like a fairy tale, and Georgia dreamed, picturing the richness of their lives, the laughter that must have rung in the air, the happiness that had once sung inside the walls.

She watched his face as he talked, really seeing it for the first time, his eyes dreamy with memory, the gray so clear, the wistful expression they held. She watched his full mouth lift in a slight smile as he talked of his mother, the realist, and his father, the idealist, and the ongoing arguments they used to have over his father's crazy schemes. He talked of his mother's garden, and how beautiful it had once been, enclosed in the stone walls that now stretched emptily to make a square at the back. He told her of how he would help his mother with the little spade his father had fashioned for him, and of his pleasure in seeing the fruits of their labor come to life. He described the stone statue that stood in the garden, a sculpture of a young child that his mother had admired on a visit to France and bought because it had reminded her of him and because, sentimental as ever, she wanted the little stone boy to have a happy home. And Georgia couldn't help feeling saddened as she thought of the little stone child who had stood witness while that home slowly died around him.

Nicholas spun his stories, and they might not have been sitting in a dark room lit only by the crackling fireplace and the single candelabrum, but in Raven's Close as it had once been, all alive and shining, just as Georgia's eyes were as she listened.

"But that was more than twenty years ago," he said, finishing with a faint laugh, and the spell was broken.

Georgia felt as if she'd been rudely jerked back to earth, and she felt the old familiar sensation of being unpleasantly returned to her surroundings. She drank deeply of her wine, suddenly nervous, knowing the evening was coming to a close and the dark night was about to begin. "What made it all change?" she asked, trying to delay the inevitable.

"My parents died. I went to Ravenswalk. And then after I left Ravenswalk for India, this happened. Georgia, I'm sorry that I've brought you to this. Truly I am."

She looked at Nicholas with astonishment. "Why should you be sorry? I knew exactly what the conditions would be—or had guessed. It is why you married me, Nicholas. You can't have forgotten?"

"No, of course not. But it still seems dreadfully unfair to subject you to such a thing."

"Anything is better than Ravenswalk. Really. In the last week I have had more hope than I have in the last eight months—no, in truth, far longer than that—and that hope is worth a great deal."

"Then I am happy. Come, Georgia, it is late. I hadn't realized how long we had been talking. Let me show you up to your room."

"My room?" she said, not quite able to believe her ears. "My room? Oh, Nicholas! Oh, Nicholas, thank you! I had thought that . . ." She stopped abruptly, coloring.

"You had thought what?" he asked, sounding perplexed.

She forced herself to go on, for her relief was so great that she felt she ought at least to thank him properly. "I had thought that you would expect . . . well, you know. I had never thought you would be so kind and thoughtful—so understanding. I cannot express my gratitude enough."

He said nothing. He only pinched the bridge of his nose, and then after a moment he leaned over and picked up the candelabrum. "Don't mention it," he said. "This way, Georgia."

She followed him, carefully walking in his path so as to avoid the occasional rotted board. Her heart was so full of relief that she felt positive fraternity with him. He stopped at a bedroom door and opened it for her, putting the candelabrum down on a table close to where logs gently hissed in the fireplace, giving off a pleasant heat.

"Here you are, Georgia. You'll find your clothes in the wardrobe, and I believe that Binkley has provided hot water. Good night."

He abruptly stepped out of the room and closed the door behind him, not giving her a chance to reply. She took a deep breath and looked about her. The room had been made comfortable, like a proper bedroom, with a dressing table, the wardrobe, a carpet on the floor, and blankets and pillows and all the rest. She had never expected so much. It was by far the most comfortable bedroom she'd ever been offered. She could scarcely believe her good fortune.

With the burden she'd been carrying for the last ten days so unexpectedly dismissed, she quickly undressed, put her best dress carefully away in the wardrobe, pulled on her warmest nightdress, and fell fast asleep.

Nicholas was not so lucky. He entered his own bedroom, where at least the ceiling was intact but the windowpane was broken. Although Binkley had apparently attempted to cover the gap with a board, a chill draft still streamed through. There was a fire burning, but it smoked and stung at his eyes. He undressed and threw himself into bed, shivering under the damp blankets. This was not exactly how he had intended to spend his wedding night. No man should have to spend his wedding night in solitude, not with a young and attractive wife sleeping only a wall away. But then, he had forgotten to take into account the fact that Georgia was a widow and no doubt still clung to the love and memories of physical affection her late husband had provided her. It would be churlish in the extreme to intrude himself on that. He would have to wait until she was ready to accept him, and wait graciously, he knew. Under these circumstances, behaving as a gentleman was his idea of hell.

He'd suspected it had all been too easy.

He wondered just how long it would be before Georgia decided to welcome him to her bed. Gallantry should never have been invented. Sainthood was not his style. He was a normal man, flesh and blood, and that flesh was burning and aching and needing release. It had been far too long since he'd had a woman, months in fact, and he'd been looking forward to this night. He had been attracted to Georgia from the first moment he'd laid eyes on her, had had his blood inflamed by that one amazingly sweet kiss, and his imagination had been playing havoc with him ever since he had seen Georgia in her turret wearing nothing more than a simple nightdress.

He had made her his wife, hadn't he? He had spent the last ten days congratulating himself on his choice, thinking about all the fine long nights they would have—starting with this one.

But virtue was virtue.

He should have thought the situation through first, instead of assuming that Georgia would automatically welcome him as her husband. He should have made his intentions clear to her, instead of standing there like an idiot while she thanked him for his understanding. His *understanding?* The only thing that he understood was that he was a fool.

"Oh, God!" He gritted his teeth and buried his head in the pillow, trying not to think of soft arms and round breasts and embracing thighs. He tried hard to think of nothing at all, but that didn't work either. He finally jumped out of bed, threw on his clothes, and went out for a long, brisk, very cold walk.

4

Georgia found Nicholas in the dining room the next morning, his dark head bent over papers that were spread out everywhere. She studied him for a moment before she entered, feeling a rush of gratitude.

She was safe, and she had this man to thank for it. She owed him a great debt. He had taken her from an untenable situation, given her his name, a roof over her head—well, part of a roof, anyway—and had asked nothing more of her. She vowed to do everything she could to see that he didn't regret his generosity.

He glanced up and saw her standing there. "Why, Georgia—good morning. Did you sleep well?"

"Very well, and far too late, I fear," she said. "My room was exceedingly comfortable. If Binkley hadn't been thoughtful enough to bring me chocolate, I might well have slept the rest of the day away."

She had no idea that the morning light was streaming in through the window, backlighting her golden hair like a halo and highlighting her slim figure through her thin, worn dress, leaving little to the imagination. She only knew that Nicholas was gazing at her in a somewhat pained fashion.

"I . . . I hope you don't mind that I overslept," she said uncertainly. "It is not usually my habit."

"I think you must have needed the sleep badly. You had dark circles under your eyes yesterday. And it is no matter to me what time you rise. Sleep as late as you wish. Now, sit down here, for I wish to speak with you." He cleared away some of the papers to make a place for her. "I've been thinking: you need a maid. Binkley might be a marvel, but we cannot expect him to help you with dressing and bathing and all the other necessaries."

Georgia looked at him with alarm. "Nicholas, that is most thoughtful of you, but I have never been dressed or bathed or looked after in my entire life, save by my mother when I was a child."

"Haven't you?" he said, unconcerned. "Well, then it's time that you should be. Furthermore, when I next go up to London, I'm buying you a proper wardrobe."

"Certainly not! What a terrible waste of money!"

"Georgia, my dear, I do believe it is up to me to decide how I will spend my money. You need decent clothes. Decently warm clothes, I mean. And in any case—"

"No," she said firmly, holding up a hand. "I can understand that you would like to have a wife who is properly turned out, but I am a seamstress. If you must, then you may buy me material, but I shall make my own clothes. But I do thank you for the thought. I am quickly discovering that you are a very thoughtful man."

"Oh, is that what you think?" he replied scratching his cheek and giving her a long, unreadable look. "I don't know about that. It is entirely possible that I am a complete imbecile. But very well, you shall have material, if that is what you wish. However, you will also have a maid. It is only proper. And I am not prepared to argue the point."

Georgia was prepared to argue the point, for Nicholas was being foolish, but then a thought struck her and she smiled. She had absolutely no need for a Bella, but she did know someone who was in need of a job, with younger brothers and sisters to feed, and she knew just where to find her.

"If you insist, Nicholas. If you will be so kind as to lend me your carriage, then I shall go immediately to hire the maid you require. I have the perfect person in mind. She was in employ at Ravenswalk in the kitchen. And Binkley will need someone to help him in the kitchen, won't he? It will kill two birds with one stone and save money as well."

Nicholas was silent for a minute, and she couldn't read his expression. "Very well," he finally said. "I think we shall call the discussion a draw. A diplomatic coup, Georgia—honor remains intact on both sides. Very clever.

I do believe I might well have taken on more than I anticipated.''

"As I told you, I only wish to oblige you—when you're being sensible. If Binkley wouldn't mind harnessing the horses? I can drive myself, of course.''

"You most certainly will not. Binkley will drive you.''

"It seems a terrible waste of his time—''

"Georgia!'' Nicholas roared. "Are you going to argue me on every point?''

Georgia, who had learned early in her previous marriage when it was unwise to push a matter, backed down. "Very well,'' she said. "But you cannot expect Binkley to play coachman to me every time I need to run an errand. I can drive perfectly well. I often used to, you know.''

Nicholas pushed out his chair and stood, leaning his fingertips on the table. "You will not drive, not while Binkley and I are here to drive you. The horses are new and headstrong and they need further schooling. Believe it or not, Georgia, there is reason rattling around somewhere inside this imbecilic head.''

"I beg your pardon,'' she said contritely. "I had not meant to challenge your reason.''

"What a relief that is. I've been challenging my reason enough for both of us. If you'll excuse me, I'll just go and instruct Binkley.''

He pushed out his chair and went through the door. But as he walked down the corridor, she heard him muttering to himself. "Bloody, blasted blockhead,'' were the last words to float down the corridor.

Georgia laughed and went to fetch her cloak, wondering what had gotten into Nicholas. Perhaps, like Baggie, he was chronically bad-tempered in the morning.

"You, married, miss?'' Lily, a pretty young girl with a heart of gold, stood in the doorway of her cottage, her mouth agape.

"Indeed, Lily, and to Lord Raven's nephew. It's all a very long story, but the long and the short of it is that we are now installed in the Close, and in desperate need of help. I was hoping I could persuade you to come and work for us.''

"The Close? But you can't live there—it's all broken-down, and not fit for people."

Georgia shrugged. "Exactly. And you needn't live at the house if you don't wish. But, oh, Lily, we're going to make it beautiful again, all on our own, piece by piece and one day it will become the grand place that it once was. Will you help?"

Lily's eyes shone with pleasure. "You know I will, and be thankful for the work, miss. You was always good to me, and I haven't forgotten for a minute, and I'd work for you anywhere, broken-down house or no, and no matter what people say. Lady Raven—she must have been fearful angry with you."

"I imagine, although I didn't consult her on the matter." Georgia grinned. "I just packed my case and walked out the door."

Lily covered her mouth with her hand, but her eyes danced with laughter. "Oh. Oh, my. No by-your-leave? The walls must still be shaking. And to run off with the black nephew? But how? You weren't allowed to talk to a soul!"

"Actually, Nicholas managed it for me. He climbed the outside wall to my room to propose."

"Oh . . ." Lily said with a great sigh. "Oh, I've never heard of anything so romantic! My heart fair bursts!"

"Well . . . it wasn't quite like that. But if you will come, I'd be so grateful. Maybe you could start tomorrow?"

"Tomorrow? Yes, miss. You can count on me. Thank you very much, miss. My auntie has moved in to look after the little ones, so I won't be needed. The money will come in handy, though. And, miss?"

"Yes, Lily?"

Lily hesitated her cheeks reddening. "Thank you for the money you sent before. I was touched. I don't know how to write, so's I couldn't send a note, and I surely couldn't come by to pay you a call, but it made all the difference in feeding our Fred and Mary and little Janie."

"It was my pleasure. I'll see you tomorrow, then."

Georgia had a pleasant feeling of satisfaction as Binkley drove her home, but speaking with Lily had brought into fine focus an aspect of her new position that had begun to worry at her ever since Nicholas had begun to talk about ladies' maids and wardrobes. She was going to have to give the matter some thought.

Binkley appeared in the attic as Nicholas was gazing up through the hole in the roof. "It's going to be a long, cold winter, Binkley," he said with a heavy sigh, contemplating the large expanse of sky.

"Very possibly, sir."

"How was your mission into town?"

"I believe Mrs. Daventry was successful. She has hired a Miss Lily Miller. Lily is young but appears competent enough, and she is a pretty girl."

Nicholas smiled. "For shame, Binkley. I am a married man."

"Indeed you are, sir, and a fortunate one at that. But as you have often said, it is always more pleasant to have a pretty face to look upon than a homely one."

"That's true enough," Nicholas said, thinking of Georgia. It would have been a great deal easier on his loins had Georgia been homely. But unfortunately she had appeared just as attractive to him first thing this morning as she had last thing the night before. He sighed again.

"Do you have an attack of melancholy, sir?"

"Not in the least. See here, Binkley, we'd better get started. The first order of business is to begin to seal up the most obvious hole. The London roofers won't be here until next week."

"I have someone who can help for the moment, sir. After bringing Mrs. Daventry back here, I returned to Polegate, sir, and had a drink at the tavern."

Nicholas gave him a long look. "And what did you discover at the tavern, Binkley?"

"It is just as you thought, sir. The tavern was full of nothing else but talk about you."

"I suppose it was the kind of talk that doesn't bear repeating."

"Exactly, sir."

"And Georgia? I hope they were at least more charitable to her."

"Yes, sir. I would say there is a degree of sympathy."

Nicholas smiled grimly. "I can imagine. Well, with luck, the talk will die down and some other scandal will come along to occupy them. What about this person you found?"

"In the course of listening, I managed to discover a Mr. Lionel Martin, who is a man of all work. He openly scoffed at the talk. I followed him outside and hired him immediately. He is not from this village, sir, but lives on the coast, at Pevensy. He will be arriving tomorrow. I also inquired at the blacksmith as to a mount for Mrs. Daventry, as you requested. There is a mare for sale at a very reasonable sum."

"Well done, Binkley. You may purchase the mare. At least the horses have a solid roof over their head."

"Yes, sir. It occurred to me yesterday upon seeing the condition of the house that you might want to take up temporary residence in the stables."

"Tempting, but no. I must draw the line at sleeping with the beasts. And speaking of that, I think we must fix the window in my bedroom. Frostbite threatened last night. It is a good thing I have a strong constitution."

"Yes, sir, although I do not recommend staying out quite so late in these extreme temperatures. Frostbite becomes a probability."

Nicholas shot Binkley an incisive look, but Binkley did not seem inclined to comment further on how his master had passed the night. "Where is Mrs. Daventry now?" Nicholas asked.

"I fear she is cleaning, sir. I could not persuade her against it."

"What, exactly, is she cleaning, may I ask?"

"The windows in the dining room. She seemed quite insistent on continuing."

"Is your sense of propriety outraged, Binkley?"

"It is not correct in the least for your wife to be washing windows, but I cannot help but admire her sense of purpose, sir."

"Yes, I am rapidly discovering that my wife has a very strong sense of purpose. It could prove interesting. I fear her gentle beauty belies a will of steel. Well, Binkley, let us leave Georgia to her cleaning while we get on with the

65

roof. In your opinion, what do you think the best approach to fixing the hole might be?''

Binkley happily launched into a technical analysis of the situation.

Georgia sat over the evening meal in an agony of nervousness. She had spent the entire afternoon trying to be realistic, and it had not been a comfortable exercise. The reality was that Nicholas was not only a stranger, he was also a stranger from a world as different to hers as night was to day. She couldn't even begin to divine his thoughts. For example, why was he so silent tonight? Perhaps he was inclined to moodiness, she decided. Cyril had problems with moodiness, and she wondered if it ran in the family, like the strong eyebrows and the striking gray eyes beneath.

She colored as she realized that those gray eyes were watching her steadily.

"Have I something stuck between my teeth, Georgia?" he said. "Or perhaps I've spilled something down my shirtfront?"

"Oh, no. Nothing like that. I was just thinking."

"And what were you thinking, may I ask, to cause you to regard me so?"

"I was only trying to work out if you like to eat your meals in silence, or if you're inclined to moods. If I'm to be a good wife, then I need to know these things."

Nicholas put down his fork. "What? What are you going on about?"

"Just as I said. I'd like to be a good wife."

"Georgia, you sound as if you're applying for a job," Nicholas said. "It's already yours, you know. And I told you yesterday that I don't wish to be accommodated. I am sure I wouldn't know what to do with that sort of thing."

Georgia fiddled with her napkin. "You don't understand." She felt the heat creeping up her cheeks.

"All right, then. Why don't you explain it to me, so that I do understand."

"It's difficult, but I'll try. You see, I don't know your likes and dislikes, or much of anything else about you.

66

And you don't know anything about me either. But you should."

"I feel a point coming on," Nicholas said.

"Yes, there is." By this time Georgia had managed to twist her napkin into something resembling a misshapen horseshoe. "I feel it is only fair to be honest with you."

"That's good. I value honesty, as I've told you before. So. What is it, Georgia? Were you a streetwalker in a previous life? Or perhaps you have six children hidden away that you're going to produce on our damaged doorstep? Fine. Whatever you wish."

"Nicholas, please don't tease."

"But I wasn't teasing. I'm quite serious. After all, I did practically coerce you into marrying me. Given that, what's a wicked past, or a child here and there?"

"But it *is* my past that's the problem."

"Oh? In what way?"

"We're from two very separate worlds, and I don't think I'd given it much thought until today, when you began wanting to shower me with clothes that you can ill afford and a lady's maid even if you do think it's the correct thing to do. I'm from a small village in the north, Nicholas. I was a simple farmer's wife. I have no proper background to speak of."

"Georgia, I cannot see anything wrong with your background. You speak like an educated gentlewoman, your manner is perfectly adequate, you seem intelligent enough. Is there a mad grandfather I should know about, some hereditary flaw?"

"I don't know. I don't know anything about my grandparents, and I have no other family. Do you see now?"

"No," he said bluntly. "I don't. What has that to do with anything?"

"You've married me, Nicholas. You, Lord Raven's nephew, have married a woman of absolutely no consequence. I don't mind for myself, but people are bound to talk."

"Georgia, believe me, it would make no difference."

"Perhaps not to you, but it does to me. I told you how I felt before I accepted your proposal, but I could see that you might lose all that you cared about if I didn't marry you, and I was in a dreadful bind myself, it is true. And so I accepted you.''

''Yes. You did. So what in the name of heaven is the problem? You haven't heard me complain, have you?''

''No. That's just it. You have been a perfect gentleman about everything, and I think I should make it up to you as best I can.''

''Make it up to me?'' he repeated slowly. ''How do you mean, exactly?'' The expression in his eyes had sharpened.

''Well, I've been thinking about it. I might not know the things I should about being a proper lady, but there are things I can do just as well, maybe even better.''

''Georgia. . . .''

''Please, let me finish. This is very difficult. You see, it's important to me that I feel I am earning my keep.''

''Earning your keep?'' He sat up straight, staring at her incredulously. ''Is that how you think of it, as earning your *keep?* What in God's name—''

''Please, don't be offended. It's one of the advantages of your not have married a lady.''

Nicholas choked, then covered his forehead with his hand. ''I see,'' he said in a muffled voice.

''It's not so shocking. You see, if you were a rich man, or even very well-off, and Raven's Close had not been falling to bits, then I should never have considered your proposal for a minute. But then, you wouldn't have had to offer for me, either, so I suppose it's a moot point. In a way it's a good thing you are poor, for I am more comfortable with you.''

''But I—''

''Nicholas, please stop interrupting me. I am quite accustomed to being poor, so you mustn't feel badly in the least. After all, I do know how to work hard. I can be useful in a hundred ways. I can paint, and scour, and . . . well, I can do just about anything.''

He looked up at her. ''You . . . you're saying you want to work?''

''Yes. Binkley did not seem to be happy to find me cleaning the windows this afternoon. But I was quite happy, and it doesn't make any sense to waste a perfectly good pair of hands when the house needs as many as it can get. I'm afraid I will never be any good about things like having a lady's maid or an enormous wardrobe, even if you could afford such luxuries. I'm not ungrateful, Nicholas. But I don't think you should try to make a silk purse out of a sow's ear.''

"Georgia—" Nicholas said again, a laugh catching in his voice.

"No, I'm not finished yet. I hope you don't mind too much about not having married a lady, and I promise I will do my best and not stand in your way when you want to go off and do the sort of things that gentlemen do. I will be quite content to stay and look after your affairs here.''

Nicholas looked as if he might sneeze at any moment, and Georgia leaned down and picked up his napkin from where it had fallen to the floor, handing it to him. He took it and stared at it, then at her.

"I hope you're not catching a chill," she said, examining his face for any other signs of a cold. His eyes did seem a little weepy. "Perhaps you should have a hot toddy before going to bed. It is damp, and you can scarce afford to become ill now. But that's something else I can do—I am quite skilled with medicines. I learned from my mother.''

"Oh, yes?" he said, his voice unsteady. "How resourceful you are, to be sure. However, I assure you my general health is excellent. It is only a . . . a slight fever." He covered his mouth with his napkin and made a coughing sound.

"Oh, dear.'' Georgia leaned over and placed the back of her hand on his cheek, then colored furiously as he covered her palm with his own.

"You do feel a trifle warm," she said, pulling her hand away.

"Yes, I know," he said. "But it's nothing that a long night in bed won't cure.''

"You're absolutely right. A good night's sleep, and I'm sure you'll feel right as rain in the morning. I shall ask Binkley to be sure to run a warming pan thoroughly over your sheets.''

"No," he said quickly. "No, don't do that, Georgia.

Please. Binkley would be offended that you thought him negligent.''

"Oh. I hadn't thought of that. You see, there is so much I have to learn about how things are done in the upper class.''

"Mmm,'' he said. "I expect they are done very much the same as anywhere else.''

"But they're not, you see. That's exactly my point. You wouldn't know, because you have never experienced anything else. I don't want you to regret your choice in wives, Nicholas, but I fear you might when you begin to know me. For all I know, you might despise me after a time for being foolish and ignorant. I could never be grand like Lady Raven.''

"And thank God for that,'' Nicholas said fervently, his face suddenly becoming serious. He threw his napkin down and his chair scraped hollowly against the floor as he stood up. "Have you quite finished?''

"Yes. I have.''

"Good. You do know how to give speeches, don't you? Now, I want you to listen to me. You're quite right: you don't know me at all. If you did, you would know that I'm not interested in such things as impeccable bloodlines, nor can I abide airs and graces. And let me tell you something about Lady Raven. Until she married my uncle, she had no entrée of her own into society. She manipulated her way into Ravenswalk, and she's played countess with a vengeance ever since. So don't you think for one moment that she is in any way your better, Georgia. The woman is a vicious, clawing witch who will walk over anyone to get what she wants. You are ten times the lady she is.''

Georgia smiled ruefully. "I wish it were true, and it was a kind thing of you to say. I have had many a daydream in my time in which I was a very grand lady indeed. Generally speaking, the more awful the situation, the more fantastic the story I would spin for myself. You would laugh if I told you some of them.''

"Rapunzel, perhaps?'' he asked with a laugh.

"Well . . .'' she answered, blushing. "Not exactly Rapunzel.''

"Georgia. Oh, Georgia, you are a dreamer, aren't you?"

"Yes, but the problem is that one always wakes up and has to face reality, which brings me back to the original point. We have to be practical, Nicholas, and make the best of our circumstances."

He was silent. He had turned away and was gazing out of the dark window. The firelight sparked and leapt in bright flame, casting shadows over his broad shoulders.

"It's like this house," she said, watching him. "Last night when you were telling me about the old days, it was like magic. I could see it all, as if it were a story that was being enacted around me, as if the rooms were just as they had been, the people still there, the parties, the laughter, the happiness. But then it was time to come back to the present. And there was this." She gestured around her.

"Yes," he said, still looking out into the dark. "That's exactly right. There was this. And what did that make you feel, Georgia?"

"Hope," she said simply. "For the first time ever, there was hope of bringing some of that magic back into real life. Usually it can't be recaptured. Do you understand? Have you ever woken from a vivid dream, thinking for a few moments that it was real, that you'd brought it with you?"

"Often," he said tightly.

"Well, then you know exactly what I mean. I used to sit and look at this house and imagine what it had once been when it was alive. I made up stories for it, gave it a past, even created a family for it. But the stories you told last night were even nicer than mine because they were true, about real people, a real family. But it was still magical, Nicholas. And now there's a chance to make it happen again, to make it right, to bring it back to life. . . ."

Her voice trailed off. She hugged her arms around herself, suddenly feeling acutely embarrassed at what she had just revealed to him, and wondering what had possessed her. She never spoke of these things to anyone. "Oh . . . now I do feel silly. You see how fanciful I am?

I promise that I shall try very hard to control these foolish tendencies.''

Nicholas turned around. "I wish you wouldn't," he said softly. "This house is going to need some serious magic if it's to be made whole again. Come, it's time to go up. The fire is dying down and it will soon be cold."

"You go, Nicholas. I'll clear everything away."

He stepped toward her and lightly took her by the shoulders with a half-smile. "Georgia. You will listen to me. You may work to your heart's content, but you will not intrude on Binkley's domain. He would not thank you, or me, for it. That is lesson one. Lesson two. You will honor your husband's wishes—within reason, naturally. Now, come."

He dropped his hands and picked up the candelabrum, leading her out of the room. Once again he left her with the candles. Once again he quietly, politely bade her good night.

Georgia lay awake for some time that night, wondering very hard about the man she had married. He was unlike anyone she had ever met.

Nicholas heard a cry. He couldn't place it at first, and then he realized it was his own. The water was over his head, and something was pulling him down and down as the water rushed up his nose and into his mouth, choking him. "No! Oh, God, please!" he cried again. "Please, no!" He couldn't breathe, couldn't breathe . . .

And then there was a figure standing over him in the dark water, someone clad all in white, and he wondered if he was dead.

"Nicholas?" came the voice, and a soft hand touched his wet brow, stroking the hair back off his face. It was an angel, he was quite sure, noting the golden hair. Who had ever heard of a dark-haired angel? The question was, had he in fact drowned, or was he still in the process? If this was heaven, it was terribly cold and uncomfortable.

"Nicholas, you're having a dream. Wake up now. Wake up." He felt his shoulder being taken firmly and squeezed by a most unangelic hand.

He shook his head hard. He didn't know where he was, but he did know he was alive and relatively dry, save for the sweat pouring off him. He shuddered, burying his face in his hands for a moment. Then he threw back his head, inhaling air as fast as he could. It was all right. He was all right. He'd made it through another drowning. He dropped his head back against the thin pillow, trying to steady the frantic beating of his heart.

"Oh, bloody hell," he said when he'd finally oriented himself. "Oh, damn." It was no angel bending over him, it was his wife, and he was mortified to have been caught in such a position. He hastily pushed himself up in bed.

"Nicholas? Is it the fever?" Georgia asked with concern, stroking his face again.

"The fever? What fever?" he asked, still confused, and then he remembered. "Oh, yes the fever. Yes, that's it. It must have broken," he said, leaping on the excuse with alacrity. "Yes, I can tell. It has definitely broken. I'm better now. Much better." He wiped his forehead with a trembling hand.

"But you're shaking, Nicholas. At least let me bring you one of my blankets. It's terribly cold in here." She looked around with dismay, noting the cold air that streamed through the broken window.

"No. No, absolutely not. I don't need another blanket."

"You're being very silly, Nicholas."

He nodded. "As I told you, I'm an imbecile." He could not help but notice the way her full breasts pressed against the material of her nightdress as she bent over him, and he turned his face away as he felt his loins begin to stir.

"Then why don't you move into my room for the rest of the night? It's much warmer."

Nicholas' head jerked back around in sudden hope. "Your room?"

"Yes. I'll sleep in here. I don't mind at all."

"That's very generous of you, Georgia," he said, suppressing a sigh. "But I'm warm enough. Thank you, but I think I would like to sleep. Yes. I feel very much better, but I think I need rest now. Good night, Georgia." He rolled over on his side and feigned a sudden exhaustion.

"If you're sure. . . ."

"Quite sure," he said with a yawn. "Now that the

fever has broken, I am sure I will sleep soundly. I do appreciate your concern, but really, there is no need for it.''

''All right. Good night, then, Nicholas.''

''Mmm.'' He forced himself to take light, steady breaths, holding back a deep sigh of relief until he heard the connecting door close.

''Oh, sweet Christ,'' he whispered, slamming his hand into his pillow. ''Oh, that was a fine performance, my man. I can see you're destined for success.''

He rolled over onto his back with a groan. It had been one hell of a fine day. The roof was half-gone, never mind the state of rest of the house, the village was rife with foul rumors, and he'd had his nightmare to finish it all off. And on top of everything else, his wife apparently had no intention of letting him come near her, now or ever. Well, maybe that was one thing he could remedy. If Georgia was not going to invite him to her bed, then he would have to find another way to accomplish his goal. Aside from the matter of his throbbing loins, he'd never have children at this rate.

He spent most of the remainder of the night contemplating the situation, his eyes fixed on the large stain on the ceiling. He had always been an accomplished strategist, but breaching Georgia's garrison was going to take more adroitness than he had ever imagined.

5

"Binkley," Nicholas said, entering the kitchen early the next morning, "there has been a slight change of plan."

"A change of plan, sir?" Binkley asked, drying a dish and putting it away. "And what change would that be?"

"It's Georgia. She's under the impression that I'm impoverished. Penniless, Binkley. All my pockets to let, except for perhaps one very, very small one, which holds just enough to keep bread in our mouths."

Binkley absorbed this. "Do you not plan to disabuse Mrs. Daventry of this peculiar notion?" he asked after a moment.

"No, I do not. I have thought about it most of the night. I have a long, hard job ahead of me, and being penniless might help."

"Excuse me, sir, but the long, hard job you refer to surely cannot be restoring this edifice? Being penniless will hinder you considerably in that endeavor."

"Yes, I know." Nicholas sliced himself a piece of bread. "I was actually referring to my wife."

"Ah," said Binkley wisely.

" 'Ah,' Binkley? Just what do you mean by 'ah'?"

"It had occurred to me, sir, that a courtship might be necessary."

"You are, as usual, quite correct. I fear the 'happy haze' you alluded to has not yet manifested."

"That is unfortunate, sir. I know how deeply you desire a family."

"Exactly. And this will be no easy conquest. You see, Binkley, I believe Georgia is still in love with her late husband."

"Oh, dear me. Yes, I can see that might create a problem."

"Yes. Furthermore, it transpires that said late husband was a farmer."

"Ah," Binkley said again, putting a chipped cup filled with tea in front of his master. "And so you will become a farmer also?"

"Well, not exactly a farmer, no, but I certainly cannot be a man of thriving business. You see, for some reason Georgia has decided that a state of reduced circumstances is attractive in a man, and so reduced circumstances she will have. I believe I shall be struggling." He waved the piece of bread. "Is there honey, Binkley?"

"Certainly." Binkley pulled a jar from the cupboard, taking care not to knock the door off the one remaining hinge. "We are not accustomed to struggling, sir."

"It will do us good. We are flexible, are we not? In any case, I always did plan to be directly involved in the rebuilding of the house. It will just take longer than I had anticipated. I've written to London to cancel the workmen."

Binkley looked eloquently around the dilapidated kitchen. "Very good, sir. And will we always be struggling?"

"Good heavens, no. I will make a fortune on the 'Change, or perhaps have an extraordinarily prosperous shipment come in. I'm not sure. But whatever I decide on, our creature comforts will have to wait until the courtship is complete."

"Then I hope that your usual skill is in place, sir."

"It is going to take more than ordinary skill, Binkley. Georgia is not quite an . . . ordinary woman. Oh, and by the by, if you are asked about the state of my health, I am much improved."

Binkley inclined his head. "Have you developed a weak constitution along with poverty, sir?"

Nicholas laughed. "No. But I made a damn fool of myself last night with the blasted nightmare, and Georgia came running. Fortunately, she decided I was fevered. Which I was by the time she'd finished administering to me. This courting business is going to be hell, Binkley."

"Most probably," Binkley said equitably. "You will have to rely on fortitude."

"Unfortunately, my fortitude is already slightly frayed

76

around the edges. Oh, and, Binkley, there is something else, and I'll be damned if I know how to deal with it. I've never been married to a farmer's wife before."

"And what might that be, sir?"

"Georgia is under the impression that she is not high-born enough for me. Therefore, she has taken it into her head to make up for her lack of birth by single-handedly rebuilding my house. I do not think it would be wise to attempt to dissuade her from any labors she decides to undertake. Do you think you can adjust?"

"If the courtship requires a lowering of standards, I believe I can manage, sir." Binkley sniffed. "I can manage anything."

"Yes, of course you can," Nicholas said soothingly. "And you needn't consider it a lowering of standards, merely a relaxing of protocol."

"A relaxing of protocol is not a problem, sir. However, I do believe it would be in Mrs. Daventry's best interests to be gently instructed to the more intricate ways of the gentry. After all, once we are no longer struggling . . ."

"As you wish, Binkley," Nicholas said, trying not to laugh. "You may instruct my wife, as long as you do it subtly. I do not wish her to feel in any way inadequate."

"I am always subtle, sir."

"Indeed you are, Binkley. Indeed you are. Now, onward and upward. I believe the man Martin has just arrived. Shall we go out to meet him? It seems that with the new plan, we might be relying on him a great deal more than we had originally anticipated. I doubt very much you're going to see any of the inhabitants of Polegate lining up for employment."

Nicholas gulped down his tea, and shoving the bread between his teeth, shrugged himself into his coat and went out through the kitchen door to deal with his new employee. Impoverishment was going to be interesting, he decided.

Christmas morning dawned bright and clear. Georgia woke to the sound of Lily coming into her room with a tray, a luxury Nicholas had insisted on the night before.

"You've been working day and night," he'd said, "and

I think one morning in bed will not hurt. Consider it a Christmas present to yourself.''

She sat up and stretched as Lily put the tray down and opened the makeshift draperies, and then she grinned as she heard the hammer start to pound. ''Is Nicholas up on the roof again, Lily?''

''Yes, missus. But he waited till I came to wake you.''

''Did he? He is considerate. I do wish he'd take a break, though. It is Christmas morning, after all.''

''Christmas or no, missus, the snow and rain still come down. The master asked me to remind you that services are at eleven, miss.''

Georgia sighed. ''Yes, I know. I've never missed a Christmas service in my life, but I must say, this is one I wouldn't mind avoiding.''

''Don't you worry about nothing. There might be gossip in the village, but it's best to face it straight on and hold your head high. You don't have nothing to be ashamed of.''

''I know that, Lily, but the villagers don't.''

''Well, like I said, nothing so exciting's happened for years. Everyone knew about the quarrel between his lordship and Mr. Daventry, and now that Mr. Daventry is back, the village is abuzz about it. And since word is out that Lady Raven isn't speaking to Mr. Daventry, and his lordship can't speak at all, and then Mr. Daventry married you in the blink of an eye straight out from under Lady Raven's nose, and now the two of you are living here, well . . . you can imagine.''

''That's just the problem, Lily. I'm not sure I can imagine. I was wondering . . . I can't really ask Nicholas, you see. Will you tell me what they are really saying?''

Lily went the color of a beetroot. ''I don't think you'd be wanting to know, missus.''

''It would be better to be prepared, especially if I have to face them all today.''

''Well . . . it's nothing against you, miss. They can understand why you'd want to be getting away from Ravenswalk and Lady Raven, and they all know how kind you was to me in my time of trouble. It's Mr. Daventry.''

''What about him?''

78

"It's all because he's part of that family. They think there's a curse on them, with the earl's brother and his wife dying like they did, and then the first Lady Raven, and then the earl himself struck down speechless. And Lady Raven, she's brought nothing but misery to the village since the earl took ill, not looking after the people like Ravenswalk has always done. And look at the strange young lord. He can't speak right, not that he'd speak to the likes of us if he could. They say that the devil's got his tongue, and his heart too, for he's cold as ice, inside and out. It gives me the shivers just looking at him, like looking at a dead man, he's that pale."

"Perhaps, Lily, although I suspect it's only because he doesn't eat properly or get enough exercise. But never mind that, what does all this other gossip have to do with Nicholas?"

"Well, missus. I can't really say, as it's not fit for my ears, my auntie said. But there's rumors, you know, about his past, and why he left so sudden-like, and why it was ordered that his name was never to be mentioned again, and his house allowed to fall to ruin. They say he's the worst of the lot. And they worry for you, missus, for they say he only married you to spite Lady Raven, and sooner or later you'll come to grief at his hand. I don't believe it for a minute, for he's been nothing but kind to me."

"I don't believe it either, Lily, and rumors are usually just that. So we'll ignore them. Nicholas is the kindest man I've ever known, and I think it's horrible that people would say such nasty things. Now, are you sure you don't want to come to church?"

"Oh, no, missus, I went to midnight services. It was kind of you to give me the night off, and we had our Christmas dinner then, so there was a tableful of people, and everyone anxious-like to know how things were over here. I told them you was doing just fine, happy as two peas in a pod."

Georgia smiled. "Thank you, Lily."

"And I told them how good you and the master was to me, and Mr. Binkley too, and how grateful I was for the wages, and that all the talk was stupid. They'll see for themselves soon enough."

"I hope so."

"So never you mind. I collected the master's present just as you asked, and it's safely put away in the stables. Now, you'll be wanting your nice dress for today, and I'll have hot water up in just a tick. The master has sent up a present for you."

"A present, Lily? What sort of present?"

"A hip bath, missus, as shiny as you've ever laid eyes on, and every bit as big as Lady Raven's! It's standing just outside, and Mr. Binkley's heating the water, and I'll soon have a fire blazing."

"An actual bath?" Georgia said with delight. "Oh, that is luxury indeed, Lily! Oh, thank you!"

"You're not to be thanking me. It's all the master's doing. You finish up your tray and enjoy your rest. You've been working your fingers to the bone."

Twenty minutes later Georgia was sitting in the hip bath, reveling in the feel of immersion in hot water. She wet her hair and washed it with a tiny slip of scented soap she'd bought in London before she'd been sent away to Ravenswalk. It had been her one indulgence, and she had hoarded it, bringing it out every now and then just to sniff the fragrance of roses.

The suds felt wonderful, and she slipped as deeply into the water as she could, closing her eyes and letting her body relax. She hadn't felt so wonderful in . . . Thinking about it, she couldn't remember when.

Reluctantly she pulled herself from the bath and dried her hair before the fire until it sprang into soft curls under her fingers. She dressed quickly, then inspected herself in the broken mirror. She looked rested, the circles gone from under her eyes, and her skin was rosy. It was Christmas morning, and it was the happiest Christmas morning she could remember in years. She heard Nicholas moving about next door and then the faint splashing of water.

She picked up her bonnet, and with a light heart went downstairs, carefully picking her way around the rotten floorboards.

"Good morning, Georgia," Nicholas said, entering the sitting room, looking splendid in his buff-colored pantaloons and black morning coat.

"Oh, Nicholas," she said, rising. "Thank you for the hip bath! Thank you from the bottom of my heart! I am sure it cost far too much, but I don't care in the least."

"That's a relief. I was prepared for a lecture. Happy Christmas, Georgia."

"Happy Christmas, Nicholas. What a beautiful day it is."

"It is indeed, and you look splendid, every inch a lady."

"I don't know about that, but I am certainly very clean."

He smiled. "Are you ready to face the village?"

"The way I feel right now, I could face anything."

"That's good. I have an idea of what might be in store, and you'll need some fortitude. The villagers are the least of our worries. Shall we?" He offered her his arm and she took it, and they went out to the carriage together, where Binkley was waiting.

She could sense the interest and saw the averted glances as they arrived at the church, but she followed Nicholas' lead and nodded her head right and left as they entered. He led her to a pew toward the front, and she gave a quick exhale of relief as they sat down.

But the worst was yet to come.

A sudden whispering and rustling began, and it grew louder. She felt Nicholas suddenly stiffen beside her, and she quickly looked to her right. Her heart began to pound and her mouth went dry.

Lady Raven was parading past them, Cyril at her side. Neither of them looked over, but it was clear that they both had seen Nicholas and Georgia and were deliberately ignoring them. She suspected that Lady Raven had a great deal to do with the fact that Cyril had not answered Nicholas' recent note to him, but she had not thought that Cyril would actually go so far as to give his cousin the cut direct. And it had cut Nicholas, not just directly, but deeply. His face was stony, and he had not betrayed any emotion with even so much as a blink of his eye, but she knew he was upset. It wasn't the first time she had seen him so.

She slipped her cold hand into his and was glad that

he let it stay. She needed to feel his strength. Inside she was shaking.

A number of other people, guests at Ravenswalk by their appearance, filed up the aisle after Jacqueline and Cyril and entered the Raven box. Their sly sidelong glances betrayed the malicious gossip that must have been flying among their company.

Georgia looked over at Nicholas again. His eyes were resting on the altar, and he appeared oblivious of the insults that had just been silently but powerfully slammed in their direction.

Again she took her cue from him and rested her eyes on the altar cross, trying very hard to remember why they were there.

It was Christmas. They were celebrating the birth of Christ. Nicholas had told her he had celebrated Christmas in this church every year for twenty years, and now, after ten years, he was back. She knew he had been christened in this church, and only three weeks ago he had been married here. He belonged every bit as much as each of the villagers, as much as Cyril did, and a great deal more than Jacqueline, who Georgia did not think belonged in church at all.

She felt Nicholas' hand go to her elbow, and she realized that they were supposed to stand for the processional.

Somehow she made it through the rest of the service.

"I do like the vicar enormously. He's a very kind man, isn't he?" Georgia said on the way home, trying to ease the discomfort Nicholas was so obviously feeling.

"Yes, and an intelligent one, thank God. He may be forced to be bipartite, but he doesn't let it intrude."

"He's the first vicar I've met who shakes everyone's hand with no hint of disapproval." Georgia pulled at the finger of her glove.

"I wonder who you think should have been given the disapproval. Surely not us?"

"I had only wondered. He must have heard the gossip."

Nicholas laughed. "Gossip? The man has been vicar for a good forty years. I'm sure he's heard a great deal worse in his time. We haven't done anything particularly interesting or exciting, save for flying in the face of Jacqueline's desires, and those I can assure you he's not interested in. The vicar is not a political creature. His career is not likely to rise or fall on Jacqueline's schemes, although he will never become the Archbishop of Canterbury, not that he'd want the position if it were offered him.''

''Nicholas?''

''Yes?''

''You're unhappy, aren't you?''

He looked at her with surprise. ''Unhappy?''

''Yes. I understand why, of course—it must have been very unpleasant for you to have to undergo such an experience. But I don't like to see this expression on your face, not on Christmas. Can we forget about the gossip and Ravenswalk and all of the other problems, just for today? I know it's asking a great deal . . .'' She trailed off, not wanting to admit that she, too, had been hurt and shaken by the coldness directed their way, although she was accustomed to being shunned. But Nicholas was not, and it had felt like death on a day that most especially celebrated life.

He rubbed his hand over the back of his neck. ''Yes of course. You're quite right, Georgia. It is not a day for these angry feelings. We will forget about the rest of the world and public opinion and have our own day of quiet celebration.''

''There's pheasant,'' she said encouragingly. ''And a carrot soup, and bread pudding to finish. And other things in between. And I have a present for you.''

''But you've already given me a warm scarf for my birthday, Georgia. You needn't give me anything else.''

''Well, I shall, because it gives me pleasure to do so. You have given me so much already.''

''What?'' he asked curtly. ''What have I given you? This house over which you insist on slaving eighteen hours a day? A new dance you have learned in order to skirt around the floorboards? What have I truly given you, Georgia? What have you let me give you?''

She thought about it with great seriousness, for it was important to her to say it correctly. ''Your kindness, for one,'' she said. ''Your conversation. Your smiles even when I've done something foolish, and your patience. You have not caviled at my lack of breeding, nor my ignorance. And you have offered up your home and let me help you to try to make it whole again. But most especially, you have respected my privacy. All of those things have a price beyond measure to me, but the last means more than I can ever tell you.''

He turned his head sharply toward the window, and she could see nothing but his dark hair. Perplexed by his reaction, she wanted to ask him why he was disturbed, but the carriage drew up to the house just then and the moment was lost.

Nicholas seemed to have regained his spirits by the time they sat down to their Christmas meal. He made pleasant conversation throughout, touching on nothing more important than the progress of the roof and the planned changes for the kitchen. But Georgia did not miss the restlessness in his demeanor and she did not know how to make it better, or how to ease whatever burden he was feeling. She imagined it was all tied up with Christmas and Ravenswalk and his family, and she did not want to intrude with questions. But she did want to make the remainder of the day a happy one for him, and so she chattered away, trying to keep his mind off his troubles.

"Come," she said when they had finished the pudding. "Let me give you your present now. You will want to take a long walk after such a meal, and you will need this first.''

'I have something for you also,'' he said. "It's over here.''

He rose and collected a large flat package that was lying in the window seat, and he brought it back to the table and put it in front of her. "Here,'' he said with a little smile. "Something I promised you. It's come from London.''

"Nicholas! You shouldn't have bought me anything else—but I'm delighted that you did,'' she said, looking up at him with a grin. "I haven't had a present in years, and two in one day! And there was the mare too.'' With fingers shaking from excitement, she untied the string and pulled the paper away. Before her disbelieving eyes appeared bolts of material, soft rich wools, delicate muslins in an assortment of colors, linens, even a length of velvet in a lovely deep blue. She stared at them. "Nicholas . . . oh, Nicholas. I don't know what to say!"

"Say that you are pleased. I hope I chose well. There are some fashion plates on the bottom that the dressmaker recommended. I hope everything is suitable."

"Suitable? Nicholas, this is wonderful—but so extravagant! These materials are the sort of thing that Jacqueline would have."

"Precisely. Now, go and change into your outdoor clothes and we'll go for that walk."

Georgia jumped up from the table, cradling the package in her arms. "Thank you," she said quickly, and ran out of the room. Then she stopped and ran back again, putting her head through the door. "I'll be back in no time, and then you shall have your present."

Nicholas looked at her, that unfamiliar expression in his eye, and it made her feel quite peculiar. "Go on, Georgia," he said, his voice slightly rough. "I want to have a quick word with Binkley." He disappeared in the direction of the kitchen.

Georgia found Nicholas waiting by the door in the front hall, also changed back into his everyday clothes. Actually, he wasn't exactly waiting: he was examining the plaster around the front windows. She had never yet seen Nicholas in a state of idleness. He was a man of perpetual movement. Even when he was sitting still, she could see that his brain was active in one fashion or another. It was little wonder that he slept so little. Night after night she had heard him pacing the floor, or coming up to bed in the early hours before dawn. One night she had crept downstairs herself, thinking to get a glass of milk from the pantry, and she had seen Nicholas in the dining room working steadily at a large pile of papers. He had not heard her, and she had not announced her presence, quietly slipping back up the stairs. But she could not help but be curious. What could Nicholas be doing in the middle of the night and with such intense concentration? She very much doubted it was anything to do with the house.

"Nicholas?" she said and he looked over his shoulder and quickly stood, brushing off his hands.

"And where is this present you have promised me so breathlessly?" he asked, smiling at her.

"We have to go to the stables. It is nothing grand, for you know I have no money, but I hope you will like it despite that."

"Georgia. You know better than to think that money is a consideration. I'm touched that you thought of anything at all. Really, I am."

"Don't be silly," she said, walking down the steps and starting toward the east, where the stables were nestled in a clearing of oak. "As I told you earlier, you have given me so very much already." She didn't wait for an answer, not really wanting to hear it. It was Christmas Day, and she would have nothing spoil it.

She heard the squeals before Nicholas did, but then, she was listening for them. "Come inside," she said with a grin, opening the door to the tack room, and then she stood back.

A small body came shooting toward them like a bullet, almost a blur in its speed. Nicholas took an automatic step backward then dropped to his knees in surprise as a wriggling body of fur flung itself against him.

It was no prize as far as dogs went, a bizarre mixture of terrier and hound, and still a pup at that, but it had heart and voice, and it gave vent to that voice immediately in an infantile attempt at a howl, then began to lap at Nicholas' hands with a frenzied tongue.

Nicholas laughed and picked the little wiry body up in his large hands, holding it up over his head. "And who are you?" he asked, looking over the undercarriage of the dog. "Ah, a young man? A very young man by the looks of you." He gently placed him on the ground again, where the pup proceeded to pull at his shoe. "Thank you, Georgia," he said quietly, turning to look at her. 'He is a wonderful present."

"You are very welcome," she said. "He is from one of the tenant farms. Lily told me about the litter. He was the scrappiest of the lot and I felt he had the most intelligent gleam in his eye."

"Yes. He does look fairly acute. Now he needs a name,

don't you, my friend. Let me see: how does Raleigh sound?"

"Raleigh? It sounds perfect, but what made you choose that?"

"I've always had an admiration for the man. He was a scrappy devil himself. Come along, Raleigh. Would you like to join us in a stroll around your new property?"

As if he not only had understood, but also had been doing it all the days of his brief life, the puppy took up position at Nicholas' heel, wagged his wiry tail vigorously, and with his tongue lolling out of his mouth, set off with his new master and mistress.

Jacqueline threw her hairbrush across the room in a fit of rage. Seeing Nicholas with his whore in church today had been almost more than she could bear. She had felt his presence behind her, had almost been able to feel the heat radiating from his strong, vital body. She had heard not one word of the service, her mind filled with images of Nicholas, hot, sensual images. In the years of his absence she had forgotten just how powerful he was, how he emanated sexuality from every pore.

But now, seeing him again, knowing he was just a mile away, she had started to burn again as if the ten years had not passed. And yet he had grown only more attractive with the years, a man now in his prime. Her hatred of him fueled her passion. Oh, yes, she remembered. She remembered everything. There was not another man alive whose nakedness had inflamed her so, and she had sampled many men since that night.

She thought she had taken care of him for good, had destroyed his precious house, had seen to it that he would never return. But he was back. He was back, and her blood was on fire. "Damn him! Damn them both!" She closed her eyes and bit the inside of her cheek so hard that she tasted blood. The thought that Georgia was now lying in his arms, was tasting his pleasures, receiving his caresses, made her ill. Of all the people in the world for Nicholas to marry, why her? It was like history repeating itself.

She rubbed her forehead hard. She still couldn't understand how it had happened at all. Georgia must have found a way to seduce him, the clever slut, although Jacqueline had taken such care to hide the girl away so that just such a thing couldn't happen. But happen it had, and under her very nose.

Well, why should she care? Jacqueline examined her face in the mirror with cold satisfaction. She was the Countess of Raven, with power and position. She might have had her birthright stripped from her through no fault of her own, but she had regained it and more. Ravenswalk was one of the finest houses in Britain, the fortune one of the largest. And she had complete control over both. She had shown her sisters. She had shown everyone. She had everything she wanted.

Everything except Nicholas. The throbbing started again between her legs at the very thought of him, and her hand went to her breast. She cupped it, her eyes halfclosed, imagining it to be his hand, remembering the feel of his palm just there.

And then she dropped her hand abruptly. There was no point in tormenting herself with memories. As for Nicholas, his life was clearly ruined, and if young Georgia thought she had married into position, she was very much mistaken. She had married herself to a man who would never be accepted back into the fold of polite society: Jacqueline had already seen to that. Let them live in their ruin and suffer. The villagers would shun them, the gentry would scorn them, their lives would be miserable.

As for herself, she would accept the invitation from the Marchese di Castagnaro and winter in his villa. She needed some hot-blooded diversion. Yes, that was what she would do. She would leave at the beginning of the new year. She certainly wasn't going to stay around Ravenswalk and watch Nicholas and his doxy any longer.

She was hungry tonight, very hungry. If she couldn't have Nicholas, she'd help herself to the next best thing. She dabbed perfume between her breasts, adjusted her dress, and started through the dark, quiet house to the east wing.

6

Georgia immediately started sewing. She created a table in the back of the sitting room and she drew patterns and cut and stitched to her heart's content. A week went by and then two, and she had a new cloak, Nicholas two warm shirts, and she had started on a day dress. Life had settled down to a comfortable routine. Nicholas worked on the roof all day while she and Lily cleaned and scrubbed and dusted, or, on fine days, worked outside. Come nightfall, she would work on her sewing while Nicholas read by the fire, or wrote letters, or did simple tasks.

Life with Nicholas could not have been more different than life with Baggie had been, she thought, cutting a thread.

Baggie had never been at home in the evenings, choosing to spend his time at the tavern. Nicholas had not once been to a tavern, at least that she knew of, and she enjoyed his quiet companionship in the evenings. Baggie had never spoken to her about much of anything except farm business. Nicholas spoke to her on a broad range of subjects, and if there was something he wanted, he requested it. He had never once treated her as a servant.

Raleigh snored in his sleep and shifted on his blanket, and Georgia rubbed his little side with her toe, eliciting a sigh of contentment. She looked up from her stitching. Nicholas was oiling the library books, his hand moving in methodical circles over the leather spines. He looked content, and it occurred to her that he no longer had such a careworn expression on his face, that he looked more at ease. It has been a gradual change: he'd been as tightly coiled as a spring when they had first come to the Close.

But now, five weeks later, it seemed as if they had alway lived this way, in a quiet harmony.

She wouldn't say he was happy. He was a very privat man who kept himself close to the chest and let no on in. She had only once seen him display any real emotion and that had been when he had thought himself to b alone. Another time, there had been a brief flash of ange when he had seen the state of the garden, but he ha quickly stifled it. No, most of the time he kept his feel ings to himself, giving little hint of what they might be She had tried hard to puzzle him out, but she had no always been very successful.

For instance, there had been the time when she ha measured him for his shirts. He had behaved most oddly coloring and pulling away as if he didn't like to b touched. He had left the room immediately afterward And yet when she had given him the shirts, he had smile with pleasure, that wonderful warm, gentle smile of his as if no one had ever made anything for him before.

He was an enigma. She liked him very much, for he was kind and generous, and she trusted him not to hur her. But he was still a mystery to her. With Baggie, she had known exactly how he would react to everything. With Nicholas, it was all guesswork.

"Georgia? What are you dreaming about now?"

She jumped, startled out of her thoughts. "Oh! Nothing. I was just thinking."

"And what were you thinking about?"

"About this, about living here."

"Hmm. Should I fear for my life?"

"Don't be foolish. I like our life here, Nicholas."

"Do you?" he said comfortably. "I'm happy to hea it. But then, compared to what your life was like at Ravenswalk, anything would seem like paradise, even this."

"Even this? But this is wonderful! I feel as if every day we are making a difference. Every day the house becomes more and more awake. Don't you feel it?"

"You are whimsical, aren't you? But I know a little of what you mean. I do feel a great sense of accomplishment at the end of every day. We no longer have rain and snow pouring on our heads, and the very worst of the damage has been cleared away."

"And soon enough the weather will grow warmer and I can begin to work on the garden in earnest."

Nicholas shook his head. "I don't know what you can do, Georgia. Everything is dead. It would probably be best to plow the damned thing under and let it go to grass."

He sounded so sad, so bitter, and it hurt her. It was horribly unfair, what had been done to him. Well, the least she could do in return for all he had done for her was to give him back his garden.

"I can make it grow again, Nicholas," she said with determination. "My mother taught me much about growing things. She could just look at the earth and things would sprout up. Her vegetables were the biggest in the village, her flowers the heaviest with bloom. She said she talked to the plants and they talked back."

"Did she? It's odd. My mother said the same thing. She said that there was a spirit in all living things and each place had its own god. She would talk to the god of her garden, leave little offerings. It's very pagan, I know, but it seemed to work, for the garden flourished. But I think the god must have left this place long ago in sheer disgust."

"We shall see, Nicholas. The first thing to do is to give the soil air and light, and then we will know better what might come back to life. And I will start seedlings, so that when it is warm enough, they can go outside. We'll breathe life back into it together."

Nicholas put down his book and came over to her. She couldn't read his face. He gently took one of her curls in his fingers and rubbed it between them, then dropped his hand and moved slightly away. She was left feeling oddly shaken by the gesture. It was the first time Nicholas had touched her in such a way, and she didn't quite know what to think of it. It had been such a tender touch. She looked down and wondered why she suddenly wanted to cry.

"You amaze me, Georgia," he said, moving over to the fireplace and looking down into the flames. "You work hard all day, doing your best under a miserable set of circumstances, and you never once complain. And now you want to take on even more."

"I told you, it makes me happy to see things come back to life. And this house especially, for I told you how sad I used to feel about it."

"Yes. You said it was like an orphan. And you said you had been orphaned. Will you tell me about it, Georgia? I know so little about you outside of these walls."

"There isn't much to tell," she said, snipping another thread and thinking back to those early, happier days. "My father died when I was seven. He was a good and gentle man, and he and my mother were very happy together, although we were poor. My father was a soldier, but he'd developed trouble with his lungs and had to retire from his regiment. So he became a schoolteacher instead, until he was too ill even for that. After he died my mother went on alone, sewing for a living, and ministering to the sick, and growing her plants. And then she died of a fever when I was twelve."

"Where did you go then?"

"As I had no relatives, I was sent to the vicar and his wife." Her face darkened with memory.

"I see. I don't think you were very happy with the vicar and his wife," Nicholas said, watching her carefully.

"Not particularly. They were good to take me in. But it wasn't home." She stabbed the needle into the material, and it went straight into her flesh. "Ouch!" She stuck her throbbing thumb into her mouth.

"Perhaps it was just a little bit more than the fact that it wasn't home?" Nicholas asked, looking at her thumb.

Georgia looked up at him and saw the amusement in his eyes. "Very well," she said with an answering smile. "If you must have the truth, they didn't like me and I didn't like them."

"And you stayed with them until your marriage?"

"Yes. I was with them for five years. They were very happy to see me go." She thought again of the day that Mrs. Provost had come into her attic room, accusing her of things she didn't even understand, and her marriage three weeks later to a man she'd not even known. Three long weeks of being locked in her room with bread and water once a day, not knowing what her future was to be. But it was the first time in five years that she hadn't

92

had to cook the meals and scrub the floors and wash the linens, or clean and dust and polish. And she had felt safe from the vicar, locked away in her bedroom, with Mrs. Provost keeping the key, for the vicar had recently developed that alarming male habit of pawing and poking and trying to plant his wet mouth on hers.

"And then?" he asked again.

"And then I married Baggie Wells." Baggie, whom she'd first laid eyes on when she'd been taken into the church. But she didn't bother to add that.

"And were you happy?" he asked quietly.

Georgia wondered at the suddenly shuttered expression on his face, and then she realized he was upset by her story, for he always shuttered his face when he was upset. She felt bad for having complained at all, but she was unwilling to lie outright.

"Georgia?" he asked again into the silence.

She smiled cheerfully, but she couldn't make the smile reach into her eyes. "The farm was nothing grand, but it was home. I can't tell you how wonderful that was, having a home again."

"I can imagine." He paused for a moment and then spoke very carefully. "And there was also Baggie."

"Yes," she agreed miserably. "There was also Baggie. It lasted three years. And then it was over." She looked down at her hands, wondering if her eyes had given her away after all. By the tone of his voice, she knew that Nicholas had guessed.

He nodded, his brow drawn down, and he turned his back and picked up the poker, stirring the fire.

"Nicholas, I don't ever want you to feel sorry for me. That time is over and done with. It will never be like that again, I am quite sure. And you have been very understanding about it."

He looked over his shoulder for a minute, then turned back to the fire. "What happened after Baggie died?"

She took a deep breath, relieved to have the subject of Baggie out of the way. "It was difficult. There were debts, and I lost the farm. I went to London and worked in a shop for a year. Lady Herton liked my designs, so I went to work for her. A year later I was sent to Ravenswalk. And I am very, very grateful to you for taking me away."

He spun around. "Damnation, Georgia! How many times do I have to tell you I don't want your gratitude! We could go on to the end of our days telling each other how grateful we are to have gotten the other out of a scrape. But that's not what I want. Gratitude is empty. It means nothing to me. I feel quite sure that Baggie wasn't interested in your gratitude either."

"Oh, please, Nicholas, can we not talk about Baggie anymore? Those memories are . . . are difficult."

"I'm sorry. I didn't mean to dwell on it. But I am only human. I begin to wonder how much you expect from me."

"But that's just the point!" she said with exasperation. "I expect nothing! I have tried and tried to make that clear to you."

"Oh, yes, you made it clear enough," he said, shoving his hand through his hair, equally exasperated. "I was just hoping that at some point you would decide that you're not averse to the idea that you're married to me."

She stared at him. Averse to the idea? Hadn't he been listening to her? She no longer lived in fear of the night, she lived with someone who talked to her and listened in reply, someone who was not an overgrown child, but a man of strength and intelligence and manners, a man who thought about her feelings, who respected her wishes.

"Nicholas," she said painstakingly, "I am not averse to being married to you. You are a thoughtful, considerate man, and I know you don't want me to say I am grateful to you, so I won't. But you have to stop thinking that I want anything from you other than what you have already given me. And I do wish you would stop asking me if I do, for it makes me exceedingly uncomfortable."

"Very well, then," he said, his voice suddenly cold. "If that is what you wish."

"Yes, it is. But why do you look at me like that?"

"Why do I. . . ? Georgia . . ." He rubbed his hand over his face. "Never mind. Never mind. It's late. I'm going to bed. Good night, Georgia. I hope that you, at least, have pleasant dreams."

He'd sounded upset, she thought as he left, and she

wondered again at the contradictions that made up Nicholas.

There was a strain between them for the next week, and Georgia knew it had to have stemmed from that night and their conversation. She realized it had not ended well, but she wasn't exactly sure why, or what she had said to upset him. She'd been over it and over it, and she could think of nothing. He had questioned her about her past, and she had answered him truthfully. Perhaps he had found the details distasteful. Still, her feelings were hurt, and she found that she missed him more than she ever would have expected.

She moved the brush rhythmically up and down over the surface of the wall, feeling very much alone, even though she knew Nicholas was working just down the hall. She missed his companionship, she missed their quiet evenings together, the walks they took together. She missed his conversation, the small courtesies he showed her that no one had ever shown her before. She also missed his physical presence, as if something vibrant and vital had been taken out of her world, and she found that she waited just for a brief glimpse of him to reassure herself that he was still there. There was no mistaking the fact that Nicholas was avoiding her at every opportunity.

She bent over and dipped her brush in the bucket of whitewash and was just about to apply the brush to the wall again when she heard a great crash, and then a shout.

"Georgia! Where in God's name have you gone to?" Nicholas' voice sounded slightly panicked and Georgia picked up her skirts and ran down the hall. When she looked around the corner, paintbrush still in hand, she could see why. Nicholas dangled half in and half out of the floor of the front bedroom. Apparently a good section of the floorboards had given in unexpectedly, and she covered her mouth for a moment, trying very hard not to laugh. It really wasn't funny, but she couldn't help herself: it served him right for being so nasty. She laughed until she cried.

"For the love of God, woman, this is no time to be amused. Fetch Binkley, will you?"

"I can't," she said, wiping her eyes. "He's gone into town for more wood."

"Then get Martin."

"He went with Binkley." Georgia grinned. "I suppose I could rescue you. If I felt like it."

"What . . . what is that supposed to mean?" he said with a pained grunt.

"Just that. You have been very short with me this week, leaving rooms when I enter, not being pleasant company at all."

"Georgia—"

"You are now in a position where you cannot leave. Perhaps you would like to explain your attitude. If you wish rescuing, that is."

"Georgia, this is no time to have this discussion, and in any case, you know damned well what's been bothering me. Avoiding you seemed to be the only sensible thing to do." He tried to push himself up, with no success. "Furthermore, I thought the subject was closed, and may I remind you that you were the one to close it?"

"I was?" she asked with a little frown, trying to puzzle this out. "I'm sure I hadn't meant to."

He groaned and hitched himself forward a fraction of an inch. "Ahh . . . my ribs."

"Oh, dear. I do think we really should get you out of there, Nicholas, before the floor gives way altogether."

"And how, my dear, do you propose to accomplish that? I weigh twice what you do."

"You'll just have to push while I pull, unless, of course, you intend to dangle there for the next hour or two? I'm afraid you have no choice." She placed her hands on the waistband of his trousers. "All right. On the count of three." And then she pulled for all she was worth.

Nicholas shoved with his arms at the same time, and he came popping out of the hole with such force that she flew backward and landed against the wall, hitting it so hard with her head that she saw stars.

"Georgia? Georgia, sweetheart, are you hurt? Are you all right?" She opened her eyes to see Nicholas kneeling over her, his hands on her shoulders, his gray eyes looking into hers with concern.

She sat up straighter and rubbed the back of her head. "I'm fine, I think. But you've torn your chest to ribbons, Nicholas. Oh, look at you! And that's the second shirt this month!"

"Never mind my poor flesh, you're worried about my shirts?" he said with a smile. "Are you sure you're not hurt?" He touched her cheek, and Georgia's face went hot. She found that she very much wanted him to touch her other cheek as well. It was so nice to see the warmth back in his eyes. "Oh, Nicholas, I have missed you," she said with a rush of relief. "If you meant to punish me, you succeeded."

"Did I?" he replied very softly, the expression in his eyes changing from concern to something else. "Perhaps the blow to your head finally knocked some sense into you. Shall we see?" He seemed to move closer to her, and then he did touch the other cheek. He took her face in his hands and his head bent toward hers. She could feel his warm breath on her cheek, the heat of his body radiating into hers, and her own breath quickened. Georgia fuzzily thought that he was inspecting her very closely indeed, and in a rush of confusion she wiggled away.

"I'm perfectly fine." She picked herself up off the ground. "But you need some salve on those scrapes. Wait just one moment, and I'll fetch some."

She was back almost momentarily with a basin of water, a cloth, and the ointment. "Take what's left of your shirt off, Nicholas. I know it's cold, but it can't be helped."

He did as he was told, and Georgia examined his chest. He really was a fine figure of a man, she thought, assessing the damage. His bare chest was shaped into sleek, strong planes, his ribs ridged with muscle. She was fascinated by the thin line of black hair that ran from a small, silky patch on his chest directly down the center of his stomach. Baggie's barrel-shaped chest had been covered in a thick mat of hair, as had his back. Nicholas was a great improvement over that design. She had an irrational desire to reach her finger out and trace the line with it.

"Will I live?" Nicholas asked, and, embarrassed, she was called back to her task.

"Probably." She dipped her fingers in the salve and carefully dabbed at his bleeding chest. Nicholas looked down at her, a pained expression in his eyes.

"Am I hurting you?" she asked with concern.

"Not exactly," he said, his breath pulling in sharply.

"Don't try to be brave. It's foolish. If it hurts, say so, and I'll be more careful." Her palm brushed over his nipple, and it went hard. She looked at it in surprise and had to force herself not to snatch her hand away.

"Oh . . ." he said with that now-familiar catch of laughter. "You're right. It hurts."

She gave him a long look, then went back to applying the salve. His skin felt hot under her fingers and she lightened her touch.

"No, you don't have to do that," he said. "It's better the other way."

She looked up at him with a frown. "You want me to hurt you?"

"I can take it. It's better to get the stuff thoroughly in the wounds and avoid infection, isn't it?"

"The wounds are not that deep, Nicholas. They are merely scrapes."

"Merely scrapes? So say you. Would you see me fester and die? Please, Georgia. Thoroughness is everything. Have you not told me so time and again yourself? Do what you must. I promise not to scream." He rested his hands on her hips and bowed his head as if to brace himself.

She carried on massaging the salve into his chest in smooth, gentle strokes, and she could not help but feel real sympathy for him, for tears had started to his eyes, and he groaned once. He was clearly in pain, even though the scrapes had not initially looked that serious to her.

"There, that should suffice," she said reluctantly stepping away, for she had enjoyed the feel of him under her fingers. Touching him made her feel pleasantly odd, and she had not minded his hands touching her in the least. She capped the jar. "Does it feel any better?"

"Yes. No. Oh, Georgia." He turned away from her and covered his face with one hand.

"Nicholas? Are you sure you have not bruised yourself

internally? You really should not be experiencing such discomfort.''

He made a strangled noise in his throat, then muttered something about finding a clean shirt. Georgia found herself alone in the room. She shrugged and went back to her painting.

But after that, Nicholas seemed to have forgiven her for whatever transgression she had committed, for he no longer left the room or spoke brusquely to her. In fact, she often found him watching her, and it was with a combination of curiosity and that other expression she did not recognize, the one he had worn when she had bumped her head and he had bent over her. All she knew was that when she did find him looking at her like that, it made her feel weak and achy and overly warm.

She didn't understand it in the least.

Nicholas carefully placed the thick, flat piece of slate on top of the foundation he'd prepared. Binkley had brought the first load from Horsham, and Nicholas was anxious to get the tiles into place before he returned with the second. Martin, who had gone off with Binkley, had shown him how to produce the correct pattern, and it was detailed work that did not allow for wandering thoughts—a blessing, for his thoughts had been wandering far too frequently recently, and in all the wrong directions.

His attention was distracted as he caught a flash out of the corner of his eye, like sun reflecting off glass, and he looked again at the woods that led toward Ravenswalk. He'd had the odd sensation over the last few weeks that he was being watched, and this indicated that his instincts might be right. He very much wanted to know who was doing the watching, and why. He knew it couldn't be Jacqueline: she had been away since early January and was not expected to return until late spring. Whoever it was, the person was being very careful to keep his presence unknown. Nicholas went back to his work, frowning.

And then he saw it again, unmistakably coming from the woods, and this time he decided he was going to discover just what was going on. He quietly made his way over the roof, ignoring the ladder in the front, instead dropping over the back side of the house and climbing down the old ivy root. He skirted the side of the wood and noiselessly came up behind the old path. He was as familiar with these woods as the back of his hand, and he knew he was well-concealed. His eyes scanned the area around him. Nothing. Absolutely nothing, except for Georgia, who was moving about in the front garden where she had been working for most of the warm morning.

And then his eye fastened upon the odd sight of a boot dangling just above eye level. He moved slightly forward and peered up into the branches. And there was Cyril, sitting in the crook of two boughs. He had a telescope clasped to his eye and his concentration was absolute.

Nicholas thought carefully. That a boy of seventeen had nothing better to do than to sit in a tree and spy on his relatives struck him as very odd. But it also occurred to him that this might be the perfect opportunity to further his acquaintanceship with his cousin. Cyril had steadfastly refused to answer a single letter Nicholas had sent to him, and he had stayed well out of sight—until now. It was clear that Cyril was not uninterested in Nicholas' activities, nor Georgia's for that matter. Nicholas wasn't particularly bothered about the reason for that interest, prurient or otherwise. He had caught Cyril red-handed.

"Good morning, Cyril," he said, and the tree shook as Cyril started and nearly tumbled down. "Lovely day, isn't it?"

"Oh, N-Nicholas," Cyril stammered, having gone first white and then red.

"Will you come down, or shall I come up?"

Cyril's mouth opened and then closed. He slung the telescope over his back and hurriedly climbed down the tree, landing clumsily on the ground.

"A good choice," Nicholas said. "I doubt it would have been a comfortable perch for two of us."

Cyril just stared at him. He couldn't have looked more guilty.

Nicholas held out his hand for the telescope. "May I?" he said, taking it and examining it. He put it up to his eye and pointed it at the Close, then handed it back to Cyril. "It's heavy, but I suppose it's been working well enough."

Cyril just nodded, then swallowed, his larynx bobbing up and down.

"Do you know, I was wondering, Cyril. You surely must have noticed the sorry condition of the Close while you were sitting up there day after day. As you have also no doubt noticed, we are working very hard, Georgia and I, to put the Close to rights."

Cyril shrugged.

"I imagine you must sympathize with the situation. After all, the property is entailed to Ravenswalk, which will one day be yours. We are very shorthanded, as you have seen, and we would be appreciative of any help we could get. I don't suppose you have any ideas? We can't afford to pay for extra help, you see. We would need someone strong, able-bodied, who had a great deal of energy." Nicholas looked at him thoughtfully. "Someone just like yourself, in fact. Someone who has time on his hands, who would like to stay out of trouble. But I suppose that to ask you would be out of the question."

"Well . . . I s-suppose I c-could help," Cyril said uncomfortably. There had been a small sharp flicker in his eyes that Nicholas hadn't missed. He wasn't sure if it boded good or ill, but he wasn't going to stop to find out. Someone needed to take Cyril in hand, and he couldn't think of a better way to do it.

"Really? You would be willing to help? Ah, Cyril. Now, that is truly Christian of you. It really is. Georgia will be so pleased." He put a firm hand on Cyril's back and gave him a pat that almost amounted to a shove, propelling the boy forward. "Come, we shall tell her together, and then you must share our luncheon with us. It will be modest, I warn you, but we can't ask you to work on an empty stomach."

"No. How k-kind."

He looked thoroughly annoyed, Nicholas thought with satisfaction as he led Cyril down the path with an iron grip.

"Cyril!" Georgia said, jumping to her feet as they came toward her. She could not believe her eyes. Nicholas had Cyril collared almost like a dog with a bird. It was a most compelling sight, for she had been feeling very annoyed with Cyril for his ill treatment of Nicholas. She was surprised for more reasons than one. For the first time she saw them side by side, and the resemblance really was uncanny. She could see how easily it was that she had mistaken Nicholas for Cyril that first day. But despite the similarities of feature and coloring, Nicholas was very much the man and Cyril the youth, and a very red-faced youth at that.

"How nice to see you again," she said, giving Nicholas a look of inquiry as if to ask whether it was nice or not. She really couldn't tell.

"Isn't it," said Nicholas. "I found Cyril studying birds, and he says he has so much idle time on his hands that he would be happy to help us in our work, Georgia. Isn't that generous of him?"

"Most generous," Georgia said. She could see that Nicholas was up to something and she waited for his lead.

"I thought that as soon as we have eaten, I will take him up onto the roof," he said. "It will help to have someone, since Martin has gone off for the day."

"Oh . . . oh, n-no," Cyril said pleadingly, looking truly alarmed. "P-please, sir, I have a f-fear of h-heights. Anything else. Anything . . ."

"Very well. Georgia has started on the gardens. I'm sure she would appreciate your help there. And you do seem to enjoy spending time in the outdoors, do you not Cyril?"

"Yes, sir."

Georgia was impressed: Nicholas had already begun to command a reluctant respect from his cousin, despite the fact that Nicholas was wearing the simplest of work clothes and Cyril was dressed in a style appropriate to the heir to an earldom.

"Why don't you come in, Cyril?" she said politely, throwing Nicholas a look of high amusement. "It is nothing exceptional, of course, but it is home, and the meal should be ready shortly."

"Very well. Thank you."

He looked around him with dismay as he entered, and Georgia watched him carefully, wondering what was going through his mind.

"It's a pity, isn't it, Cyril?" Nicholas said, leading him through the hall. He pointed at the high ceiling, where the plaster, once ornately molded, was buckled and peeling. "They're all like that," he said. "Mind your step. We've shored up the worst of the floor, but it can still be dangerous. Here. The dining room is in better order, and not all the furniture was taken, so there is a table off which to eat."

Cyril's face went redder and redder as Nicholas spoke, and Georgia was glad for his embarrassment. If Cyril had chosen to side with Jacqueline against Nicholas, at least he could see with his own eyes what his stepmother had done.

"Lily," Nicholas said as she came out with a platter of cold meat and potatoes, "lay another place, please. Lord Brabourne will be dining with us today."

Lily's eyes widened with surprise, but she curtsied and did as she was asked.

Cyril said very little during the meal, and he kept his eyes down. Indeed, Nicholas did most of the talking. "It was a shame to have to bring my wife home to this, but I had no choice," he said. "I've tried hard to describe to Georgia the beauty of the Close before it was pillaged and then allowed to fall to bits. It appears as if there must have been a bad storm at some point, which ripped half the roof away. We've had some cold, wet nights, I can tell you. I look forward to the spring. More water, Cyril? Georgia? It doesn't help to be only a few miles from the sea, either, for that only encourages the damp and rot. Oh, by the by, Georgia, I asked Binkley to bring the seedlings you requested when he returns. You can start them indoors in my mother's old room off the buttery."

"Thank you, Nicholas," she said. "You are always so thoughtful."

Cyril frowned.

Nicholas stood and went over to the window, looking out over the garden where the hedges and shrubs ran wild and the weeds stood tall in the old beds. A dead tree, once a magnificent elm, stood blackened and forlorn, its branches hanging over the wall as if they were sadly trying to reach in and touch the past. "If you really can bring this back to life, Georgia," he said, "there is no effort too great."

He looked over at Cyril, whose eyes slid away.

"Well," Nicholas said, "we had better get back to work. There's much to be done before dark sets in. Cyril, go with Georgia. She will let you know what needs doing."

He walked out the door without looking back.

"Come with me, Cyril," Georgia said. "And try to look pleasant. You don't want to wither what few growing things there are."

"I . . . I'm only doing this because I w-want to," Cyril said belligerently.

"I'm sure you are. And both your cousin and I appreciate your help."

"It didn't t-take him long to s-seduce you, did it?" he said nastily. "All your talk about p-propriety, and you ran off with h-him the first chance you g-got."

Georgia glared at him. She knew this mood well enough, and she also knew how to deal with it. "You wouldn't dare to say that in front of Nicholas, would you? And you won't speak like that to me either. Whatever your feelings might be, you can keep them to yourself, because I'm not interested in hearing them."

He scowled and kicked at the floor with the toe of his boot.

"It might surprise you to know that Nicholas cares about you very much, and I think it's very bad of you to have treated him as you have. But that's between the two of you. However, while you're on this property, you will behave with decency and respect. Now, come along. You can start by pulling up the weeds out front. Lily and I are digging up the beds."

She marched out, and Cyril followed like a sullen, chastised puppy at the heel.

"How did it go?" Nicholas asked Georgia over dinner that night. "There didn't seem to be much conversation, from what I could see."

"I boxed his ears and he sulked the rest of the afternoon, which was just as well, for I didn't feel like speaking to him in the least. When he gets into these moods, he is impossible.''

"He worked hard enough," Nicholas said.

"Yes, and it's probably the first day's work he's done in his life. There are times I feel sorry for him, locked away at Ravenswalk with Jacqueline and a sick father, but the fact is, the boy is spoiled, Nicholas.''

"That won't last for long. I have a plan.''

"I thought you might. What is it?''

"Well . . . it was a stroke of good fortune to catch him spying today. He's no doubt terrified that I'll tell Jacqueline, for I'm sure he's been told to keep away on pain of death. But I have the feeling that Cyril secretly longs to make a friendly overture. He can't have completely forgotten how he used to tag along at my heels everywhere.''

"No, I imagine not. But then, he's been under Jacqueline's influence for so long, and there was the problem between you and your uncle . . .''

Nicholas nodded. "Yes, I know. And I plan to begin to visit my uncle while Cyril is busy over here and not inclined to interfere. I might as well take full advantage of Jacqueline's absence.''

"She's gone?'' Georgia said with surprise. "How do you know?''

"Binkley has his sources in the village. She is most definitely gone, and she won't be back for a good long time.''

"Oh, that's wonderful news.''

"It is indeed. And good for Cyril too, I think, not having her influence. I think what the boy needs more than anything is fresh air and hard work. And he needs to be exposed to a family, some normalcy. Well, relative normalcy. He's been too much alone. He needs a man to show him how to go on, and I'm sure he'll soon learn that I'm not the ogre I've been made out to be. You might think me an ogre, Georgia, but I promise you, underneath this repulsive exterior, I'm not all bad. Mostly, but not all.''

'Nicholas!'' she said in laughing protest. "You know

I don't consider you repulsive in the least, nor an ogre. Are you fishing for compliments?''

"I wasn't," he said wistfully. "But should I? Would you give them to me?"

"You know perfectly well that you are an extremely attractive man. In fact, no doubt you not only know it, but I imagine you have been told so time and time again by an enormous assortment of women.''

"But never by you," he said softly.

"Well, you are. You have only to look at Cyril to see yourself.''

"I don't see it. In what way do I resemble Cyril?''

"Your coloring, for one thing. You both have exactly the same black hair and gray eyes. And then there's the arch of your brows, and also the shape of your mouths.''

"Oh?" he said. "And what shape is that?''

"Well, wide, I suppose. And full, although your bottom lip is slightly fuller than the upper.''

Nicholas ran his finger over his mouth. "Interesting." He leaned over and reached the same finger out, touching her lips. "Yours is different," he said, outlining it. "Yours is shaped like a bow, with two little curves upward at the corner. Oh, and it's rosy. Did I mention rosy?''

"No," she said, thinking the accursed fever was coming upon her again.

"Well, it is. I don't believe my mouth is rosy in the least.''

"No. It's . . . it's the same color as the rest of you.''

"Flesh-colored?" he said.

She nodded.

"How dull. Excuse me. May I?" He leaned even further forward as if he were reaching for something, and the next thing she knew, those lips were on hers. The touch was very light, and his mouth, slightly open, moved softly, as if he were tasting.

A moment later he had pulled away and was sitting back in his chair as if he'd never moved. Georgia stared at him, touching her mouth with shaking fingers. "What did you do that for?" she said, her voice unsteady.

"I wanted to see how rosy tasted. Sweet, I discovered,

and soft. I would say like early strawberries, but that's not quite it. How did flesh-colored taste?''

Georgia was thoroughly rattled, but she couldn't really refuse him an answer. "It was like . . . like flesh."

"Oh, Georgia, you disappoint me. Flesh can taste any number of ways. Salty, dirty, soapy, fresh, stuffy, like camphor—''

"You did *not* taste like camphor," she said, unable to resist laughing. "If anything, you tasted like wine and sunshine. Or maybe the smell of sunshine was from your hair. I'm not sure. Smell and taste go hand in hand."

"Yes, quite right. But if anyone's hair smells of sunshine, it is yours." He casually rose and bent his head to her cap of curls, and Georgia found her heart was beating wildly.

"Yes, I was right. Sunshine, just as I said. It's appropriate, given its color." As he straightened, his fingers lightly brushed the side of her neck.

She clenched her hands together in her lap.

"Georgia," he said, taking his seat again and regarding her with grave concern, "you're not catching cold, are you? You're shivering, and your face is flushed."

"I don't think so," she said, wishing the shivering would stop. "I'm probably just tired."

"Tired?" He leaned his chin on his fist and regarded her lazily, with that look in his eyes. "You're tired? Are you sure that's what it is? You don't usually tire easily."

"I know, but it has been a long day. I think I'll retire early. Forgive me if I don't sit next door with you this evening."

"Don't trouble yourself in the least," he said, looking extremely amused. "But should you need anything, you know where to find me."

"Good night, Nicholas." She nearly fled the room, and she heard his soft laugh follow her down the hall. She was beginning to think there was something very wrong with her.

She mixed a strong cup of nerve relaxant before going to bed that night.

7

"Tea?" Nicholàs asked the next morning, putting down his quill as Georgia entered the dining room. "There's a pot just here, and I think it's still hot. Lily can make fresh, if you'd prefer."

"No, that will be fine. Thank you," she remembered to say, for she was preoccupied.

He poured her a cup and handed it to her. "And how are you this fine morning? I thought I heard you tossing and turning in the night."

"You did?"

"Yes," he said cheerfully, and bent down to feed Raleigh a piece of toast.

"Well, I slept soundly as far as I am aware. Although I did have a very peculiar dream, so perhaps that is why I tossed."

"Tell me, Georgia, sweet. I am a master at peculiar dreams," he said with a touch of irony. "Please—don't think you'll bore me for a moment."

"Well . . . it's all a bit vague, but I remember that I was in a strange place, somewhere I didn't recognize. It was dark and cold, and there was an ogre—don't laugh, Nicholas."

"Oh, dear God," he said, putting his head in his hand for a moment. "Sorry. Go on."

"I am sure you put the idea of ogres in my head last night with your silliness. Anyway, there was an ogre—or actually, it was more like a troll. Do you know about trolls?"

"I do, indeed," he said, making a valiant effort to keep a straight face. "I had an Orkney nurse who told me terrible stories about them."

"Really?" she said, her face lighting up. "My father

was from the Highlands. He was very fond of troll stories. My mother could never understand why he persisted in terrifying me with them."

"I can imagine. Which is no doubt why you are dreaming about them to this day. And what did this particular troll do?"

"That was the odd thing. He was chasing me, and I was trying to run away, with that awful feeling that my feet were stuck and I couldn't move, do you know?"

Nicholas nodded. "And then?"

"I was very frightened. There was a table, and I knew that if I didn't escape, the troll would tie me up on the table and eat me for his supper. Alive."

Nicholas grinned again and shook his head.

"So there I was, trying to run and not getting anywhere, and I looked over my shoulder to see how close he had come, certain it was the end of me. But when I looked, the troll had shrunk. He grew smaller and smaller as I watched, and the voice he was shouting in became higher and higher until it was just a tiny squeak. And then he went up in a wisp of smoke."

"Really? How fascinating."

"Wait, I haven't finished. Once I knew I was free, I caught my breath and looked around. I was in the cellar of a house. I couldn't think how I had come to be there, or what had made the troll vanish. And then I saw. There was a man standing in the doorway. He was dressed in a suit of armor and he had a lance—"

"Not the *prince,*" Nicholas said. "Oh, Georgia, you are incorrigible."

"He wasn't a prince in the least. That was the other odd thing. This man's armor, it imprisoned him. I couldn't see his face, but I knew it was sad, that he'd been locked away inside this horrible thing for years. I thought he must have been another prisoner of the troll's, but the troll hadn't been able to eat him because he couldn't get him out of his armor. So in a way, he'd been lucky, even if he was trapped and uncomfortable."

Nicholas leaned forward, his eyes dancing wickedly. "Let me guess. You ran over to him on tiptoe, of course, and you kissed the chin piece on his helmet—I assume there was a chin piece?"

"There was, and I certainly did not. I am not given to kissing strangers, Nicholas, despite what you might think. I went over to him, and I asked him to tell me what I might do to help him."

"Oh, of course. How silly of me."

"Nicholas, I will not go on if you persist in teasing me."

"Sorry. My humble pardon. Please, don't stop now."

"I asked him what I might do to help him, and he said in a deep, melancholy voice, 'Inside my breastplate there is a seed. You must take this seed and plant it in the earth. Your love will be its sunshine, your tears its water. From this seed will grow a mighty tree, and the tree will bear fruit. Take the first of the fruit and bring it to me.' "

"I'm telling you, it's the prince."

"And I'm telling you, he was *not* the prince. Whose dream is this, anyway?"

Nicholas grinned. "It's certainly not mine. It has your trademark all over it."

"So let me tell it my way. I reached my hand out, wondering how to get through the breastplate."

"This is going to be good," Nicholas said with a choked laugh. "Maybe it will give me some insight into the tactics of frontal assault."

"Nicholas, I really will not tell you the rest if you keep interrupting," Georgia said, pouring herself another cup of tea. "And there is no insight to be had. I should never have taken the tisane before bed, that's all. Anyway, I reached my hand out to his breastplate, and suddenly in my palm lay a tiny golden seed. I took it outside—"

"I thought you were in a cellar."

"Well, I was, but this is a dream. The next thing I knew, I was outside in the most beautiful garden. In the very center of the garden was a little piece of tilled earth. I carefully placed the seed in the earth, and I patted it down. I thought of the poor sad man, and I cried, and then I thought of how happy he would be to be free after all this time. The earth trembled, and a shoot appeared, and it grew before my eyes into an enormous great tree. I'm not sure what kind. But it was big." She looked at Nicholas suspiciously, for his shoulders seemed to be shaking. But his head was turned away, so she couldn't see his expression "And on the tree was an apple—stupid, I know, for it certainly wasn't an apple tree."

"Golden?" Nicholas asked breathlessly, looking back at her.

"What?"

"The apple. Was it golden?"

"No. It was an ordinary old apple. Well, it wasn't ordinary. I mean, it wasn't riddled with worms or anything. It was red and ripe and quite beautiful."

"Oh, my God," he said, looking completely disbelieving. "What did you do with this red, ripe, beautiful apple?"

"I picked it, naturally, and I took it back to the man in armor."

"Yes?" he said, his lips trembling. "And what did you find, my sweet Georgia? Tell me quickly, love, for I cannot bear the suspense."

"That was the saddest thing. He was dead."

"Dead? What do you mean, he was dead? He can't have been dead." Nicholas looked mightily surprised, even disappointed, and Georgia saw that he'd become involved in her story, despite his teasing. Well, she could tease as well as he.

"He was quite dead. He lay there on the ground in his heavy armor, and I didn't know what to do. Here I was with his apple, having done everything exactly as he'd said. But he hadn't said anything about dying. I didn't think it would be right to eat the apple myself."

"No, absolutely not. You certainly couldn't have done that. I can see you were placed in a very difficult position. And what did you do?"

"I placed the apple in his gloved hand. And then I went back outside to the garden. I was very worried it might have wilted because he had died."

"Dear heaven, this is getting better and better by the moment. And what did you find?"

"Well . . ." Georgia said slowly, reeling him in. "I found the troll."

"Not the troll? Surely not the troll? Oh, Georgia. Why the hell did it have to be the troll? I thought we'd dispatched the troll."

"We had. But that's the thing about trolls. They keep

coming back. And my feet were stuck, and I was trying to run, and I looked over my shoulder . . .''

Nicholas burst into laughter. "You're a wicked woman, Georgia Daventry. But it doesn't wash, and you haven't bested me yet. Now, tell me the truth. How did the dream really end?''

"And you won't laugh at me if I tell you?''

"I'll try very hard not to, but I cannot guarantee it. Back to the apple. What did you do with it?''

"I did put it in his hand. And I did go outside. But what I found was very different. There was a garden, but it was this one, and you were on your knees digging in it and swearing under your breath as you tried to dislodge a root. There was no great tree and no apple and nothing other than the soil and the cross expression on your face. And I'm deeply sorry, but there was no prince.'' She grinned.

Nicholas laughed even harder. "Oh, Lord. And that really is the truth?''

"Yes, that is the truth. Boring, isn't it?''

"Boring? Dear God, you're anything but boring, sweetheart.'' He dissolved, burying his face in his arms, his shoulders shaking so violently that Georgia almost worried for him. He looked up at her, tears streaming down his face. "Oh, Georgia, I do find your way of expressing yourself most elucidating. I don't know whether to be downcast or elated.'' He fell into hoots again.

"Nicholas, you make no sense. What do you find so amusing?''

"I can't quite explain—it must be an aberration of the brain. I have a tendency to have these storms. Please, Georgia, forgive me. It is of little import. I am often foolish.''

"You are not often foolish in the least, and I shall not ever tell you another dream as long as I live, if this is the way you choose to behave. I feel very silly.''

"If you feel so silly, then why is your smile so wide? I know it was your dream, but you did tell it to me, and tell it charmingly. I think you enjoyed the telling as much as I enjoyed the tale.''

Raleigh gave a low growl, and Nicholas' expression suddenly sobered as his eyes went past her to the door.

"Good morning, Cyril," he said, his voice now cool. "How long have you been standing there, I wonder?"

"Long enough to hear a s-stupid s-story about apples and armor," Cyril said. "Oh, and let us not forget t-trolls."

"And let us not forget, my dear Cyril, that it is impolite to let one's presence go unannounced. Don't let it happen again. We might appreciate your help, but we also appreciate our privacy, and you seem to have developed a habit of, shall we say, watching others?" Nicholas stood, and Georgia was amazed by the severity of his voice. She had not heard the tone from him before. "Now. It is time to set to work," he said more kindly. "Georgia, I will meet you and Cyril back here for luncheon. Cyril, I trust you will help Georgia in every particular that she asks."

"Wh-whatever you w-wish, sir." Cyril's intonation in no way agreed with his words.

"It is exactly what I wish. Actually, there are a great many things that I wish, but this is what I would ask of you. Thank you, Cyril." He gave his cousin a long, undecipherable look, which seemed to have the desired effect, for Cyril's eyes shot to the ground and his open defiance vanished.

Nicholas then gave Georgia a warm smile and touched her shoulder as he passed. "Have a happy morning digging."

"I will, thank you. We start cultivating the back garden today. The front is finished for the moment. Cyril did a brilliant job yesterday of taking out the remainder of the weeds."

"I saw. I hope you are as successful on the other side."

"I am sure we will be." She smiled in return, and Nicholas shook his head again and gave a short laugh, gave Raleigh a pat, then strode off to his work by way of the kitchen.

"Cyril, do try to be more gentle," Georgia said for the tenth time as he took the hoe to the earth with a vengeance. "As I've told you, I suspect that there might be bulbs under there, and you don't want to cut them to bits, do you?"

He just looked at her.

"Very well," she said, trying to control her temper, for he had been behaving like this for almost all of the morning. "If you insist on cutting things to bits, why don't you start with that dead wood over there? It all needs to be cleared out. There's a hatchet in the shed. Raleigh, stay. Good boy."

Cyril threw the hoe down and marched off. Georgia watched him as he went, feeling as if she had an extremely recalcitrant child on her hands, not a situation she might have wished for, but one which she was stuck with nevertheless. But if Nicholas was right and they could help him somehow, then it was worth whatever strain he created. Perhaps being around growing things would help, and bringing the garden back might give him a sense of purpose, which he was sorely lacking. But she really didn't know how to deflect his seething anger. She was seething herself, which didn't help.

The puppy gave a happy bark, and she looked up to see that Nicholas had been watching them from his perch on the roof. She spread her hands out with a little shrug, and he shrugged in return, but he was smiling. He reached into his pocket and pulled something out, then tossed it down to her. It landed close to the statue of the child, and she saw that it was a handkerchief wrapped around a small round object. She picked it up and, mystified, untied it. Inside was a red apple, one of the fall's crop, slightly withered, but still sweet-smelling. Georgia started to laugh, and then laughed harder as the humor of the situation took over. She laughed until her sides ached and tears rolled down her cheeks. Her peals rang out over the garden, washing away the pall of bitterness and anger that Cyril had so effectively spread over the morning.

Nicholas grinned down at her, then disappeared over the gable, and Georgia breathed a deep sigh, remembering the pleasure she usually took from life at the Close. Nicholas had an uncanny gift for putting things into perspective, she thought, and went back to her work with a broad smile.

When Cyril returned, he was unable to make a dent in her mood, as hard as he continued to try.

* * *

After lunch, Nicholas set off for Ravenswalk, without giving any indication to Cyril of his intention. He knew it might be a battle gaining entrance, but that did not concern him. This was one garrison he knew exactly how to breach.

"You will stand aside and let me enter," Nicholas commanded the terrified footman, "and you will do it now. I am not interested in what you have been told by Lady Raven or any other person. Lord Raven may be ill, but he is still your master, and he would not thank you to keep me from him."

The footman hesitated, intimidated by the sheer force of Nicholas' presence, and then, unable to bear being drilled by those sharp steely eyes another moment, he crumbled.

"Very well, sir," he said in a nervous whisper, "come this way. But come quickly, if you please. The fewer people who see you, the better."

"Nonsense," Nicholas said. "I have nothing to hide. Nor have you, my good man. And I will find my own way, thank you." He marched into the front hall, gave the footman his coat and hat, and went directly up the stairs to his uncle's quarters. The old manservant came to the door, greatly surprised to see that Lord Raven had a visitor at all. But his face lit up to see Nicholas there. "Master Nicholas!" he said with pleasure. "It is a long, long time since I've laid my eyes on you. Welcome home, sir."

"Thank you, Jerome," Nicholas said, relieved by the man's reaction. Nicholas had known him since childhood, and it would have hurt to have been shunned by him as well. "I am home, and to stay. I had not realized that you were still in my uncle's employ, but I am delighted. Tell me, Jerome, how is his condition today?"

"Much the same, sir. But no one is allowed in here except her ladyship. I wish I could allow you to stay, Master Nicholas, but I am sorry. Her ladyship gave express orders, about you in particular."

"And those are orders that you and I are going to ignore, my dear Jerome. Her ladyship is not here, is she?

And I believe you know how much my uncle means to me. I will say nothing to her ladyship if you will not."

Jerome thought this over, then shook his head. "I am sorry, sir, but I cannot."

"But why not, Jerome?" he said, trying to keep his growing desperation out of his voice. "It would stay just between the two of us, I assure you."

"But it would not, sir. The walls have ears, and eyes too, in this place. It is not like the old days."

"That much I've understood," Nicholas said tightly.

"I am truly sorry, Master Nicholas. But if I should lose my job, for I certainly would once her ladyship came to hear of it, there would be no one loyal to his lordship to look after him. And then there is the fact that his lordship cannot be upset by anything or anyone, in case it drives him to another stroke. It is why he is allowed no visitors."

"Is this on the doctor's orders?"

"Not exactly, sir. Lady Raven does not hold with the doctor and his ways, and that much I can understand, for he tends to do more harm than good, and that we will all swear by."

"I see. So what is being done for my uncle?"

"His basic needs are seen to, sir, and I give him a healing tea twice a day, but quite honestly, I fear his brain has been damaged beyond repair by the apoplexy. He does not understand things. Even if I were to let you in to see him now, he would not know you. Please, do believe me, for I do not keep you from him for any reasons of my own."

"I do not blame you, Jerome. I know you are a man of good judgment and principles."

"Thank you, sir. I have always thought the same of you."

"Oh?" Nicholas said dryly. "I find that hard to believe."

"It is quite true, Master Nicholas," Jerome said. "I never believed a word of what was said." He lowered his voice even further. "It was I who discovered his lordship's letter to you and saw it posted without her ladyship's knowledge. He must have written it in the night before his illness struck him, for I found him the next morning, as he is now."

"Thank you, Jerome. Thank you very much, for that at least. And for your good faith."

"I wish I could do more, Master Nicholas. I truly do. But you must understand the situation."

"I am afraid that is one thing I will never understand, nor accept," Nicholas replied, trying to stifle his anger and the helpless frustration that coursed through him. "I am deeply sorry that I have put you in such a difficult position. I will not do so again. Good day, Jerome."

He went quickly out, far more quickly than he usually moved, barely noticing the curious servants who were peeking out from around almost every corner. He managed to maintain some semblance of dignity until he reached the safety of the deep woods. And then he fell to his knees, slamming his fists into the earth.

"Why?" he shouted furiously, and his cry echoed hollowly around him. "Dear God, explain this to me! Please explain this to me," he said again, his voice now faltering. "Where is your Almighty righteousness? First you take my parents, then my aunt, and then you unleash Jacqueline de Give? It was not enough to have her destroy my house and my honor—you had to rob me of my uncle in the process? Sometimes I wonder why you bothered snatching me back from the sea at all if this was what you had in mind."

He slowly doubled over until his forehead met the earth. His body rocked not with tears, but with a dry, futile anger. And then he stood and started in the direction of the stables. The only thing to do was to ride, and ride so hard that there was nothing else. He felt in that moment as if he might lose his mind.

"Nicholas? Nicholas, what is it?" Georgia asked as he came in the door. His face was pale, and he just shook his head and went past her, straight up the stairs.

She squeezed her arms around herself. It couldn't have been Cyril. He had left long before Nicholas had returned, having succeeded in making her afternoon a misery. It had to have something to do with his uncle—or perhaps it was just Ravenswalk, she reasoned. It had that effect on people. But she was frightened. She had never seen Nicholas look so, and it came on top of the merriment he had shown just that morning.

If Binkley had been there, he might have understood what was wrong, or known what to do. But he wasn't, and she was, and Nicholas needed someone. She steeled her will and then she went upstairs after him.

He opened the door to her knock. His face and head were wet, and he was dressed only in his trousers and a half-open shirt. A towel was slung over his shoulder. "Yes?" he said curtly. "What is it?"

"Oh, Nicholas," she said, "whatever has happened, I think you must tell me. If you must be alone, then I will understand, but I could not leave you by yourself in this condition without asking. Perhaps I can help."

He put both hands on the door frame and bowed his head slightly. "Georgia."

"Yes?" she said anxiously.

"Georgia." He looked up, and she was amazed to see a slight smile. It was a weary smile, but still, it was something.

"Please, Nicholas. I already know my name well enough. You have not enlightened me in the least, and I wish you would."

His smile widened. "Yes. I can see that. You do make it easier, I must say. I had momentarily forgotten. In truth, Georgia, you do make it easier."

"I'm glad. So share your troubles. That is what I am here for."

Nicholas bowed and waved his arm. "Please, enter my palatial quarters and sit down."

She marched in and sat in the one armchair in front of the fire. "What happened?" she said again.

"What happened?" he said, drying his face and hair with the towel. 'Today I met the troll. I met the troll head-on, and it nearly conquered me. You said yourself that trolls have a habit of returning."

"Oh, no. Jacqueline wasn't there, was she?"

"No. She wasn't there, although she might just as well have been. You can smell her poison everywhere. But then, Jacqueline's not really the troll. She's just its handmaiden."

"But something dreadful must have happened. You're hurt, I can tell."

"Hurt? I would say more maimed. It's not important."

"But it is important, Nicholas. It's very important. You're very upset, more so than I've ever seen you. Please, Nicholas, I think you must tell me."

"There's nothing to tell. Nothing actually happened. I was refused admittance to my uncle's bedchamber."

He sat down and began to tug off his boots, and Georgia automatically leaned forward to help, which caused Nicholas to look at her with surprise, but he obligingly stretched his leg out and let her pull. "Thank you," he said with an amused smile. "You're very adept."

"Baggie could never get his boots off on his own," she said absently, her eyes lingering on the small scar on his chest, a result of his accident with the floorboards. "Why?"

"How am I supposed to know? Maybe they were too tight."

"What?" she said, looking up at him. "Oh. No, I meant why weren't you allowed to see him?"

"Oh, I see. Jacqueline left orders. It's all the same old nonsense."

"Nicholas, I don't mean to pry, but perhaps I can understand better if I know what happened originally, why you and your uncle quarreled."

He shrugged. "It's a long story."

"I have all the time in the world."

Nicholas hesitated, then let out a deep breath. "Very well, Georgia. I suppose you have a right. But first I have to explain the background. My uncle and I had always been very close. We'd had our share of disagreements, naturally, the sort that happen between two strong-willed, stubborn people cut from the same cloth, but they never amounted to anything. Anyway, I was away when my uncle married Jacqueline. I'd never met her and when I returned home six months after the wedding, I knew instantly that my uncle had made a bad mistake. I could see that he was besotted by her, and I could also see that she knew it and would use the fact to get whatever she wanted. She knew immediately that I couldn't bear her."

"Not surprising," Georgia said with a laugh.

"What, that I couldn't, or that she knew it?"

"Both. So what did she do?"

"She felt threatened. I think she was afraid I would warn my uncle away from her and she would lose her power over him. So she manufactured an unsavory story about me, basically calling me a debauched, immoral rakehell, and she convinced my uncle that it was the truth. I found myself out in the cold. I think it must have half-killed him to believe I was capable of such behavior and to feel forced to send me away. I know what it did to me."

"Oh, Nicholas, how awful!" Georgia said, appalled. "I am sorry, for I know that you're not like that in the least! But what brought you home again after all these years? Was it your uncle's illness?"

"No. I had no idea about that. He wrote me a brief letter, asking me back. I assumed he must have realized his mistake. But I'll probably never know now—apparently he became ill the same night he wrote to me, and there has been no improvement in his condition since then. His manservant believes his brain has been damaged by apoplexy. He has no cognizance, no movement."

"Really?" said Georgia with great interest. "Perhaps the right herbs—"

"Georgia, my sweet," Nicholas said wearily, "believe me, there is nothing we can do. No one is allowed in, not even the doctor. You and I most especially would be refused. It is Jacqueline's command, and there is no one who will disobey."

She tugged on her lower lip with her teeth. "It is a pity."

"Yes, it is. But enough about it. The past is the past, and it's best if we keep it like that."

"But you were so upset, Nicholas—you can't bury your feelings, for they will only worry at you."

"It was only my anger getting the better of me. We all have trolls, I suppose. It's just that mine is more active than some. Tell me, how did the afternoon go with Cyril?"

"The same as the morning. He was sullen, resentful, angry, and silent all at the same time. But at least he took his mood out on the wood. We now have a fine pile for the fireplace.''

Nicholas nodded. "That's good. I am sorry that he's being so difficult, Georgia, I really am. But he'll come around.''

"I hope so. I know I should feel sad for him, for he's clearly unhappy, but he is the most infuriating child, self-ish and malicious. And—oh, do you see? Just as I promise myself that I won't become annoyed, all my good intentions go by the wayside.'' She smiled. "And thank you for the apple.''

"You're most welcome. And if you'll excuse me, I'm going to change for dinner. I'll be down directly.''

"Oh! Oh, yes, of course," she said, jumping to her feet. "I need to get back to the kitchen and make sure Lily has everything going according to plan. She has wonderful intentions, but she does need guidance. Rabbit again for dinner, but I've used your apple to sweeten it. I hope you don't mind.''

"Mind? Not in the least," Nicholas said. "Maybe Binkley will bring back a small side of beef from Horsham. Pray God he will, and knowing Binkley's ingenuity, he will not need God's help. We will have a celebration. Oh, lovely side of beef. I can taste it now. Not that I'm decrying your skills in the kitchen, which styare superb, but rabbit five nights out of seven would challenge the most prodigious of appetites.''

"You should have been in the diplomatic service," she replied tartly, and shut the door behind her, but privately she was celebrating the smile that was back on his face, and she hummed a little song as she went downstairs.

Cyril demanded his dinner early and sat down to yet another solitary meal. But he liked eating alone, and to-night it was a relief to eat alone, for he found it sickening to eat and at the same time watch the disgusting interplay between his cousin and Georgia as they cooed to each other over their food. He'd never seen anything like it, this lower-class display of blatant sexuality. Nicholas may always have been tainted, but to have lost all the standards of his upbringing, to stoop to marrying a woman no better than a scullery maid, to live with her in squalor and behave as if it suited him perfectly? That was a true disgrace.

He would never behave as Nicholas had, at least not in that manner, although there were other appetites it seemed he shared with his cousin. He shifted uncomfortably, then pushed the thought to the back of his mind, for there were some things that didn't bear thinking about. Guilt ate at him whenever he didn't take care to keep it at bay, and he still couldn't help flushing whenever he passed his father's door and thought of the broken man behind it. He had found himself taking a circuitous route downstairs in order to avoid the unpleasant reminder of his culpability. But still, the old man had been almost as useless before the stroke had felled him, so what difference did it make? Had he been any kind of a father, any kind of a man come to that, Cyril might have been able to respect him. But he hadn't been. He hadn't been at all. Cyril might just as well have been an orphan for all the attention his father had paid him. Life just wasn't fair. In fact the only fair thing about it was that one day Ravenswalk would be his and sooner rather than later would suit him very well, not that he had any control over the matter. At least Ravenswalk was one thing Nicholas couldn't stick his filthy hands into. And when Cyril was earl, Nicholas would regret ever coming back. Cyril would see to that. The thought gave him great satisfaction and served to distract him from the unpleasant stirring of his conscience, which lived like a small, sleeping animal on the inside of his brain. It was deceptive, innocent while dozing, but when it awoke it attacked viciously and without warning with sharp, rabid teeth. He wished he could kill it as easily as one could kill the real thing, for wasn't blood meant to be cleansing? He had often thought that if he could bleed himself dry and start over, he might be cleansed. But that was foolishness, of course. He supposed that was why animal sacrifice had been so popular in pagan rites: animal blood was a replacement for human blood, and symbolically animals took on the sins of man. Didn't they?

He frowned, for he was beginning to think that there was a certain pleasure to be gained in controlling life and death. And that could only be had when the powerful vanquished the weak. Cyril shifted again. He still wasn't clear on that point, despite how powerful he felt after the fact, for the animal tended to haunt him in his sleep. That made no sense when it was supposed to be dead.

He was distracted by the footman removing his soup bowl and placing the fish course in front of him. He ate his turbot quickly, his appetite like a great gnawing thing inside of him, then called for the next course. He impatiently watched the footman carve the saddle of mutton, thinking all the while of how he'd like to carve Nicholas just so, and he knew exactly where he'd make the first slice. If ever there was a man who deserved it, it was Nicholas Daventry, who seemed to feel he could conquer the world by the sole means of his genitals. There were some things Cyril would like to say to his high-handed cousin.

"Would you care for gravy, my lord?" the footman asked.

"You kn-know I never take g-gravy, fool," Cyril answered petulantly. "And k-keep the vegetables well away from the m-meat."

"Certainly, my lord."

Cyril looked at the man suspiciously, for he was sure that he wore a slightly smug expression. But he was too hungry to delay the delivery of his food by filling the minion's ear with the chastisement he so richly deserved.

He dived into the plate that was put before him and polished it off in no short order. "M-more," he said, and the footman looked astonished.

"Did you say *more,* my lord?"

"I did. M-more, Harrington. And I would like it n-now, not t-tomorrow."

"Certainly, my lord. The cook will be most pleased to know that his efforts have met with your approval." He refilled the plate with alacrity, and Cyril dived in once again. When he had finished with his second helping of pudding and drained his tankard of ale, he threw down his napkin and set off for the billiards room with the intention of practicing a few shots. It was one of the few things in life he did well, other than shoot, and he was religious about keeping his hand in.

He sighted the ball, imagining it to be one of Nicholas', and he hit it square on with a great deal of satisfaction. Who did Nicholas think he was, anyway, ordering him around as if he were a servant? If it hadn't been for the fact that Nicholas had something to hold over his head, he wouldn't have tolerated it for an instant. But at last this way he could keep a closer eye on the goings-on at the Close, even if he did have to put up with his cousin's foul presence in the process.

He pocketed all of the balls swiftly, with intense concentration, and then he started off to bed. But he halted as he heard voices speaking in hushed tones. Hushed tones always meant secrets, and he had learned to listen well over the years. He pressed himself back against the wall and he listened for all he was worth.

"It was a brave thing, Mr Daventry walking in just as if he still lived here," the voice was saying. "I was that astonished. And he's the finest figure of a man," she added with a giggle. "All strong and tall and dark, with those eyes . . . Ah, those eyes is enough to send the chill up your spine and right down into your privates."

"I wouldn't mind a quick roll in the hay with him myself," said the second voice. "I haven't seen one that fine for many a year, although I don't think I'd have a bit of luck casting my eye that way. Lucky Mrs. Wells, is all I can say, not that I can't see the match—her with her fair beauty, him with his good looks. Must be nice on the cold nights, putting the two together. From the look of him in them tight pantaloons," and she lowered her voice, "he has all that it takes and more. Not that I don't love my own Frank when I have the chance to see him, but he never did stir the imagination quite the same."

"I know just what you mean," replied the first voice, and it was all Cyril could do to control his rage and remain hidden. "I wonder if it's true what they say about his evil ways."

"I can see it myself. If you looked like that, wouldn't you take advantage every chance you had? He could be the very devil, and I'm sure I wouldn't care. If he tilted one of those eyebrows in my direction, he wouldn't have time to drop it again before I was on my back."

"Nice of him, though, to want to see his lordship. Too bad Mr. Jerome had to refuse him. Seems there's not another soul save for Mr. Jerome who cares whether the old man lives or dies, the young lordship included—not that he isn't the strangest, coldest thing that ever was.''

''And never mind her ladyship,'' the second voice said with a snort. ''But now mayhaps things will change for the better if Mr. Nicholas Daventry and his packed pantaloons regularly come a-visiting. You won't hear me complaining.''

They both cackled furiously, and then their voices faded as they disappeared down the hallway.

Cyril, now that they had gone, found that his fingers were digging violently into his face and he was shaking all over. A terrible, ungovernable rage poured over him, through him, obscuring thought, reason, everything but a need for revenge.

How dared he? *How dared he?*

He wanted to strike out, needed to strike out, to hurt the man who had brought him to this humiliation. He would show him that he could not invade his life. So Nicholas thought he could just walk in the front door, did he? He thought he could flaunt himself, make the staff drool with desire? It wasn't enough that he had married the seamstress. He had to have them all. And as if that wasn't bad enough, he thought he could march into Ravenswalk and ingratiate himself? Not likely.

It would not happen. It could not happen. And Georgia? She would pay for her insolence. A lowly seamstress giving him orders? She who'd had the temerity to refuse him and then run off with his vile cousin? He would make her very sorry indeed.

And he knew just where to start.

Nicholas buried his head in his pillow, then swore and impatiently rolled onto his back in an attempt to take the pressure off his groin. He had been ready to jump out of his skin all night. Dinner had been a living hell. Georgia. He was getting to the point where he couldn't even look at her without becoming aroused. Night was the worst. This night took the prize. Georgia had been nothing but sweet, amusing, and good company. And he had done what? Responded like a primitive beast, watching her, thinking about how it would be with her, only vaguely attending to her conversation.

He had known from the beginning that he wanted her. Oh, yes. He had wanted her as any sane, hot-blooded male would want a woman, especially a woman with her unusual fair beauty. But now it was different. He didn't know how, or when it had happened exactly, but everything had changed, and he knew that he needed her, and needed her in a way he had never needed before.

Gone was the desire for just a woman. He wanted Georgia, the woman who cried over his house, who worked on his lost garden, who laughed and delighted in the simplest of things, yet was so deeply attuned to nature, to life. What other woman would have given him a mangy dog for Christmas, and yet Raleigh was the most perfect present she could have found. What other woman would insist that he not buy her things, but would smile as if he'd given her the world when he presented her with a simple piece of material, and then make a shirt for him out of it. A woman who made him *shirts?* And yet he treasured the shirts she made for him, as if they came from the finest tailor in London. In truth, they weren't far off.

He was living in poverty for her sake, and yet he felt more alive, more full of purpose, than he had felt in years. Georgia made him laugh, she made him angry at times, certainly frustrated, and she startled him often. But from the very beginning she had touched him. It had been so long, so very long, since anything, or anyone, had touched him. And then he had returned home, and in one fell swoop he had been thrown back into the maelstrom without so much as a chance to take breath. Except for Georgia. Georgia might be a constant torment, but she was also a lifeline. If there was any hope for him at all, he suspected it rested in her.

After all, he hadn't drowned in nearly two months, he considered, and that was a record. It was probably the physical punishment that was responsible. He never slept deeply enough to dream. He barely slept at all.

He rolled over onto his side, wishing his erection away. It had become a constant and unwelcome companion, but like a toothache, it had settled in for the duration. And, like a toothache, it was of no use at all. He would think of the roof. No, he thought of that all the time. He would think of his business affairs. Yes, that was it. He'd think of business, of the latest reports. The figures looked promising, profits were up again.

Nicholas groaned. Those were the wrong words for his state of mind. He needed release. He needed Georgia.

An hour later she came to him.

"Nicholas? Nicholas, wake up," she said, touching his shoulder, then shaking it hard.

He sat up abruptly, wondering if he'd had the accursed dream. But he was breathing normally, and his mind was clear.

"Georgia? What are you doing in here?" He reached out and touched her arm to make sure she was solid and not a figment of his imagination. He couldn't quite believe his luck. It was the middle of the night, Georgia was in his bedroom, and he was in bed. Best, he was sure he was awake.

But she did not look like a woman with ardor on her mind, he quickly realized. She was white as a sheet and she was shaking from head to toe. "Georgia, for the love of God, what is it? What happened?"

"I think you had better come and see," she said, turning and going back through the door to her room. Nicholas quickly followed. Georgia stood in the middle of the room, her head bowed, and in the better light he saw her face more clearly. She looked sick.

"Georgia? Georgia, what is it?"

She pointed at her bed without looking up, and he turned his head. There, lying on her pillow, was a cat. Its throat had been cut, and cut so deeply that its head was almost completely severed from its neck. Its eyes were half-open and staring. The bed was soaked in blood.

"Oh, dear God." He went over and pulled the sheet off the mattress, wrapping the poor animal in it. "Wait here. I'll be right back." It took him only a minute to take the bundle down the hall and leave it in one of the spare rooms. He would dispose of it on the morrow. Right now Georgia needed him.

She was still standing in the middle of the room when

he returned. He poured some water into the basin and quickly rinsed his hands, then went over to her, pulling her into his arms without thinking. He held her tightly against his chest. "Georgia, Georgia, sweetheart. I'm sorry. I'm so, so sorry."

Her only response was to bury her head more deeply into his shoulder.

Not wanting her to stay in the room for another minute, he scooped her up in his arms and took her through to his own bedroom, firmly shutting the door behind them. The fire still crackled in the fireplace and gave off some decent warmth without smoking, now that the chimney had been cleaned. Nicholas sat down in the chair next to the fire, cuddling her in his lap. Her face stayed buried in his shoulder, and he knew she was trying not to cry. He held her tightly against him, stroking her back, her soft hair, his cheek resting on her head. She was cold as ice. She must have learned long ago not to give in to emotion, nor fear, nor despair. She must have learned a number of protective devices to shield her from the harsh world. He knew. He had an arsenal of them himself. But to see her so vulnerable, so hurt, to see her without any protective clothing at all, made his heart ache. Her fantasy had been sullied, her happy dream bloodied with reality.

"Georgia," he whispered. "Georgia, love, listen to me. It was a cruel joke, that's all. A horrible, cruel joke."

She didn't move at all, and he knew by that just how badly upset she was. "I'm sure it was meant for me, sweetheart. I don't know how anyone got into the house without someone hearing, but we did spend quite some time in the dining room tonight. You're safe, love. You're safe now."

He felt a nod against his shoulder.

"I won't let anyone hurt you," he continued softly. "I promise you that. Please don't be afraid. Please, Georgia? I can't tolerate the thought that this vicious act might take away whatever small happiness you've had here."

She suddenly raised her head and met his eyes. The fierce expression in them took him by surprise. "Nothing will take that away," she said. "Nothing and no one. And no one will take Raven's Close away. I don't care what they try to do."

"Good girl. That's good." Very gently he took her face in his hands and held it between his palms, his thumbs stroking the hair off her temples. "You're right. No one will take it away. Wherever this attack has come from, we'll meet it head-on."

"Oh, Nicholas, the cat—the poor, poor cat . . . How could anyone be so cruel? Why would someone do such a thing?"

"I don't know, sweetheart. I really don't, except to say there are people in the world who do horrible things for inexplicable reasons. I don't know why in this case, although I intend to find out. It was a terrible thing for you to have witnessed." He held her tightly against him, stroking her back, her hair, trying to avoid anything more personal.

"I'm sorry to have made a fuss. It was a shock, pulling the cover back and seeing the poor thing there. She'd been nursing kittens, Nicholas."

"Had she, sweetheart?" He tried to keep his voice even, but now that the initial shock was over, heated anger welled up in him. He had a terrible feeling that he knew exactly who had done this thing and why, but he wasn't going to put the idea in Georgia's head. She had enough to worry about. "What were you doing up so late?" he said, trying to distract her. "I thought you were going to come to bed straightaway."

"I decided to do some sewing. There was a piece I wanted to finish."

"Georgia, you work too hard. You need your sleep and you don't get enough of it."

"I don't need much. And I enjoy sewing. It's soothing, now that I don't have to do it day and night for other people."

"You amaze me," he said, resting his head on her hair.

"So you keep telling me, although I cannot understand why I should do so."

"To explain that would take all night. And I think you should try to get some sleep. I think it would be best if you stayed in here tonight. Tomorrow we'll find a clean mattress for you. I'll sleep here in the chair."

"You are a good, thoughtful man," she said, looking up at him through the flickering light, her eyes a deeper blue than he had ever seen them before. Her hand went out to his face, and she hesitantly touched it. "Thank you, Nicholas. Thank you for caring."

"Georgia . . ." He wanted to cover her mouth with

his, to cover her body with his own, to make her forget everything in the heat of lovemaking, but he instinctively knew that would be a foolish mistake. He couldn't afford to shatter her trust now. But his body wasn't listening to him, insisting on its own course of action.

Oh, sweet Jesus, Nicholas thought fervently. Help me. Help me, Lord, in my hour of need.

The Lord did not answer him.

He stood quickly, lifting Georgia off his lap before she could divine his thoughts, and he carried her over to his bed, depositing her in the middle of it and pulling the covers up around her. "Do you think you might be able to sleep now?"

Georgia smiled up at him. "I think so." She moved onto her side and tucked her hands under her cheek. Nicholas bent down and kissed her cheek, then stepped away and looked at the bed with slight disbelief. Then, pulling an extra blanket from the foot of the bed, he settled himself back into the chair.

"Good night, Nicholas," Georgia said.

"Good night," he replied as evenly as he could manage, thinking that life at that moment bore a strong resemblance to hell. "Sleep well."

"Thank you. You've been very kind to me. I do thank you."

"Please, don't give it another moment's thought." He squeezed his eyes shut and gave a resigned sigh, knowing he'd have little sleep that night, and it had nothing to do with the damned chair. He had come to an astonishing realization.

His condition had not so much to do with his groin as with his heart. Oh, his groin was needy, but his heart was needier. Of all the futile, idiotic, harebrained things he might have done, he had gone and fallen in love with his wife. And his wife was in love with a dead farmer with the absurd name of Baggie Wells.

Nicholas prepared to tally his accounts well into the following morning.

8

Georgia woke to the sound of pelting rain. She sat up, wondering for a brief instant where she was, and then she saw Nicholas asleep in the chair and she remembered. His legs were propped up on the table and his head was slumped back against the cushion. She could hear the rhythmic pull of his breathing—actually, it was more of a rhythmic snort.

Georgia smiled. She had grown very fond of Nicholas Daventry, had thought she was coming to know him well, but one thing she hadn't known about him was that he snored.

She pulled her knees up to her chest and rested her chin on them, watching him. People asleep seemed so vulnerable. She never normally would have used the word to describe Nicholas, but that was exactly how he appeared, his hair tousled, a dark shadow of beard on his cheek. At some point he had exchanged his nightshirt for trousers and a shirt, she noticed.

He had been so good to her the night before, so tender with her, holding her on his lap as if she'd been a hurt child in need of comfort, tucking her up in his bed and kissing her cheek. It had given her the strangest feeling, a warmth inside that had started in her middle and spread out, making her feel languid and heavy. And when she had slept, she had dreamed that Nicholas was still holding her close in his arms.

She had liked being held by him, the heat of his body warming hers, the feel of his hard muscles against her, the way his hands had gently stroked her back. She'd never felt anything quite like it, and when she had stopped shaking and begun to relax in his embrace, she'd discovered that she had wanted to hold him in the same way, to put her arms around him, to touch his skin, to feel his mouth on hers again, as it had felt the other night, his lips slightly parted, his breath mingling with hers. But she had been afraid.

Even though she knew she was in no danger from him, she'd been afraid—afraid that she might arouse him, afraid that it might lead to the other thing. But most of all she was afraid of these strange new feelings in herself that she didn't understand.

Nicholas stirred and his eyes groggily opened. He rubbed them with one hand, and then he suddenly sat up straight and his eyes flew to the bed as he became fully alert. He saw her watching him, and she thought he looked almost embarrassed. "Georgia . . . um, good morning," he said, and cleared his throat. "What are you looking at?" He looked down at himself as if to find the answer there.

"You snore," she said with a grin.

"Snore? I most certainly do not."

"You most certainly do. You might only snore when you sleep sitting up, but you do snore."

Nicholas considered this. "And you couldn't wait to point out this fact to me? Suppose I told you that you snore too? How would you feel?"

"But I don't," Georgia said practically. "I'm a light sleeper, and I'd wake myself up if I did."

Nicholas rubbed his eyes again. "I've just realized something," he said. "I've never woken up with you before. You start right in, don't you? You don't even wait until breakfast until you start handing out your extraordinary version of logic."

"I don't know. I don't usually have anyone to talk to before breakfast, except for Lily when she brings the water. It's rather nice."

"Is it, sweetheart? We should do it more often."

"Really?" she said, her face lighting up. "And I always thought you preferred having your tea in peace."

He looked surprised. "That's why you always come down after I do? You thought I wanted the privacy?"

"Yes, of course. Why else?"

"I had no idea. Is that how Baggie liked it?"

She shrugged a shoulder. "Well . . . we had no servants, so I was always down first to light the fire and prepare his breakfast, but he couldn't bear talking in the early morning. Of course, it was the very early morning, before dawn, as we had animals to feed and the milking to be done. The vicar never talked in the morning either, and his wife never came down before eleven. She said men liked their morning peace, so I assumed you would too.''

Nicholas laughed. "I don't think I'd put much stock in anything the vicar's wife had to say. And as for my morning peace, don't give it another thought.'' He came over and sat down on the bed, leaning back on his elbow. "You know, thinking about it, with the exception of Binkley, I haven't ever woken up with anyone. At least not that I can remember.''

"Really?'' Georgia said with interest. She had no idea what the etiquette of gentlemen was when dealing with their mistresses and other ladies of the evening, or what they did with such ladies when the evening's activities had been brought to a conclusion. But then, Nicholas was no ordinary gentleman, she had discovered.

"Really,'' he replied. "It seems appropriate that the first time I should do so it is with my wife. Even if she does tell me that I snore.''

Georgia reached out her hand and rubbed his cheek. "And that you need to shave. I've never seen you before with a beard. You look very rakish.''

"Do I? Maybe I should go unshaven more often.''

"Binkley would be outraged.''

"Binkley, my dear Georgia, is never outraged. That is why he is such an exemplary manservant.'' Nicholas sighed. "I have missed him, however. He does a much better job of shaving me than I do.''

"But, Nicholas, why didn't you say something? I can shave you, and I'm sure I could do it every bit as well as Binkley—well, maybe not with quite such expertise, but probably better than you can shave yourself, if those nicks on your face are anything to go by. I hadn't thought about it before.''

"You want to shave me?'' Georgia wondered why he looked quite so appalled.

"Don't you trust me?'' She jumped out of bed and

went to the door. "Lily," she called, and heard an answering query. "Lily, bring hot water to Mr. Daventry's room, if you please?"

"Georgia . . . Georgia, wait. Oh, help."

"And I thought you were a gambling man," she said, turning back to him, and found him lying flat on his back, his hands flung over his head, his eyes closed.

"If you're trying to simulate a faint, it won't work." She fell onto the bed next to him and dug her fingers into his ribs. Nicholas' eyes shot open and he gave a howl, then grabbed her wrists and flipped her over onto her back in one swift movement, pinning her down beneath him.

"You dare to tangle with me, madam? First you threaten my face, and then my ribs? And this after I gave up my bed to you? You have a strange notion of repayment for extreme gallantry."

"Extreme gallantry? I think you are painting it a bit thick, sir."

"Am I? And should I attack your ribs, I wonder?"

Georgia squirmed under him, laughing. "Oh, please don't, Nicholas. I am fearfully ticklish. Oh, please, no," she begged as he easily grasped her wrists between one hand and lowered the other in the direction of her side. "No!" She twisted to no avail, and then she suddenly found her wrists released. Nicholas still leaned over her, but the expression in his eyes had changed, and her breath caught.

He shifted his weight onto his forearms, and he looked down at her, his breath coming faster, as if he'd been running. "Georgia," he whispered. "Georgia . . ."

Her arms slowly came down from over her head, and she touched his face with her fingertips, and then the corner of his mouth. There was an undefinable ache inside her, and all she knew was that she wanted Nicholas to fill it somehow. Her fingers slipped into his thick hair, her eyes questioning his, her heart beating faster at what she saw there.

He bent his head and kissed her.

He took his time, softly brushing his mouth against hers, and she gasped as she felt his tongue stroke her bottom lip, then seek entrance inside. She could not help herself. Her mouth opened against his and she shuddered as his tongue touched hers. He played with her lightly, drawing her into the kiss as an equal partner, not like Baggie, who had stuffed her mouth as if he were trying to suffocate her. Oh, this was a different thing entirely, soft as velvet, hot as fire, scalding, and the only thing that she thought might suffocate her was her heart, which threatened to dislodge itself and leap into her throat.

"Georgia," he said with a choked laugh, disengaging his mouth from hers, and she gazed at him, stunned. Through the haze in her head she vaguely heard a knock at the door, and then it came again. Nicholas looked down at her with a rueful smile. "Your timing, sweetheart, is abysmal. I think you had better answer, for I cannot quite find my voice."

Indeed, he did sound hoarse, and certainly shaken, Georgia thought as he left her and went to the window, his back turned to the room. She was shaken as well, terribly shaken. But she collected herself as best she could.

"Come in," she called, sitting up and straightening her shift.

Lily entered with the water. "Oh! I beg your pardon," she said, nearly dropping the pitcher as she saw Georgia in her nightclothes sitting on her husband's bed. She curtsied, managed to put the pitcher down without spilling it, and hurried off in record time.

Georgia looked at the water, then at Nicholas' broad back, and back at the water again. Now that she'd had a chance to recover herself, she felt terribly foolish. What had she been thinking, to behave in such a way? Nicholas must think her the most awful wanton, practically begging him to ravish her, when that was the last thing in the world she wanted. But she couldn't help running her fingers over her mouth, remembering the feel of his lips just there, and his tongue . . . She blushed furiously, then quickly removed herself from the bed before such a thing could happen again. She would give Nicholas his shave, and they would pretend it hadn't happened at all.

Nicholas turned around, rubbing the back of his neck. "Georgia," he said. "I think we need to talk."

"Oh, no," she replied, pointing at the chair. "You're

not escaping with an onslaught of words. Sit, sir, while the water is still hot. Where do you keep your razor?''

''You can't be serious,'' he said. ''You really cannot be serious.''

''But I am, and that look of alarm will do you no good.'' She poured the water into the basin, found his shaving equipment in the cupboard, and tested the blade with her thumb. ''Perfect.''

''Dear God,'' he said.

''Sit.'' She advanced on him with the razor, and he fell backward into the chair.

''Georgia, no . . . oh, Binkley, where are you in my hour of need?''

She wet the towel and put it over his face. ''That's quite enough, Nicholas. Any more and I shall be offended. Now, relax, while I work up a lather.''

''It won't be the first time,'' he said with a muffled laugh. ''Are you sure your hands are steady?''

She ignored him, whipping up a good foam, then removed the steaming towel and spread the foam over his face, bending over him with the razor.

''For my sins,'' Nicholas said, then closed his eyes.

Georgia firmly gripped the ivory handle and carefully applied the straight edge to his cheek, pulling downward in short scrapes. She methodically worked first on one side of his face, and then the other, thinking that it was more challenging shaving a face with angles than it was shaving one that was simply round. Satisfied with the appearance of his cheeks and chin, she said, ''Tilt your head back.''

Nicholas opened his eyes. ''Is this the part where you do me in?''

''You're not very trusting, are you? If I had wanted to do you in, I shouldn't have wasted my time first making sure you were clean-shaven.''

Nicholas swallowed, but obliged. Holding his chin in one hand, she made a few long clean sweeps upward. She savored the feel of his warm skin beneath her fingers, the beating of the pulse in the hollow beneath his ear, the damp curl of hair over her fingertips. She was almost sorry when she was done.

She took the towel and wiped the soap off his face, then stood back. "There. And not a single nick."

"That's it?" he said, running his hand over his face. "You're finished?"

"What else is there? There's not a whisker left."

"There's my bath."

"Nicholas!" she said, truly shocked. "Don't tell me that Binkley bathes you too. You couldn't possibly be that lazy."

He laughed. "No," he said reluctantly. "I can actually manage to wash myself without doing too much damage."

"Oh, well—that's good. I'll leave you to it, then, while the rest of the water is still warm."

"Thank you for the shave," he said softly, pushing himself to his feet. "I enjoyed it."

"I'm happy it pleased you," she said, looking down at the floor, for the warmth in his eyes was giving her that peculiar feeling again.

"Oh, it did. It did. You have a certain touch that Binkley could not equal. Georgia, about earlier. We really should talk about it, don't you think? After all, it was a fairly interesting exchange."

"Nicholas," she said in a small voice. "I'm sorry."

He stared at her. "You're sorry? What the devil is that supposed to mean?"

"I didn't mean to . . . to inflame you."

Nicholas covered his eyes with his hand. "To inflame me. I see. You're sorry to have inflamed me." He looked up again, and this time Georgia really couldn't read his face. "There are not words for this," he said. "There are no words and I am not sure if there is any appropriate behavior. Tell me something, sweetheart. You liked being kissed, didn't you? It's not the sort of thing that can be pretended, not like that."

"Yes," she admitted. "I did like it. I liked it very much. But oh, Nicholas, I shouldn't have. I shouldn't have liked it, not at all."

"Why not, Georgia? Why ever not?"

"Because of what it leads to," she said in a choked voice.

Nicholas massaged the palm of one hand with the thumb of the other. "This is about Baggie, isn't it?"

She dropped her head.

"Yes, I thought as much."

"I'm sorry," she whispered, knowing now what a terrible mistake the kiss had been.

"Please, don't be sorry. You cannot help your feelings, any more than I can help mine."

"Your feelings?" she said in confusion.

"Did you think I had none? I'm flesh and blood, Georgia, not a statue."

She blanched, suddenly understanding. "I'm sorry," she said stiffly. "I hadn't realized. If you want more from me, then you must say so, and I will accommodate you."

"You will not!" he roared, and she jumped.

"I'm sorry. Forgive me. But you will not accommodate me, and I don't want to hear that blasted word again! I am not a brute, Georgia. I would never ask such a thing of you. I want only what you are prepared to offer with open arms and an open heart. Anything else I would find distasteful. Do you understand me?"

She wasn't quite sure she did.

"Georgia, now why do you look at me so? Surely I made myself clear to you from the very first. To force myself on you would be repugnant to us both. I would far rather have your affection, and perhaps that will grow with time."

Comprehension finally dawned, and she couldn't help but stare at him in disbelief. He also found the sexual act repugnant? "Truly?" she said, unable to hide her astonishment. "You truly mean that?"

"Yes, naturally I do. Have I in any way indicated to you anything else?"

"No . . . no, you haven't. Oh, Nicholas," she said with a great sigh of relief. "Oh, Nicholas, you are wonderful."

"Am I?"

"Yes, you are. You have taken a great weight off my mind. I have always thought you a man out of the ordinary, and you are indeed. You truly are."

"I'm beginning to think I must be," he said, looking baffled.

"No, really you are. And my affection for you grows by the day."

"Does it? I hope it is growing by leaps and bounds, for I find myself in great need of it."

She stepped forward and placed her hands on both sides of his smooth face, looking up into his eyes. "You must know that I think of you as my friend. My good friend."

Nicholas looked down at her mouth. "Your good friend," he said. "Yes, of course you do. I don't know what I could have been thinking. Well. That's quite enough of that, for I hear the word 'gratitude' threatening." He moved away and gazed out of the window. "The rain shows no sign of stopping. We'll be working inside today. Cyril should have the good sense to stay away until the weather clears, so it looks as if we might have the day to ourselves, Georgia. What would you like to do with it?"

"The kitchen could use some attention," she said, returning to practical matters. "Let me dress, and I'll meet you in the dining room. Raleigh is probably wondering what's happened to his breakfast."

She went through to her own room and, avoiding looking at her bed, started to wash in the now-cool water that Lily had left. Only a moment later she heard a crash and a howl from the next room, and then a volley of swearing.

She laughed and shook her head, reasoning that Nicholas must have dropped something on his foot.

The kitchen door banged and all three of them looked up from their various tasks in surprise. Binkley stood there, and he was soaked from head to foot.

Lily was the first to speak. "Mr. Binkley, sir! We had wondered where you'd got to. A bit wet out there, isn't it?"

"A bit wet?" Binkley said indignantly. "It is a full gale, Lily." He turned his attention to Nicholas, shaking the water off his cape, uncharacteristically ignoring the puddle of water that was accumulating about him. "I fear it is heading in this direction, sir. We were lucky to have been coming from the north, so the roads were still passable yesterday, but the inn we put up at last night was full of people who had been caught out. They are saying it is going to hit the coast, and the storm seems to be building in force.''

This was an unusually long speech for Binkley, who normally kept himself abbreviated, and Georgia's concern grew. She looked over at Nicholas, who was leaning against the kitchen table, his arms folded, his brow drawn down.

"The wind direction, Binkley?''

"South-southwesterly, sir.''

"Trouble, Binkley.''

"I believe so. It should arrive shortly, if my estimate is correct.''

"Oh, hell. Well, there's nothing we can do but wait and pray. I don't suppose you managed to bring back a side of beef?'' he added hopefully.

Binkley's mouth twitched. "Indeed I did, sir. It resides just inside the door. I shall prepare it for dinner this evening. Everything else is best stored in the stables until we have more clement weather. We had a most successful trip. Martin is looking after the horses, and I have instructed him to return to his family immediately after. As you know, they live on the water, sir.''

"Very well. Thank you, Binkley. You have been efficient, as ever. Why don't you retire to your room and change into something dry? We'll carry on here.''

"Very good, sir.''

Georgia picked up her rag, thinking how very lucky they were to be safe and snug in their part of the house. They were also lucky to have such loyal and reliable help, people not inclined to panic. For Nicholas' worry did not escape her.

The wind picked up that afternoon, increasing in force until it was howling about the house. They'd given up working in the kitchen in favor of the superior warmth of the sitting room. Nicholas once again stuck his head out of the window with an anxious frown.

"Nicholas, do stop worrying. There's nothing you can do to stop the wind, or even the rain for that matter.'' Georgia secured another pleat in the draperies she was making. She was just as worried about the roof, but determined that someone had to remain calm, even though she was ready to jump out of her skin with fear.

"I just don't know if the coping is strong enough to hold," he said, pulling his head in and shutting the window. "This is a full-blown gale, Georgia. We sometimes get them down here at this time of year, and they can wreak serious havoc. This one seems particularly fierce, and the roof is only temporarily secured." He paced up and down the floor.

"Why don't you try to relax and do something useful? There must be something that will take your mind off the storm."

He turned and gave her a long look, then went back to his pacing. The wind continued to howl, a primitive, almost terrifying sound, and Georgia wanted to bury her head under the sofa every bit as much as Raleigh.

"Nicholas," she said under her breath, desperately wanting to have him take her into his arms and comfort her as he had the night before, but she wanted to be brave. Being brave was what Nicholas would want, and she would do it well for him. So she continued her stitching and hoped the storm would soon abate.

And then there was a terrible crack from the back and moments later a great crash. Georgia jumped to her feet, her nerves finally shattering. "Nicholas!"

Raleigh howled, then buried himself more deeply beneath the sofa.

"Oh, hell!" Nicholas ran for the back door and grabbed up his coat as he went. "Binkley!"

Georgia ran after him, but he had already disappeared. He was back a moment later.

"It's the old elm. It's been torn up by the roots and thrown down on the middle wing. I'm going to have to go and try to shore up the roof or we're going to lose the entire top floor. Tell Binkley to get up to the attic and work from below. And hurry."

He was gone in a flash.

"Nicholas, don't do anything stupid . . . Nicholas, please, it's dangerous out there! Oh, Nicholas, be careful . . ." Georgia whispered as the door slammed behind him.

It took every ounce of self-control she had not to go

chasing after him, not to try to pull him off the ladder, but she knew that would be foolish. Nicholas would not thank her for it. She had learned that he had an iron will and did not appreciate interference. Instead, she went to fetch Binkley, and then she found Lily and asked her to start the kettles for filling the bath, for she knew Nicholas would need one when he finally came in.

She went up to the attic to see how bad the damage was. Binkley was already up there, and he nodded at her politely, while at the same time trying to secure a board over the gash. Rain was pouring down on his balding head.

"Ah, Mrs. Daventry," he said. "Nasty weather we're having, is it not?"

Georgia couldn't help smiling. "Yes, Binkley, perfectly foul. Here, let me hold that board for you, and you can fasten it."

"Very good, madam. If you'll just pull over the stool and stand on it, you can take the corner here. Thank you very much. That's it exactly. A pity there's so little light."

They worked in tandem, Georgia alternately fetching boards and nails for Binkley, then holding them while Binkley hammered. And while she worked, she worried. She jumped half out of her skin when she heard another slither and crash.

"Not to worry, madam," Binkley said reassuringly. "Mr. Daventry is a capable man. I believe he also has nine lives. He has used up only two or three to date. I am sure he will be perfectly all right."

"Thank you, Binkley," Georgia said in a small voice, the most she could summon over her fear. "I am sure he will."

"That's the spirit. If you would just hand me the next board . . ."

Another hour went by. Lily came up with linens to try to soak up the worst of the water. They did everything they could, and then went downstairs as the gray of the afternoon drew down to dusk and they could see no more. And still Nicholas had not come in. She could just hear the banging of his hammer over the wailing of the wind. She went out once to see if she could see him, but with no luck. The rain came down in sheets and the wind nearly blew her off her feet, and she went back inside, saying a small prayer. And then finally, as she was about to give way to her panic, the front door opened and Nicholas came staggering through.

"Oh, thank God!" she cried, running to him. She threw her arms around his back and pulled him against her, burying her head in his shoulder. "You *idiot!* You might have been killed—blown off the roof, or hit by lightning, or any number of things! It's amazing you didn't break your neck!"

He put her away from him. "But I didn't, and we have a roof again. At least for now. And I didn't know my neck mattered quite so much to you," he added.

"You really are an idiot," she said furiously. "Now, go and stand in front of the fire and take your clothes off. If the storm didn't kill you, the aftereffects will."

"No doubt," he said dryly, "given my congested state."

"You're not already feeling congested? Oh, Nicholas, what am I to do with you? Go on. Do as I told you. Binkley will bring in the water for your bath. We put it on hours ago. You're going to sit in it, too, until you turn as red as a boiled lobster. I'll make you a hot tisane."

"Thank you," he said, stripping off his sodden coat, his teeth chattering.

"I don't know what makes you think a chunk of roof is more important than your health, Nicholas," she said, taking it from him.

"But you have told me time and time again how important a roof over your head is," he said with a wicked grin.

"Don't try your foolish joking on me now. The effect is utterly ruined by blue lips. Now, go."

He obediently disappeared in the direction of the sitting room, and Georgia went into the pantry to fetch her medicine chest. She prepared a preventive brew made of healing roots and herbs. No man should have blue lips as Nicholas had, nor look quite so exhausted. It took what seemed to her forever to properly prepare the tisane, but one could not neglect the correct steeping time of all the elements. Her mother had admonished her over and over about too much haste in these matters. She finally took the steaming cup out to the sitting room and pushed the door open with her foot.

Nicholas was indeed in the hip bath, steam rising about him, his back to her. She was about to step forward, when he put his hands on the sides of the tub and rose, reaching for a towel. She stood transfixed, the tray forgotten. He was the most beautiful thing she had ever seen. His long legs were powerfully built, the thighs bulging in two separate muscle groups. His buttocks were defined by hollows at either side, and a ridge of muscle ran over the top of each hip. She saw the muscles flex smoothly in his back as he moved. She had never, never imagined that the naked male form could be quite so magnificent.

And then he suddenly turned around and saw her, and her hand went to her mouth as she understood, as all the pieces finally came together.

"Georgia," he gasped, staring at her in return, and then the tub almost tipped over with his violent response as he fell back into it, water sloshing over the sides. "Georgia, for the love of God, what are you doing in here?" He drew his knees up to his chest, looking thoroughly disconcerted, and she understood why he would be. She wanted to cry for him.

"I've brought you a warm drink," she said haltingly.

"A warm drink? Oh, yes, of course. But in here?"

"It was wrong. I can see that now. I hadn't realized. Oh, forgive me, Nicholas," she said with a choke of remorse. "I didn't know. I'll leave it over here on the table, and I'll go. Please, forgive me. . . ."

"It's all right, Georgia, really. You surprised me, that's all."

"I . . . I'm so sorry." She quickly put the cup down and flew out of the room. Only after she had closed the door behind her did she cover her face and let her tears of embarrassment and concern come. Poor Nicholas. Poor, poor Nicholas. No wonder he had been such a gentleman, no wonder he was not interested in asserting his marital rights.

He couldn't.

"I am sorry for the lateness of the meal, sir, madam," Binkley said, presenting them with the first course of soup. "It was unavoidable, given the circumstances. I took the liberty of taking Lily home in the carriage, madam," he added. "She was worrying over her family in the storm, and I felt it best she be with them."

"Thank you, Binkley," Georgia murmured, keeping her eyes down, and Nicholas wanted to laugh. The poor girl was in agonies of embarrassment. She still had not lost the flush that covered her from head to, no doubt, toe. Although he hadn't included the earlier incident in his strategy, he hadn't thought the sight of his naked body would rattle her quite so much. Georgia had stood there staring at him as if she had never before seen a man in her life, and he had begun to wonder if she had. He was truly beginning to wonder. Her innocence was astonishing for a woman who had been previously married. He had begun to wonder about it the day he had fallen through the floor and she had pulled him out. She'd had absolutely no conception of what she was doing to him with her touch. And yet she had deeply loved her husband. It was most odd.

Georgia cleared her throat. "It is very good soup Binkley has made, is it not, Nicholas?"

"Delicious," he agreed, trying to hide his smile behind his napkin.

"I was wondering. How much damage was done to the roof?"

"Not enough to be a serious setback. I don't believe we'll have any more water coming in as a result. It's a damned waste of the slate and the time, but if the wind doesn't take anything else off, we should stay dry and moderately warm."

"That's good." She bowed her head again and concentrated on her soup.

He admired the long sweep of her neck, where the soft little wisps of hair curled, wishing very much to place his lips just there. He could think of a number of other places that he wished to place his lips, but realized that such thoughts would do him no good at the dinner table, save to create a physical reaction in him far too common these days.

"Nicholas," she said suddenly, putting down her spoon with a clatter, "I want to apologize again for coming into the sitting room unannounced. It was unforgivable of me to intrude on your privacy."

He managed to keep a straight face and match her gravity. "As I told you, Georgia, there is no need for repentance. You were bound to see me in a state of undress at some point or another during the course of our marriage. I only hope the shock wasn't too great."

She went bright red. "No, of course it wasn't, Nicholas. I just didn't want you to feel bad."

Nicholas rubbed the bridge of his nose. "No. No, naturally you didn't."

"I think you are very fine in every regard."

"Thank you, Georgia," he said solemnly, not quite able to believe the conversation they were having. "It is kind of you to say so."

"The side of beef, sir," Binkley said, entering with the platter, and it was everything Nicholas could do not to burst into hysterical laughter.

"Please, do serve it up," he said, barely able to speak at all.

Binkley set to the task, and then his head came snapping up with sharp attention. "Excuse me for just a moment, sir, but there seems to be someone pounding on the door."

Nicholas cursed the intruder, whoever it was, for keeping him from his well-earned, long-awaited meat. But at least it served as a distraction and gave him a chance to bring himself back under control. And then Binkley returned, and Nicholas wondered at his tight expression. "Yes?" he asked, his spine already beginning to prickle.

"I am very sorry, Mr. Daventry, but the message is urgent. It is the village teacher, Johannes Helmut, outside. A ship has foundered, sir, on the Head. All men are urgently needed." Binkley cast a quick look in Georgia's direction. "What would you like me to tell him, sir?"

Every muscle, every nerve violently protested, screaming for him to pretend that he hadn't heard. Of all things—of all the awful things that he might have been asked to face, that had be the worst.

Maybe it was just another bad dream. Maybe if he just sat there long enough it would all go away.

"Mr. Daventry, sir?"

Nicholas blinked. It was no bad dream—it was all too real, and he couldn't ignore the summons. He pushed back his chair, hoping the cold, sick fear that had taken hold of his gut did not show on the outside. "Tell him we are on our way. Get whatever ropes we have. We'll need brandy, blankets, whatever else you can think of. Load everything into the carriage. I'll go directly to harness it. And, Binkley," he added, walking over to him and lowering his voice, "before you do that, send Mr. Helmut to Ravenswalk. Insist he go. Tell him to ask for Lord Brabourne, on my order. Tell him that the young lord is to see to provisions of every sort, including men, and that I expect him to appear along with them. Tell him to be sure to inform Lord Brabourne that it is in payment of his account to me and to some orphaned kittens. Thank you, Binkley."

"Very good, sir." Binkley vanished, as did Nicholas, and Georgia moved just as quickly to gather what she needed.

"Georgia, I will not say it another time. It is no place for you." Nicholas adjusted the harnesses of the horses. "It's too dangerous."

"Don't be absurd, Nicholas. If there are injuries, then I'll be needed. And there is no telling what has happened. I'm sorry, but I cannot allow you to argue with me on the matter." She threw her medicine chest into the carriage.

"You cannot allow *me* to argue with *you?*" he said incredulously. "I beg your pardon, madam, but I think you have no choice but to do as I ask." He looked down at his heel, where something was tugging. "Raleigh, what the devil are you doing here? Stop that pulling at once."

"He must have followed me from the house."

"And he will follow you right back again."

"Very well. If you are determined to take such an attitude, then I warn you. I will go straight to Ravenswalk and have them take me in one of their conveyances. I will not be turned away from a situation where I can help."

"Georgia, I will not tolerate this! You will return to

147

the house straightaway and you will stay there until I return! Raleigh, stop your infernal barking!''

"Raleigh, that's enough. Nicholas, please listen to me. You cannot expect me to sit still and wait here when there might be people hurt. What good is it to pull them out of the water only to have them die of their injuries?''

Nicholas paused. "Oh, very well,'' he said with extreme annoyance. "Suit yourself. There's no more time to aruge. Binkley's coming now with the last of the supplies. But you will stay out of danger's way, do you understand me? And put that dog away in the tack room. He'll be far safer than you. My God, neither of you listens to me.'' He snapped the final buckle into place.

"I will be safe enough,'' she said with equal annoyance, putting a struggling Raleigh away. His frantic barks came only slightly muffled through the closed door. "You have an irritating fashion of issuing commands, Nicholas, without listening to reason.''

"Inside the carriage, Georgia, and let us be on our way. And not another word from you. I haven't the patience. Binkley, take the carriage out. I'll close the doors behind.''

A minute later Nicholas joined her inside. He sat in silence, his arms folded across his chest, a scowl on his face, and Georgia was equally determined not to talk to him if he was going to be so stubborn. The carriage jerked and swayed in the gusting of the wind, which only became more fierce as they approached the coastline, and the horses struggled headlong against it. Georgia saw a cluster of horses and carriages gathered near the cliff's edge, and she knew they were arriving. She swallowed hard, fear gripping at her, not for herself, but for Nicholas.

Nicholas suddenly turned to her. "Listen to me, Georgia,'' he said, taking her hands between his. "Listen to me well. It might be bad—very bad. I'd rather you were safe at home, but since you insisted on being here, please promise me . . . Promise me, Georgia . . .'' He sounded almost anxious.

"Promise you what?'' she said, perplexed.

"Don't go near the water. Please. Don't go near the water.''

"All right, Nicholas. I'll do my best."

"*No!* Not your best. Tell me you'll stay well away. I want your promise. Give it to me."

"Yes, all right, if it is so important."

"It is." He took her face between his hands, and then he pulled her roughly to him and kissed her hard. His mouth took hers as if it were the first and last time it would ever do so, and his arms pulled her close against him, so close that his buttons bit into her skin and she could feel the pounding of his heart beneath. She kissed him in return, held him equally tightly, feeling his apprehension as if it were her own, and she was suddenly afraid.

"Nicholas," she whispered against his mouth as the carriage came to a halt, "take care. Don't do anything foolish. Please don't do anything foolish."

He didn't answer. He buried his face in her hair for one last brief moment, and then he was gone into the dark.

9

Georgia's first impression when she alighted from the carriage was of the deafening sound of surf pounding against the rock. The next was the spray, exploding off rock in great white fans against the dark of the night, so powerfully that it hit her face even where she stood. And the third was of the distant cries of people mingling with the high wailing of the wind and the roaring of the waves.

"If you will hold the horses' heads for a moment, madam, I will unload the supplies," Binkley said quite calmly, and Georgia hurried to comply, talking soothingly to the poor shaking beasts. Someone came out of the dark and relieved her of the task, and she went back to fetch her medicine chest, then headed for the beach.

But the sight that met her eyes as she came over the edge of the cliff was worse than she had imagined. It was chaos. The beach was full of people rushing about and calling to each other, their voices barely audible over the shrill howling of the wind. Bodies were strewn about above the tide line. She frantically scanned the shore looking for Nicholas, but he was nowhere to be seen.

"This way, Missus Daventry," said one burly man, coming up and taking her arm, leading her down the steep, rocky path to the sea. "Mr. Binkley said to keep an eye out for you. He said you could help them poor souls left alive. This way, over here."

Tripping and stumbling, impeded by skirts that were already soaked and heavy, Georgia made her way down to the beach. It was then that she saw the ship for the first time. It had struck the treacherous jut of rock that pushed out from the foot of the cliff, and it lay like a broken toy, the mast cracked, the bow crushed. Tiny objects bobbed about, appearing and disappearing in the white spume of the waves that broke along the rocks, and with a sick sense of recognition Georgia realized they were people—people who could not possibly survive being thrown against the vicious teeth of the reef. She wondered how many had already died in such a way, or drowned beforehand. Men secured only by ropes held fast on the shore were out in the water trying to bring people to safety without being battered to death themselves.

She had one brief glimpse of Nicholas. He had stripped off his coat, shirt, and boots, and he was tying a rope around his waist, talking to a man she recognized as Martin. His face looked ghostly white in the eerie light. She squeezed her eyes shut and whispered a brief prayer for him, and then she turned away, unwilling to watch anymore.

She started moving among the injured, trying to see what could be done for them. Binkley had taken control of the proceedings on the beach and soon had an organized system in place. The dead were taken to one end of the beach, the wounded to the other, where Georgia was stationed, working frantically to salvage those she could with her limited abilities and materials. A doctor appeared at some point, but there was more than enough work for them both, and as he ignored her, she was left in peace to do what she thought correct.

She was attending a man whose arm had been badly gashed. He was bleeding heavily, but Georgia could do nothing for him while he thrashed so violently. "Please, you must let me help you," she said. "Please, try to be still so that I can help you. I imagine the pain must be great." She wiped the rain off her face and bent down to him again.

"I c-can hold him," said a voice over her shoulder, and she looked up with surprise to see Cyril standing there, staring down at the man's arm.

"Oh, thank God you've come, Cyril."

"That man B-Binkley told me to help you," he said in a sulky voice. "Where's N-Nicholas?"

"In the water," she said curtly, wanting to slap him. "Look here, just hold his shoulders down so that I can wrap his arm. That's it. That's the way. Good. That's good." She quickly closed the jagged edges of the wound together, fastened the bandage, and watched to make sure that the bleeding had stopped. "There you are," she said. "Wrap this blanket around you and stay very still. Someone will be along to look after you."

She moved to the next man, who was lying on his side, feebly coughing up blood. She pulled back the blanket, and knew instantly that he would not survive. His eyes opened for a minute, and he mumbled something.

"It's all right," she said, kneeling down and stroking his hair. "It's all right. It's all over. You're safe now."

He shuddered once, and then he was still. "Go with God," she said softly, and closed his staring eyes. She heard retching behind her, and she looked up to see that it was Cyril, who, having seen the extent of the man's injuries, had gone white as a sheet. She ignored him, pulling the blanket up over the man's face, and she moved on.

So it went for the next hour. There were far more dead brought out of the water than living. She moved as quickly as she could, but still some died before she could reach them. She pumped water out of heaving bodies, insisting Cyril help her. He had quickly lost his sulkiness, shocked into compliance, and he did as he was told, sticking to her side as if his life depended on it. She wondered if he was not afraid that he would be sent into the water if he didn't stay to help her. But she hardly cared what he thought. All she knew was that she was grateful for the extra pair of hands.

And all the time that she worked, her eyes strained for a sight of Nicholas, terrified that he was going to be brought to her next.

Nicholas came out of the waves shaking with cold. He couldn't quite believe it was over, that they had taken in everyone, dead or alive. He heard voices around him, felt hands on his back, something being put around his shoulders, and he sank to the sand and put his head on his knees, trying to catch his breath, which was not easy. Something heavy had smashed into his side and his ribs felt as if they'd been broken. He looked up and out into the pitching sea and shuddered, not quite able to believe he had survived. And then his eye caught something, and he looked more closely. He could have sworn he'd seen something small and pale tossed on a wave. He forced himself to his feet and strained to see. And there it was again—a child, he would swear it, a young boy, for he saw his face as plain as day.

"Oh, Jesus . . . sweet Jesus," he cried, throwing off the blanket and retying the discarded rope around his back.

"Daventry, what the hell do you think you're doing?" someone shouted, seeing him.

"There's a boy out there," he said. "I swear it to you—I just saw him."

"There is no one left out there, Mr. Daventry," said Johannes Helmut. "Please, you will kill yourself if you go out again. You have done enough—more than enough. Talk some sense into the man, Mr. Binkley," he pleaded.

"It is true, sir. You will be no good to anyone in your state of exhaustion. Leave it to the others, now. You have been at this far too long and will likely drown yourself if you continue. It's a miracle you haven't drowned already."

"I must go back in, Binkley," Nicholas said, bending over and coughing. "You don't understand."

"I am sorry, sir, but I must insist that you not drive yourself anymore. If there is someone out there, there are other men who can help. And no one can be left alive."

"I don't give a damn," Nicholas said. He shoved off the hands that tried to restrain him and plunged back into the icy water, ignoring their shouts. He forced his arms to move, his legs to kick, beating in the direction of the shape he had seen. He ignored the water that rushed up his nose and mouth, the waves that dragged at him. He, at least, had a lifeline to the shore, and if he went under, they would pull him in. The boy had nothing. He went under time and time again, almost too exhausted to try to keep his head up. It was dark, so dark, and he couldn't see. The salt stung at his eyes, and the cold numbed him so that his limbs didn't want to move. Only his desperation to save the child drove him on. Another wave washed over him, and he swallowed a great mouthful of water and then fought his way back to the surface. Nothing. He could see nothing. And then, as if God had thrown the child to him, he saw him again to his right, and he swam as fast as he could, catching him up in his arms before another wave could take him away. Nicholas threw the boy onto his back, holding on to his arms with one hand and beating his way back to the shore with the other.

"Binkley. Binkley," he gasped, forcing his way through the last of the surf and struggling up onto the sand, his hands holding on to the arms that were slung over his shoulders. "I found him, Binkley. Thanks be to God, I found him."

He stood quite still as Binkley pulled the child off him, and then he automatically turned to go back into the roaring sea.

"No, sir, I think not this time," Binkley said very gently, passing the boy to waiting arms and putting a hand on his shoulder. "Come with me. Your wife is here."

"Georgia?" he said, dazed. "Oh, God—she's not hurt, is she?"

"She is tending to the injured. Look. Look up there. They are taking her the child you have brought in. Why don't you go to help her?"

Nicholas nodded, not feeling Binkley's hands untying the knots of the rope around his waist, or the blanket that was thrust around him. His body had started to shake uncontrollably. Somewhere in the deep recesses of his mind he understood that he didn't have to go out into the water again. He had brought the boy in, and he was safe. He stumbled toward the higher beach and Georgia, not aware of the hands that helped him.

She was bending over the boy as he reached her, and he shoved through the crowd of people who had gathered around.

"How is he?" he managed to say, dropping to his knees, his lungs heaving for air.

She looked up, and her face went white. "Nicholas! Oh, Nicholas, thank God! They said you wouldn't come out of the water!"

"The boy, Georgia? How is the boy? Please, tell me he's alive. Please. Tell me I wasn't too late."

"Oh, Nicholas . . . I'm so sorry. He's not breathing." She quickly turned back to the limp form and continued to pump on his back.

"Not . . . not breathing? Oh, God, no. Oh, please, no. . . ." He let out a great long anguished cry, then pushed her aside and began to pump on the child's back himself. "Come on, breathe, boy. Breathe! You can do it if you put your mind to it! You're not dead. You can't be dead! Breathe, I say!"

Binkley took him by the shoulders and gently moved him away, and he was too weak to resist.

"Leave your wife to it, sir. We must get you warm and dry."

"Damn you, Binkley, stop telling me what to do! Someone has to help him. Someone . . ." And then he felt something inside snap. Everything seemed to spin around him as if he were being sucked into a whirlpool. And there was nothing more.

"Binkley! Binkley, help him," Georgia cried as she saw Nicholas collapse. "Oh, please, help him." She continued pumping on the boy as she spoke, afraid to take her hands from him.

Binkley bent over Nicholas, listening for the sound of breathing. He looked up, relief on his face. "I believe he is suffering from exhaustion and exposure, madam. He needs warmth and shelter. Martin, if you would help me carry him, and you, Mr. Jerome. Do not worry, Mrs. Daventry, we will see to him. You look after the child."

"Thank you, Binkley. For God's sake get him warmed as quickly as you can." She rolled the boy over and breathed into his mouth, reasoning her breath had to be better than none at all. "Come, little one, you can do it," she muttered, fiercely willing him to live. "Come along, now, help me. Breathe. Oh, please, breathe. Do it for Nicholas if you won't do it for yourself." She didn't know exactly why she wouldn't give up, except that Nicholas had seemed so terribly distraught, had risked his own life for this child. And then there was also a small voice inside of her telling her that there might still be life somewhere. She knew it was quite impossible, but she had never before ignored an instinct, and now was not the time to start. So she pumped, and she breathed into his mouth, and then she pumped some more, trying to stimulate his lungs into breathing for himself.

Cyril, who had been standing back watching all of this, said, "He's d-dead, Georgia. He's p-probably been d-dead for ages. Why don't you j-just leave it?"

She looked up at him furiously. "Because your cousin went out into those waters to save him."

"Well, it w-was a s-stupid thing to d-do. Look at them both."

"Keep your opinions to yourself and help me. I didn't see you out there risking your neck, did I? Nicholas brought this boy in, and I'm going to do everything I can to see that his efforts weren't wasted. I don't care if I have to stay here all night. I don't care, do you hear me? And don't you dare say another word about it." She bent her mouth and breathed another breath into the boy's body.

Cyril sighed and moved down next to her, taking over the pumping while Georgia breathed. They went on like this for what seemed like a lifetime as people continued to stand and watch, transfixed. And then the body stirred. It stirred, and then coughed, and then coughed again, and Cyril gave a shout and jumped back. A murmur went up in the crowd, and people began crossing themselves, and some furtively made the sign against evil. Georgia sat up, astonished. She quickly collected herself and rolled him onto his side. Water dribbled out of his mouth, and he moaned.

"Oh, dear God," she said, not quite able to believe it. "He's alive. He's alive! Cyril, go tell Nicholas. Quickly! Go tell him!"

Cyril, who was staring at the boy as if it were the second coming, scurried away. Georgia scooped the boy up into her arms and held him close to her for warmth, rocking him against her. He couldn't have been more than nine or so, she estimated. He felt so light, so fragile, his bones all thin and sharp.

"It's fine now, little one," she whispered against his temple. "You're safe now. All safe and sound." She took the blanket off her own shoulders and wrapped it around him, then pulled him against her again and continued to rock him as if he were an infant. She didn't know what else to do. She felt that she had to shelter him from the wind and rain and cold, and from the stares of the people who crowded around as if they didn't have better things to do. She wanted them to leave, she wanted to be left alone. She wanted to cry.

Cyril appeared back at her side. "N-Nicholas is still out c-cold," he said, "and B-Binkley's had him taken up to the c-carriage. He says you're to c-come along and b-bring the boy. There's nothing more we can d-do here. I've arranged for two men to c-carry him up. And I've d-directed the other wounded to be taken t-to Ravenswalk. They c-can stay there until they've r-recuperated."

"Why, Cyril . . . that is very good of you." Georgia looked at him with extreme surprise. This was not the Cyril she knew. But she did not have the time or the inclination to think about the sudden change in his attitude. "I must go now. The child needs shelter."

"I . . . I would like to c-come with you, if I m-may. I would like to assure myself that the b-boy will recover."

"And that is good of you too, but you'll be far more use at Ravenswalk overseeing things here. Binkley and I will look after him. I fear the child has a battle ahead of him. He will probably be staying with us for some time."

"Then m-may I come t-tomorrow?"

"Of course you may, Cyril. You have been a tremendous help tonight. Nicholas will be very pleased to hear it, I know."

He colored. "Here are the m-men to take the b-boy up. I will w-watch over the others t-tonight."

"Thank you for everything, Cyril. I will see you in the morning."

He nodded and disappeared, and Georgia handed the limp boy into the keeping of the men who awaited him, and wearily followed them up the path.

The journey back was like a procession. Half the village accompanied them on horses and in carriages. Nicholas' rescue of the child was seen as a small miracle; the larger miracle was the return of life to the child's body.

Georgia had already heard the whispers start, and she could only hope they did not lead to trouble. Her mother had been called a witch often enough. Georgia had never understood the ignorance or the lack of gratitude that tended to follow her ministrations. But she had more important things to think about just now.

"Nicholas," Georgia said gently, stroking his wet head where it lay in her lap. "Nicholas." He still had not regained consciousness, and she was becoming worried. "Nicholas, it's over. We're going home now. We have the child. Everything's going to be all right. Wake up, my love. Please wake up."

But he did not stir.

She looked over at Johannes Helmut, who was still holding the child in his arms. He met her eyes and shook his head. "I have never seen anything like it, Mrs. Daventry," he said. "Never. He went back into that water as if he were a man crazed. A hero, that's what he is. A hero."

"He'll be a dead hero if we don't get him home soon," she said angrily. "How could you have let him go out there time after time until it came to this? How, Mr. Helmut? You must have known what would happen!"

"It was not our choice, Mrs. Daventry. It was his. He could not be stopped. Look, now. He is alive, and so is the boy, who would be dead if it had not been for him—and for you."

Georgia just bent her head. She couldn't help herself. The tears came unbidden, unwanted, and she cried silently, her hot tears falling off her cheeks and onto Nicholas' cold face. She would not lose him now. She could not lose him, not Nicholas of the laughing eyes, the kind heart, the enigmatic soul. She couldn't bear the thought that he might leave her, all because of a storm and a foundered ship.

And then she looked over at the child, and her own heart turned over. It was because of Nicholas' kind heart that he had found the strength and courage to go back out, to save this young one's life. How could she rage against that, when it was his very being that made him capable of such things? She thought of all the men she had ministered to that night, who never would have lived at all if it hadn't been for Nicholas and men like him. Georgia ran a hand over her face, wiping away her tears.

"I beg your pardon, Mr. Helmut. I did not mean to take my anxiety out on you. Please forgive me. I know you risked your own life in the same way."

"Mrs. Daventry, you are a good woman. You saved many a life yourself, and we are grateful to you—and this child here should be most especially grateful. Please, do not fret yourself. Your husband is an unusually strong man, as he proved tonight. With God's help he will recover."

"With God's help, yes. And I swear to you it won't be without mine to urge God along. I will see him well. I will."

"I am sure you will, and the child as well. And now here we are. Let the men take your husband from you and bring him inside."

Binkley directed the men to carry Nicholas up to his bedroom, and he went up with them. She showed Johannes Helmut into the sitting room and he carefully put the boy down on the sofa, then stripped his wet clothes off and wrapped him in the blanket as Georgia stirred the dying embers of the sitting room fire into life. All of this was done without a word spoken. Georgia then examined the child, listening carefully for his breathing. It was quick but steady. She had no doubt that there were crises ahead, despite the outward signs that all was well.

"We have little left in the way of dry blankets, Mr. Helmut," she said apologetically. "If anyone outside has any to spare, I would be grateful. As you can see, our situation is not one of luxury."

"I understand, Mrs. Daventry. Let me see what I can do."

He was back shortly with an entire armful. "Will this do?"

"Thank you," she said, extremely grateful. "And if you will show those waiting outside back into the kitchen, I am sure that Binkley will make you all something hot to drink, as soon as he has seen my husband safely settled."

Johannes Helmut bowed his head and cleared his throat. "I am very sorry, Mrs. Daventry, that we of the

159

village have not been more generous in nature, or more forthcoming. We thought your husband to be connected to Ravenswalk, you see, and like them. And there was talk, although any fool could see your devotion to each other, so it's not to be considered again. I'm sorry, ma'am, if we've caused you pain. Rumors are hard to dispel. But you and your husband both seem fine people, and that man Mr. Binkley too. What was done tonight is surely proof that the talk has been wrong. Please accept my apologies.''

Georgia bent back over the child, not wanting Johannes Helmut to see the tears that had started in her eyes again. "Thank you," she said. "You are very kind.''

"It is of no consequence compared to what you and your husband have done this night. I will leave you, Mrs. Daventry, if there is nothing further.''

"Nothing," she said, then laid her head on the child's chest and cried as if her heart might break.

It was Binkley who came to her and stood her up, Binkley who quietly led her upstairs to her room and handed her dry clothes, Binkley who waited outside until she was changed and then led her downstairs again to the waiting crowd who were amassed in the kitchen.

"They need to hear something from you, madam," he said. "Some words from the mistress of the house. Think of what your husband might want to say in these circumstances,'' he added tactfully as she looked at him in dismay. "Perhaps he would want to encourage and give thanks?''

Georgia nodded, then squared her shoulders and walked into the kitchen.

"Thank you all," she managed to say. "You were so brave and good tonight, each and every one of you. Let us pray to God for the souls of those who perished, but also pray that those who have survived so far will continue on a course of recovery. You should be very proud of yourselves and your village.''

A great cheer went up, and Georgia found herself bewildered by this sudden approbation after months of being snubbed. But at least they weren't hissing and calling her witch, or Nicholas the devil.

"If you'll excuse me now, I must attend to my husband and the child he brought in. Please, make yourselves warm and comfortable before you go back out into the elements. I wish we had more to offer you . . . Binkley? The beef, perhaps?"

Another cheer went up, and Binkley bowed to her. "As you wish, madam. These good people need nourishment. I will do what I can to provide it."

"Excellent. Good night, and I thank all of you again."

She left with as much dignity as she could gather, checked one more time on the sleeping child, then tore up the stairs to see Nicholas.

They had stripped him and put him into a nightshirt. He lay unmoving in his bed, the same bed where they had talked and laughed and kissed only that morning. It seemed a lifetime away. His skin was pale and cold as death. Binkley had put warm bricks in the bed and layered blankets on top of him, and she went to the fireplace and pushed even more wood into it, until the room blazed with heat. She didn't know what to do beyond that.

She sat down on the side of the bed and tried to feel inside of him, the way her mother had taught her to do with all living things. But there was nothing there, nothing to catch hold of. Even the child downstairs had more of a feel of life to him than Nicholas did. Her heart went quite still. Deathly still.

"The hot drink you asked for, madam," Binkley said, entering the room with a tray sometime later.

"Thank you, Binkley, but it won't do him much good if I can't wake him to make him take it," Georgia answered. "It's not a good sign."

"He is exhausted, I think."

"It's more than exhaustion. I don't know why, but it's something I feel in my bones. But maybe tomorrow he will have improved. How is the boy?"

"He is sleeping still, madam, but his breathing is quite normal now, and he seems warm enough to the touch."

"Good. And you, Binkley? You must be exhausted yourself. At least you are now dry."

"It was you I was concerned about, madam. You have endured much tonight."

"I'm perfectly well, thank you, although I do believe I will stay in here tonight."

"A wise decision, if I may say so, madam. I will stay with the boy in front of the fire downstairs and keep a close eye on his condition. Should there be any change at all, I will alert you."

"Thank you, Binkley. Have the men left?"

"Yes, madam. I gave them all hot coffee and a bite to eat, along with more of your thanks."

"And you have mine as well for all you did tonight. I don't know what I would have done without your help."

Binkley inclined his head, and softly shut the door behind him.

Georgia ended up drinking the tisane herself, as she could not rouse Nicholas. She quickly changed into her night shift, then shored up the fire again. And then, since she could think of nothing else, she climbed into the bed and pulled Nicholas against her, trying to warm him with the heat of her own body.

"Nicholas," she said. "Oh, Nicholas, please be all right. Sleep if that is what you need, but come back to me. Please come back. Oh, please. . . ." She ran her hands through his hair, not soft and silky as it had been that morning, but stiff with salt. She held his cold face between her hands and pressed her mouth against his, but there was no answering pressure, no movement of his lips. She wrapped her arms around him and stroked his strong back. She pressed her cheek against his chest, willing him back, but there was no response.

"Oh, Nicholas," she whispered. "Nicholas, my love. . . ."

She held him through the rest of the night. It was the longest night she had ever known.

The next morning when Georgia woke, Nicholas was still in her arms. He had not moved, and when she touched his face, it was not to discover that he was hot with fever, as she had expected, but to find that he was still cold, far colder than he should have been. She rolled him onto his back and pressed her ear to his chest, trying very hard not to panic. His heart beat slowly, but in an even rhythm, and his chest continued to rise and fall. She knew there was something terribly wrong. She sensed it in every fiber of her being, had sensed it from the night before.

"Binkley," she called from the bedroom door. "Binkley, come quickly!"

Binkley appeared only moments later. "What is it, madam? Has something happened?" He spoke evenly, but he was more shaken than she'd ever seen him.

"No," she said, trying to be calm. "That's just it. Nothing has happened. Nothing at all. I think you had better come and see."

Binkley entered the room and went over to the bed, looking down at Nicholas. He picked up his hand and let it drop. Then he gingerly opened Nicholas' eyelid and gazed at his eye. It did not move, not did it see.

Binkley stepped away and carefully folded his fingertips together. "It is curious," he said.

"Curious?" Georgia said, wanting to scream. "Binkley, it is unlike anything I have ever seen! He should be recovering from exhaustion by now—or at least have a fever in reaction to the exposure. But instead he is still cold. I cannot understand this. He did not strike his head that you know of? I have found no evidence of it, but sometimes there is none."

"No, I saw no indication that Mr. Daventry might have had a blow to the head. He was shocked, yes, but that is not surprising after he had pushed himself beyond his limits. Perhaps he only needs rest, a very long sleep."

"I agree, but this is not a natural sleep. Oh, Binkley, I cannot bear that Nicholas might have saved all those lives only to give up his own. I really can't." She pushed her hand into her forehead hard, willing herself to stay strong. "He must get better. He must. I could not bear it if anything happened to him."

"I am pleased to hear it, madam," Binkley said.

Georgia's eyes shot to his in dismay. "Binkley! How could you ever think otherwise?"

"It is not what I think that matters. It is what Mr. Daventry thinks. But I should return downstairs. The boy

163

has begun to toss and turn, and his skin is very warm to the touch.''

"He is most likely the one coming down with the fever. I will be down directly. I must just dress,'' she said, blushing as she realized she was standing there in her nightclothes.

"Very good, madam,'' Binkley said calmly, as if he hadn't noticed a thing, nor spoken so personally to her. "I will bring up hot water to your bedroom. Lily is not yet returned.''

Georgia sat down on the bed again and took Nicholas' hand in her own. Binkley's words had shocked her, and she needed to think. Was it possible that Nicholas did not know how deeply she cared about him? It was not as if she hadn't told him, after all. But he must have said something to Binkley to indicate that he thought her indifferent. Why? Why would he think such a foolish thing? And why did it matter so much to him?

"Nicholas,'' she said, looking down at him with tears filling her eyes. "You really are an imbecile. Don't you know I'd be lost without you?'' She pulled his hand to her mouth and kissed his fingers, then curled his hand in hers and held it against her chest, which hurt so much she could scarcely breathe.

She remembered how he had kissed her in the carriage before he had gone, and the words he had spoken to her, the promise he had insisted on. "Don't go near the water,'' he'd said, almost desperately. He had held her to him as if he would never hold her again, as if he were impressing her on his soul.

Georgia covered her mouth with her fist, her tears spilling over. She suddenly understood. "Oh, Nicholas,'' she whispered. "I'm the one who's been the imbecile, haven't I?''

She put her head in her arms and she wept.

10

Georgia knelt down beside the child and touched his flushed cheek. His eyes flew open, and she saw for the first time that they were a deep brown.

"Hello, my friend," she said gently. "How are you feeling this morning?"

"*Aidez-moi*," he cried, his eyes unfocused. He coughed, and turned his body into the pallet. "*La mer . . . elle moi submerge . . .*"

"*Soit tranquille, mon enfant*," Georgia replied, stroking his hot brow. "*Tu es sain et sauf. Tout est bien.*"

He sighed and his eyes closed again. She sat for some time, murmuring to the child in his own language. She had hope for him, if he could survive the fever he was building and his small body could find the strength to overcome his experience.

Nicholas was another matter altogether.

She bit her lip, trying very hard to attend to the child, but the thought of Nicholas lying upstairs in his unnatural sleep would not leave her. She was frightened, so very frightened. She really did not know what she would do if he died. For not only would it break her heart, but it would be too late to tell him how she really felt.

Cyril arrived later that morning, full of news. "We have twelve m-men at the house," he said breathlessly, entering the sitting room and looking curiously at the pallet where the child slept. "All survived the n-night. How is it h-here? H-how is the b-boy?"

Georgia looked up from sponging the child. It was almost more than she could do to look at him. Her emotions had already been pushed to the edge, and she knew one more thing, one more insult, one more demand, and she would snap.

"Hello, Cyril," she said tightly. "To answer your question, the child is feverish. His lungs are congested. But he is taking liquids. Your cousin, on the other hand, is in a state near death. Were you going to ask about him, or is it of no interest to you at all?"

Cyril blanched. "N-Nicholas? N-near death?"

"I believe so. You can go and see for yourself. Binkley is with him."

"Georgia . . . I m-meant to a-apologize to you. For what I s-said last night. About N-Nicholas, I m-mean. And the b-boy. It was f-foolish."

She took in a quick breath, praying for patience. "Yes, it was foolish, and it was thoughtless. But it is good of you to recognize that fact and to offer an apology. You might give it to Nicholas."

"H-he is upstairs?"

"Yes. You can sit and talk to him, even though he probably cannot hear you. But it might do you some good. I think you have a very misguided idea of your cousin, Cyril, and if he is fortunate enough to survive, perhaps you will manage to change your attitude. And then you can come back down here and sit with the child. He needs constant attention, and I want to go over to Ravenswalk and check on the injured."

Cyril nodded and left the room, but she could see how reluctant he was to go. She could well imagine why. She hoped Cyril was thoroughly ashamed of himself. No, more than ashamed. She hoped he saw what a spoiled, whining, dreadful child he was. She was hoping for yet another miracle, she thought bitterly. And if she were to line her miracles up, Nicholas was first on the list.

"Mrs. Wells!" said the footman, opening the door. "I . . . I mean Mrs. Daventry. How is your husband? He was so very brave last night. As were you, ma'am."

"My husband has still not awakened, but thank you for asking, James. If you would take me to wherever you've quartered the injured men? I'm sorry to be so curt," she added, hearing her tone of voice. "It is only that I am in a hurry to return home."

"Naturally, ma'am. And the boy? How is the boy?"

"He is fighting. Has the doctor been?"

"Yes, ma'am, earlier this morning. But they'll be happy to see you. They've been talking of nothing else. An angel, they're calling you, ma'am, with the touch of the good Lord himself."

Georgia colored furiously. "I am nothing of the sort," she said. "I don't know where they've come up with such a fanciful idea."

She followed James to the ballroom, only to see it had been turned into a ward, mattresses laid out on the marble floor. With a brief flash of humor she thought of Lady Raven and the horrified reaction she'd have when she eventually discovered the use her precious ballroom had been put to. She colored again when a murmur went up as the men saw her.

"Good morning, gentlemen," she said as briskly as she could manage. In truth, she was happy to see each and every one of them, for she vividly remembered what had gone into their rescue.

She moved among them, talking quietly to them, discovering that they had been the crew of a trading vessel returning to England. "And the child?" she asked. "Can you tell me about him?"

"A Frenchie, missus," said the man whose arm she had bandaged the night before. "Pascal LaMartine is his name. Only eleven, the poor lad, hired on as cook's assistant, although a touch above us all. Did he make it through the night? We've all been afraid to ask."

"He did," and she smiled at the sighs of relief. "I am hoping he will make a full recovery, as will all of you. How did he come to be aboard?"

"He'd just joined us. Thought he was a goner, we did, not that he had any family to worry about him. He lost them all in the sickness that ran through Paree last year, and gentlefolk they were, from the little he said—or didn't say. The troubles, you know. Things haven't been so good for the gentlefolk since then, you see, so he weren't talking much—in truth, the lad's not talking at all, not at all. He did a proper running-away after his family died. He's more educated than the lot of us, that's for certain. But his language is halfway decent so you won't have no real trouble understanding him, miss, though he confounds my brain with all his odd prattle. He's a good boy, don't misunderstand me. Didn't deserve to have this happen. Thank God for your husband is all I can say."

"Yes. I know. This might hurt, for I am going to apply a mixture to your arm. It will prevent infection."

"But the doctor stitched it only this morning, missus. I'm sure it don't need nothing else," the man said, alarmed.

"Yes, I can see he stitched it, but that doesn't prevent infection; it only ensures that the edges will heal together."

"Not dung?" the man asked, shuddering.

"Certainly not," Georgia replied with a smile, pulling out her jar of unguent. "I have no intention of killing you. It's a mixture made from hedge woundwort, and will speed the healing. There you are. Your name, sir?"

"Jeremiah Briggs, missus."

"Well, then, Jeremiah Briggs. You'll soon be better, see if you aren't."

She rebandaged his arm and moved on to the next man.

A half-hour later she was finished, well-pleased. They were a ragged bunch, and would need some time to recover, but they looked well enough, given everything.

She went down to the kitchen to mix some medicines, and she found Jerome there, engaged in the process of making an herbal tisane.

"Mrs. Daventry," he said, looking up from his work with surprise. "Good morning. How is Mr. Daventry this morning?"

"He is not well, Mr. Jerome," she said, setting down her box. "But I am hoping he only needs rest. You were all so wonderful last night."

"We did nothing compared to him," he said, pouring boiling water onto his mixture, and Georgia looked over with curiosity.

"What are you preparing?" she asked.

"It is a tea for his lordship," he said. "He receives it twice daily."

"Oh? May I ask what the ingredients are?"

"I don't really know, madam. You appear to be far more conversant with the art than I."

"I wish I knew more," Georgia said, finishing the fever reducer. "Perhaps I could smell? I am curious."

"Certainly, madam," he said, stepping away from the bubbling pan.

Georgia bent her nose to the steam, then looked up in sudden alarm. "May I see the dry mixture?" she said, sure she had to be wrong.

Jerome took a tin off the shelf and opened it. "It is not the most pleasant of odors, I know. I sweeten the tea with honey and add a touch of brandy to make it more palatable."

Georgia took a pinch between her fingers and smelled again. "Surely," she said slowly, "the doctor did not prescribe this?"

Jerome shook his head. "Not Dr. Lythe. He is overly fond of the leeches and the blade. It is Lady Raven's remedy. Her ladyship is well-versed in herbal lore. She is most insistent on mixing the herbs herself."

Georgia frowned, finding that an extraordinary piece of information, for she had unmistakably smelled monkshood. A very small amount, but monkshood nonetheless. "I see . . ." she said. "How long has Lord Raven been receiving these tisanes?"

"From the very first. I feel quite sure it is the tea that keeps his lordship alive."

"I could not persuade you to change the formula?" Georgia asked. "I feel sure I could produce one more beneficial to his lordship."

"Certainly not, madam," Jerome said, looking shocked. "I would not think to interfere with her ladyship's orders. I am sure you are very knowledgeable, but I will not in any way risk his lordship's health."

Risk his health? The poor man was imbibing a deadly poison twice a day. It might have been a mistake caused by ignorance, for there were those who used monkshood in an ill-advised attempt to cure gout or rheumatism, or even neuralgia. But none of those was Lord Raven's problem. A tiny prickle of suspicion formed in the back of her mind and wouldn't let go.

She really didn't know what to do. She couldn't accuse Jacqueline of deliberately poisoning her husband, for she had nothing to go on. If she even suggested such a thing, it would create the most terrible scandal. But there was poor Lord Raven's health—if not his very life to consider. Still, he had survived well over a year, so a few more days would make no difference. She would wait until Nicholas was better, and then she would find a way to broach the subject.

Georgia found Cyril still sitting by Pascal's side. She'd been sure that he would have tired of his duties, but instead, and very much to her surprise, he refused to leave.

"Y-you have enough to d-do, l-looking after N-Nicholas," he said. "L-let me help. P-please."

"Very well, Cyril. If you are really sincere, then it would be a great help."

"I am. S-sincere. I will do whatever you s-say."

"And I will hold you to your word. Now listen carefully. Here is what you must do. . . ."

As soon as she was finished giving him instructions, she went upstairs to relieve Binkley.

"Has he stirred?" she asked anxiously as Binkley stood.

"I'm afraid not, madam. However, I took the liberty of washing Mr. Daventry as best I could. I did not like the thought of all the salt water on his skin. He has some cuts and bruises that you might want to examine. But I believe that his skin does seem warmer to the touch."

Georgia touched Nicholas' cheek, then looked up at the older man, who was standing with hands folded in front of him. She knew Binkley well enough by now that she knew his facade of calm concealed a terrible worry, and she smiled at him.

"Do you know, you're right, Binkley. He is warmer, and that's a good sign. A wonderful sign. Now, where are these cuts you have found?"

Binkley pulled up Nicholas' nightshirt, careful to keep the sheet over his hips, protecting his modesty. Georgia wanted to tell him that he needn't worry, that she already knew about Nicholas' impediment, but she didn't want to embarrass either Binkley or herself. She leaned over Nicholas, seeing where the skin was badly bruised around the left side of his ribs and the marks where the rope had chafed at his waist. He had some nasty cuts on his back, which she treated with the salve, and then Binkley adjusted the sheets and showed her his leg.

"And here, also, madam." There was a wide, angry-looking scrape on his calf, and Georgia applied some salve to that as well. And then her eye caught a thick white scar on his thigh. It was long and jagged, and it ran from just below his hip nearly to his knee.

"Goodness," she said. "What caused that, Binkley?"

"I have no idea, madam. Mr. Daventry said only that it was a childhood injury. It never seemed to give him any trouble." He pulled the blankets back into place. "I will go and prepare a meal, madam. You must keep your strength up if you are to look after the sick. We cannot afford to have you become ill yourself. Will Lord Brabourne be staying?"

"He's offered his help, Binkley, but we shall see how long that lasts. I would expect he will stay through luncheon, however. I don't suppose there is any of the beef left?" The mention of food had made her realize she had not eaten anything since the soup at dinner the night before, and she was terribly hungry.

"The beef is gone, madam. However, the village people have been very kind, and food has been brought to the back door. I will find something suitable, I am sure."

"Thank you, Binkley." Her attention went back to Nicholas and she did not hear him leave.

Lily returned that afternoon full of excited stories. "I couldn't believe my ears, missus, when I heard what happened last night! You should hear what they're saying in the village. They're calling Mr. Daventry the 'savior of sailors.' He's a right hero, missus! How is he today? They said he went out cold, just like that."

"He is still sleeping, Lily." Georgia took the kettle off the stove and poured the boiling water onto the crushed roots of Solomon's seal, making a poultice for Nicholas' bruises.

"Ooh. And the boy? They said you brought him back from the dead, missus. The master saved his body and you saved his soul. A miracle, they say it was."

"Lily, that's absurd. Pascal just needed a push in the right direction. He's in the sitting room if you want to go see him. It's a pity we're so short of usable bedrooms, but I thought we might temporarily turn my room into a bedroom for him. I'll move in with Nicholas, for he needs full-time attention anyway. Pascal really should be in a proper bed.''

''And there's the nice fresh mattress for him and clean sheets that I put on just yesterday. I'll go straightaway and make a fire, and you can bring him up.''

By that evening Pascal was coughing in earnest. Georgia finished mixing the mustard paste for his chest, and she handed it to Cyril to apply. ''Don't forget the hot cloths,'' she said, washing her hands. ''I'm going back to Nicholas.'' She bent over Pascal and brushed the hair off his face. ''Did you give him the last infusion?''

''Y-yes. He took it all.''

''That's good. And, Cyril . . . thank you. Lily will be in soon, and you can go home.''

''N-no. I will s-stay here. He is m-my charge. I w-want to stay.''

She gave him a long look. He was slightly flushed, and there was a look in his eyes that was different, a sense of purpose, perhaps, of genuine concern for someone other than himself.

''Very well, Cyril. If you insist. But I warn you, it will no doubt be a long night. I'll ask Lily to make you up a pallet on the floor.'' She stroked Pascal's fevered brow one more time, then went into the next room and closed the door behind her.

She sat in the armchair and picked up her mother's book of medical notations, but she could find nothing that approximated Nicholas' condition. His skin had warmed, his lungs were clear, his heartbeat was back to a normal pace. And yet she could not rouse him. She prepared to wait out the night.

By the third night Georgia was at her wits' end. Pascal's fever had not broken, and he was delirious. And yet she was more worried about Nicholas than she was about the child. She knew that if Nicholas did not wake soon and take nourishment, he would die. But what could she do? There was no point trying to dribble liquid down his throat, for it would only choke him.

"Nicholas, I'm just going to put some more of the poultice on," she said, pulling back the covers and lifting his nightshirt. Binkley would no doubt have been shocked, but he wasn't there to see, for he was finally getting some much-needed sleep. She rubbed the poultice on his poor ribs, wondering what he had come into contact with to create such bruising.

"Oh, Nicholas," she said, wondering if he could hear her. "You must get better. You really must." She replaced the covers and rested her forehead on his chest for a minute, so exhausted she didn't know what to do with herself. "I miss you, you know. I miss your silliness, and hearing you laugh. I even miss arguing with you. I miss everything about you, Nicholas. And Raleigh misses you too."

Raleigh, hearing his name, lifted his head and nudged at her feet. She'd been amazed by his devotion. When Binkley had remembered him the morning after the shipwreck and let him out of the tack room, he had barreled directly up to Nicholas' bedroom, refusing since to leave him except to eat and briefly go outside so as not to disgrace himself. Georgia wondered if his frantic behavior before they had left that night hadn't been some sort of premonition. Animals were uncanny in that way. She sat up and gave him a pat. "You must be worried too, my friend. I'm sure you love him every bit as much as I do."

Raleigh yawned and licked her hand, then put his head back down on his paws and closed his eyes.

Georgia stood and went to the connecting door, putting her ear against it. She heard nothing, so she carefully opened it and put her head through. Pascal was finally sleeping, and Cyril was stretched out on his pallet, his arms flung over his face. She quietly shut the door again and went over to the window, where dawn was just breaking. Everything was quiet. It was as if the whole world slept, except for her. And Nicholas slept most deeply of all.

Helpless frustration washed over her, and she slammed her fists against the wall. Why wouldn't he wake? Why? It was as if he'd lost the will to live, as if he'd just given up. She couldn't do a thing for him, and he wasn't doing a thing for himself.

"What am I to do with you?" she shouted furiously,

turning around to glare at him. "You haven't much time left, you know. Do you want to die? Do you? It would seem so, for there is nothing else wrong with you that I can find. Very well, then. You've always been mule-headed. If you want to die, go right ahead. Don't worry about the fact that I love you, that you'll break my heart. Oh, and don't worry about Binkley's heart either, even though he loves you as if you were his son. Then there is your uncle—you said it half-killed him the first time you went away. What do you think your permanent departure will do to him, especially in his condition? But fine, Nicholas. Be stubborn. Off you go, leaving a trail of heartbroken people behind. I suppose we'll all find a way to get on without you, even though life will never be the same. I think it is extremely inconsiderate and unfeeling of you. The least you could do is to put up the semblance of a fight."

She took a deep breath, having worked herself into a righteous fury, and marched over to the bed, glaring down at him. "I just want you to know one thing, Nicholas. If you die, the troll wins. And I don't think I could stand it."

She went back to the armchair and slumped down into it, her body shaking with spent emotion. And then she picked up her mother's notebook again and began to read through it, not taking in the words.

An hour later Nicholas opened his eyes.

Georgia came awake with a start, the book having fallen open in her lap, and she realized she'd been dozing. She rubbed her burning eyes, then pushed herself to her feet and went to check on Nicholas.

There had been no change. She sighed heavily, then went next door to see how Pascal was. He and Cyril were both still asleep, and she had no intention of disturbing them. She closed the door and went to stir the fire.

She thought she heard someone whisper, and she spun around, thinking she was beginning to imagine things. Nicholas had not moved. She started to turn back to the fire, when it came again.

"Water. . . ."

"Nicholas?" she said, running to the bed, almost

174

knocking the chair over as she went, and banging her shin in the process, but she didn't even notice. "Nicholas?"

His eyes opened, and she covered her face with trembling hands for a moment, trying to collect herself. Her relief almost sent her to her knees. "Nicholas, thank God . . . oh, thank God." She poured a glass of water from the carafe next to his bed, her hands trembling so badly that she nearly dropped it. "Here, my love, here you are. Let me help you."

She held his head for him as he drank deeply, and then she helped him to lie back. He was weak—terribly weak. But he was alive and awake, and she couldn't have asked for more.

His eyes fluttered closed again, and he turned his cheek into the pillow with a sigh. Georgia, her entire body shaking, sat down on the side of the bed, holding his hand. She avoided the temptation of shaking him to see if he would wake, although it took tremendous willpower. She bit her lip, not knowing how to contain her happiness.

Nicholas had come back. Everything was going to be all right. She covered her face and gave in to her tears, but for the first time they were tears of relief.

She was still sitting there when Binkley came in with hot water. "Binkley," she said, looking up through swollen eyes, and Binkley very deliberately set the pitcher down and straightened.

"Is it over, madam?" he asked with great dignity.

"Oh, Binkley, no! It's not over in the least. He was awake—only for a very brief time, mind you, but he asked for water, and he drank an entire glassful!"

"Madam! Madam, this is true?" He approached the bed and peered down at Nicholas as if to find some illumination there.

"It is true. I think he is sleeping a natural sleep now."

"Then I must prepare gruel, for when he wakes he will need nourishment. And I have already made broth. Good strengthening beef broth from the bone I saved. And then no doubt after his meal he will want to be shaved. And a bath. I am sure he will want a proper bath." He cleared his throat and turned away for a moment, wiping at his eyes.

Georgia smiled, thinking Binkley's priorities perfectly in character. "It sounds wonderful, Binkley. It really does. I think the broth first, for his stomach might rebel against solid food.''

''Indeed, madam. I bow to your superior judgment in these matters. Perhaps the boy, Pascal, will want the gruel.''

''Binkley . . . you have already prepared the gruel, have you not? There is no point prevaricating, for I can see that you have.''

Binkley sniffed. ''I had hoped it might be needed, madam.''

Georgia's smile widened. ''And so it shall be. You are an excellent man, Binkley, as Nicholas has said repeatedly. He will be very happy to wake and find himself in competent hands.''

''I do not feel your hands incompetent in the least, madam, although there are certain tasks that a gentleman's gentleman is meant to perform. I will be most happy to see to those details, for Mr. Daventry will no doubt be bedridden for a short period.''

''Thank you, Binkley.'' Georgia smothered a laugh as Binkley took himself away. Binkley had a way of leading her through the maze of correct behavior without ever making an exact statement. She was learning all sorts of things about life in the upper class in a most unconventional fashion, and Binkley was an education unto himself.

Nicholas slept the morning away, which gave Georgia a chance to turn her attention to Pascal. When she went next door, she found Cyril still sound asleep and Pascal tossing and turning, muttering all sorts of things that made little sense. His fever still burned, and his chest was more congested than ever. She quickly administered an infusion of betony to help ease his chest, then sponged him with cool water.

''G-Georgia,'' Cyril said, sitting up and digging at his eyes. ''I f-fell asleep. I'll d-do that.''

''It's all right, Cyril. I'm nearly done.''

''B-but how is he? Is he improved at all?''

''No—the worst is yet to come, I think. The best we can do is to keep him comfortable. The herbs will help a little. The rest is between God and Pascal. And as I believe Pascal has already had a word with God, we might be lucky. Cyril, are you sure no one is worrying about you at home?''

''Who is there to w-worry about m-me?'' he said with a shrug. ''They know where I am.''

''Yes, I suppose. Well, I'll leave you now to look after Pascal. Nicholas is slightly improved, you'll be happy to hear. He woke briefly.''

''Oh,'' he said with a return of his former sulkiness. ''I s-suppose that's g-good news.''

''Don't stretch your concern,'' Georgia said with disgust. ''I'm sure he'll survive without it.'' She went out of the room, and this time she slammed the door behind her.

Later that morning Nicholas rolled his head on the pillow with a low moan. Georgia was immediately there. ''Nicholas? It's all right. Everything is going to be fine. Wake up, for you need to drink something now.''

He obliged her by opening his eyes, and she smiled as if he'd just given her an enormous present. ''Hello, Nicholas,'' she said very softly. ''Welcome back.''

He looked at her without speaking.

''We've all been terribly worried about you. It's been three days, did you realize? I have some broth warming by the fire. Let me get it for you. The very first thing you need is some nourishment.''

She fed him from the cup, and he drank it all, and then drank a glass of water, and Georgia was very pleased. ''Would you like to sleep again?'' she asked when he had finished. ''You should know that Binkley is most anxious to shave you and bathe you, and goodness only knows what else. He has been beside himself with worry, Nicholas, only he has disguised it in a more becoming fashion than I. I have been unfashionably frantic.''

Nicholas continued to look at her, and it was only then that she realized his eyes were blank. It was as if he didn't recognize her, or know what she was talking about, or even care.

Her heart froze as she understood.

Nicholas hadn't come back at all.

Binkley came out of the bedroom with the slightest crease of frown on his brow. ''He does not know me, madam. You are quite correct. His eyes are open, but he does not really see. Yet he hears, and he does respond to simple requests. I was able to shave him and bathe him with no trouble. But it is as if there is no one there."

"And what does that tell you, Binkley?" Georgia asked, anxiously pacing back and forth.

"In truth, I do not know how to answer, madam. I am perplexed. Mr. Daventry has always been possessed of a superior intelligence. I am puzzled indeed."

"As am I, Binkley. But there is reason in this puzzle. Somewhere there is reason. I have been thinking this through for the last hour. Nicholas responds to basic needs. He knows he is thirsty, for example. He will no doubt soon know he is hungry. I believe he has everything necessary to recover his physical health. But the one thing he does not have is his cognizance. There have been no signs of injury to his head, and although injuries to the head can have odd manifestations, I do not believe this is the case. I do not think it is his brain that has been damaged."

Binkley pulled on his ear. "What are you implying, madam?"

"I'm not sure exactly. I really don't know. It's the most peculiar feeling. As you said, it's as if Nicholas has gone away somewhere. And if you trace it to an exact point, it was when he collapsed after he brought Pascal in."

"But he collapsed from exhaustion," Binkley said. "There is nothing uncommon in a reaction of that kind."

"No, but there was nothing common about the way in which Nicholas rescued Pascal, was there? They told me that Nicholas could not be dissuaded from going back into the water. They told me that he was frantic, that his strength was extraordinary—he could not be stopped by anyone."

"It is true," Binkley said.

"So you see, I think there is a connection."

"A connection, madam? What sort of a connection?"

"I don't know. That's the problem. I just don't know. It doesn't make sense to me."

"In truth, madam, none of it makes sense. I was astonished that Mr. Daventry went into the sea at all. He has always had the most terrible fear of the water. In all the time I have known him, he has avoided it at all costs."

"Oh, dear heaven, Binkley," Georgia said, shocked. "You cannot be serious? He is terrified of water?"

"Yes, madam. Mr. Daventry had to drink himself into a stupor just to cross the English Channel. He is usually very accomplished at masking his feelings, but he could not disguise his terror on this occasion."

"My God . . . and yet he went into a raging sea? Why would he do such a thing?"

"I do not know, madam. It has puzzled me."

"He p-probably thought p-people would think him p-particularly brave," Cyril said from the other door, and Georgia jumped.

"Cyril! You will not keep eavesdropping! If you must interrupt, the least you can do is announce your presence."

Cyril scowled. "I was only g-going to add a useful c-comment," he said. "But if you have no use for me, I'll k-keep it to myself."

"Oh, for the love of God, Cyril. I have no patience for your games. What is it?"

"Y-you d-don't know, do you?"

"Know what?" Binkley and Georgia asked in tandem.

"About the shipwreck."

"Make your point, Cyril. I cannot think you know anything more about the shipwreck than we do," Georgia said impatiently.

"N-not that shipwreck. The f-first one."

"The first one?" Georgia said, her brow drawing down. "What do you mean, the first one?"

"In F-France. A f-few years b-before I was b-born. Uncle D-David and Aunt Elizabeth d-drowned."

"What? Surely you don't mean Nicholas' parents?"

Cyril nodded, looking as if he could have cared less.

"Good heavens," said Binkley. "How dreadful. It is no wonder Mr. Daventry does not like the water."

"W-well, he only s-survived by the s-skin of his t-teeth."

Georgia took Cyril by his arms, her fingers digging into his flesh. "You're saying that Nicholas was there?" she said, biting out every word. "He was there with his parents when they drowned?"

Cyril nodded again, but he looked slightly frightened by the fury on Georgia's face. "S-some fishermen r-rescued him or s-something. He was the only s-survivor."

"You *knew* this," she said, "and yet you said nothing. You knew what Nicholas had been through, and you stayed quiet. You watched him struggle in that water, knowing that? You loathsome child—you little maggot. I should strangle you—"

"Madam," Binkley said, restraining her. "If anyone strangles the boy, it will be me. But he is needed just now to look after young Pascal. And it is true, he could not know that Mr. Daventry has never spoken of the accident."

"I . . . I thought everyone knew," he said in a high voice.

"Cyril, get out of my sight," Georgia said, releasing him. "Now, before I do you damage."

Cyril vanished at lightning speed, and Binkley actually smiled.

"I believe you made your point, madam. It was not a bad thing to see."

"I haven't even begun to make my point. How self-centered can the little beast be?"

"Extremely," Binkley said succinctly.

"Poor Nicholas. I can't even begin to imagine what it must have been like for him the other night! It must have been his worst nightmare come true!"

"Yes . . ." Binkley said slowly, hand on chin. "I do believe you might have hit on something, madam."

"What are you talking about?" she said, perplexed.

"His recurring nightmares, madam. He is prone to them on a regular basis. He cries out over and over and cannot seem to catch his breath, and then he wakes up in a cold sweat, disoriented and shaking. But he has never said what the dream is about. He did, however, mention you had attended one, so perhaps you have seen his terror for yourself."

"Oh, dear God, Binkley. Oh, the poor man. The poor, poor man. He must be dreaming he's drowning." Georgia slipped to the floor and pulled her knees up, lost in thought, and equally lost to the impropriety of sitting on the ground. But Binkley didn't bother to correct her, lost in his own thoughts.

Georgia sat there for some ten minutes, trying to put all the pieces together. And then it suddenly came to her.

"That's it, Binkley!" she said jumping to her feet. "That's it! I think I have the connection!"

"Oh, yes, madam?"

"Yes—listen. I can understand why Nicholas was willing to overcome his fear of the water to help the sailors. No doubt he couldn't bear the thought of anyone drowning when he could help. But his desperation over Pascal, that was different, wasn't it?"

"Yes, madam, it is true. It was a state almost beyond desperation."

"Exactly. He saw a child, a young boy. It would have been like seeing himself. So in his mind, the two events came together. And then he thought he'd been too late and the boy was dead."

"I am sorry, but I do not follow your train of thought, madam. Why would that leave him as he is now?"

"I don't know, Binkley; I am inventing as I go along. I have heard it said that a terrible shock to the emotions can do strange things to people. And Nicholas had had a series of emotional shocks that night, never mind the physical shock. And now he has put himself someplace where the horror can't touch him."

"It is an interesting theory, madam. You are most imaginative."

"Yes, I know. And maybe that's why I can understand a little. It's the damned troll, Binkley."

"Madam?" Binkley said, looking horrified.

"Oh, I beg your pardon. It's what Nicholas would have said."

"Yes, madam. More than likely. But what is a troll? I have not heard of such a thing before."

"Oh. They're nasty mythological creatures who live underground and do terrible things to people. Nicholas equates the troll to everyone's worst fear, and that's what Nicholas was faced with that night."

"I see. Yes, I do believe I see."

"So," she said, thinking hard, "if I'm right, then it's not Nicholas' brain that has been injured, it's his heart. We must do what we can to heal it and bring him home to us."

"Yes, madam. But how does one go about healing a broken heart?"

"With love, Binkley. Simply with love."

11

"L-look here, Pascal," Cyril said with irritation. "You c-cannot play the game that way."

"Pourquoi pas?" the boy asked, throwing down another card. "This is how the sailors play." He coughed. "Just because you are a lord, Cyril, it does not mean that you can make all the rules. And there. I have won. Again."

"V-very well. I shall teach you another game, and this time we will p-play according to my rules."

"No, I am tired of these cards, Cyril. We have played them all of the morning. Now I would like to rest."

"You're not feeling ill again?" Cyril said anxiously. It had been a week since Pascal had passed the crisis, but Cyril worried constantly about him. "I will make you a t-tisane if you like."

"You are very kind, but I am only a little tired. I had the bad dreams last night."

"You did? What did you dream?"

Pascal wrinkled his nose. "I would not like to talk about it. How is the monsieur this morning?"

"He's exactly the s-same. Personally, I think Georgia should l-let the d-doctor bleed him. But instead she t-talks to him all the t-time as if he c-could understand her, and tells him s-stupid stories about knights and d-dragons and m-magic gardens. And he just s-sits there staring into space like a m-madman. He c-can't even f-feed himself. I d-don't know how long this c-can go on. He should b-be committed to B-Bedlam. That's where they put people who have lost their wits."

"You do not like the monsieur, I think, or you should not talk like this. Why do you not like him? He is a good man to have taken me from the sea, and the others too."

"Y-you do not know him, Pascal. He may have taken you from the sea, but that d-doesn't make him a h-hero."

"No? And why not?"

"It just d-doesn't. Underneath he is b-bad. He uses p-people to g-get what he w-wants, without regard for their f-feelings. He h-hurts people. He's d-done some very w-wicked things in his time."

"Yes?" Pascal said, fascinated. "This is true? What kind of wicked things?"

"N-never mind. He should n-never have come b-back to R-Ravenswalk."

Pascal laughed. "But me, I am very pleased that he did. And the madame, she does not think he is wicked. She loves him very much, I think. It is very hard to love so much and have this great sadness inside. I know how this is. And the madame, she is worried all the time for him, that he will not come back to her."

Cyril didn't answer.

"Do you not care for her either, Cyril?"

He shrugged. "I d-don't think about her one w-way or the other."

"I care for her very much. She has been very good to me, very tender. I care for all of you, even you when you make such faces when we play cards. But you saved my life, so I cannot be annoyed. And I think that you must care for me, Cyril, for you have stayed by my side all these days, looking after me in my time of need. But I have been wondering . . ."

"Yes?"

"What will become of me when I am all well? I have no family to go to, no ship, no work."

Cyril smiled and ruffled his hair. "Don't you worry about that, little m-monkey. You're not going back on the s-sea again, and as for work, we will find you something. We're your family now. You d-don't bring someone back from the dead, then toss him out on his ear when he is recovered. Now, s-slip under the covers and sleep."

Pascal did as he was told, and Cyril collected the cards and then pulled the covers up around him. *"Merci,* Cyril. You are like a brother to me."

"I am glad. Now s-sleep, Pascal. I have some work to

do in the garden, but I'll be b-back later to see you." He went out and closed the door quietly behind him.

The days passed. Pascal's health improved to the point that he was allowed out of bed, and he quickly regained his stamina, eager to help out around the house and in the garden. Georgia had grown extremely fond of him, for he was an affectionate, quixotic child, and his cheerful presence and obvious devotion to all of them helped to lighten her spirits. She could have done without Cyril's constant companionship, but he and Pascal were inseparable, and they seemed to be good for each other. Pascal was thriving on having a hero to follow around, and she knew that Cyril was thriving under Pascal's unconditional worship.

Georgia turned on her pallet, tucking her hands beneath her cheek. She could hear Nicholas' even breathing through the dark. He never snored: there was only this quiet, steady breathing. He never tossed in his sleep: he woke in the same position he had gone to sleep in. He might just as well have been a statue. Despite the love and the constant companionship, he responded to nothing and no one.

She missed him. Despite the people she was surrounded with, she was lonely. She missed him in a way that made her ache inside. It was not hard to be strong during the days, but the nights were so empty, and she felt so alone.

Sometimes she would get up and watch him while he slept, for in his sleep he looked almost like his old self. One couldn't really tell that he was in a place beyond dreams, beyond feeling, beyond reach. She could imagine for a time that he was back with her, and it gave her solace of a sort. But then would come the morning, and his eyes would open. And every single day her heart wanted to break when she saw that terrible blank look in them.

She wished she could find the key to open his mind. She wished she could somehow touch him and heal his wounded soul. If it had been possible, she would have given him her own heart.

Georgia turned her face into her pillow and wept.

184

* * *

It was late, and Georgia was trying to finish the draperies she was making from the blue velvet Nicholas had given her at Christmas. The front bedroom was almost ready. She intended to move Nicholas into it as soon as possible, for the views were fine, and nicer than from his present window, and it would be warmer as well. Now it just remained to finish the woodwork around the long windows, and Cyril was making great progress with that. It would be a wonderful room when it was done. She jumped as the door to the sitting room opened.

"Pascal, what are you doing up at this hour? What is it, *chéri*?" she asked more slowly, taking in the look on his face. He had been unusually quiet that evening, and she had wondered why. "Come, sit here with me by the fire." She put her needle and material off to one side and patted the sofa.

Pascal sat down, pulling his legs up under him. "I could not sleep, madame. I was afraid."

"Afraid? And what were you afraid of, little one?"

"I cannot say. I am ashamed."

"Oh, Pascal. Whatever it is, there is nothing to be ashamed of, I promise you. You don't have to tell me if you don't want to, but it might help if you shared it."

"But if I tell you, then you might send me away. And then I would be very unhappy."

Georgia laughed. "Listen to me, little one. We love you. This is your home now, for as long as you choose to stay, so you needn't worry that we will send you away. So tell me what it is, and we'll both feel better."

"It is a promise, madame?"

"Yes, of course it's a promise."

He thought for a moment. "Then I believe you."

"I'm very happy. Now, what is it? Did something happen to frighten you?"

"Today in the afternoon I went with Cyril to the village to fetch the things you needed. It was the first time I have been out to the village, and I was curious. We went in the carriage. Cyril drove very nicely."

"Yes?" she said, gently prompting.

"When we arrived, the people, they stared. I did not mind at first, but when I was with the horses, waiting for

185

Cyril to come from the store, I heard them talking. They did not know I could hear, or perhaps they thought I could not understand.''

"Oh, dear,'' Georgia said. "More gossip? The villagers tend to indulge themselves overmuch in the habit. What are they saying now?''

He blushed. "It is very bad, very wicked, madame. It is about me and the monsieur.''

"About you and Nicholas?'' She frowned. "What about you and Nicholas?''

"They say that I am the reason the monsieur lies upstairs in bed with no mind.''

"And how have they reached that absurd conclusion?'' she asked, trying not to let her impatience show.

"This is the wickedness, madame. They say that I was dead when the monsieur brought me in from the sea. Is it true?''

"It is true that you were not breathing. You had a little water in your lungs, Pascal, that had to be taken out. But I've explained this to you.''

"Yes, I know, madame, but is it true that I was dead? It is important. Cyril said something like this before, also.''

"I am sure Cyril would like to think he brought you back from the dead, Pascal, but I think you must have had a spark or two of life in you. What has this to do with Nicholas?''

"They say that I came back from the dead because monsieur's soul went into mine. And now he has no soul, madame. Is it true, do you think?'' he finished anxiously. "Did I steal the monsieur's soul?''

"Oh, Pascal—no, of course you didn't. One has nothing to do with the other. And in any case, you can't steal someone's soul.''

"No?'' he asked hopefully.

"No. No and no. Your soul is your own, for always. And you came back because you are strong and determined, and because you and God decided it wasn't time for you to go to heaven. You were needed here for other things.''

"Like building the house and gardens with you?''

"Exactly. And because Binkley and Cyril and Lily and

Martin and I all were waiting for a little boy named Pascal LaMartine to love and care for, and Nicholas too, although he hasn't been properly introduced to you yet. But he knew enough to take you from the sea and bring you to us, didn't he?"

"That is a very big relief, madame, to know I did not rob the monsieur of his soul."

"Good. Because you are your very own unique person, and so is Nicholas, and believe me, I would know the difference between you in a flash. When Nicholas is better and you meet him, you will see for yourself."

"But there was another woman who said that the monsieur was mad, madame, and will never be better. She said there is a curse on him, and that is why his mind was taken from his body. It was in payment of his wickedness. And Cyril told me before—"

"Listen to me carefully, Pascal," Georgia said, cutting him off, unwilling to hear another word. "I know how much you adore Cyril. However, you must not listen to him on the subject of the monsieur, for Cyril does not know Nicholas at all. He believes foolish lies about him, lies made up by other people. It is like the villagers. They make up silly stories, and then they end up believing their own nonsense."

"Then why does the monsieur stay upstairs with no mind and no soul? I do not understand."

"Of course he has a mind and a soul, Pascal."

"But if so, then where are they?" Pascal said logically. "Even Cyril says he has lost his wits."

Georgia sighed. "All right. All right, Pascal. I will try to explain so that you do not think any more about these other ridiculous tales. When Nicholas was a boy, somewhere around your age, he was in an accident very like yours. . . ."

She told him the entire story, down to the nightmares and Nicholas' fear of the water, leaving out nothing. "And so you see, it was a very terrible thing for him that night. It takes time to heal from a shock of that sort. Do you understand better now?"

"Oh, madame . . . madame . . ." Pascal wiped away tears from his eyes. "That he would do such a thing for me. To have such courage. I am now even more ashamed.

I didn't know. But in a way, you see, I did steal his soul, did I not? If it had not been for me, then he would not have gone back into the water, and he would not have brought me out and thought me dead.''

''I honestly don't know how it would have turned out if Nicholas hadn't gone back for you. But these are the sorts of things that are impossible to answer. We only know what happened, not what might have happened.''

Pascal nodded. ''Yes. And I owe the monsieur an even greater debt than I had realized. Madame, I would like to see him.''

''You would?''

''Yes. I would only like to look upon his face, madame. Please.''

Georgia smiled, unable to resist his earnest expression. ''All right, Pascal. Why not? Come, I'll just put my things away, and we'll go upstairs.''

He entered the room hesitantly, almost as if he were afraid of what he might find. Georgia put the candle down next to the bed. The light flickered on Nicholas' face, lighting the strong bones, now pronounced from the weight he'd lost.

Pascal came over to the bed and looked down at him, and he released a long breath, as if in satisfaction. He stood perfectly still for some ten minutes, gazing at Nicholas as if memorizing every detail. And then he spoke, very softly. ''Thank you, good monsieur. Thank you for my life. I would now lay down mine for yours if I could. But as I cannot, know you have my undying gratitude and my love.''

He looked over at Georgia, where she sat on the other side of the bed, watching. ''I am finished, madame. Thank you.''

Georgia took him through to his bedroom. He was very quiet as she tucked him up. ''Is everything all right, little one?'' she asked. ''You are not upset?''

''No. I am deeply moved. He is very beautiful, the monsieur. I had not realized—it is as if I have seen him in my dreams. He is like Cyril, but not. He is as an angel to my eyes, a strong, magnificent angel with great white wings. I cannot describe it to you. But I know that in my heart I love him.''

"I am glad," Georgia answered softly, wondering at the gift that had been given them in Pascal. "I love him too."

"I know this, madame. And together we will make him well. This I swear to you. I can see that his soul is firmly in his body, and he does not look the least mad. Sad, perhaps, as if he were lost and did not know how to find his way home, but he is also at peace, and perhaps this is what he needs. Madame?"

"What is it, Pascal?" she said, trying not to cry, for his words had touched her deeply.

"I would like to spend time with the monsieur. If you think it is correct, of course. Surely someone who loves him cannot be bad for him?"

"No. Someone who loves him cannot be bad for him. Let me think it over, Pascal. You might be right. He is much stronger now, I think, and it might be time for Nicholas to begin living more of a normal life. But now it's time for sleep. I'll see you in the morning." She bent down and kissed his hair, then went back into the other room to prepare for bed.

Georgia looked up at the sky, pleased to see that the weather was holding throughout the day. They'd been spending most of their time in the garden, trying to get it into shape, and she was finally satisfied. She'd been right about the bulbs. They had poked up tips of green with the very first of the warm weather, and now that she and Cyril and Pascal had succeeded in clearing away most of the debris, they had room to breathe. Crocus, anemone, and cyclamen peeked up along the walkways and tulips pushed up at the base of the little stone boy. The willow tree was swollen with buds; the rosebushes even looked as if they had some hope. Sap was rising everywhere, new life pushing forth. Nicholas would have a garden that summer, she was certain of it.

"Madame," Pascal whispered, nudging her a few minutes later. "Madame! Look! Look, madame, it is the monsieur! And the little Raleigh is with him!"

Georgia looked up. Binkley was leading Nicholas to the bench that sat under the willow tree. He moved like a man walking in his sleep, and in the outdoors the weight he'd lost seemed more apparent. His clothes no longer hugged his once energetic body, but hung from him. "It is indeed, Pascal," she said quietly. "I thought today would be a nice day for him to sit outside and enjoy the sunshine. Now that the weather is fine, I think it won't harm him to join us, and maybe it will help."

"He looks very sad," he said. "Even sadder than in his sleep."

"Yes, I know, Pascal. But somewhere deep inside of him there is great happiness and laughter. You will see. One day you will see." She got to her feet and went over to them. Binkley was just settling a warm blanket over Nicholas' knees. "Hello, Nicholas," she said as casually as she could manage. "I'm glad you've come out to enjoy the day. Look, the garden is beginning to come back, can you see? And there is Cyril up on the wall, which he has been repairing."

"Hello, N-Nicholas," Cyril said, although Georgia could see it was an effort for him to sound cheerful. Still, she was pleased. She'd had a long talk with Cyril concerning his cousin and had made it very clear that she would not tolerate any sort of negative attitude, or he would never be welcome at the Close again, and he hadn't argued the point.

Georgia went back to the bed where Pascal was pretending to work. "Pascal, don't stare," she said. "It's important to behave as if there is nothing unusual. If you would hand me the next plant, please?"

He obediently dragged his eyes away, but she noticed how often his eyes flew over to Nicholas.

"The monsieur is very brave," he said after some time. "Very, very brave. I would like to do something for him."

"I d-don't know what you think you c-can do, Pascal," Cyril said, coming down for more stone. "It's c-clear that he's touched in the head. Here, hand the rocks up to me one at a t-time."

"You are very wrong about the monsieur, Cyril. I have had a long conversation with madame, and she has assured me that the monsieur is not mad, only far away. So because I love him, I want to do something for him."

"How c-can you love someone you've never met?"

190

"It is not difficult. And I have met him. Twice. It is too bad, because the first time I was not awake, and the second time he was not awake. But one day soon we will both be awake at the same time, and then we will meet formally."

"You are the s-silliest child," Cyril said, reaching down for another rock.

"I am not silly. Look at him, Cyril. Is it not sad to see him so, a man so strong and brave? He is in very much pain, can you not see it? I think you should find it in your heart to love him. Be careful, it is heavy."

"Why should I f-find it in my heart?" Cyril asked. "Just because he is a relative?"

"No. Because you love me and I love him, and I ask it of you."

"That makes absolutely no s-sense, Pascal," Cyril said, but he was smiling.

"Perhaps not to you, but it makes sense to me. And it is very important to have people to love. I have told you this before."

"And I have told you that love is a d-dangerous thing. You should be more d-discriminating, I think."

"If people were all as careful as you, nobody would be loved at all. Look at you. You do not love your father or your *belle-mère,* or your good cousin, or your new aunt. The only people you say you care about are your *maman,* who is dead, and me, and that is only because you saved me and looked after me, and it makes you feel important to have done so. If you had met me on the street you would not have given me a second look."

"Pascal, I begin to b-believe that you are the one who is t-touched in the head."

"You are very unkind. I shall not talk to you again until you can say nice things." He left the ladder and went back to Georgia, who had been trying very hard to pretend she wasn't listening and also to keep a straight face throughout this exchange. Conversations between Pascal and Cyril were almost always highly entertaining, and usually quite illuminating.

"I have been thinking," Pascal said to her. "It would be permissible to give the monsieur a flower, madame?"

"A flower? I cannot see why you shouldn't give him a flower. Nicholas loves flowers."

"I know there are not all that many yet, but I thought one would not hurt. Perhaps one of these new red ones over here?"

"A tulip? Of course. What a nice thought. It's an especially lovely flower because it's the very earliest of the tulips, Pascal, and a special kind, so it's one of the bravest, willing to face the difficult weather that might come. I am sure it will be a fine gift for the monsieur."

"I understand. I will not say anything to remind the monsieur of the badness, I promise, madame."

Pascal went to the bed and carefully plucked a single bloom, then brushed off his hands and shyly approached Nicholas. "Monsieur?" he said, holding it out, and Nicholas brought his gaze to rest on him. "You do not know me, as we have not been introduced. I am Pascal, and I live with you now. I have brought you a flower, monsieur. It is one of the first of the spring, a tulip, madame calls it. It is for you, to remind you of happy, beautiful things." He took Nicholas' hand and carefully placed the flower in it, looking at him with very solemn eyes. "It is strong, this flower, for it comes back year after year, despite the cold of winter. When the sun warms the ground, it stirs, and then it remembers and stretches itself up to the sun and shows us its joy. It has a fine color, has it not? It is greatly satisfying, being a gardener. Madame Daventry is teaching me much about growing things."

Then Pascal smiled his warm, sweet smile and turned away, going back to his work.

Nicholas stared down at the flower for a long time. When he looked up, there was a single tear rolling down his cheek.

Georgia didn't know what to make of it. Nicholas still did not speak, nor did he actively respond. Binkley brought him out to the garden day after day. He sat quite still for long hours as they worked. But there was a stirring in him that she felt as clearly as she felt the stirring of life under her fingers, and for the first time she had real hope.

They talked and laughed among themselves, Lily joining in when she wasn't required elsewhere. Cyril even tolerated Lily, treating her almost as a friend when he wasn't remembering that he was a lord. Their mixed laughter and conversation tumbled together, Pascal joining in his sweet high voice. Georgia began to feel as if there really was a family back in Raven's Close, and the house and the land knew it and were answering.

As they worked together and the days went by, the garden began to truly come to life, little by little. The willow sprouted pale green leaves and violets threw a heady scent into the air. The white, starry flowers of saxifrage fell in mossy sheets over the garden wall. Lantern roses and snowbells, their little bells daintily hanging from upright stalks, danced together with the blue stars of hepatica in a riot of color. Buttercup had seeded itself in an unruly but brilliant carpet along one side of the wall, and Georgia didn't have the heart to dig it up. It was a wild garden, but a garden nevertheless, and her heart was glad for every single blossom.

She was also fascinated by the small changes that seemed to be occurring in Cyril. He was growing up. He no longer indulged himself in bated comments or barbed insults, and he rarely sulked. He threw himself into his work with great pleasure, and although he still had his odious moments, it seemed that there was a happiness growing in him. He had even unbent toward Nicholas, maybe beginning to see that he was not the wicked man he'd been painted, but just a poor ill man damaged by events beyond his control. Pascal might have had something to do with the change in Cyril's attitude, for he unabashedly showered Nicholas with his love and attention. He delighted in presenting him with bouquets of wildflowers that he picked, describing the contents of each one as he brought them and placed them on his lap. He received no answer, and he didn't mind in the least, for he chattered away quite gaily. But Georgia noticed how Nicholas' hands later moved in the flowers as he sat, and her heart sang with happiness. He was coming back. She knew it. Now it was only a matter of time.

* * *

It happened the third week in March, late at night. She was sleeping soundly on her pallet when she was startled awake by a cry and Raleigh's barking.

"Georgia . . . Georgia, help me!" Nicholas' voice was filled with terror. "Help me!"

She was with him in an instant. "Nicholas? It's all right. It's all right."

His eyes were open and they were looking at her, not blankly, but with panic. "Georgia? Oh, God. You're here. Thank God you're here."

She stroked his face, his hair, his face again. "Of course I'm here. Right here with you, Nicholas. Where else would I be?"

"I don't know . . . I dreamt . . . I dreamt . . ."

Georgia gathered him up into her arms and held him tightly. "It's all right, Nicholas, it's all right," she whispered. "You're safe. You're safe. You're safe now. You're home, Nicholas. You're finally home." She rocked his shaking body in her arms, and he held her so tightly that she could hardly breathe.

"Oh, God," he said in a choked voice. "Oh, dear God . . . it was no dream, was it?"

"No. It was not a dream. But it's all right now. It's over, Nicholas. It's finally over."

"The boy. I'm so sorry. I'm so sorry. I tried . . . I tried, Georgia, but I was too late, may God forgive me. The poor child."

"Nicholas, there are things you don't know yet, that you don't understand." But as she spoke, the connecting door burst open and Pascal stood there in his nightshirt. "Like this," she finished, thinking that God worked in his own mysterious way, and Pascal and Nicholas were both firmly in his hands. And this was one shock that could only be beneficial.

"Madame?" Pascal said in alarm. "I heard crying! The monsieur, nothing has happened?"

"Come over here, Pascal," she said, standing. "It is time for you to meet your beloved monsieur."

"He is awake, madame? God be thanked!"

"He is awake. And, Nicholas, it is long past time that you meet Pascal. You have much in common." She took Pascal's hand and drew him from the dark of the doorway into the moonlight that streamed down near the bed.

Nicholas pushed himself up and stared.

"*Bonsoir,* monsieur," Pascal said with an enormously pleased grin. "I am overjoyed to meet you."

"It is the boy . . ." Nicholas said, stunned. "It . . . it is the boy."

"Yes, the child you rescued."

"But . . . but it is not possible. Just tonight I . . . he . . . he was dead. And now . . . My God, how is it possible?"

Pascal took Nicholas' hand. "You saved me, monsieur. I did not die after all, thanks to your courage and the care of madame and Cyril."

Nicholas gazed at Pascal as if he were a phantasm. "I am dreaming again," he said.

"Do not be so silly, monsieur. I am very real. Pinch me and I will shout."

Nicholas gave the ghost of a smile. "I believe it is I who should be pinching myself. Would you like to do the honors?"

Pascal considered. "I do not know if it is correct to hurt you, monsieur. But I will oblige you if you like." He took the hand that was not holding Nicholas' and he squeezed the flesh of his cheek.

Nicholas yelped, and Georgia laughed.

"It is good, monsieur," said Pascal. "Even this morning you would not have made a response. Tonight you give a healthy cry. I am pleased."

Nicholas rubbed a hand over his eyes. "You are pleased," he said. "And I am baffled."

"But it is simple, monsieur. I am Pascal LaMartine, the boy you took from the sea. And you are the great hero Nicholas Daventry, but now you know who you are for yourself."

"Yes, naturally," he said, rubbing at his eyes again. "Why would I not?"

"You have been in a deep sleep, recovering from your efforts. Do you not remember?"

Nicholas shook his head. "No. . . . How . . . how long have I been sleeping, Georgia? It must have been a full twenty-four hours." He looked down at himself. "I seem to be clean and dry, and in one piece." And then he frowned, feeling his ribs. "That's odd. . . ." He

195

threw back the sheets and looked at his leg, then up at Georgia. "How long have I been sleeping?" he demanded.

Georgia heard the alarm in his voice, and she came and took Pascal by the shoulders. "Bedtime, *chéri*. Tomorrow perhaps you can spend more time with the monsieur."

Pascal slipped off the bed and gave her a quick kiss. "I am very happy, madame. Very, very happy. And now I leave you to the monsieur. Good night, monsieur. It is a great pleasure to finally meet you properly. I am very honored."

Georgia waited until the door had closed behind her. And then she sat down on the bed and took Nicholas' hand.

"How long has it been, Georgia? That child couldn't *possibly* have recovered that quickly from drowning. And my ribs—I know I did them some damage. In fact I feel quite well," he said, "although I do feel weak. What has happened to me? Have I been fevered?"

"It is just as Pascal said. You've been in a deep sleep, recovering."

"Days? I've been sleeping for days?"

"It's been six weeks, Nicholas," she said gently.

He stared at her. "Six weeks?"

"It's the seventeenth of March."

'The seventeenth . . . Oh, dear God. But that's not possible. It's just not possible."

"It may not seem so, but it is the truth."

"But what happened?"

"I don't exactly know myself," she said. "You remember nothing?"

He shook his head. "Just the storm. And the water, and the men. And the boy—Georgia, it really is the same boy? He survived?"

"Yes," she answered gently. "Pascal survived. You did not do quite so well yourself. I worried about you terribly. Everyone did. But I never stopped believing you would come back to us. I only wish you had not been so long about it."

"But, Georgia, there's a point. Surely if I had slept six

weeks away, I would have starved to death? I would have starved within the first week!''

''Well . . . you weren't exactly asleep the entire time. You woke in the morning and went through the day.''

''Then why don't I remember it!'' he said frantically. ''I don't understand. How can someone lose six weeks of his life, as if they had never existed! Explain this to me, Georgia.''

''I can't really. It was as if you weren't here, as if your body functioned, but your mind was elsewhere.''

''Are you telling me I went crazy?''

''No, not crazy. I just think you had too many shocks that night, and so you needed time to recover from them. So your mind protected you by taking you away until you were strong enough to deal with what happened.''

''Sweet Christ,'' he said softly. He threw the covers back, and Raleigh licked furiously at his feet as he placed them on the floor. ''Hello, Raleigh,'' he said, absently patting him. He gingerly stood, as if he was not quite sure his legs would hold, and he walked to the window, looking out over the moon-washed woods. There was new leaf on many of the trees. The grass was silvery green, and narcissus bloomed in the stretch of lawn that reached down to the old pond. He turned around, running his hand through his hair. ''I was hoping it was a joke,'' he said. And then his eye caught the pallet on the floor, and her night robe next to it, and he looked at her again. ''You have been sleeping in here?''

She colored. ''Yes. Pascal needed his own bedroom while he recovered, and I thought it was best to be in here anyway, in case you needed something in the night.''

He reached out and pulled her to him. ''Georgia. Sweet, sweet Georgia. Do you know, for a man who has slept six weeks away, I feel uncommonly tired.''

''I'm not surprised. It must have taken tremendous strength for you to come back to us.'' She reached up and gently kissed him. ''You have no idea how wonderful it is to be able to do that and know you can feel it.''

''Have you been doing much of that?'' he asked with a smile.

''Oh, yes. Lots.''

''I really must have been ill to have slept through it,''

he said. "And speaking of sleeping, no more sleeping on the floor for you." He took her hand and led her to the bed. "Do you think you might be willing to share? I cannot have fond feelings for the floor myself."

She slipped under the covers.

"That was almost too easy," he said dryly, joining her. He lay back with a sigh. "I feel exhausted. It's ridiculous. Georgia, are you sure it's safe to go back to sleep?"

"You can't go through the rest of your life without sleeping, Nicholas. And yes, I think it's very safe. You've remembered that night, and you've seen Pascal is safe and sound, and you're safe and sound, and what else is there to worry about?"

He rolled onto his side and looked at her through the dark. He swallowed. "You can't think me any madder than you already do, so I suppose it won't hurt to tell you. It's a long story, but sometimes I have dreams. Bad dreams. Nightmares, actually. . . ."

"Yes, I know. Binkley told me, and he also told me about your fear of water. And then Cyril told us about your parents drowning, and what happened to you. It's how we put the pieces together."

"You know everything?" he said, sounding shocked.

"Yes, I know."

"Oh, dear God. I feel like an idiot."

"Nicholas, you're anything but. We all think you extraordinarily brave. Listen to me, now. Listen. It all makes sense in a peculiar way. That night, you lived your nightmare. Do you understand me? You lived it as if it were happening all over again. You thought the boy had died, and the shock was too much for you. But he hadn't died at all. This time you saved the child. You saved the child, and you saved yourself in the process."

He was silent for a long time. She reached out for him and took him in her arms, and he held her hard against him.

"You've vanquished the troll, Nicholas. You went off somewhere and battled it, and you were victorious. You won't have to dream anymore. And you saved so many lives—not just Pascal's, but others too."

"I can't believe it's over," he said, his voice breaking. "I can't believe it's over."

"You were magnificent," she said, stroking his hair. "Unstoppable."

"Georgia . . . I meant to tell you so many things that night, but there wasn't time. I meant to tell you so many things. . . ."

"I know. We'll talk more tomorrow. Sleep now. Sleep and be safe." She settled into the crook of his arm, and Nicholas rested his cheek against her hair.

"Good night, my love," he whispered, and then his eyes closed.

12

Nicholas was gazing out the window lost in thought when a knock came at the door and Binkley entered with a breakfast tray. "Good morning, sir," he said to Nicholas' back. "A fine morning it is."

"Indeed, Binkley, an extremely fine morning," Nicholas said, turning around, and Binkley nearly dropped the tray.

"Oh, good heavens. Oh, good heavens," he said. "Oh, my goodness! You're back, sir!"

"Binkley, you're babbling," Nicholas said with a smile.

"I most certainly am not," Binkley said, recovering his dignity, but he couldn't disguise the tears that had sprung to his eyes. "Will you be taking your breakfast by the window, sir?" he said, blinking rapidly, and Nicholas grinned.

"Is that where I have been taking my breakfast to date?"

"Yes, sir. Is Mrs. Daventry aware of your recovery?"

"She is. She is across the hall, dressing."

"And when did the recovery take place, if I might make so bold as to ask, sir?"

"In the middle of the night. I was gone one minute, and back the next, with no idea that there had been any passage of time. Most bizarre."

"We have all been extremely concerned about you, sir."

"And I am sorry for worrying you, but I couldn't really help myself."

"You had no business going in that water in the first place," Binkley said severely.

"Yes, I imagined you would have a lecture to give me.

Well, I'm sorry, Binkley, but lectures will go straight over my head. I'm too happy at being alive to feel remorseful. A nice shave, perhaps?''

"Certainly, sir. A nice shave it is, as soon as you have eaten your breakfast. You have lost weight, and you must apply yourself to recovering it if your clothes are to fit properly. I am very pleased you have decided to rejoin us, sir. Aside from our concern over your health, there has been much to do. Papers have been coming in from London and Bombay, and I have had no idea how to deal with them, other than writing to the necessary offices to inform them of your illness. You left me no instructions how to cope in such an eventuality.''

"Perhaps because I had no such eventuality in mind,'' Nicholas answered with a smile. "Never mind. I don't think too much harm can have been done in six weeks. Funny, isn't it, the idea that one can disappear for six weeks?''

"I did not find it amusing in the least,'' Binkley said. "I found it extremely alarming, and poor Mrs. Daventry was beside herself. First you won't wake up at all, lying like a man cold in his grave, and then when you do finally wake up, you don't bother to do the job properly.''

"I know, Binkley. It's no way to behave.'' He wobbled, and sat down abruptly.

"Sir? Are you feeling unwell?'' Binkley asked with concern.

"It's foolish, but I'm as weak as a babe. I suppose it will take a bit of time to get my strength back.''

"Fresh air, good food, moderate exercise, sir, should see you fit in no time. But Mrs. Daventry will no doubt see to your full recovery. Very skilled, she is, in the medical arts. And no woman should have to cry so many tears over her husband, I might add.''

"Tears, Binkley?'' Nicholas said softly.

"Indeed, sir. A great many. And all I have to say is that I think we may cease struggling, sir, for if you think your wife is still in love with her farmer, you are very much mistaken.''

"In truth, Binkley? In truth?''

"In truth, sir.''

Nicholas sighed and ran a hand through his hair.

"Thank God. Well, in that case, let the struggling begin to ease. Most gradually, mind you, but a few small luxuries might be in order?"

"Thank you, sir."

"And I promise you, as soon as I've regained my strength, I will bring this courtship to a conclusion."

"Very good, sir. It is high time. Now, if you will excuse me, sir. I have things to attend to downstairs. I shall return shortly with water for your shave."

Nicholas settled down to his breakfast with a tired smile. Life had never felt finer. He just wished he were stronger so that he could take full advantage of it.

Georgia was out in the garden later that afternoon with the boys. Nicholas had gone back to sleep directly after his breakfast, and she hadn't wanted to disturb him. It had been all she could do to keep the boys' voices down, so as not to wake him. And then she looked up to see Nicholas standing in the back doorway, blinking at the sunlight.

"Monsieur!" said Pascal, jumping to his feet and running over to him. "Monsieur, you are awake finally! I have waited all this day to see you—look over the wall, Cyril! Your cousin is here."

"Hello, Nicholas," Cyril called, climbing up the ladder on the far side of the wall and peering down at Nicholas.

"Hello, Cyril," Nicholas replied, squinting up at him.

"How are you f-feeling?" Cyril asked politely.

"Better, thank you," Nicholas replied equally politely, and Cyril nodded and disappeared again. Nicholas just shook his head, then looked down as Pascal took his hand and carefully led him down the steps and out into the garden.

"What do you think, monsieur? We have worked very long and very hard, and we are pleased. Are you pleased? Do you remember sitting out here with us? You did, day after day, and I would pile flowers onto your lap. I will still pile flowers onto your lap if you would like."

Nicholas just stood there looking about him speechlessly, and Georgia went over to them. She could see that Nicholas was overwhelmed, and she gently removed Pascal. "Back to cultivating the rosebushes, *chéri*," she said. "The monsieur is not yet accustomed to all our chatter. Come, Nicholas, there is a bench over here, if you'd like to sit."

"Georgia. Oh, Georgia . . . you've brought it back after all."

She smiled up at him and wiped his cheeks with her fingers. "It just needed some tending. And the boys have been wonderful, and Lily also." She swallowed against her own tears. To see his pleasure only magnified her own.

He put his arms around her and held her close. "Bless you. Bless you, sweetheart."

"All this time I've been waiting for the moment when you would see it, really see it. And I don't think I even knew how happy I would be. Sit over here, Nicholas, and enjoy the sunshine."

And so he sat and watched, and Georgia moved to work near him, talking about small things, things that had happened while he had been ill.

"It is the oddest feeling," he said. "I stopped and the rest of the world went on without me." He looked up and his gaze fell on the roof. "Good heavens," he said with surprise. "That looks very much better than the last time I saw it, when that blasted tree had just come down on it."

"It is nearly done. People from the village have been very generous about lending a hand when they had time to spare."

Nicholas looked incredulous. "From the village?"

"It is true. You are a hero to them. They felt so bad about what happened to you that they wanted at least to be sure you had a secure roof over your head while you recovered."

"What . . . what happened to the others?" he asked, his eyes pinching slightly at the corners.

"The others? Well, all the men from the village survived their soaking, although there were a couple of cases of pneumonia."

"No. I mean the others."

"Oh, the survivors? There were twelve, Nicholas, not

including Pascal, and they all recovered and went home. Cyril put them up at Ravenswalk for the duration.''

"*Cyril* did?''

"Yes. There's been quite a change in him. I think the night of the shipwreck was the beginning of it. Pascal has made a big difference too. In case you haven't noticed, Pascal has a way of throwing his love around. He thinks Cyril is perfectly wonderful, and as a result, Cyril has obliged him by trying to become so.''

Nicholas raised an eyebrow. "How interesting. I'm delighted to hear it, although I'll have to see the full evidence with my own eyes.''

"That won't be a problem. Cyril as good as lives over here these days, and by his own volition. He's been a great help.''

"Amazing. And the boy, Pascal? What of him? He seems fully recovered. When will he be returning to his family?''

"Well . . . you see, Nicholas, he doesn't actually have a family. So I offered him ours. If it's all right with you, of course, but I didn't think you'd mind, given everything. And I'm sure you'll come to love him very quickly. It's impossible not to. Nicholas?''

"You're saying he's ours?'' Nicholas said very quietly, looking over at where Pascal worked, his tongue poking out of the side of his mouth in concentration.

"In a manner of speaking, yes. Is it all right with you?''

"Georgia,'' he said shakily, "it is more than all right. It is a great gift. I have . . . I have always wanted children, you see. To have a child given so unexpectedly to me, and in this manner . . . I'm sorry. I seem to be awash with emotion. It is not my usual habit.''

Georgia came over to him and put her arms around his neck. "It is perfectly acceptable to be awash with emotion. We all are at the moment. And it's a wonderful thing to actually be able to see how you feel. You've always been so good at disguising your emotions.''

"I have, haven't I?''

"Too good, Nicholas. I have spent a great deal of time trying to divine you. You even went so far as to disappear where no one could divine you at all.''

"Least of all myself," he said with a little laugh. "But I will try to do better from now on. Georgia, will you forgive me? I find that I am terribly tired. I think I'll go back upstairs."

"Take as much rest as you need. I'll be in to see you later." She kissed him on the forehead, but watched him carefully as he made his way back to the house.

Nicholas slept away most of the next five days. He took his meals quietly in his room, spent small periods of time with them in the garden, but his body needed sleep more than anything else, other than food. He couldn't seem to get enough of either, but Georgia could see that with every day that passed, he improved. All the energy that Nicholas normally exhibited physically, he now focused internally, determined to recover his health and strength as quickly as possible.

Pascal understood that Nicholas needed peace and quiet for the time being, and he exhibited unusual restraint in allowing Nicholas both, but then, Pascal was imbued with an unusual wisdom that many people did not gain in a lifetime. For his part, Cyril was happy to leave Nicholas alone. Georgia had not missed Cyril's nervousness now that Nicholas was back, and she knew he was probably afraid that the happy life he had carved out for himself at the Close would change. He was so careful not to offend that it would have been amusing had it not been so sad. And because she felt sorry for him, she doubled her efforts to make him feel included. Pascal, naturally, did not miss any of the subtle currents running at the Close, and in his sweet, solemn way he also tried to make Cyril feel more comfortable with the situation. But Georgia knew that the only thing that would really help would be Nicholas and Cyril sitting down and talking things through. Georgia was not foolish enough to think that the outward changes in Cyril reached down into his true feelings for Nicholas, whatever their basis. Cyril was manipulative enough to do what he had to in order to preserve his tenuous position and his access to Pascal.

Georgia, who was sensitive to Nicholas' every move, especially at night when he was sleeping, felt the mattress shift and lighten, and her eyes flew open to find Nicholas sitting on the side of the bed, scratching Raleigh's ears. The first of the light was streaming in through the window, and she yawned. "Nicholas . . . it's dawn. What are you doing up at this hour?"

He turned to look at her. "I think I've had quite enough sleep. It's high time to start living fully again."

"How do you feel?" she asked, sitting up and rubbing her eyes.

"Like a new man, strong as an ox. So up you get and dress, for I would like to go for a walk."

"A walk?" she said sleepily, thinking that he did look better. His eyes were bright and his face no longer appeared drawn. In fact he appeared to have put on weight just in the night alone.

"Yes. Let's go and look at the world, just the two of us. I haven't had any real time alone with you, not between the boys and Binkley. I'm jealous; I am accustomed to more of your company."

"All right. Whatever you wish. Give me a few minutes and I'll be with you." She went across the hall to the room she'd been using to dress and put on warm clothes. Nicholas was waiting for her downstairs, Raleigh at his heel.

He took her hand, and they strolled in the direction of the woods, which smelled fresh and crisp with dew. And then they walked behind the house and down the wild lawn to the pond, Raleigh gamboling along in front of them, every now and then attacking a stick with a great show of ferocity. Nicholas sighed with satisfaction and put his arm around her. "It's good," he said, stopping and looking back at the Close. "It's very good."

"It is, isn't it?" Georgia replied. "You see, dreams can come true."

He laughed and tugged at her hair. "Maybe they can after all. Maybe they can. Georgia . . . do you realize that we've been married nearly five months?"

"Yes," she said, smiling. "We've come a long way since the day I met you in front of the Close."

"We have indeed. I was a desolate man. And I was very chagrined to have been discovered by a beautiful woman, weeping my heart out."

"A beautiful woman? Really, Nicholas."

"But you are, you know. That ghastly cap did nothing for you, but nonetheless my eyes were not deceived. I grabbed you and kissed you, if you remember. I do not usually grab and kiss beautiful women without a proper introduction first, mind you, but I could not resist."

"I remember," she said. "I was shocked by your impetuousness."

Nicholas grinned. "Would you be shocked if I grabbed you and kissed you now?"

"No. I would like it very much, I think."

"Let us see," he said, pulling her to him. He covered her mouth with his and kissed her much in the manner he had done that first day, but this time she did not push him away. Her arms went around his neck and she returned his kiss in full measure. She felt his laughter vanish as he deepened the kiss, opening his mouth against hers, tasting her with his tongue until her bones turned to water and she gave a little moan deep in her throat.

"Georgia," he said, lifting his head and looking down at her, his breath coming fast. "Georgia." His hands cradled her face, his thumbs stroking the line of her jaw. "There's so much—I don't even know where to begin. And I don't even know how you will feel about what I want to tell you."

"Nicholas . . ." she whispered, alarmed by the anxious expression in his eyes. "What is it? Please, just say it, whatever it is."

"Just like that?"

"Just like that."

He looked down at the ground for a moment.

"Nicholas, surely it can't be anything too terrible? Whatever it is, we can deal with it. We've dealt with everything else, haven't we?"

He looked back at her. "It's not quite the same sort of thing. Georgia . . . when we married, it was out of necessity. We both understood exactly what the other had to offer—well, perhaps not exactly, but that's beside the point. The point is, everything has changed. I never expected it, but there it is, and I'm afraid there's nothing I can do about it."

"What are you saying?" she asked nervously, for she

had never seen him so rattled. "Please tell me, Nicholas, for my mind is racing to all sorts of dreadful conclusions."

"No—it's nothing dreadful, sweetheart, or at least I hope it isn't. Actually, it's quite simple." He took a deep breath. "I love you."

Georgia's heart tightened in her chest. Here was a man so strong, so brave, and yet so vulnerable that he found it difficult to speak of his feelings. And yet he had shown her in every other way. "Nicholas," she said softly. "I love you too, with all my heart."

"You do?" he said, sounding surprised. "Are you quite sure?"

"Very sure. It seems as if I have known it for always, but I only realized when it was too late to tell you, and I was so afraid I would never have the chance."

His eyes closed for one brief moment. "I'm glad you told me now. I'm very glad. I've waited a long time to hear it."

"I'm sorry," she said. "I didn't know how you felt either, not until the night of the shipwreck."

"Why then?" he asked, frowning. "Of all times, why then?"

"You were so angry with me. I know now it was because you were frightened for me. It was also in the way you kissed me and held me. And then I had nothing but regret for having let you go without at least telling you that you went with my heart. And afterward, when you were so still and cold and I was desperate about you, Binkley pointed out to me that you had no idea of my feelings for you. I felt like a fool."

"Georgia," he said hoarsely, drawing her against him and resting his cheek on her head. "Sweetheart. We've both been foolish. But I can only thank God that he sent you to me, and I am exceedingly grateful for what we have. Five months ago I had nothing. Today I have a wife I love to distraction, a little boy named Pascal, whom I'm sure I will come to love, a half-restored house, and a garden."

"And Binkley," she added. "You mustn't leave out Binkley."

Nicholas smiled and kissed her forehead. "How could

I leave out the inestimable Binkley? You are absolutely right. And speaking of Binkley, do you think he's up yet? I'm famished.''

''I very much doubt it, and you will not wake him. I'll make you breakfast myself.''

They walked back and Georgia showed Nicholas where Cyril had been working on the wall, and the progress he'd made. And then she sat him down in the kitchen and made him an enormous breakfast of scrambled eggs and kidney and toast and last night's ham.

As she cooked, he watched her, his chin in his hand. ''Do you know, I never did get my side of beef,'' he said.

She looked over her shoulder. ''You didn't, did you? I am sorry, for I know how you were looking forward to it. Actually, Binkley fed it to the men that same night.''

Nicholas groaned. ''Gone in a puff of smoke.''

''What was gone in a puff of smoke, monsieur?'' Pascal asked, padding into the kitchen and sitting himself down at the table.

''My side of beef, Pascal. But never mind, for it is too complicated to explain. Good morning, my fine friend. And how are you?''

''I am happy to see you so. Madame said you had much happiness inside of you, and today I see it shining in your eyes. You are no longer sad?''

''I am no longer sad,'' he agreed. ''And you, Pascal? You were not sad?''

''I was sad, it is true, monsieur. When my parents died I was very sad, and I had no home. And then I was put on the ship to work, and I did not much like that, although it was better than the orphanage. And there was the storm, of course, and that was not nice at all. But now I have a true home and true friends. And as you are better now, monsieur, how can I find anything to feel sad about?''

Nicholas looked at him thoughtfully. ''You are happy here?'' he asked gently.

''But yes, monsieur. Very happy. But you are now regarding me with great seriousness. You want to send me away, perhaps?''

''No, Pascal. I most certainly do not. Georgia has told

me that she has asked you to live with us permanently. I only wanted to hear from you that this is what you want, to have us as your family.''

"Oh, yes, monsieur. Oh, yes, this is what I want! All that I want. I will work very hard to pay my way.''

Nicholas laughed. "Now you are sounding exactly like Georgia. It makes me wonder if there's not something about me that appears mercenary. You need not pay your way, Pascal. Believe me, there is no need to consider it.''

"It is very good of you to take me in, monsieur. I shall try hard not to disappoint you.''

"And I shall try very hard not to disappoint you, Pascal,'' Nicholas said gravely.

This statement had the effect of sending Pascal into gales of laughter. Georgia put two heaping plates of food in front of them, along with steaming mugs of tea, then sat down to join them. They ate and talked and laughed, and as Georgia cleared up, she had the happy feeling that Nicholas had just been indoctrinated into his new family.

"Good morning, madam, sir, young Pascal,'' Binkley said, entering the kitchen not much later. He did not so much as blink an eye to see the three of them sitting around the table.

"Ah, Binkley—just the man I wished to see,'' Nicholas said, throwing down his napkin. "If you'll excuse me, Georgia, I have business with Binkley. Come along, Binkley. We have important matters to discuss.''

"Certainly, sir,'' Binkley said, untying the apron he had just put on. "Lily will be back shortly from her night off, madam. Is there anything you desire before then?''

"No, thank you, Binkley. You had better go with my husband before he drags you away. I fear his energy has returned in full force. Come along, Pascal. We might as well get started on the garden. What do you suppose the surprise is that Cyril is bringing over today?''

"It is furniture, madame. It is for the monsieur's room.''

Georgia gave him a sharp look. "Really? That's interesting. How did that come about, I wonder?''

"I became very angry with Cyril this week after the monsieur became well.''

"Yes? And then?"

"And then I told him he was selfish. And I told him that I had heard Monsieur Binkley saying that there were things in Cyril's grand house that belonged to the monsieur, and it would be nice to have them back in their rightful place. I said that it was not right for Cyril to have so much and the monsieur to have nothing, and that Cyril could help to make it correct, now that he knew the truth. I told him that I had great respect for his fairness. And then there was the fact that Cyril has worked hard on the new room for the monsieur. It is no good for it to stand almost empty after all of that."

"You're a clever little devil, aren't you, Pascal?"

Pascal looked very pleased. "You think so, madame? This is good. And does not the monsieur look wonderful today? Full of life and merriment. And he is very kind to allow me to stay. It should have broken my heart to have to leave him. Here, madame, look! There are buds on the rosebushes . . ."

Nicholas sat Binkley down, despite the fine man's protests. "Binkley, be sensible," Nicholas said impatiently. "I have a campaign to plan, and I cannot crane my head up and around just to suit you whilst I do it."

"You seem to be restored to your old spirits, sir," Binkley said, carefully perching himself on the edge of the chair. "And may I ask what the campaign consists of?"

"In the first particular, I intend this night to be my proper wedding night. I would like for you to arrange the details—every last glorious detail to set the scene, and I leave it entirely up to you, for I trust your exquisite sense of scenario implicitly. I want to be hampered by nothing. Second, I am now prepared to tackle my business affairs, for my mind feels fully clear. Bring me my boxes, Binkley, and let me embark."

"Certainly, sir. As you wish. All other matters will be managed quite discreetly, for I feel it is important that nothing feels alarmingly different to Mrs. Daventry. One does not wish to frighten the newly tamed bird from the hand."

Nicholas gave him a look of slight disbelief. "I realize

I have only recently returned to my senses, Binkley," he said, "but I have not lost all my power of reason. Now, let us begin where we left off. My boxes. And I will take my luncheon in here, for I do not want to be interrupted."

"Very good, sir," Binkley said, bowing and looking mightily pleased with the return of his crusty employer.

Nicholas worked away the morning and afternoon mysteriously closeted away in the sitting room, and Georgia used the opportunity to put the finishing touches on Nicholas' new bedroom. Cyril had indeed seen to the delivery from Ravenswalk of a bureau, a mattress, and a sofa and chairs. He then helped Georgia hang the draperies, and Pascal helped Lily make the bed and clean up the last of the dust. Binkley moved clothes into the wardrobe. It was a great moment when they were finished. The wood on the four-poster bed gleamed, the bureau sat in its proper place against the wall. The sofa, table, and chairs had been arranged in front of the fireplace. There were rugs on the floor, and the place where Nicholas had once gone crashing through looked as good as new.

"It's p-perfect," Cyril said, looking around in satisfaction.

"It is perfect," Georgia said, her hands on her hips.

"*Magnifique,*" Pascal added proudly. "The monsieur will be very pleased.

"Indeed, it is quite suitable," Binkley pronounced, and Lily giggled.

"Fit for a king is more like it," she said. "Fit for a king."

"When are you going to tell him, madame?" Pascal asked breathlessly.

"If none of you has any objection, I'm not going to say a word. I'm going to surprise him at bedtime."

"A very good idea, madam," Binkley said, looking extremely satisfied and rather pink in the cheeks, Georgia thought. "You could not have picked a better time. Lily and I are preparing a celebratory dinner of a selection of the master's favorite foods, now that he is well enough to sit downstairs."

"Surely not a side of beef?" Georgia asked with a laugh.

"Yes, madam. A particularly fine side of beef, provided by the butcher, who would accept no payment. I also have a bottle of Mr. Daventry's favorite burgundy. A nice long sleep this afternoon should find him in excellent form."

"And, Pascal," Cyril said, "I thought you and I might spend the night at Ravenswalk. I would l-like to teach you billiards." He gave Binkley a sidelong glance, and Binkley nodded approvingly.

"Ravenswalk? I would like very much to see this grand house you have told me of. *Merci, Cyril.* If it is correct with you, madame?"

"What? Oh, yes, of course. Whatever you like, Pascal. It's very kind, Cyril. Now, we should all be out of here before Nicholas comes up and finds us. Thank you. I thank all of you so much for helping."

"The hip bath is in Pascal's bedroom, missus," Lily said. "The water should be ready by now."

"The hip bath?" Georgia said, mystified. "But it's not Saturday."

"No, missus, but Mr. Daventry has requested a bath later, and so it seems only sensible to use it while it's up here. If you're going to have a nice dinner and all, you might as well feel all rosy-like."

Cyril turned away with a laugh.

"That is most thoughtful, Lily," Georgia said. "I would appreciate a nice bath, although I hate for you to go to the trouble."

"No trouble, miss. Martin will help me carry up the buckets, and the boys will too. Won't you, boys?"

"Absolutely," Cyril said. "And then Pascal and I must be off before d-dark. Come along, Pascal. Let us start hauling w-water."

"Why is it I feel there is some sort of conspiracy afoot?" Georgia asked suspiciously.

"No conspiracy in the least, madam," Binkley said blithely. "We have merely had a discussion amongst ourselves and decided that you have worked and worried overly hard since the unfortunate incident, and you need a touch of pampering, as does Mr. Daventry. And so we thought we would see to an enjoyable evening for both of you, with nothing more strenuous than each other's company.''

"Oh, I see. And you are very considerate indeed,'' Georgia said. "Really, I do appreciate your concern. But there is no need—''

"M-must you always argue, Georgia?'' Cyril said, sounding exactly like his cousin.''Why can't you l-let people do something nice for you for once? Now, do as you're told and prepare for your b-bath.''

Georgia laughed. "Oh, very well. If you insist on overworking yourselves on my behalf, who am I to argue?''

They all looked very pleased, and Georgia went off to oblige them.

"Cyril . . .'' Pascal, who had been hopping with excitement, stopped dead in his tracks as they broke out of the woods and the first sight of Ravenswalk came into view. "But this is a house of the greatest magnificence! It is the finest house I have ever, ever seen! Oh, my. But since you are a lord, it is only right, is it not?''

"It's not m-mine yet. It belongs to my f-father,'' Cyril said, his voice heavy with bitterness.

"Yes, I know this. And you should not sound like this about your father, for you are fortunate to have one at all. It is a pity he is not well, but perhaps he will recover as the monsieur did.''

"Hardly likely,'' Cyril said darkly. "The best thing he could do would be to d-die.''

"Cyril! You must not speak so! It is very bad to wish for such things. It is a terrible, terrible thing to lose a father. Just as bad as losing a mother, and this you already know about. But come, show me this house of yours, for I want to see all the things inside, and outside, and up and down! And then I would like to eat in the very grand dining room, and learn to play these billiards.''

"Very well, little m-monkey. Come along. I w-will show you.''

He took Pascal by the arm and pulled him along, explaining about the layout of the gardens, the exterior design of the house, its history. And as he did so he found that he was seeing it with fresh eyes. He loved Ravenswalk with an all-consuming passion, but he had resented the fact that it did not belong to him—not completely, as it should. It belonged to a broken, foolish shell of a man, and it was run by Jacqueline. The day that his father died it would be his, and Jacqueline would finally have to bow to his dictates instead of the other way around.

That would be a fine day indeed. That would be the day that he would finally be a true man. He would be the Earl of Raven, and the world would look up to him, would respect him. At the moment the only person who looked up to him was Pascal. He didn't mind Pascal's adulation in the least—in fact he enjoyed it extremely, for Pascal was the first person who had properly appreciated him in a great many years, the first person who he knew would not cast him to one side as his own family members had done. Pascal's love for him was as all-consuming as Cyril's own love for Ravenswalk. Immutable. Infallible. Eternal.

It was what happened when you saved someone's life.

13

Nicholas was in the sitting room, reading through some papers in front of the fire, Raleigh at his feet. Georgia drew in a quick breath at the familiar scene. It was as if no time had gone by, and yet a lifetime had.

He looked up as she came in, and the smile faded from his face as he rose. "Georgia . . ." he said on a long exhale.

"Is something wrong?" she asked with dismay. "Do you not like my dress? It is the first of this kind I have made for myself . . . is it too daring?" She looked down at the neckline, wondering if she had cut the muslin too low after all. She'd been in an agony of indecision, for this was the sort of evening style that was worn by ladies, not the seamstresses who executed it. She'd never before put in such time on a dress for herself.

"Sweetheart, you look wonderful," he said. "Absolutely glorious. It is only that I've never before seen you so that I stare. Come, sit down here with me. Talk to me. I have missed your conversation. I have, in fact, missed many things about you these last few days, given that I've slept so much. I suppose I have missed a great deal these last few weeks, but you must understand that it seems no time at all to me."

"I know, Nicholas. I know. It's not important anymore. I missed you most dreadfully, but you are here now. Nothing else matters."

"No. It seems that very little matters other than the fact that I have you."

"And the Close," she added.

"Yes, but as I told you this morning, it all goes together. I used to worry so much about other things, things that now seem foolish. But life suddenly seems so simple. I can't really explain it, sweetheart, save to say that I feel happy."

"You were not happy before? Not at all?"

"It wasn't that I wasn't happy with you. I had just begun to realize that somehow in you I had stumbled on the most extraordinary good fortune, quite by accident. But deep down, I was still chasing shadows. And those shadows don't seem to be there anymore. It's not that the fears, or regrets, or even the anger have vanished. It's more that they aren't very important. I feel altered, as if something important happened to me, although I don't know exactly what it was." He took a deep breath and released it. "I suppose I feel at peace. I'm afraid that's the best I can do to explain."

"I think I understand," she said, stroking the back of his hand. "I have felt that way for some time. When you took me away from Ravenswalk, I was chasing shadows too. And then you gave my life a substance, a happiness that hadn't been there for a very long time."

"But you are sure now?" he said, gathering her hand up in his. "Sure of that happiness, I mean?"

"Yes," she said, meeting his eyes steadily. "Very sure."

"Georgia," he started to say, when Binkley appeared in the doorway, and he sighed heavily.

"Dinner is served," Binkley said in his grandest fashion, which was very grand indeed, Georgia thought with amusement. They might have been dining in state, and given the meal that Binkley had produced, they might well have been.

They were presented with salmon and Nicholas' beloved side of beef. There were various baby vegetables and puddings. And there was also the wine to accompany it all, dark and full and heady. There wasn't actually all that much time for conversation, for Nicholas was bent on eating. He put away plate after plate, and then, when he was finished, he looked over at her apologetically.

"I seem to have a prodigious appetite," he said. "But I am duly ashamed of myself for having been such poor company. Speak, Georgia, and tell me what you are thinking. You are looking exceedingly dreamy."

"It is most likely the wine. But I must confess, I was

217

watching you, thinking how happy I am to see you sitting here again."

"And I am exceedingly happy to be here. Life positively bursts in my veins."

"Does it, Nicholas? It is wonderful that you feel so."

"Yes. It is." He grinned. "I hope it is bursting in your veins as well."

"I think it must be," she said. "Along with all that happiness."

"Oh, good. And given that, surely it must be time to go upstairs?"

"Already? Oh, yes, of course. I had forgotten. No doubt you want to go to bed."

"In a manner of speaking," he said with a smothered laugh. "Come along, Georgia." He drank the last of his wine, then held out his hand to her. He stopped only to put a very disappointed Raleigh in the library.

"You do not want him in your room any longer?" she asked with faint surprise.

"I don't particularly need an audience," he replied enigmatically.

"Oh," she said, thinking the wine had dulled her wits. She followed him up the stairs, and he started down the hall in the direction of his bedroom.

"No—wait. I have a surprise for you," she said, stopping outside the front bedroom.

"What is it?" he asked impatiently.

"Look and see for yourself." She stood back and indicated the door.

He turned the handle and pushed the door open, then stopped in his tracks, stunned. Lamps burned brightly on the tables and a fire crackled in the hearth. The bed with its counterpane looked comfortable and inviting, and the new draperies were closed against the night.

"Dear Lord. Dear, dear Lord," he said, taking it in, then turning to look at her. "How ever did you manage to do this?"

"We all did it. And you have Cyril to thank for the furniture and much of the labor."

He just shook his head. "I cannot tell you, sweetheart. I cannot tell you what this means to me. It is almost as it was when my parents lived in it." He walked inside and looked some more, then sighed deeply. "Thank you," he said simply.

"It gave us all hope when you were ill, making something for you that you could enjoy for the future. And here you are."

She came to stand next to him, and he wrapped his arms around her. "How I ever came to be so fortunate is completely beyond me. But I am not one to argue with good fortune." He brushed her lips with his. "I really do thank you, sweetheart," he murmured against her cheek. "You couldn't have planned a nicer surprise for this night. I think you must have read my mind."

"Well, I'm going to read your mind again," she said, disentangling herself. "Binkley has moved all of your clothes, and you'll find everything you need. Good night, Nicholas. Sweet dreams."

"Good night, Nicholas?" he said incredulously, catching her wrist. "What the devil do you mean by that?"

"I thought you were tired," she said, looking down at where his hand held her, then looking back up at him.

"I'm anything but tired. And even if I were tired, where were you intending on going?"

"To your old room. Don't you want your bed to yourself, now that there is one to spare?"

"I certainly do not, not now or ever again. Unless we should have an argument and I need to sulk, in which case I will remove myself to my old room."

"Oh," she said in a small voice.

"Or such time as you are brought to childbed," he continued, "in which case I shall remove myself until such time as you welcome me back."

"Childbed?" she said, bewildered. "I cannot see how that could happen."

"Well, neither can I, if we don't stop having this absurd discussion."

"But, Nicholas," she said, now truly confused. "You cannot have children."

"I cannot?" he said, looking at her with a combination of amusement and exasperation. "May I ask why not?"

Georgia turned bright red. "Because . . . Oh, Nicholas, surely you must know how children are created?"

He frowned. "This has nothing to do with my recent illness, has it? Georgia, if it has, then you must tell me."

"No, nothing like that. It is your impediment, Nicholas."

"My impediment? What impediment?"

Her eyes dropped to his groin, then fell to the floor in an agony of embarrassment.

Nicholas followed the direction of her gaze, and then to her astonishment he burst into howls of laughter. He fell into one of the armchairs, gasping for breath. "Oh, dear God, Georgia, I have heard it called many things, but never an impediment." He covered his face with his hands for a moment, unsuccessfully trying to sober. "Oh, please . . . please, no more."

"I cannot think why you find this so funny," she said. "I had thought you would be upset."

"Why in heaven's name would I be upset? I don't think of it as an impediment in the least."

"You don't?"

"No. Why should I?" He started to laugh again. "Oh, I do love you, sweetheart. And what makes you think I cannot sire children? I am perfectly normal, you know."

Georgia's eyes flew to his face. "Normal?"

"Yes. Normal." He grinned, and then his amusement faded as he took in her expression. "Georgia . . . you cannot possibly be a virgin, can you? After all, you were married for three years."

Georgia looked away. "No. I am not a virgin."

"Then what, sweetheart? What is it?" He pushed a hand through his hair, regarding her quizzically. "If you're not a virgin, then you must be familiar with male anatomy."

"Yes," she said hesitantly. "That's just it. . . ."

"Oh, dear heaven," he said, grinning. He got to his feet and walked over to the window. "I'm afraid," he finally said, "that there's absolutely no room for delicacy here, not if we're to get to the bottom of this." He turned to face her. "I know you have seen me unclothed once before, and probably on a number of occasions I'm not aware of. And I do well remember the expression on your

220

face on that first occasion. Somehow you have reached the extraordinary conclusion that I have . . . I have an . . ." His face screwed up again. He turned his head away for a moment, his shoulders shaking. And then he collected himself and looked back at her. "That there is a problem," he managed to say with a relatively straight face. "Now, applying logic to an illogical situation, the only thing I can think of is that it is a question of . . . of proportion."

Georgia nodded, wanting to drop straight through the floor.

"Very well. And applying further logic, I would assume that you feel I am, shall we say, too generously endowed to safely manage? Going by your previous experience, that is."

Georgia looked at him as if he were completely mad. "Too generously endowed?"

"No? Oh, dear. I was sure that was it. I wish you would just out and out tell me, then, sweetheart, so that we don't have to play guessing games all night."

"It was quite the other way around," she said, almost wishing Nicholas back in his stupor so that she didn't have to answer any more humiliating questions. "I thought you couldn't."

Now Nicholas stared at her. "You can't be serious?"

"Nicholas, please. Can we not—?"

"Georgia, forgive me, but you did see Baggie when he was not in a state of arousal, didn't you?"

"Yes," she said, concentrating very hard on a knot in a floorboard. "That is why I thought you couldn't."

He slumped down in the chair again. "I see. Or at least I think I see. This conversation is so peculiar that I'm not quite sure I'm having it."

"Then let's not have it at all."

"No, we're going to finish it, Georgia, for I'm damned if I let Baggie Wells come between us anymore. I do love you, you know. Surely that counts for something."

"And I love you, Nicholas, and that means everything to me."

"Then let us stop all this nonsense and do something about it, now that we've established that I'm perfectly capable. I've been waiting months, sweetheart, and it's been half-killing me.''

''You . . . you're saying that you want to assert your marital rights?'' she asked, her heart sinking.

''Well, I wouldn't put it quite like that,'' he said. ''But I would like to make love to you.''

Georgia just nodded, her eyes still on the ground.

''You don't look very enthusiastic, Georgia. What in the name of heaven is the problem here? This can't possibly still be about you and Baggie, can it?''

''Oh, Nicholas, don't you understand, I have no idea at all of how to feel in these circumstances!'' Tears sprang to her eyes. ''I love you, I do, and I am sure that you will not smother my mouth with your hand, and you will probably ask me, rather than force my legs open, but I don't know if I can bear having you tear me apart.''

Nicholas was across the room in a flash. He took her by the shoulders and lifted her face to his. He looked angry and upset, and even shaken. ''Georgia. Georgia, what are you telling me?''

''It is only that I am afraid,'' she said, tears falling down her cheeks. ''But I will not refuse you, Nicholas. And I will try to be brave.''

''Sweetheart,'' he said very gently. ''Are you saying that this is what Baggie did to you?''

She looked at him, bewildered, wondering if she hadn't misunderstood his intentions again. ''Yes, of course.''

''Of course? And yet you loved him?''

''Loved him?'' she said, wiping her eyes. ''I didn't love him. I didn't even hate him. I felt nothing at all.''

Nicholas looked away, stroking his eyebrow. ''You're going to have to give me a moment to absorb this.''

''But, Nicholas, I thought you understood that I had been very unhappy with him. It wasn't really Baggie's fault—he couldn't help being what he was.''

''I think we had better have a talk,'' he said, drawing her over to the sofa, and he sat her down. ''I have been going at this completely backwards, haven't I? Here I've been thinking all this time that you were deeply in love with some handsome farmer, living poorly but in wedded bliss.''

''The only thing that is true about that statement is that

we were poor. Baggie was short and squat and stupid. And there was certainly nothing resembling wedded bliss."

"Then why did you marry him? Please, Georgia, I need to understand this. I can see you don't want to discuss it, but it's important. It's very important. I've been laboring under a gross misconception from the beginning, and behaving accordingly. You have been laboring under some misconceptions yourself. So let us have the truth out and be done with it. Start at the beginning. Why did you marry him?"

"If you really must know, I had no choice. Mrs. Provost—"

"The vicar's wife?"

"Yes. She made up stories about me. She discovered that her husband had been chasing me about, and she accused me of trying to . . . to seduce him. Why she thought I would even want to look at a skinny old man with bad breath and a worse temperament, I cannot imagine, especially when I had done everything I could to evade him. But she locked me away anyway, and then after three weeks I was taken to church and married to Baggie. I didn't even know him."

"Oh, Georgia. Sweetheart. I'm sorry."

She kept her gaze fixed on the fire. It was still all too real, too immediate, even after all this time, and her shame burned through her.

"Please, love, tell me the rest. I'm sorry if it's painful, but I really do need to know. What happened after the wedding?"

She shrugged. "We went back to the farm. He got very drunk. And then he took me."

"He . . . he took you?"

"Yes. He told me that he was my husband and he had his rights. Which he did. And I had my wifely duty. Which I did."

"I see," Nicholas said tightly. "I imagine Mrs. Provost had told you all about your wifely duties."

"Yes."

Nicholas' hands clenched. "And it happened just as you described before."

"Yes."

223

"Was that the only time?"

She stared at him. "The only time? Nicholas, he took his rights nearly every night for almost three years. Baggie would go to the tavern and come home in his cups, and then he would come to bed. I cannot understand why you look so appalled. It is only what every husband does to his wife, although I am sure you will be much kinder. Baggie didn't deliberately mean to be unkind, but I don't think he knew any other way. I know you will try not to crush me with your body, nor smother me, for I will try very hard not to scream."

Nicholas jumped to his feet and slammed his fists against the mantelpiece. "Damn him!" he cried. "Damn him!" He spun back and looked at Georgia, his eyes burning with a pained rage. "Don't you understand, that is not what lovemaking is about? It is most certainly not what every husband does to his wife. And on top of it all, it sounds as if he was the man with the impediment. Georgia, I swear to you that I really am a perfectly normal man. I hate to ask, but I'm trying to put this damnable situation into perspective. Was Baggie really that . . . that large?"

She colored again. "He was like a bull. I thought all men were."

Nicholas choked. "Oh, sweetheart . . . oh, my poor love. It's no wonder . . ."

"What is no wonder?"

"Everything. All of it. Why you were so relieved when I didn't outright ask the same thing of you. Even why you drew the conclusion that I couldn't. Your sweet response when I've kissed you, and your quick withdrawal after, they've all baffled me. I thought it was because you had loved Baggie and you weren't ready to be with another man. So I waited, as patiently as I could, thinking you would let me know when you were willing to take me to your bed. But now I understand. And, Georgia, there are so many things you need to understand. So many things."

"Nicholas, I'm sorry. I hadn't realized you were waiting for me. I feel very bad about having neglected your needs."

"My . . . Georgia, listen, sweetheart. Listen to me." He took her hands between his. "This isn't about my

224

needs. It's about a very real fear you have that Baggie in his blasted ignorance and selfishness gave you. I understand just how frightened you must have been that I would do the same, and it only shows your generosity that you have offered yourself, despite your fear."

"But, Nicholas, I am not withdrawing that offer. Please, do not concern yourself just because I am afraid."

"I most certainly will concern myself, and it is no good your trying to argue me out of it, for I refuse point-blank to rape you, my love. I'm afraid I'm too greedy. I want to see you writhe under me in helpless lust while I take you to the stars and shatter your senses—and mine."

She opened her mouth, and then closed it, looking at him as if his senses were already shattered. "Nicholas. I have just *told* you . . ." And then she looked at him a little harder. "Have you ever done this thing?" she asked, and frowned as he gave a great shout of laughter.

"I'm afraid I have," he said. "Many times, although I'm not sure that's the correct thing to say to one's wife. I'm told I do it rather well."

"I'm sure you do, Nicholas," she said, glaring at the fire, now annoyed. "And it's all well and fine for you. But then you should know why it is that I am afraid."

He smiled at her and chucked her chin. "What does not seem to have sunk into your stubborn head is that there is no reason for you to be afraid, and certainly no need for you to feel you have to martyr yourself on the altar of my male desires. I've martyred myself on them quite enough. I'm not interested in unleashing terror on you, Georgia. It's no bloody fun, terror. Believe me, I should know."

She looked at him then, and he saw that the tears were back in her eyes. "I know," she said softly. "But it's not as bad as that. Not as bad as yours, I mean. I don't mind."

Nicholas' heart gave a great aching pull, and he instantly sobered. "I'm sorry, sweetheart. I didn't mean to tease. Well, I did, but I forgot for a moment what it is like to have horrible, unreasoning panic, no matter what logic—or other people—might tell you. I didn't mean to diminish your fear, only to tell you that I'd like to take it away." He reached out and very gently touched her cheek. "Listen, love. It was you who explained to me about how it is possible to be healed, and I believed you. You have held me when I've been afraid, more frightened than I can ever express in words. And you have seen me through the worst of nightmares and offered your love as a balm. Will you not let me do the same for you?"

"But how, Nicholas? How?" She found she was trembling.

"I am a troll-slayer, am I not?"

She gave a shaky laugh. "Yes, I suppose you are."

"Very well, then. I shall slay your troll as well."

"You are very silly, Nicholas."

He wiped away the trail of tears with his thumb. "No, not silly. I love you, Georgia. I love you with all of my heart and soul. I would never do anything to hurt you, ever, at least not consciously. I would certainly never force myself on you. But we cannot go through the rest of our lives with this dread haunting you. And I know I cannot go on much longer in this inflamed state. I can show you, Georgia, how it is meant to be. But you have to trust me, sweetheart, or I cannot help either of us."

"I do trust you," she said, but her lips were bloodless.

He gave her a long look. "All right, then," he said. He stood and started to take his shirt off.

"What are you doing?" she asked nervously.

"I'm undressing. We're going to bed. And I don't plan on asserting anything other than a few words unless you want me to. That's not too frightening, is it? Have I not held you against me night after night now? You have come to no harm, and I will not harm you now."

"Nicholas, you are so good to me. I promise you I will try to come around to the idea."

"Oh, I have no doubt at all that you'll come around to the idea. It's just a question now of when."

Georgia stood and started toward the door. "My nightdress is next door. I'll be back directly."

He gave a short laugh, pulling off his trousers. "What do you need a nightdress for?"

She turned and stared at him. He was standing there stark naked and completely unconcerned about it.

"Nicholas . . ." she said uncertainly.

226

"Yes?"

"Are you suggesting that I should take all my clothes off?"

"Unless you wish to sleep in that very attractive dress, which I doubt you do."

"But why must I take all my clothes off?" she finally asked.

"Because I want to hold you against me, skin against skin. You'll like it."

"I will?"

"You will. Trust me, Georgia. We have to start somewhere, don't we? I can't slay a troll with both hands tied behind my back."

Georgia, who had not been seen naked by anyone since her mother, could not imagine liking it, but she couldn't see how she could refuse what seemed to be a reasonable request. Nicholas came over to her and unfastened her dress from behind, then slipped it over her head, leaving her in nothing but her petticoat. Cheeks aflame, she crossed her arms over her breasts, then turned and hurried to the bed, slipping under the sheets and removing her petticoat only after she was safely covered. She turned on her side and squeezed her eyes shut.

Nicholas laughed softly, then opened the curtains nearest the bed, letting in the moonlight, extinguished the lamps, and joined her.

Georgia felt the mattress shift with his weight, and then the touch of his hand on her shoulder. "Georgia," he said, the laugh still in his voice. "You can come out now. It's just me."

She rolled onto her back and looked over at him, the covers pulled up to her chin. "I knew that," she said with a tentative smile.

"Clever girl. Now, move over here a little. I can't see a thing, I swear it. I could see more of you five minutes ago than I can now."

Georgia inched over and Nicholas leaned on his elbow, watching her. "I know you can do better than that," he said.

"Nicholas, I feel very foolish."

"So you should, for I have told you that you can trust me."

"But I have never lain naked in a bed with a man before."

"There are a great many things you have never done before. This is the least of them. What is so different about me now? I am the same man I was when I was dressed."

"I am not frightened of you. I just feel very unclothed."

He chuckled. "Georgia, relax. I am not going to eat you. I only want to talk to you."

"What about?"

"To begin with, I cannot begin to think what Mrs. Provost might have told you about sexual matters. Will you tell me?"

"I already have. She said it was a wife's duty to submit to her husband, whenever he wished."

"Did she give you any detail?"

"Not really. She told me it would be painful but that it was a woman's lot in life to bear pain and not to complain. She said I should close my eyes and say prayers."

"That sounds unbearably dreary. I wonder if she followed her own advice."

"I don't know," Georgia said with a grimace. "I can't imagine Mrs. Provost in that position at all. Maybe that's why the vicar was chasing after me."

"Oh, I can well imagine why the vicar was chasing after you. Poor Georgia. You do not have a very high opinion of men, have you?"

"I have of you," she said.

"And probably because I'm one of the few who has not pawed at you. Although there was that one snatched kiss, I'm afraid."

"Yes, there was that. But it was the nicest snatched kiss I've ever had. All the others were quite repulsive."

"I can see why you were averse to kissing in the beginning. It is something that many people do very poorly. There are those who slobber, and those who twist up their mouths as if they were having arsenic forced on them, and those who kiss as if they were chewing on a piece of meat."

Georgia laughed. "Really, Nicholas, what a disgusting description."

228

"My point exactly. Kissing is a sensual art and should be approached as such. Tell me, did Baggie ever kiss you?"

"Yes," Georgia said. "But his idea of kissing was to stuff his tongue down my throat and half suffocate me."

Nicholas shuddered. "It sounds extremely unpleasant. Baggie altogether sounds extremely unpleasant. But I am happy you have no objection to the way I kiss you."

"Oh, no—that's entirely different. You make me feel wonderful."

"Wonderful? In what way do you feel wonderful?"

She considered. "Generally, I would say that when you kiss me I feel flushed and weak, and I ache."

"Georgia! You make it sound as if I am giving you influenza, not pleasure."

"I did think at first that it might be influenza," she said with a tender smile, touching his mouth with her finger.

"It is not the first time you have mistaken passion for illness," he answered, taking her hand away. "Had I been ill all of the times I have touched you, or even looked at you and felt fevered, I would be dead by now. And when you touch me like that, I might as well be, at the rate I'm going."

"Passion?" she said, extremely surprised. "Are you quite sure?"

"Quite sure."

"How peculiar," she said, thinking this over.

"It serves its purpose." Nicholas rolled onto his back, pulling one knee up, and regarded the canopy over his head. "Or at least it can."

"But how, Nicholas?" she said intently, determined to get to the bottom of the matter. "I cannot see the use in becoming dizzy and fevered and generally useless every time one kisses. It's true that it feels very nice at the time, but it makes me very distracted, and I can't accomplish anything at all afterward."

Nicholas seemed to find that extremely amusing, and she frowned. "It is no good your explaining matters if all you do is laugh in between. I am not stupid, Nicholas."

"Oh, beloved, you are anything but. You are only in-experienced."

"I do not think you can call me that," she said indignantly. "And your words are all well and fine, but the fact of the matter is that you are a man, and I am a woman."

"Exactly," Nicholas said with satisfaction.

"Yes, exactly. And no matter what you might choose to believe, you experience things differently. You have no idea what it is like to be in my position."

"No . . . I haven't, it is true. But I do have a very clear idea of what it can be like for you."

"Then why would you want to do such a thing to someone you love?" she asked almost desperately. "I can see the need to get children, but why must it be so brutal?"

Nicholas abruptly sat up and turned to look at her. "That's precisely what I've been trying to tell you. Georgia, it's not meant to be a brutal thing. Not in the least. You've been very badly used, and hurt, and disenchanted. But if you look at me now, do you truly believe I would treat you so? Do you believe I would tell you lies to gain your trust and then blithely rend you apart for my own satisfaction? Lovemaking is meant to be a wonderful experience." He pushed his hand through his hair in frustration, then reached out to her. "Here, feel this," he said, taking her hand and placing it on the muscle of his chest.

"Your heartbeat?" she asked in confusion.

"Yes. It is fairly normal, is it not?"

"Yes. I think so."

"All right. Now." He leaned down and kissed her, slowly, gently, inviting her to open her mouth, and he lightly touched her tongue with his own, then pulled away. "Oh, Georgia, these lessons might be more than I can bear," he said hoarsely. "Give me your hand again." He took it, and she could feel his heart hammering wildly and his skin flaming beneath her palm.

"I feel the same way," she said softly, her hand still on his chest.

"Yes, I know. I have not been oblivious of your reaction. But what you don't know is that kissing is just a pleasant prelude to lovemaking. It only gets better, sweetheart, and more passionate, and when you reach the actual act itself, the pleasure is so intense that it can be almost unbearably good—for both the man and the woman."

"No," she said. "That I do not believe."

"Believe it. It's absolutely true. But like kissing, love-making can either be done very well or very poorly. When it is done very poorly, as in the case of Baggie, then it has exactly the opposite effect. And here ends the first lesson."

"But you can't end there, Nicholas."

"Why not?"

"Because I don't understand."

"I'm not surprised. It's the sort of thing that needs to be demonstrated. But you have to want to have it demonstrated—that's the key to the whole thing."

"Oh," she said. "But what would ever make you want to have it demonstrated?"

"That's where passion comes into it. Now, come over here, and let's go to sleep." He reached out for her and pulled her to him before she could object.

His arms went comfortably around her, and she found that her breasts were pressed against the smooth skin of his chest. She could feel the beating of his heart, and it was still pounding. His hands slowly stroked her back, and as she relaxed into his embrace, she found that she enjoyed the touch of his hands on her bare skin. And the feel of his hot chest against her breasts. She was amazed that it felt so nice, and she slipped her arm over his lean waist and moved closer, resting her head on his shoulder. Nicholas rolled slightly onto his back and kissed the top of her head.

"Good night, sweetheart," he said softly.

"Good night, Nicholas," she said, wondering why she felt disappointed and empty.

She settled down to sleep, but she couldn't help thinking about everything he had said about passion and pleasure. She knew how it felt to be kissed by him, and how it felt to be held by him. She also knew how it felt to hold him, and how many times she had been seized with the desire to run her hands over his body, that beautiful male combination of grace and strength, solid muscle under smooth skin, slight hollows and flat planes and hard curves just waiting to be touched. The thought made the strange ache start inside again, and she shifted against him, drinking in his now-familiar scent.

He was gentle, so gentle with her, consciously restraining all that power, and yet she remembered his crushing her against him, his mouth taking hers in a desperate grip, and she knew that he was capable of unleashing his power when he chose. How would it be when he took her? She could not compare him to Baggie, she knew, for they were as opposite as night and day. It would be like equating Nicholas' sharp intelligence to Baggie's dull brain, like comparing Nicholas' refinement to Baggie's coarseness, Nicholas' tall, beautiful form to Baggie's stumpiness. No, he surely couldn't take her in the fashion Baggie had. And yet she was still terribly afraid.

But she found that beneath her fear, curiosity burned. Everything Nicholas had said led her to think that she might, in fact, be mistaken, that she was ignorant. And he had promised he would not hurt her, just as she had promised to trust him.

Ten minutes later she sat up, the sheet clutched to her chest.

"Nicholas?"

"Mmm?"

"Are you awake?"

"Yes."

She looked down at him to find him watching her steadily, his eyes undecipherable, his expression neutral.

"Nicholas," she said carefully. "I have been thinking."

"Good," he said, casually lacing his hands behind his head. "And?"

"And I think I . . ." She swallowed, then summoned up her bravery. "I think I would like you to demonstrate it to me."

"That took even less time than I thought it would," he said with a slight smile. "But plant a seed in fertile soil . . ."

"Nicholas, did you understand me? What I meant?"

"Perfectly."

"Then why are you just lying there as if I'd said nothing of any significance?" She wanted very much to throw something at him, but she was too intent on clutching the sheet. "I don't understand you in the least!"

"Have you gone so quickly from reluctance to impatience?" he asked, his smile curving up at the sides.

"It is just that I think we should get it over and done with. And there is no need to be so blithe about it. I will lose my nerve in another moment."

"Georgia," he said, pushing himself up on his elbow. "Listen to me. This is not exactly the sort of thing that you get over and done with, like an unpleasant chore. It is meant to be enjoyed."

"So you said, and I still find that very hard to believe," she said, unwilling to admit to the paralyzing terror that had begun to clutch at her stomach again.

"I am sure you do. But you shall see." He lay back down again.

"Nicholas . . . Nicholas! You are making this very difficult."

"Am I, love? How is that?"

"Because I do not know what it is I am meant to do! This is not how it ever happened before, although I know that Baggie was just a simple farmer and didn't know much about anything. But he was the one who would come and . . . well, I told you. Oh, for once I wish I had Binkley to instruct me in the correct behavior. I'm sure he would tell me exactly how a proper lady would go about matters."

Nicholas burst into laughter. "I think that is where Binkley would draw a very firm line. I can just see his face now if you asked him. And I certainly do not want to make love to a proper lady."

"Then what you do want, Nicholas? Please tell me, for I am confused."

"I want to make love to you, Georgia, all of you, just as you are."

"But, Nicholas, I am serious. I feel very awkward. Here I sit and there you lie, and you do not seem to be doing anything about it. I begin to think you are politely waiting for me to give myself to you. Am I to lie down on my back?"

"Whatever for? I am already on mine. It would be rather silly to have the two of us lying side by side like sausages in a pan."

She looked at him nervously. "Do you tease me?"

"Never. I never tease." He smiled and picked up her hand, kissing the palm, then laid it on his chest. "Touch me, Georgia, for it feels uncommonly good."

She tentatively moved her fingers where he had placed them on the firm muscle. This was something that was familiar, and she relaxed, sliding her hand over his smooth torso, exploring the planes she had just been thinking about. He had regained some of the weight he had lost, but he was still thin, and her fingers caressed the slight indentation under his ribs.

"You feel nice," she said shyly.

"So do you," he replied, catching his breath as she trailed her fingers over his nipple and the nub sprang to life as it had the first time she had accidentally touched him. It sent a little thrill through her, to see him react so to her touch, and she became a little bolder. Taking the tip of her finger, she ran it from the patch of hair on his chest down along the silky line to where the sheet covered him at the waist. "I have wanted to do that for so long," she said on a sigh of satisfaction.

"Oh? And what else have you wanted to do?" he asked, his voice husky.

"I have wanted to kiss you just here," she said, and bent her lips to the exact point where his neck met his ear.

"Mmm," he said on a long sigh. "That's not bad at all. I don't suppose you've wanted to kiss my ear? Maybe trace its outline with your tongue? It's not such a bad ear."

"No, it's a lovely ear. I hadn't thought of it—but I could try." Adjusting her grip on the sheet, she moved up and did as he had suggested, finding it most interesting, and actually very pleasant, to feel his ear under her mouth. She became absorbed in her task, exploring the crevices with the tip of her tongue, when he turned his head away with a little laugh. "That was extremely nice. But there is my neck, you see. It feels neglected." He tilted his head back and exposed it for her.

So she bent her head to it and she kissed it, rubbing her mouth up and down, savoring his warm, slightly salty taste, and she couldn't help herself. Her tongue came out to run over the vein that pulsed just there. And then she moved down to kiss the hollow of his throat, and she ran her tongue over that too.

"Georgia—oh, Georgia—my mouth. You forget my poor mouth," he said even more hoarsely. "How am I to survive this sensual assault without being kissed as only you can do?"

She smiled and she lowered her mouth to his, brushing his lips as he had taught her, then opened her mouth and shyly touched his tongue with hers. And she became lost in the kiss as he responded, his arms going around her, drawing her down against him, playing havoc with her senses as his tongue tangled with hers in a wild dance.

Nicholas buried his fingers in her hair, then rolled her over onto her side. The sheet began to slide off her chest, and she hastened to adjust it, but he stopped her hand.

"No," he said, hooking the sheet with his finger and slipping it down even lower, exposing the top of her breasts. "No. You have had your way with me, and now it is my turn." He kissed her neck, his mouth open and warm, and he traced a line down it and then back to her ear, pulling the lobe into his mouth and nibbling it. Georgia shivered with pleasure.

"Do you see how very nice that is?" he said. "And this too?" and his tongue traced a path directly down her neck, his mouth suckling the skin at the base of her throat. "And this?" He pulled the sheet lower and his warm mouth ran down the side of her breast, his breath burning into her. She tensed.

"Wait, sweetheart, wait," he murmured. "Relax." He kissed her throat again, and the underside of her jaw in the same way, and then traveled back to her mouth and tongued the corners until she opened her mouth and gave him entry. Waves of hot pleasure coursed through her as he suckled her tongue as he had her ear and her throat. The hand on her waist moved restlessly, wandering over her hip and back again, his fingers spreading around her back, then traveling up over her ribs. They stroked just under the swell of flesh; then his hand moved up and over, touching her sensitive breast as lightly as a feather.

"Nicholas!" she gasped against his mouth.

"What?" he asked with a lazy smile, his fingers coming to rest on her nipple. "You don't like it?"

"No, I think I do. I . . . I was just surprised."

"Mmm. I can imagine. I doubt very much Baggie paid any attention to your breasts."

"Yes, he did," she said stiffly. "He tended to crush them in his hands. It hurt."

"Oh, Georgia. Georgia, we do have some educating to do." He impatiently pushed the sheet all the way down to her waist, and she blushed and turned her head away, horribly embarrassed.

"Sweetheart . . . sweetheart, look at me. Look at me." He turned her face back to him. "Let me pleasure you. Please. Let me show you how nice it can be." He bent his head to her breast, and Georgia wanted to scream. Until she felt his mouth gently taking her nipple, nursing on it, his hand cupping her breast, stroking it with his thumb. She could not help herself. Her back arched and she pressed herself closer, her breath quickening until she made little whimpers of excitement in her throat, and Nicholas groaned and bent his head to the other breast, now swollen and aching with excitement.

She took his head in her hands and tangled her fingers in his hair, her hips squirming with delight at the new sensations, pressing against him harder. Her hand came down to his cheek and he stroked it, then touched the corner of his mouth, and she pushed her finger into it, touching his tongue and her damp, throbbing nipple at the same time.

Nicholas' head shot up and he gave a low laugh as he saw the heated expression in her half-closed eyes. "Little seductress," he said, his body so quickened by desire that it was hard to speak at all. "You learn quickly. My God, you learn quickly."

"You are beautiful," she said shakily. "So beautiful."

"Oh, no," he said. "You may call me handsome, or virile, or even magnificent, if you really must. But you may not call me beautiful. That is reserved solely for you." He molded her breast in his hand, then kissed it again. "And you are gloriously passionate. Do you think you like all this passion, Georgia?"

"Oh, yes. Yes, I think I like it very much."

"Then come closer to me." He urged her hips toward his.

Georgia twisted around to press herself against him, moving her hands over the breadth of his shoulders, his back, dropping down to the corded muscle of his hip, and he shook with torment. And then the lovely swell of her belly touched his engorged length, and he could feel the soft, moist brush of curl against his thigh. He breathed out a long, jerky sigh. Torment. Sweet, sweet torment. He ached to bury himself in her, and it was everything he could do not to move against her. It was more than he could do, for his hips took over, shifting against her, just a small rub, one very, very nice rub.

Georgia suddenly pulled away.

"It's all right, sweetheart," he said, desperate to have her back touching him again. "It's all right. You're going to like that part too, I promise." He knew she would, he was as sure of it as he was that he breathed, but he wasn't sure how much longer he could play cat and mouse, not with this beautiful, fabulously erotic woman in his arms. "Don't be afraid of me, or that part of me," he said, trying to sound rational. "When you touch me there, it makes me feel as you do when I touch you like this. Even better." He brushed his hand back over her nipple and she shivered, and then he ran it down over her waist, spreading his fingers to touch the small of her back. "You like that, don't you?"

"Yes, Nicholas. . . . I do. Oh, I do."

"You are so delicate, so soft," he murmured, lowering his head again to her breast and drawing it into his mouth, breathing on it, pulling on it, teasing it with his lips and tongue until she cried with pleasure and pushed herself up against him. And this time when she felt him against her, she did not pull away. "Oh, God," he said. "Oh, God. That feels . . . that feels good."

"Nicholas . . ." she said hesitantly, looking away.

"Mmm?" he replied, lost in the excitement of the feel of her soft skin pressing on him.

"I would like to give you pleasure too," she said shyly.

237

"You are, my sweet. You are."

"I would like to touch you," she said, her voice barely audible.

"Touch me? Oh, please," he said, raising his eyes to the ceiling in silent thanks. "Certainly. Do feel quite free." He hardly dared breathe as her hand crept down between them, then, light as a breath of air, skimmed over him, and came back again, settling as delicately as a butterfly landing on a rose petal. She ran her fingers up and down his blazing skin, and then her whole palm, and Nicholas stiffened his thighs, trying not to shake.

"I do not hurt you?" she asked, her own breath coming faster as she explored him with amazingly accurate instincts.

"No, my love," he croaked, "you do not hurt me. You give me great pleasure. Very, very . . . great . . . pleasure." He clenched his teeth and twisted his hands through her hair, breathing shallowly into her soft curls. And then her fingers moved up and encircled him and he grasped her wrist in desperation. "Georgia . . . oh, Georgia, love . . . I think maybe a little break would be in order."

Georgia sighed, for touching him had caused a shower of heat to explode through her body, centering between her legs in sweet desire. It was as if some unreasoning part of her had come awake and wanted to discover, to feel, to experience him, to hold the silky steel of him in her hand, to see his brow knot and know that he was caught up in the same passion she was feeling. "Nicholas, may I look?" she asked, possessed by a sudden need to see, to know.

"Look? You want to look?" he said, making a noise somewhere between a laugh and a groan.

"Yes. Oh, yes, I do. You are not embarrassed?"

"Embarrassment has nothing to do with it," he said. "Look to your heart's desire."

Georgia, her cheeks flaming with a combination of embarrassment, curiosity, and arousal, sat up and pulled the sheet away. She dragged her eyes down to his groin and drew her breath in sharply as she saw his masculine shape. He was nothing like Baggie at all. Nothing. Baggie had been terrifying. Nicholas was in perfect proportion to the rest of his body. He was beautiful. She knew she ought to be afraid, but she wasn't afraid in the least: she was fascinated. Her eyes roamed up and down his length, taking in every detail. "It's . . . you are . . ." She paused, searching for the right word to describe such a thing. "You are very nicely made," she finally said, and Nicholas burst into laughter, then pulled her down on top of him.

"I am delighted that my proportions finally please you," he said, entwining her fingers with his, then gently moved her onto her back. "And now it is my turn to look." He pushed away the sheet and gazed down at her.

She felt she should be shy, but she was inflamed by the hungry way his eyes traveled over her body, by the impassioned look in his eyes as his hand stroked over her hip, came to light on the triangle of curls between her legs, moved away to her thigh, stroking the skin until she shook violently under his touch.

"You are exquisite," he said. "You are the most exquisite woman I have ever laid eyes on. God, look at you. It's enough to make me lose what's left of my mind."

Georgia looked into his eyes. The gray glittered as silver as the moonlight that washed over him, and she saw the laughter that still lingered, and the heat and the desire that burned over it. Her heart ached as strongly as her body, and she wanted to enfold him, to offer herself up to him, but she didn't know how.

"Georgia," he whispered. "What is it? Now why do you look at me so?"

She raised her mouth to his and softly kissed him. "Show me, Nicholas, for I am not afraid anymore. I want to give myself to you. I want you to take me."

"Georgia, what do you do to me? It is not enough that I want you beyond any sane desire, but I must feel as if my heart is being torn from my chest as well?"

He bent down and kissed her soft belly, and then the indentation of her waist. He lifted her arms over her head and ran his mouth down the sensitive insides, then took her breast into his mouth, drawing heated circles with his tongue until he captured her nipple and tugged on it, sending shocks of fire through her. She writhed under him, whimpering, wanting everything he could give her, greedy for more, and his hands cupped her buttocks and shaped them to his palms. She jerked, her hips lifting, pushing against him, her legs opening in mindless need. She needed something, for his hand to touch her there, to take away the heated ache. And as if he had read her mind, he moved to his side and his hand traveled down to the juncture of her legs, tangling in her curls, pulling gently, sliding over the outside of her mound, and she twisted impatiently, pushing against his hand, wanting him to open her, to touch her more deeply. That she could be so wanton only dimly occurred to her, her wits occluded by this fierce, overpowering desire.

"Oh, Nicholas," she sobbed. "Oh, please. I can't bear it anymore." She pulled up her knees, opening wider for him, and he obliged her, the tips of his fingers sliding along her cleft, gently parting the delicate flesh, and moving between the swollen folds. The breath caught in her throat as he ran his finger back and forth, homing in on a place that sent her nerves not just sparking, but into full conflagration. She cried out with a shock of pleasure, her back arching, pushing herself harder against his hand.

Nicholas knew he was lost. The feel of her hot, slick, quivering flesh under his fingers inflamed him to the point where he knew he would never be able to stop. They'd have to shoot him first. He dropped his open mouth to hers and invaded her with his tongue, and at the same time he pushed two fingers into her tight hot passage, reveling in the feel of her female muscles contracting around them as she buried her fingers almost painfully in his hair.

Georgia was not shy. She thrust her pelvis against his fingers and rocked, sliding herself back and forth with sweet little whimpers of excitement, and he watched her face, her lip caught between her teeth, her eyes closed, her head turning on the pillow, her breasts rising and falling in shallow pants. No, Georgia was not shy in the throes of passion. It was more as if she were lost. She grasped his buttocks and kneaded them, then pulled him down to her, her legs spreading for him, her hips pushing upward.

He wasn't about to stop to ask her whether she was quite sure that was what she wanted him to do. He slid between her legs, rubbing himself between her silky folds, reveling in her heat, her arousal, her little cries.

"Oh, you truly were made for passion, weren't you, my sweet," he murmured hoarsely, burying his face in her neck. "You just didn't know it." He braced himself on his forearms and pushed against her entrance, and she yielded to him, her skin stretching to embrace him. He pushed a little harder and he was home, buried in her moist, heated flesh, her muscles gripping around him. She cried out, and he knew without doubt that it was in pleasure, not pain, from the way she trembled around him.

He leaned down to kiss her.

"Georgia," he said on a groan, staying perfectly still in hopes of preserving himself. "Oh, you feel good. You are perfect, just perfect—even more perfect than I ever imagined. And oh, *God,* how I've imagined." He began to move his hips, slowly at first, adjusting her to the feel of him inside of her. He brought his hand down between them, moving in her damp curls and touching her gently on her exquisitely sensitive nub, and she sighed and moved against his fingers.

"Nicholas," she whispered against his cheek. "Why did you not teach me before? It is the most wonderful thing in the world."

He wanted to cry from frustration. He had waited four months to hear this now? She might have been his that much sooner if he hadn't been such a gentleman? He groaned, cursing himself for a fool.

"Nicholas?" she said, wriggling against him, pushing him more deeply into her.

"Patience, love," he muttered. "Patience." He took a few deep, shaky breaths, decided he had calmed enough that he could function again, and repositioned himself, slipping his hands under her buttocks and lifting her even closer to him.

Georgia wrapped her legs around his hips as if she had been doing it always, reveling in the fierce swelling of his body in hers, pushing up against it, feeling him slide in her in a pounding rhythmical dance, filling her one minute, nearly gone the next, then driving home again, causing her to sob with her pleasure. She rained kisses upon his face, his mouth, anywhere she could reach, her tongue tasting the salt of his sweat, her hands slipping over his slick torso as his muscles worked under her fingers. She closed her eyes and lost herself in the waves of sensation that rolled through her, and with each thrust she felt an exquisite building of tension, a movement toward something unknown but terribly important.

Nicholas kissed her neck and her mouth and then her neck again, and she opened her eyes to see him watching her, his eyes fixed intently on her face.

And then with a low moan he pulled his hips back and plunged into her hard and deep, holding fast inside her. It was as if a storm had been gathering, waiting for the first clap of thunder, the first stroke of lightning, for it broke over her violently, the lightning striking sharply, the thunder answering a second later in a great roar through her very core, echoing over and over and over. She was at the epicenter and she heard herself crying out, and then she heard Nicholas cry out as well, sharply, as if he were caught in the storm with her. She was no longer sure whose body was pulsating, for it felt one and the same.

And then finally, finally, the storm passed and it was quiet again.

Nicholas dropped his face onto her shoulder and kissed the place it landed on. He was still breathing heavily, and Georgia ran her hands over the back of his neck, his shoulders, his arms, trying to work out what had just happened. She knew she had loved and been loved. She knew that she had just experienced a shared physical communion that bound her more strongly to Nicholas than anything she had experienced before. He had taken her, not in an act of violence, but in an act of love. She had trusted him, and he had proved himself not only trustworthy but also infinitely patient. For she finally understood what it was that he had been waiting for, and she knew that the price he had been forced to pay for his patience must have been steep indeed.

Her hand crept to her breast almost with reverence, then to the cheek that lay upon her shoulder, and she stroked his face.

"Nicholas," she whispered, her hands smoothing over

his skin, moving into his hair, and she relished the feel of the damp, silky strands under her fingers.

"Mmm," he said, turning his face into her breast and kissing it.

"You were right."

He lifted his head slightly. "Of course I was," he said, then dropped his head back down on her shoulder.

"And you waited so long."

"I know," he murmured.

"I love you for it."

"You love me for many things," he said. "You're just in the throes of sexual aftermath. You'll remember the rest in the morning."

"Nicholas!" she said, laughing softly and tugging on his hair. "You're being exceptionally casual, considering that you just ravished me."

"Excuse me, madam, but you ravished in equal part. I am too much a gentleman to take all the credit. By the by, you ravish rather well."

"And you ravish in a most devastating fashion. I hope you will do it again very soon."

Nicholas pushed himself up and looked at her. "I am a man, merely a man."

"And a very fine man at that. And I'm sorry for thinking you were impeded."

He smothered a laugh against her shoulder. "It was a blow at the time. But I am relieved we have it sorted out now. And if you give me an hour—no, maybe a few hours—I will impress my incredible manliness upon you again. I am full of tricks." He kissed her mouth. "I think I love you."

She smiled and snuggled up against him. "Your brain has been overheated. I know you love me. Now, sleep, my dear prince. I will look forward to dawn."

"I'm no prince," he muttered, and his breathing deepened.

"But you are mine," she whispered, and held him safe into the night.

14

Georgia rolled over on her side and smiled in her sleep. Nicholas was panting from exertion, the point of his sword resting in the dirt, both of his hands on its hilt. At his feet lay something that looked like a small shriveled piece of cloth.

"I have conquered it," he said proudly.

"But what was it?" she asked curiously.

"A balloon. What did you think, silly girl? It was a very large balloon, naturally, and it took a great deal of skill to bring it down to earth, for it flew about all over the place. However, I bested it in the end." He straightened the gold band that circled his head, for it had slipped slightly over one eyebrow. "Are you not impressed?"

"Oh, yes," she said, trying very hard not to laugh. "I am very impressed indeed. But, Nicholas, do you not think you should be chasing after dragons? Isn't that what princes do?"

"Dragons do not interest me in the least," he said, scoffing. "Every run-of-the-mill prince and his brother chases after dragons. I prefer more elusive challenges."

"I see," she said gravely.

"Now, kiss me as my reward," he said, pulling her into his arms and shaping his mouth to hers. She felt his warm breath, his lips moving back and forth across hers, and she inhaled softly against him, feeling a sharp throb of desire between her legs. Georgia's eyes slowly opened and Nicholas' mouth was indeed on her, moving in a most seductive fashion. She slipped her arms around his strong back, answering him.

"Good morning, wife," Nicholas said, lifting his head and kissing her nose. "Enchantress." He kissed her ear.

Georgia responded by touching the curve of his shoulder with her open mouth and the tip of her tongue, and pulling him down to her.

"Wanton," he said with a laugh, but she felt his hard arousal against her thigh, and she pushed against it, positioning herself so that he touched against her nest of curls. She opened her legs to him, and Nicholas made a guttural noise as she closed her thighs, capturing him between them.

"Oh, sweet Jesus," he choked as she slowly moved her hips back and forth so that he slid against her delicate flesh.

His head fell back and his eyes closed, and Georgia delighted in his knotted brow and his suddenly rough breathing. "Good morning, husband," she said, and reached her hand down to cover him with a little shudder of pleasure at the feel of his maleness in her hand. She felt terribly bold, but she couldn't help herself. There was something about touching him like that that she found wildly exciting. Apparently he found it exciting too, for he inhaled sharply and cupped her buttocks.

"You want to play erotic games, my love? Very well. Lie still and let me show you another way." He moved his hands lower still, and he slipped down the bed, gently urging her knees further apart and slightly up.

"Nicholas, what are you doing?" she asked in alarm as his mouth traveled up and down the inside of her thighs.

"Pleasuring you," he murmured, kissing her downy triangle. "Relax, sweetheart."

"But, Nicholas . . ." she said, coloring with embarrassment as he spread her open to his gaze.

"Beautiful," he murmured, and Georgia felt his warm breath mingling with the cool air running over her hot flesh. "Sweetly scented, like the most glorious of fruit. Does the description remind you of anything?" But he didn't give her a chance to answer, for he had placed his mouth on her.

"Oh, Nicholas," she whimpered as she felt the touch of his lips. She knew she should be shocked with herself, with her wantonness, but she couldn't have cared. All she wanted was more—more of this reckless excitement, more of Nicholas' touch, more of everything. He obliged her, tracing her open cleft with his tongue, finding the hard bud of nerves and very gently tugging on it with his lips.

"Oh," she gasped, and dug her fingers in his shoulders, which only served to bring him more forcefully against her. She sobbed with pleasure as he pulled her more deeply into his mouth, licking, stroking, penetrating her with his tongue until she was shaking from head to foot. And then he raised his head and kissed her neck, and her breasts, and he shifted over her, pulling her leg over his hip. He entered her in one powerfully smooth stroke, his body hot and full inside of hers.

"How the hell did I ever last so long without you?" he said roughly, pulling his hips back and pushing into her. "In the same damned house, day after day, night after night?" He thrust. "Tortured." He withdrew and thrust again, and Georgia pressed up against him, drawing him deeper into her center. "Without hope." He pulled her leg higher and thrust again, and Georgia trembled violently as she felt her tension building to breaking point. "Anguished," he said, and caressed her exposed flesh with his fingers. "Unappreciated." He took her nipple between his teeth and bit it lightly.

She exploded. "Nicholas!" she cried sharply, as wave after wave of furious release crashed through her. Nicholas trembled and pushed even deeper as she contracted in a fierce rhythm around him, and then he shuddered and drove into her with a strangled sob. She could feel his heavy release and she bit her lip against the new rush of pleasure that swept through her. Nicholas' mouth came down on hers and his hips pushed her back against the bed as she thrust up against his still-engorged shaft, seeking the source of her desire. He moved slightly, and she was there again, crying out, falling, her body shattering into a million brilliant stars. Her whimpers finally faded as the paroxysms released her from their grip, and she slowly relaxed in Nicholas' arms, hardly able to think at all.

"Oh, my God," Nicholas groaned a few minutes later, collapsing onto his side, carrying her with him, his body still buried in hers, his breath still labored. "Oh, my God. Georgia. Georgia."

"Nicholas, what is it?" she said in alarm, thinking that perhaps he was not yet strong enough for such excitement. "You're not ill, are you?"

"I am a mightily sick man," he said with a snort of laughter. He flung one arm over his head and stroked the hollow of her back with the other. He appeared extremely healthy to her, and she looked at him suspiciously.

"And what exactly is wrong with you?" she asked.

"I have just suffered a high fever, heart attack, and seizures, all at once. I am quite sure I was near death."

She turned her face in the curve of his shoulder to hide her smile. "How tragic for you," she said sadly.

"But is there a cure, O wise woman?"

"I'm afraid, my poor stricken husband, that the only cure for such a battery of illnesses is abstinence from such strenuous activity."

"No!" he said. "Surely nothing quite so drastic. I think the only cure is to attempt to work this terrible thing out of my system with vigorous exercise. That is what I think. I would confine myself to my sickbed, of course."

"Of course."

He moved his arm and stroked her hair. "Do you know," he said softly, "I never in my wildest dreams imagined it would be like this with you. You're so damned responsive that it sends me reeling."

"I feel most terribly shameless, Nicholas," she said hesitantly.

Nicholas sat up abruptly and looked down at her, anger sparking in his eyes. "Shameless? You should thank God you are able to respond at all after what you've been through!"

"Yes, I know, but still, I know it is wicked of me to behave with quite such . . . such abandonment."

"You listen to me well, Georgia. You're a fantastically sensual woman, and it is your birthright to be so—anyone who has told you otherwise is not only wrong but also twisted. You are my wife. I love you. Why should we not pleasure each other? There is nothing wicked about it."

"But to *want* you to do such things to me—and to want to do them to you just as much, that is not wicked?"

"God meant it to be so, sweetheart, or he wouldn't

have created us as he has, with the ability to feel such things, to desire such things, to come together in such a way. I'm going to murder the vicar's wife for putting such ideas in your head, see if I don't, and she can roast in hell. And I'll murder the vicar while I'm at it, and he can roast with her. And it's a damned lucky thing for Baggie that he's already dead, or I'd kill him too for what he did to you." Nicholas looked away, his hand clenching. "I hope he is burning in hell."

"We are the ones who will be burning in hell, Nicholas, if we carry on like this," she said with a small smile.

"If I burn in hell, it will not be for that, I promise you," he said, looking back at her. "I am quite sure that God is happy with your pleasure, which means that for once he must be happy with me for giving it to you. And if I would like for God to continue to regard me with benevolence, then it only follows that I must continue along this course. You don't want me to burn too, or at least not in hell, do you, Georgia?"

"And you think I have a peculiar brand of logic, Nicholas?" she said, slipping her hand into his. "I think you could talk any situation around to suit yourself."

He lay down again and pulled her back into his arms. "Whom would you rather believe on the matter? Me or Mrs. Provost, who sounds exactly like a prune, all dry and wrinkled, with a large stone in her middle. No doubt she thinks in the same manner."

Georgia burst into laughter. "You have her exactly."

"I'm sure, although I find it terribly difficult imagining you in those circumstances. I cannot help but feel angered by the injustice of what was done to you. And I'm afraid I cannot be even remotely rational on the subject of Baggie. I still cannot credit the fact that all these months I thought you were passionately in love with him. I pictured him a Nordic god, you see."

She shuddered. "If you had seen him, you would have understood how ludicrous the idea. He was covered everywhere in hair, Nicholas, and shaped exactly like a barrel. And his eyes, they never seemed really focused. He liked his drink overly much, but it wasn't just that.

He wasn't capable of much real understanding. I am sure that was how Mrs. Provost convinced him to marry me.''

Nicholas groaned against her hair.

"But he meant no real harm, Nicholas, really he didn't. I think he needed a wife to help him on the farm, someone to cook his meals and to look after him, someone he could take out his male needs on. I am sure he did not realize that the pain he was giving me was unusual.''

"Georgia, you are far too forgiving. He forced you to an act you did not wish, and he hurt you terribly in the process. I cannot even imagine what you must have suffered.''

"It is in the past," she said. "It is finished.''

"Thank God. But, Georgia, do you mind if I ask you something? I have wondered why there were no children.''

"I found a formula in my mother's book of medicines to prevent conception. I didn't want Baggie's children.'' She ran her fingers over his nape, thinking how very much she did want his.

"Yes . . . I can well understand why not. It was a blessing you didn't have any, either, or I cannot think how you might have ended up when Baggie died. By the by, what happened to him?''

"Who?''

"Baggie," he said, smiling.

"The early mail," she replied absently, wondering how someone as completely masculine as Nicholas could have such extraordinarily soft hair.

"What?'' Nicholas pulled slightly away and looked at her. "What in God's name do you mean by that? Did he have a shock of some kind?''

"Oh, no—Baggie couldn't read. It was the mail coach. The wheel ran over his head.''

"How in hell did that happen?'' Nicholas asked incredulously.

"He made his bed on the side of the toll road the night before. He'd had too much ale. I found the horse outside the barn the next morning.''

"You're serious?'' Nicholas gave a choked laugh. "He managed to be run over by the mail coach?''

"I told you, he was not much for brains.''

"And I imagine even less by the time all was said and done," Nicholas said dryly. "Well, thank God for the Royal Mail, I say." He swung out of bed and went over to the basin, pouring some water into it and wetting a cloth. "It's cold," he said, coming back to bed, "but you'll want to wash. Shall I help?" He gave her a particularly wicked grin.

"No, thank you," she said, taking it from him. "I know exactly where that would end, and we need to get on with the day, as tempting as spending it here with you sounds."

"Very tempting. But you're right. I have a great deal of work to do today. I've seven weeks of idleness to make up for. And, Georgia—thank you."

"Whatever for?"

"For letting me love you. For loving me. For looking after me when I needed it, and for trusting me when I asked."

"Nicholas, you are far more sentimental than you would have people believe."

He bent down and kissed her. "For God's sake, don't tell anyone. I have a devilish reputation to uphold."

"You must have nurtured it carefully. You have never been anything other than good and kind that I've seen. And patient. I love you, Nicholas."

"You do, don't you? It astonishes me. I've never considered myself particularly lovable." He kissed her one last time, then quickly washed and dressed and disappeared downstairs.

Lily delivered the hot water along with a look of satisfaction when she saw Georgia in bed, her shoulders bare. "It is nice to see the master back to his old self," she said, pouring it into the basin for Georgia. "He was singing a nice little song when he came down for his breakfast, and he put all of it away too. Never did see an appetite like his has been the last week, missus. He liked his new room, did he?"

"He did, Lily, very much."

"That's good, then, missus. He needs a few pleasures, does the master. Mr. Binkley was smiling himself this morning, though I don't expect he thought I was watching. Mr. Binkley don't like folks knowing he's human, if you know what I mean.''

Georgia grinned. ''I know exactly what you mean. Never mind, Lily, he's a good man, and better than most. And speaking of good men, how are you and Lionel Martin coming along?''

Lily blushed scarlet. ''How did you know, missus?'' she asked in a near-whisper.

''Oh, Lily, it hasn't been difficult to work out. The two of you have been smelling of April and May since February.''

''He asked me to marry him, missus. I don't know what I should do!''

''Why ever not? Do you love him?''

''Oh, yes, but there's the children, aren't there?''

''Lily, don't you worry about all of that. Your aunt is looking after them beautifully. There's no need for you to sacrifice your own happiness.''

''Well, it's been harder and harder being under the same roof, specially in the nights, with Lionel so close. You understand, feeling about the master the way you do. A body has urges, doesn't she? And you know what the men can be, all impatient-like.''

''Oh, yes,'' Georgia said, smothering a laugh. ''I do know. Well, perhaps you had better accept him and have the banns called, Lily, before there's a child to baptize. If you love him, and you want to be with him, then there's nothing in the world that should stop you.''

''Oh, thank you, missus,'' Lily said with a great sigh of relief. ''I wasn't sure that you'd approve. I wasn't even sure it was the right thing to do, marrying a man not from my village, what with living here and all.''

''What has that to do with anything?'' Georgia asked, frowning.

''Well, nothing, really, missus, except people already say that I've overstepped myself.''

''*Overstepped* yourself? How, Lily? It isn't as if you've been living in a palace. You've been struggling harder than most of the villagers.''

''No, it isn't that—it's not that at all, for folks know how it is here. It's Lord Brabourne, missus, and all the time he spends here, and things he's been saying at Ravenswalk about him and me, and they're not true, missus, sure as the day is long.''

''Oh, Lily . . . oh, of course. I see. I do see. I know how awful it feels to be subjected to such rumors, believe me. I'll have a word with Cyril. Don't you worry about it. I'm sure no one really believes it anyway. Gossip is only the work of idle tongues. Lionel Martin doesn't believe it for a minute, does he?''

''No, but it angers him. You'll notice how he stays out of his lordship's way, for fear of losing his temper and knocking him down.''

''He's a fine man, Lily, and a handsome one.''

Lily giggled. ''Well, missus, he's brawny enough, isn't he, and he'll be a good provider too. I'll have a word with him today, and we'll be making our plans. His mum will be glad enough that he's settling down, that's for sure, for she'd been after him to get a wife and babes. And we may stay on here afterward?''

''Yes, naturally. I don't know what we'd do without you.''

''Your water's cooling, missus. Thank you, missus.'' She curtsied and hurried out.

Georgia felt a surge of impatience with Cyril for bandying Lily's name about so. There were times she wanted to shake the boy until his teeth rattled, despite his improved attitude. Cyril would have to do an extraordinary amount of improving before he was actually likable. For him to be roostering around, crowing that he had in some way compromised Lily when the situation could not have been more different, was absolutely infuriating.

But there were a great many things on her mind, and Cyril was the least of them. She also had to find a way to broach the subject of Lord Raven and the monkshood to Nicholas, now that he was well. She knew how upset he'd be and so she was reluctant, but it really couldn't be put off. Someone had to intervene. She'd been thinking for weeks on it, wondering how to counteract the harm that had been done, playing with different herbs in her mind. Now that the spring had finally arrived, she had the opportunity to cull new, fresh herbs, if she could only think of a combination that might be fitting. There was no time like the present, she decided, for if she was going to give Nicholas the news, she really ought to have some sort of remedy in hand.

She slipped out of bed, looking down at her naked body with a certain degree of amazement. And then she gave herself a thorough wash and, wrapping herself in a towel, went next door to dress.

Georgia was busily collecting hawthorn from among the hedgerows alongside the road into the village when a female voice came unexpectedly over her shoulder in a slight French accent.

"Ah," it said mischievously, "the sign of rebirth, and also the flower of lovers. I wonder which it is in this case?"

Georgia straightened to find a most attractive woman regarding her quizzically. She was beautifully dressed, her pelisse cut in the latest fashion, her chestnut curls most becomingly arranged beneath her fashionable bonnet. But her face was open, her expression warmly amused, and Georgia relaxed, relieved to see the woman had not spoken mockingly. Georgia knew exactly how she looked in her worn dress, down on her knees in the dirt. "You seem to know something about herbs, ma'am," she said, standing and brushing off her dress as best she could.

"A little something. I could not help but notice that your basket also contains shepherd's purse and deadnettle. I therefore deduced that you knew something of the healing arts yourself."

"A little something," Georgia replied with a smile. "Nowhere near as much as I'd like."

"Yes, one can never learn too much. Is it a particular remedy you are gathering? You must forgive my curiosity. I am a stranger here. My carriage had a small problem and I am walking while it is being seen to. I could not resist intruding, for I find herbs a fascinating subject."

"You do not intrude in the least, ma'am. It is not often that I meet someone who has any real knowledge. In truth, you might be able to aid me, for I confess I am confused."

"I would be pleased to try," the woman said, appearing delighted. "Why don't you give me the instance?"

"There is an elderly gentleman, ma'am, who was stricken by apoplexy—at least, that much I believe is true. However, since the original incident, he has been administered a strange herbal tisane. Peppermint, chamomile, a number of other harmless ingredients make up the majority of the herbs, but there is also a small amount of monkshood."

"Monkshood—good heavens!" the woman said, looking shocked. "What fool would add such a dangerous thing?"

"That's just it, ma'am. Very few people are aware of the long-reaching effects. It is not given in such a quantity as to be deadly. In my estimation, taken twice daily in the amount present, it is just enough to be extremely incapacitating to the nervous system, certainly enough to render the poor man useless. The person who prescribed the herb was either very ignorant or very, very clever."

"Yes . . . I would have to agree. And my first assumption would be ignorance, although human nature is unfortunately flawed in other ways. Would there be a reason for deliberate mischief here?"

"I believe so, although that would be a terrible charge to bring. Unfortunately, the circumstances are not such that there is much I can do. Even if I could find an antidote, administering it would be very difficult, for I do not have access to the gentleman in question. And in the meantime, the poor man suffers. But even if I could help him, what antidote could I give him? I thought a nerve stimulant would be helpful, but I cannot think what would counteract the effect of the actual poison."

"No, I cannot think of anything directly," said the woman, tapping her mouth. "He would have to have his system cleaned of the monkshood first. So initially a purifier would be necessary—speedwell, perhaps, the entire plant infused and given three times a day. And then, something to restore strength and clarity. Vervain? It grows down here, doesn't it?"

"But does not flower until June, ma'am. However, I do have some dried betony."

"Yes—yes, that might do. Let me see. Let me see . . ."

Georgia listened carefully as the woman rattled off a list of possibilities. After a long and elucidating discussion, a footman appeared.

"My lady, we have repaired the damage to the wheel. We are ready to proceed."

"Thank you, Penally. My dear, it was a great pleasure speaking with you. I do hope you find a solution to your difficulty."

"Thank you. And thank you so much for your advice. I shall give it great consideration." Georgia went back to her collecting, her mind working over the information she'd been given. It made her smile to think that Frenchwomen not only knew their clothes and their food, but apparently they knew their healing herbs as well.

Not much later, her collecting done, she made her way back to the Close, thinking that it surely must be coming up to lunchtime and wondering if the boys had returned from Ravenswalk. But the garden was quiet for once, and she went through the back door. Her ear was caught by the murmur of voices in the sitting room, and she started toward it, then stopped directly outside the open door in astonishment as she recognized the voice of the woman she had been conversing with not even an hour before. She could see only her profile, but she was sure she was correct.

"Nicholas, I do not understand this nonsense," the woman was saying. "I have not come all the way from London to have you fly in the face of reason and your own reputation. What must I say to you to convince you?"

"There is not much, Marguerite. Let Jacqueline do her worst. She's done it already. I can't see how I can possibly pretty the picture at this point."

"But that is my point exactly. Jacqueline has only just returned to London from her Italian sojourn. She is already planting the stories in influential ears. Nicholas, she wasted no time. You never bothered to defend yourself the first time around—you simply left the country. What were people to think? I never believed the story myself, but then, I know Jacqueline. But you cannot allow the old rumor to resurface, nor this new nonsense she is putting about concerning your wife!''

"And what nonsense is that?" he asked wearily. "That Georgia was her bloody seamstress? That Georgia has no proper connections?"

"That she was Herton's whore, and after that, his son's," Marguerite said harshly, and Georgia, who had just been about to walk in, froze, her hand creeping to her throat.

Nicholas stared at Marguerite. "No—she wouldn't go so far. Oh, damn the bitch!" And then he caught himself. "I beg your pardon, Marguerite. I did not mean to insult you in any way, but it is beyond belief."

"Nicholas, we might not know each other very well, but my husband and his sister have always thought very highly of you, and the few times we met, I shared their opinion. George does not know I have come down, for he would no doubt tell me not to interfere. But I thought that I must, for the situation does not seem right, and I feel a certain responsibility. Jacqueline told me why you married, and she was annoyed in the extreme about it, I might add. I know nothing about your wife, but your judgment—with the exception of leaving the country in the wake of Jacqueline's accusation—strikes me as being sound. But I do not understand why you are being so stubborn. Why will you not go to London and defend yourself and your wife? Surely she cannot be that unpresentable?"

"Georgia is not unpresentable in the least," Nicholas said, his voice tinged with anger. "However, she is shy. She also is uncomfortable with the idea of mixing with the *ton,* for she comes from a different world. She is accustomed to a very simple life."

"Ah," said Marguerite. "Perhaps that explains why you are living like this?" She waved her hand around her.

"We are living like this, Marguerite, because this is what Jacqueline allowed to happen to Raven's Close."

"Nicholas, it is no good trying to flummox me. You could easily have afforded to refurbish this house properly, and done it immediately upon your return. George has many interesting sources, and he tells me that you took the money your father left you and turned it into a substantial fortune. A very substantial fortune."

Georgia waited for Nicholas to deny this. But instead he only rubbed his neck and then dropped his hand. "You surprise me," he said. "It is not common knowledge."

Georgia stared at him, not at all sure she had heard him correctly.

"Yes," Marguerite said. "I think perhaps you must care for your wife very much to choose to live in these conditions, for I can think of no other reason. I assume your wife does not know the truth?"

"You are far too astute, Marguerite."

"It is my French blood."

"And perhaps using that French astuteness, you will understand now why I am reluctant to take Georgia to London and expose her to a life she might find painful. My reputation is not of consequence next to her happiness. I am sure that in time she will be more secure in her position, but for the time being, we live quietly and simply."

"Nicholas?" Georgia said from the doorway, her throat so tight it was hard to speak.

Nicholas' head snapped around, and he stood, his face mirroring his dismay. Marguerite looked equally dismayed as well as very surprised, but Georgia did not even take her in.

"Georgia, I didn't mean for you to hear—" Nicholas started to say, but she cut him off.

"Is it true? You have a fortune?" She walked into the room, so shocked she was almost numb.

"Yes," he said uncomfortably. "It is true." He rubbed his neck again and looked down.

"You've been willing to suffer these conditions when you didn't have to at all? And you say you did it for me?"

"Yes."

"But why, Nicholas? Why? You did not even know me at the beginning! Why should you care how I felt?"

"You were my wife," he said quietly. "I did not want to frighten you away from me."

"Frighten me away? How would you have done that? You were nothing but kind."

His mouth lifted in a half-smile. "If you recall, you

257

made it very clear that you only married me because I was poor.''

Georgia slowly nodded. ''Yes. That's true. But at the time I believed you *were* poor. Why else would you have married me? No doubt there would have been a hundred women willing to marry you for a fortune.''

''Perhaps. Perhaps not. It doesn't matter—you were the one I wanted. And you needed rescuing. And you loved the Close.''

''Yes . . . but so did you. You could have afforded skilled workmen to restore it, and yet you have labored until your hands were raw and your body stiff with cold, and you have gone hungry—oh, Nicholas, just think of all the sides of beef you could have had!''

He burst into laughter. ''I have—oh, believe me, I have.''

They had both forgotten about Marguerite, who had moved over to the window and was watching them, doing her level best to keep her face composed.

''I cannot understand it,'' Georgia said. ''You might have told me the truth and saved yourself a great deal of trouble and suffering.''

''No, I don't think the truth would have done at all. It would have been a serious stumbling block in your courtship.''

''My courtship? What courtship?''

''Sweetheart, what in God's name do you think the last four months have been about?''

''I have no idea, save that you said you thought I was accustomed to poverty. Which I am, but your deliberately pretending to be impoverished is the strangest notion of a courtship I have ever heard.''

''Well, you have to remember I thought I was battling your love for a poor but handsome farmer. And you did say that my being poor made you more comfortable with me. You wouldn't let me get a word in edgewise to correct your mistaken assumption, and as I wanted to win you over sooner rather than later, I decided to use everything at my disposal. My strategy worked, didn't it?''

Georgia considered. Little vignettes of their life over the last few months flashed through her mind: Nicholas balancing precariously on a ladder, calling something down over his shoulder to her about a dropped hammer; Nicholas, Raleigh at his heel, swearing fluently under his breath as he tried to dislodge his ax from the block where it had become stuck; Nicholas coming in soaking wet from yet another sojourn on the roof and presenting her with a scraggly bird's nest as if he had been presenting her with the finest of jewels—which, as far as she was concerned, he had been. And there had been the expression on his face when she had presented him with his shirts, a look first of surprise and then genuine appreciation, this when he could no doubt have ordered as many shirts as he pleased from London. None of the struggling had been necessary and yet he had managed it all with good grace while constantly stoking fires and carrying water and battling with the elements. Would she have fallen in love with him so easily had she not had the advantage of knowing him in that way? Perhaps not.

"Georgia? Don't tell me after the fact that it was all for naught. Oh, please don't. I don't think I could bear it."

She smiled. "It wasn't for naught in the least. I have enjoyed the last months in the extreme—save for your illness, but you couldn't help that. I've loved working next to you, seeing our labors bear fruit, and the long winter nights, trying to keep warm in the sitting room, and all the conversations we had, and . . . oh, all sorts of things. And I think that perhaps you have enjoyed them too. You have, haven't you?"

"I must confess, there has been something very satisfying about rebuilding this house with my own hands, raw or no. But I think it might be time to hand the hammer over to more competent workers and get on with other things. I do have a business I've been neglecting." He ran his hand through his hair and regarded her carefully. "You have taken the news much better than I ever anticipated, Georgia. Are you truly sure you don't mind about my not being impoverished?"

Georgia tilted her chin. "It is you I love, Nicholas, not your financial condition. If I could love you when you were impoverished, then I can just as easily love you now that you are rich. I do not think you have much faith in my ability to adjust. I am very flexible, you know. In fact, now that I have had a few minutes to think about it, there is no reason I shouldn't be pleased that you have money to spend, for now you can lavish it on the house, and we can buy a much larger assortment of plants for the gardens, and maybe even some furniture. We can turn the library into your study, and you will have a nice private place to sit and do your business—Nicholas, what *is* your business?"

"Export," he said, his gray eyes alight with laughter.

"Oh. You will have to tell me all about it . . . Good heavens, Nicholas—Binkley! Oh, poor Binkley. Really, you have been most unfair to him, forcing him to live like this for my sake. He does have his standards, you know. I shall have to apologize to him."

Nicholas grinned. "Oh, don't do that. Binkley would be most upset. God, how I love you, sweetheart. I'm still not sure how I ever became so damned lucky as to find you." He took her chin and was just bending his head to kiss her when he was distracted by a discreet cough and glanced over to see Marguerite gazing out the window. "Oh, good Lord. I beg your pardon, Marguerite. I quite forgot you were there."

"I can understand why you might have. Please, do not concern yourself in the least. I found the period of your forgetfulness most illuminating."

"Illuminating?" he said dryly. "I should think it would have been the exact opposite. But allow me to introduce my wife. Georgia, Lady Clarke."

"What a delightful surprise," Marguerite said with a smile. "Your husband is an old friend of my husband's family. I am pleased to see he is so happy in his marriage."

Georgia blushed. "You must think our situation most peculiar."

"I think the situation is one of the most enchanting I have ever come across. I am a great devotee of love matches, having made one myself. But this marriage positively shines with originality, and as I am also a great admirer of originality, I am doubly enchanted. Nicholas, you really must bring your wife to London. Not only is she a beauty, she is unaffected. Jacqueline would spit with fury, for Georgia is bound to be an instant success, and all of Jacqueline's rumor-mongering would instantly be dispelled.''

"Marguerite, I have told you, Georgia is not interested in—'' Nicholas began, but Georgia interrupted him.

"I beg your pardon, Nicholas, but I would like to speak for myself,'' Georgia said, turning to Marguerite. "I did not mean to eavesdrop, for I am forever scolding Nicholas' cousin for the practice, but I overheard what you said about Lady Raven and the stories she is spreading about Nicholas. I do not know what they are, but I do know what she is capable of, for I spent nearly a year in her employ, and she can be very vicious. I cannot stand by and let her once again drag Nicholas' name through the mud, most certainly not on my account.''

"Georgia, it is *not* on your account,'' Nicholas said with frustration.

"Even if it is not, if I can help by going to London, then I shall. But I am afraid I have no proper education in such matters, Lady Clarke. You have already seen how appalling my manners are. I would not want to do Nicholas any more damage.''

"Your manners are charming, and as I said, unaffected. I find you infinitely refreshing, my dear Georgia. And if you decide to come up to London, then I shall be more than happy to help you in any way that I can, not that I can see anything that needs improving.''

"Oh, but there is, for I am not the least respectable! I fear making a terrible fool of myself and embarrassing Nicholas. But thank you so much for offering to help me. Between yourself and Nicholas and Binkley, I should find a way to manage.''

"And who is this Binkley I keep hearing about?''

"My manservant,'' Nicholas said. "And before you throw yourself headlong into this foolish scheme, Georgia, I must caution you, the situation is a great deal more complicated than you realize. You have no idea what you would have to face. If you thought Christmas services were bad, London during the Season would be a hundred times worse. I will not put you through that.''

"I am much stronger than you think, Nicholas. And if Jacqueline is saying damaging things about you, then you must stand up for yourself. Furthermore, it would be better if I was at your side while you do it, for I will not have it said about you that you married a . . . a whore. I won't, for it only damages your reputation more.''

''Georgia—''

''I can do anything I set my mind to, and if I set it to being a lady, then that is what I will be, even if I wasn't born to the part.''

Marguerite clapped her hands together. ''Bravo, my dear! An excellent speech! You see, I knew you had fine judgment, Nicholas. I believe you may have outdone yourself in your choice of wife. What say you now?''

''I say that I stand firm in my position. I will not drag Georgia through a bed of scandal.''

Georgia stubbornly dug in. ''Nicholas, look at what you have already gone through because of that dreadful woman. And it is no good using me for an excuse, for I am more than willing to help you.''

''Georgia, I don't want your help in this. For the love of God, can't you see that I'm doing everything I can to keep you out of it? Jacqueline has already done you enough damage. I will not see her hurt you any more.''

''And can't you see that she hurts me by hurting you? Nicholas, you are the bravest man I have ever known, and you have fought many difficult battles and won. Why do you shy from this one?''

''It is a very good question,'' Marguerite said. ''Have you an answer for us?''

Nicholas raked his hand through his hair with a noise that sounded remarkably like a smothered curse.

''Nicholas?'' Georgia echoed.

''It's a damned conspiracy,'' he said.''One would think the two of you were working together.''

''Not working together,'' Marguerite said, ''but we both care about you. Nicholas, I only came down because I could not bear to see my sister start up the same old stories and create new ones. My intentions were to warn you and to discover the truth of the matter for myself.''

''Your *sister*?'' Georgia said, appalled. ''Lady Raven is your sister?''

''She is, and I have no more liking for her than you, so you needn't worry in the least about offending me. However, you told me a story earlier on the verge of the road when neither of us realized the identity of the other. Now that I know your connection to the family, I find myself greatly disturbed. I am correct in believing the man in question is Lord Raven?''

Georgia bit her lip, knowing what was coming. "Yes. You are correct.''

"And the person you suspect of mischief is my sister, is it not?''

Georgia bowed her head.

"And so. It is as I thought. Please, my dear, do not feel bad. I admire you for your concern. And if you are correct, then a very great mischief has been done indeed, and must be corrected.''

"Georgia, what is this?'' Nicholas asked, his voice suddenly sharp.

"I met Lady Clarke earlier,'' she said. "I was gathering herbs for your uncle, and as she expressed an interest, I told her I was seeking a remedy for monkshood. It is a poison, Nicholas. According to Mr. Jerome, your uncle has been ingesting it since the onset of his illness.''

"Sweet Christ,'' Nicholas whispered, the blood leaving his face. "She's been poisoning him?''

Georgia gripped her hands together, feeling terrible. But she could not deny the facts. "Mr. Jerome was very clear on the fact that Jacqueline had prescribed your uncle's medicinal tisane and mixed it herself. Perhaps her inclusion of a pinch of monkshood was intended as a cure.''

"Jacqueline would know its poisonous properties well enough,'' Marguerite said as calmly as she could manage.

"Oh, dear God in heaven,'' Nicholas said. "But why? Why would she do such a thing? She surely wouldn't want him dead, for then all control of the properties would pass away from her to Cyril.''

"But you must understand that it's not a large enough dosage to kill. Only a tiny amount, enough to incapacitate. I could not convince Mr. Jerome to let me offer another remedy. Jacqueline has him convinced her tisane is keeping your uncle alive, and his first loyalty is to Lord Raven.''

"How could she do such a spiteful thing!'' Nicholas

said furiously. "The poor man—poisoned by his own wife!"

"I have always wondered," Marguerite said, thoughtfully tapping her mouth, "whether Jacqueline had not had a hand in her first husband's death."

"Oh, surely not!" Georgia said, shocked.

"I have no actual proof, and I have never mentioned my suspicions to another soul, but you must understand how angry and bitter she was about her marriage."

"He was a wealthy tradesman, was he not?" Nicholas asked, frowning.

"Yes, and a great deal older than she. It was an ill-advised marriage, and loveless."

"Was she forced to it?" Georgia asked, thinking of herself and Baggie.

"Oh, no. It was her own choice. She thought to escape what she considered the shackles of her family. Jacqueline married Francis Humphrey because she thought she would rise in the world. It did not happen as she had anticipated."

Nicholas ran his hand over the arm of his chair. "Do enlighten us some more, Marguerite," he said, examining his fingertip as if it were the most fascinating thing in the world.

"You must remember that we grew up under straitened circumstances, Nicholas. Jacqueline always felt deprived of what she saw as her correct position in life."

"She was lucky that your father managed to get you out of France at all," Nicholas said tightly. "As I remember hearing, it was an extremely close call."

"Yes, it is true. And I am fortunate, for I was too young to remember, whereas my sisters could never forget. Perhaps that was part of the trouble with Jacqueline. She never forgot for a moment what it had been like being the daughter of the respected Comte de Give, living in a grand chateau with many servants, beautiful clothes, plentiful food. But here in England there were so many refugees, and without money, a title meant nothing. Our father lost his health, and our mother supported us by working. We lived above the shop and we all helped out. But Jacqueline resented having to work at all, and she made life very difficult for everyone."

"Why do I find that so very easy to believe?" Nicholas said. "Was there ever a time that Jacqueline didn't make life difficult?"

Marguerite smiled and shrugged. "Not that I can remember, but my father said the de Gives always bred true and she was the image of *grand-mère*. I don't believe he meant it as a compliment. We tried to get along, but Jacqueline never failed to find something to complain about, or some way of taking out her petty jealousies, especially on our sister, who had the misfortune to be beautiful and also blessed with a sweet temperament. Jacqueline did not grow into her looks until later, and was awkward and bad-tempered as a child, so it only made the situation worse. At least I was young enough that Jacqueline usually ignored me. She never considered me competition."

"It seems to me that situation rapidly changed," Nicholas said curtly. "As I heard it, Jacqueline was not very pleased when you married George."

"Well, yes, but that takes me back to the original story. You see, Jacqueline married Francis Humphrey against our mother's wishes and found herself not only unhappy but also trapped. Francis Humphrey may have had money, but he had no inclination to spend it, and worse, no entrée at all into society. Instead, she found herself firmly entrenched in the *bourgeoisie*. There were no gay parties, no extravagant clothes, nothing that a seventeen-year-old girl might desire. She had married into a stolid respectability, and she was miserable. I felt terribly sorry for her."

Nicholas snorted. "Why should you have felt sorry? She got exactly what she asked for."

"Yes, she did," Marguerite said gently. "And although she had always treated us all very badly, and I could not like her, I could still see her misery. She would come home to play the gracious benefactress, but beneath it all I could see her unhappiness and even her desperation."

"Oh, how sad," Georgia said. "To throw away one's life on nothing more than misplaced ambition seems a terrible shame. And look at her now. It is as if she sold her soul to the devil for nothing more than a title and a big house and limitless funds.'' Georgia suddenly pressed her hand over her mouth, hearing what she had said. ''I beg your pardon, Lady Clarke. I forgot myself. I should never have spoken so of your sister.''

''Please, you must call me Marguerite. And you are very insightful, Georgia, for that is exactly what has happened. Jacqueline was always chasing after position and attention, never seeing the things that really mattered. Her vision has only become more narrow with time, until she can see nothing else. Unfortunately, human nature is such that when bitterness and jealousy take hold, they are sometimes impossible to dislodge. It is as if Jacqueline has been consumed by her need to be better than everyone else, more important, more powerful. It does in truth sadden me.''

''Your generosity is extraordinary, considering how she behaved toward you,'' Nicholas said. ''Do not think I didn't hear the stories from Louisa, Marguerite—how Jacqueline behaved at your wedding breakfast, sitting there with eyes narrowed, looking as if she might do you murder.''

''Yes, I remember it well. I was quite upset at the time, although not surprised. Jacqueline was the only family left to me by then, and I had hoped she might be happy for me. But that would have been too much to ask, I realized. After all, I had married not only the man I loved, but I had also married into one of the oldest families in England. It infuriated her, especially as I had met George only because I went to be companion to Louisa after our mother died. Jacqueline was quite pleased when I was the servant, but she hadn't counted on my marrying the eldest son. Suddenly I had not only a young, attractive husband and a beautiful house but also a title.''

Nicholas looked down at his boot. ''How did Humphrey die? It wasn't very long after your wedding, was it?''

''It was only three days later. He died of a broken neck. Jacqueline said he'd tripped and fallen down the stairs. She pretended grief, and I could not challenge her.''

''Oh, damnation,'' Nicholas said tersely. ''Knowing Jacqueline, she probably did push the poor man down the

266

stairs in a fit of pique. And yet you let her come live with you?''

''How could I refuse her, Nicholas? She had no one else, and a year of mourning to observe. She was unhappy where she was, and I had no proof that she was guilty of any crime. We really had no choice.''

''George has always been an extraordinarily patient man.''

''Yes, he has. It was a difficult time, especially seeing Jacqueline carefully stalking all of George's friends and acquaintances during that year of supposed mourning. Unfortunately your uncle became her prime target. But there was nothing I could do to stop it. Your uncle was a close friend of George's mother, and I could not really say that my sister was a viper in pursuit of one of her oldest friends, a man who had only recently lost his wife. Jacqueline behaved so properly. I think everyone but me was astonished when at the end of their respective mourning periods they suddenly married. Jacqueline got exactly what she wanted. Title, position, money—and another loveless marriage, for although your uncle was entranced by her, I know she did not love him.''

''That is an understatement,'' Nicholas said. ''That's the greatest understatement of this entire sorry conversation. No, she didn't love my uncle. And now she's poisoning him, no doubt so that she can retain control over all his affairs. And so here we are. Well, Marguerite. What are we to do now?''

''It is quite simple. Jacqueline must be stopped. She may be my sister, but after learning about this, I cannot sit back and let her continue along this destructive course.''

''And how do you propose to stop her?'' Nicholas said, crossing over to the window and looking out over the garden.

''With the best weapon we have, Nicholas. With the only weapon we have. You.''

He spun around. ''*Me?* Marguerite, you must be mad.''

''Indeed, who else? You are the only person who is capable. We must go immediately to London. . . .''

15

Nicholas took Georgia by the shoulders the moment Marguerite's carriage started off down the drive. "You and I are going to have a long talk," he said. "A very long talk. There is no way in heaven or hell that I will let you go up to London and be attacked by those vultures."

"You may talk as long as you like, but you will not change my mind."

"I have never in my life come across a person as stubborn, as pigheaded, as you, Georgia. Never."

"With the exception of yourself," she said, folding her arms and preparing for battle, for she knew there was a fight ahead. "Marguerite is absolutely right, you know. There's no other way."

Nicholas' brow snapped down. "You may think she's right, but you are sadly lacking in information."

"And whose fault is that? If you choose not to tell me anything, then how am I expected to know? I only discovered you were not poor because I happened to overhear. You keep going on about all the reasons why I shouldn't help you stop Jacqueline, but you have given me nothing concrete. Not one thing."

"Very well," he said curtly. "If you are so damned determined to know, then I will tell you, and to hell with trying to protect you."

"Nicholas, I don't need protection. I know you love me, and I am grateful for that, But I am not a hothouse flower. I have not had a protected life. It seems silly to begin one now."

"Come inside."

"No, let's go into the garden. You're angry and upset, and maybe being out there will help."

"Fine. Whatever you please. It hardly matters to me

where you hear the truth of the matter." He grabbed her hand and pulled her through the house and out the back door into the garden, sitting her down on the bench under the willow. He did not join her, instead choosing to face her, his eyes the color of dark slate.

"All right," she said. "Go ahead."

He pushed his hand through his hair. "Georgia, this is . . . difficult."

"But why, Nicholas? Why?"

"Because I love you. Perhaps if I didn't, it wouldn't matter so damned much to me. I've lived with disgrace for a long time, and I taught myself not to care. But to have you involved, after everything you've already been through—it only makes it ten times worse."

"I don't mind for myself. I'm accustomed to being accused of things I haven't done. But I do mind for you, Nicholas, because you shouldn't have to defend your name against lies. Now tell me. Just what was this rakehell behavior that Jacqueline accused you of?"

"You know, the timing of this mess is fairly unbelievable. Had this been yesterday, I would never have said a single word. Today not only do I find I have little choice, but I worry more than ever over your reaction. I trust you, Georgia, but I do not know how far you are prepared to trust me."

"I showed you how far last night. And that should tell you everything."

"Yes," he said, his voice rough. "But this is different."

"It's not different in the least. Anyway, you can't possibly think I would believe Jacqueline over you. Your uncle might have done, but he was blinded by her. I am not, not at all. Aside from the fact that I know what kind of woman she is, I also know how much she dislikes you."

"No, you don't. And you don't know why she hates me as violently as she does."

"No, I don't. And I wish you would tell me. Whatever it is cannot be that terrible."

He met her eyes evenly. "No? Not even being accused of rape?"

"Rape?" she whispered.

"Exactly. It's an ugly word, isn't it, and one that no doubt strikes a particular horror into your own heart."

"But how? Whom were you meant to have raped?"

"Jacqueline."

"Oh, Nicholas—no. . . . No, it is not possible."

"I'm afraid it is true. Not that I raped her. But that she accused me of the act, yes."

"Oh, God—of all things to have picked, she could not have found one more unjust. . . ." Georgia lifted her head and met his eyes. "Tell me what happened, Nicholas. Please. Tell me exactly how it happened."

He drew in a deep breath and released it, almost as if relieved to have the words finally out. "I told you that I disliked her on sight, the minute I first walked in the door of Ravenswalk. But for her it was a different matter. She knew I disliked her, but that only made it more of a challenge for her. She took one look at me and decided that I was fair game."

"Fair game for what?" Georgia asked. "Surely not to accuse you of rape just because you didn't like her?"

Nicholas managed a smile. "No, sweetheart. Quite the opposite. She had it in mind to seduce me, you see. I was nearly twenty, not altogether inexperienced, and it became quickly obvious that she wanted me as a lover. She was subtle, but not so subtle that I did not catch her meaning. I, in a fashion equally as subtle, let her know I was not interested. But Jacqueline persisted. She wanted something she could not have, and she wasn't going to stop until she had attained it. I cannot tell you the times that I caught glimpses of flesh I most certainly should not have."

"Nicholas. I think I am shocked. I had thought that this morning I had learned I could not be shocked by anything, but I think I am."

"This morning was a bit different, my love. The natural things that happen between two willing people, most especially two willing people who love each other and happen to be married, is absolutely acceptable. But the point here is that this was my uncle's wife, not all that much older than I, and she was pursuing me like a hungry tiger after a piece of flesh. There was nothing more to it than that—it was lust, and lust alone."

"Nicholas, what happened? What *happened?*"

"I woke one night to find her in my bed. She was naked, pressed against me, and at first I didn't know where I was, or even whom I was with. My hand was on her breast. I think she must have put it there, for her hand was covering mine and moving on it, but God only knows. Anyway, I'd been fool enough in my sleep to become aroused, and I think for a moment or two I thought I was elsewhere—with some insignificant woman or another, for her other hand was . . . she was stroking me. Georgia. Forgive me. You shouldn't have to hear this."

"Don't be absurd. Go on."

"I kissed her. God help me, I kissed the bitch and didn't even know whom I was kissing until I smelled her perfume and came to my senses. That happened quickly enough, like having a bucket of ice water thrown over me. I pushed her away from me and told her that if she ever came near me again I would tell my uncle exactly what she was. She was frightened, for she stood to lose everything. I think she must have believed that once she was in bed with me I would succumb to her, give her what she wanted. I told her to leave and she did. It never went beyond that, I swear it."

"Oh, Nicholas—I am sorry. But how did your uncle find out?"

He rubbed his forehead. "That was the ultimate irony, although if I'd had any sense, I should have anticipated it. I made an appointment to see him the next afternoon. It was about arrangements for the Close, but Jacqueline didn't know that. She thought I was going to tell him what had happened. So she panicked, and she went to him first and told him I'd forced myself on her. Not just attempted it, but had succeeded."

"And your uncle believed her? He believed such a thing of you?" Georgia was trembling with outrage.

"Yes. He did. He called me into his study. She was there. And that was an end to it. There was no point in trying to defend myself. As I told you before, he was besotted with Jacqueline. No doubt he imagined I was likewise besotted and was also young and hot-blooded enough to lose my reason over her. He threw me out, and

I left Ravenswalk, only to discover that everywhere I went, the whispers had gone before me. So I went to India. It didn't matter there, for there were many scapegraces in similar situations. I put all my energies into building a fortune. But I never forgot. Not for a moment. And I never forgot the Close.''

Georgia couldn't bear the stark, drawn expression on his face. To have his honor taken from him over such a filthy accusation cut her to the quick. She thought of the first day she had met him, the tears wet on his cheeks as he absorbed the shock of what the Close had become. She thought of the courage he had shown, forcing himself into the sea to save men from the fate he had once nearly met. She thought of his anguish over the small lifeless boy he had brought in, and the long weeks he had been off battling demons too terrible to contemplate. And she thought of his patience with her and the incredible gentleness with which he had tempered his passion. That this same man should be accused of an act as violent, as despicable as rape was beyond belief. It was enough to break her heart. She covered her face with shaking hands.

"Oh, Georgia . . . Georgia, love, don't. Please don't, sweetheart. It's over, it's finished. It happened long ago, and we're here now." He dropped to one knee and gathered her into his arms. "Please don't cry," he whispered against her hair. "Please. I cannot bear it." He moved her hands away and kissed her wet cheeks. "Do you see why I didn't want to tell you?"

"No," she said, sniffling. "If you thought that by keeping it from me you were protecting me, then you were being very silly."

"Was I?" he said with a hint of a smile. "Perhaps I was. I am never quite sure what you will find foolish. But understand that I didn't want that ugly part of the world intruding here, not here where you and I have been happy. It has felt at times as if the outside world could not touch us. I think we both needed a bit of that."

Georgia gave him a long look. "That's another reason you didn't want to tell me, isn't it? You were thinking about Baggie."

"The circumstances may have been different, but it is the same violent act, Georgia," Nicholas said very

272

gently. "And I think you know it now as well as I. And yes, I was concerned that somewhere in the very back of your mind a doubt might linger that I might have done such a thing in some mindless moment. If one man, why not any other?"

"Because I know you, Nicholas. I know you would never be capable of such a thing, despite how hot-blooded and hot-tempered you can be. It's absurd. I'm amazed anyone would believe it."

"But they do, Georgia. They do. Think. In their minds Jacqueline would have no reason to lie about such a thing. She pretended to be terrified of me. She pretended immense relief that I hadn't put my brat in her. Oh, I heard. I heard it all. It didn't seem to occur to anyone that I might have scorned her, that her spite stemmed from that—and her fear of me, which was genuine. So now I stand accused not only of rape but also of raping my uncle's wife. Do you understand how serious a charge that is?"

"I may not be from your world, but I am not stupid," Georgia said indignantly, wiping her eyes and nose on her sleeve for lack of anything else. "It is a terribly serious charge. And Jacqueline has great power and influence, I know. But just as I know that you have told me the truth, apparently Jacqueline's own sister knows it too, and she has offered you a way to amend things. What happens after that is solely up to you, Nicholas, but we must make a beginning."

He dropped to the ground and shoved his hands against his temples. "Do you have any idea—any idea at all—of what you would be facing if we went up to London?"

"I think so. But with Marguerite's patronage behind you, Nicholas, surely people would think twice. After all, she would be publicly flying in her sister's face. What other way to clear you name is there?"

"Damnation!" he finally said. "You're determined to put yourself through this, aren't you?"

"Yes," she said calmly. "I am. What you have been through is too awful, and the unfairness is too much. And then there is your uncle to consider, and Cyril also. You cannot let Jacqueline continue along her present course, Nicholas. As Marguerite pointed out, you are the only person who can change it. I will help you as best I can. You thought I would be discouraged, but I'm not. I'm not. I hate her. I hate her more than I ever thought it was possible to hate another human, but I do, and I want to see justice done for everyone. And that includes our un-born children, Nicholas. It is wrong for them to be born in shame for no good reason.''

He pulled absently at the grass. ''You are right, of course,'' he said after a long silence. ''Perhaps I've been dreaming. I suppose I was foolish to think that it might all evaporate, that people would forget with time—even that Jacqueline might choose to forget her hatred and ob-session in favor of some other distraction. But it has not proved to be true, has it? Never mind Jacqueline. Im-mediately I returned, the village was rife with the old rumors.''

''Yes, I know. And yet when they needed you, they came to you, and you proved yourself a very good and courageous man. Do you think they would have helped as they did during your illness if they had truly believed you were guilty of debauchery? Nicholas, believe me, I know. My mother was accused often of being an accom-plice of the devil's, for our village was small and ignorant and her healing arts were extraordinary. But they forgot soon enough when one of their own was ill. If they had really believed they would be tainted by the devil, they never would have come again, but they always did. It is the same with you. I cannot believe many a person in the village, and most likely not very many of the *ton*, truly think you're really guilty. But accusations are terrible things, for they leave doubt unless proof is offered up against them.''

''And that's just it, sweetheart. That's just it. How does one offer proof against a thing that can't be proved? Who is to say that I did not commit this act? I have no influ-ence. I have no title. I have only Jacqueline's word against mine, and my uncle's censure. Even Cyril believes I did this to Jacqueline—that much is more than apparent. Do you see what I have done to you, Georgia? Do you see what you have married? And you thought you were a threat to my respectability.'' He laughed harshly. ''It's a damned joke, isn't it? Here you discover in one day that

274

your husband has a fortune, and there is nowhere to spend it save the two-mile periphery of the Close.''

"And that is quite enough," Georgia said firmly. "I will not listen to you indulging yourself in self-pity, not when there are solutions at hand. Now. To begin. We will go to London. We will accept Marguerite's offer of hospitality."

"There is no need," Nicholas said, pushing himself to his feet and straightening to his full height. "I have a town house of my own. It is not only large, it is also respectably located."

"You have a house in London? My goodness. Wait— does that mean you agree? Oh, Nicholas!"

"I will not have you look upon me as self-pitying. It is a most unattractive trait. And if you are bound and determined to do this thing, then who am I to stand in your way? But, Georgia, I will not warn you again of the hell you will be put through." He smiled briefly. "I admit, if you hadn't brought our children into it, I might have stood my ground forever. I am sure you introduced the subject quite deliberately in order to twist my arm."

"Oh, Nicholas," she said lightly, "never mind the children. What about Binkley? You forget his reputation. He deserves to have some respectability after everything you've subjected him to."

"Yes, in truth, I hadn't considered Binkley. I am sure he will be pleased in the extreme to return to London and force sartorial splendor upon me. Very well, Georgia. You will have it your own way, and the consequences be damned. But when you walk into the full force of the havoc Jacqueline has wreaked, then remember it was you who asked. You have never experienced the sort of snubs and subtle digs the *ton* is capable of producing."

"It will be perfect," Georgia said with satisfaction, standing and looking across the garden. "We will bring Pascal, naturally, for we cannot leave him behind, and Cyril is guaranteed to insist on coming, for he will not be willing to let go of his personal crusade. It might, in fact, be a perfect solution to the problem of Cyril, for he needs an introduction to life outside of Ravenswalk if he is to properly take on his responsibilities. He has been shut away too long. He's been bandying about Lily's name, by the way, implying all sorts of things between them. Martin is not in the least pleased. I said I'd mention it to you.''

''The blasted young cub,'' Nicholas said impatiently. ''I'll have a word with him. And you're right. He could use some town polish—and apparently some exposure to young . . . young ladies. I suppose he is that age, isn't he?''

''Apparently,'' Georgia said dryly. ''I think he's been coming to it for some time. He showed up one night in my turret with a most interesting suggestion. I dispatched him. In fact it was the night before I found you in the woods. I thought Cyril was upset that I'd given him an earful.''

''Good God. I don't know whether to laugh or to take his head off. Ah, well. No harm done, and he hasn't tried it since, has he?''

''Certainly not. He was a bit miffed that I married you so shortly thereafter. I think it must be hard on him, resembling you so closely but not yet being grown.''

''I would imagine so. In fact I've worried a great deal over the fact that Jacqueline would not be pleased by the resemblance and would take out her pique on him. I wonder how she'll react to Cyril coming to London with us— and that's a problem, isn't it?'' He frowned heavily. ''I hadn't thought about that.''

''What, Nicholas?''

''I certainly don't want any of my reputation rubbing off on Cyril. If things do not go well, and they might well go very badly, it wouldn't be fair to have Cyril connected to me. I'll have to have a talk with him about that as well. He should certainly be set straight on some things, and it is only fair to forewarn him. We are inviting him to a bloodbath, after all. Georgia, sweetheart, are you not frightened?''

''Naturally I am,'' she said cheerfully, ''but it is only because I have much to learn. Nicholas, you cannot so quickly have lost sight of what is important?''

''I know that I love you. Other than that I know that I would like to have this damned onus off my head. I know that I would like to see my uncle well again and free of Jacqueline. And I know that I would like many children, and that you will no doubt refuse to give them to me until I have accomplished the second and third matters. So. I will send a note around immediately to Ravenswalk to let Marguerite know of our decision.''

"There is no need. You can tell her yourself. She will be coming by later this afternoon to help me mix the medicine for your uncle. We've agreed it is best if it is she who gives the formula to Mr. Jerome, saying that Jacqueline sent it with her from London. That way he will have no doubt about administering it. It is a very new remedy Jacqueline discovered in Italy, a wonder cure. He is to dispose of the old medicine immediately. Naturally Marguerite hurried down with it when Jacqueline found herself taken with a chill and unable to travel.''

"You sly puss—when did you have this conversation, may I ask?''

"When you went out to call for Marguerite's carriage.''

Nicholas chucked her chin. "You are dangerous. It's a very good thing for me that you're on my side.''

"Nicholas, I am always on your side—except when I'm arguing with you,'' she said with a grin. "And then it's only because you make no sense.''

"I'm not even going to attempt getting into that with you. I've had quite enough conflict and emotion for one day. And where are those confounded boys? Surely they should be back from Ravenswalk by now? I miss their noise.''

"I am sure that they will be returning any moment. No doubt Cyril is showing Pascal over every square inch of his vast property.''

"Then I shall get on with catching up with my paperwork. I may not have a property anywhere near the size of Ravenswalk, but I do have a small empire on paper. Georgia, love, you're quite sure you can deal with it?''

"Nicholas, I've always longed for an empire, didn't I tell you?'' She laughed and kissed him. "Now, I must get on with my gardening, for if we are to go to London shortly, there are things that need doing. Go about your business, for no doubt there will be many other matters to claim your attention before we leave.''

"No doubt,'' he said. "You being one of them. All

right, sweetheart. I'll begin preparing for the onslaught. God only knows, we're going to need preparation. A good two weeks should be appropriate."

"For a troll-slayer you are extraordinarily reticent," she remarked. "Or perhaps you are just extraordinarily modest. Whichever it is, sharpen your sword, for you're going out to do battle again, and this time you're going to have me at your side."

His face sobered and he touched her cheek with his finger. "Do you know, my love, with you at my side I believe almost anything is possible. But we shall see. We shall see. This is still against my better judgment, I'll have you know. But who am I to refuse you anything you desire?" He kissed her softly, and Georgia watched after him until he had disappeared through the door. She was not going to let Nicholas know in any fashion just how terrified she really was.

Marguerite, who had been delighted to hear of Nicholas' decision, chatted easily as she worked side by side with Georgia, and Georgia found that she felt surprisingly comfortable in her company, for Marguerite had no grand airs at all. "Have you any clothes that will suit for London?" Marguerite asked.

"Only one simple muslin dress I made myself, and a winter walking dress. We have not needed finery down here."

"It is time for all of that to change. If Nicholas does not plan to leave for two weeks, then I shall take your measurements and have my modiste begin work on a wardrobe immediately."

"It is an extraordinary thought, having someone else make clothes for me."

"And a nice change. Have no fear. You can have absolute faith in Madame Girondaise. She is deliciously expensive, and worth every penny."

"Oh, but Nicholas—"

"Is a very wealthy man. He will be delighted to finally be allowed to lavish money on you."

"I haven't quite adjusted to the idea," Georgia said, a dimple appearing in her cheek.

"He most certainly had the wool pulled over your eyes.

What a very wonderful story it makes. And what a dear man to court you as a pauper. I like him more by the minute. Was he correct, my dear? Would you have refused to marry him had you known the truth?''

"Most probably," Georgia said, "for it would not have seemed right. I would have felt I was taking advantage of his plight. But now it is hard to say, for I did not love him, nor even know him at the time. I was in desperate need of escape, and Nicholas' offer was the only avenue open to me.''

"Was my sister really that cruel to you?"

Georgia hesitated. "She kept me very busy," she finally said as tactfully as she could manage.

"What you mean is that she exploited you."

"I have never needed much sleep," Georgia said, a little smile creeping onto her face. "What are a few lost nights here and there? And as I was not to leave my turret unless I was taking exercise or attending to a fitting, sewing gave me something to do.''

"Oh, my dear—it was worse for you than I thought. Jacqueline never has liked to have anyone prettier than herself about, so no doubt that was why she kept you shut away. She's always been dreadfully jealous. And here you are, so young and fresh and attractive, as sweet as she is sour. I should think it drove her quite mad.''

"I don't know," Georgia said dryly. "She never said."

Marguerite laughed lightly. "She wouldn't, though, would she? She would only gnash her teeth and make your life as miserable as possible. I've seen it before. And it sounds as if she succeeded.''

"She did—until the night that Nicholas scaled the walls and came through my bedroom window, suggesting that I marry him.''

Marguerite grinned with delight. "He didn't."

"But he did. He was very businesslike about it. He had a problem, and I had a problem, and it made no difference to him in the least that we'd met only once before in the woods, or that I had absolutely no breeding. He wanted the Close, and he needed a wife in short order if he were to have it. He was very much a gentleman," she hastened to add.

"I begin to see the origin of Jacqueline's rumors. But

the truth could not be more different. I was most interested," she continued, cutting a piece of dried root and putting it in the mortar, "to hear at Ravenswalk of a ship foundering off the coast. I also heard that Nicholas became gravely ill as a result of his actions that night, and that he was ill until very recently."

Georgia explained everything that has happened, and her theory about it. "There has been a change in him since his recovery," she said, taking the ground angelica Marguerite handed her and adding it to the bowl. "I don't know quite how to explain it, except to say that he seems more at peace with himself."

"It is a most fascinating story," Marguerite said, considering. "And I think your theory sound. How fortunate that you kept the doctor away from him."

"I felt Nicholas needed every drop of blood in his body," Georgia said, smiling. "My mother taught me a healthy disregard of most doctors."

"She was very wise, your mother. You learned about herbs from her?"

"Yes, although she died when I was fairly young, so much of what I know I have taken from her notes. But I could not find anything at all about mental absentia. I had to improvise as best I could."

"You were very successful. Nicholas seems perfectly well. I would never have guessed anything had been amiss. Tell me, what sort of treatment did you use?"

Georgia happily launched into a description, and was in the middle of giving Marguerite a formula she had devised, when Pascal came flying through the door. "Pascal, where have you been? I was beginning to worry!"

"Je m'excuse, madame," he said to Georgia, looking at Marguerite curiously. "Cyril took me out on a horse and taught me almost all of the day. It was *fort amusant.* I fell many times. Did the monsieur enjoy the surprise?"

"He did, very much. Pascal, make your bow to Lady Clarke, please."

"Madame," he said, bobbing at the waist.

"Enchantée," Marguerite replied, and Pascal's face broke into a huge grin.

"Vous parlez français!" he said with delight.

"I do indeed. So, you are young Pascal, the Frenchman. I was just hearing all about you."

"From the madame? She has been everything that is good to me, and the monsieur also. Did you know he saved me from the sea? He is a very brave man."

"Yes, indeed," Marguerite said. "I believe he is. I cannot be surprised."

"He is the finest man I have ever known—except for my dear *papa*, of course, but he is dead. And Cyril is very fine too, naturally."

"And where is Cyril now?" Georgia asked. "Did he stay at Ravenswalk?"

"But no, he has just gone into the sitting room with the monsieur. The monsieur appeared very grave. Is there trouble, madame? Did we stay away too long?"

"No trouble. But there are plans, and I believe Nicholas must have wanted to discuss them with Cyril."

"Because Cyril is a lord?"

"No, because Cyril is his cousin, and the plans concern him—and you too, *petit*."

"Me? It is a good plan?"

She knelt down and touched his face. "How would you like to go to London?"

"To London, madame? Truly?" And then his face fell. "Are you sending me away?"

"Oh, no, *chéri*, not away, not ever. I have told you, you belong to our family, for always. Nicholas and I are going as well, and I believe he is inviting Cyril to join us. And Lady Clarke will be in London also. There are all sorts of wonderful things that we can do."

"I have a little boy just your age," Marguerite said. "His name is Rupert, and he will be delighted to have someone to play with. He finds his younger sisters a terrible trial."

"It sounds very nice, madame. Thank you."

"Now. Georgia, I have been thinking. There are a great many things that must be planned. . . ."

"Please sit down, Cyril." Nicholas indicated a chair, but elected to stand. Cyril appeared uncommonly nervous, and Nicholas imagined it was due to being shut up in the same room with him.

"H-have I done something?" Cyril asked, twisting his hands together.

"Not recently that I'm aware of. Relax, Cyril. I'm not g_ _ _g to box your ears. However, it's long past time that we had a talk, and there are a great many things I wish to say to you."

"Oh?" Cyril said, the word dripping with sarcasm. "I cannot think what you could p-possibly wish to say to m-me."

"To begin with," Nicholas said, trying to keep a hold on his temper, "I would like to thank you."

"Thank me?" Cyril said with surprise. "F-for what?"

"For a number of things. For all you have done here, which has been considerable. And for the return of the bedroom furniture and your hard work there too. You did an excellent job. I was mightily impressed."

Cyril flushed a deep red.

"And I'd-like to thank you for looking after Georgia while I was ill, and Pascal. You acted with honor and I am grateful to you."

"Thank you," he muttered.

"Not at all. There is one small matter which I think I should address, however, and don't bother flying into the boughs over it. It has come to my attention that you've been exaggerating your . . . ah . . . your relationship with Lily. I can quite understand why, as she's a pretty thing, but it is making both her and Martin unhappy. If you want a woman, it's easy enough to arrange."

"How d-dare you!" Cyril hissed, leaping to his feet, his eyes flashing with anger. "How d-dare you speak of such things to m-me? Do you think I am s-some innocent? And you, corrupt as you are, offering to f-find me a woman, that's laughable."

"Ah, so. The gloves are off, are they? Very well, Cyril. Then it's time for plain speaking."

"As you w-wish. But j-just remember you invited it."

"I not only invited it, I welcome it. So let's have it out once and for all. Just what have you been told I did that caused your father to send me away?"

Cyril looked at him with contempt. "D-do you think I don't know the truth? P-perhaps you hope I think it was a g-gambling offense, or maybe that you impregnated one of the ch-chambermaids? Wake up, N-Nicholas. I know all about your d-debauchery, what you d-did to Jacqueline.''

"Do you? But then, no one has bothered to mention that the whole thing was fabricated."

"Why do you try to lie about it n-now? D-do you think I will believe you?"

"I have no idea. It's a complicated situation. I'm not surprised you believe the old story, for after all, your father did."

"What you d-did half-destroyed his health. I d-don't know why you b-bothered to come back."

"I came back because he asked me back, Cyril. He wrote to me in India and asked me to come home. And so I came."

Cyril went white as a ghost. "No—I d-don't believe it."

"Would you like to see the letter?" Nicholas went to the table where he kept his papers and opened a leather box. He withdrew the sheet and handed it to Cyril, who was standing frozen, an expression of real dismay in his eyes.

"Do read it. It's only two lines."

Cyril glanced over the page and handed it back to Nicholas, not meeting his eyes.

"I don't know what happened to change his mind," Nicholas said. "I do know that was the night he fell ill. Do you really think he would have asked me to come home if he believed I had raped his wife?"

Cyril said nothing.

"Cyril, surely you must know what Jacqueline is like by now. I have no idea what your life has been like at Ravenswalk, but I cannot imagine it has been very happy. I was very upset when I met her after your father had married her, for I knew she would not make a good mother to you."

"Certainly not a m-mother," Cyril spat.

"I thought not," he said, putting the letter down on the mantelpiece. "And one of my greatest regrets about leaving England was leaving you, for I loved you very much and worried about your happiness."

"You expect me to b-believe all this d-drivel? You expect me to s-swallow this s-sad tale of poor Nicholas, unfairly m-maligned? You expect me to believe you c-cared about me? If you had, you would n-never have d-done what you did. Never! You think y-you're so f-forceful, so handsome that you c-can take anything you want. You m-must have thought she'd j-just give in to you. You did, d-didn't you?''

''That's not how it happened,'' Nicholas said quietly.

''So—you admit something happened b-between you.''

''Yes. That much is true.''

''Oh, G-God. You are d-despicable. Now you will try to m-make it sound as if she w-was willing, as if she w-wanted you.''

''Yes.''

''L-liar! Liar!'' he shouted. ''She never wanted you. N-never!''

''Cyril, I don't know why the thought upsets you so much. It was not my idea, believe me. It was the last thing in the world I wanted.'' Nicholas raked his hand through his hair. ''Jacqueline had been after me for weeks—she was like a bitch in heat. There was no getting away from her. Every time I turned a corner, she was there with her smiles and insinuations. My God, I even found myself hiding in a closet one day when I heard her coming, just to avoid her. Can you imagine it? Hiding in a broom closet at the age of nineteen? God, I couldn't wait to escape back to university. And how was I supposed to behave around Uncle William, when his wife was chasing me like a light-skirt, exposing herself at every opportunity? I couldn't meet his eye across the dinner table, not with Jacqueline trying to paw me with her foot under the table. He must have thought I'd developed a nervous condition, what with the way I was moving my chair around to avoid her.''

Cyril's face was stained with color, and Nicholas suspected he saw a glint of tears in his eyes. ''It . . . it is not t-true,'' he said. ''N-not true. She h-hates you.''

''Yes. Because I rejected her.''

''*You* r-rejected *her?* That I will n-not believe.''

''It is the truth. The night in question, I'd gone to bed early, for I had important business to discuss with your father the following day and I wanted a clear head. I woke at about two to find Jacqueline in my bed, very much uninvited. I was very angry, and I threw her out. She was resentful, and humiliated, and frightened that I would tell your father, so she turned the tables on me and accused me of raping her.''

"I d-don't believe you!" he cried. "I know the t-truth!"

"Cyril, think. Really think. I am not a stupid man. Nor are you. I would no more have taken my uncle's wife to bed than I would take my own sister to bed, if I had one. Do you understand? It would not only have been monumentally stupid, but also morally wrong, for so many reasons that I won't even bother to go into it. And I most certainly would never force myself on a woman, any woman. Ever.''

"You're j-just trying to t-twist it to m-make yourself sound b-better. And anyway, she w-wasn't related. N-not properly. N-not by blood.''

"What the hell difference does that make?" Nicholas said, seeing no sense in the statement. "She was a member of my family. It comes down to the same damned thing. It would have been incest.''

"It's *not* incest! It's n-not! You have to share b-blood!''

"And now you're suddenly defending the thing? Why the hell would you. . . ? Oh, my God, Cyril." Nicholas turned away as it began to come chillingly clear. He gripped the mantelpiece with his fingers, feeling as if he might be sick. "Dear Lord," he whispered. "Did she succeed with you where she failed with me?''

Cyril didn't answer, and Nicholas turned to look at him. Cyril's face had completely drained of color save for two bright spots that flamed on his cheekbones. He was staring at the floor, his hands working at his sides.

"Is it true?" Nicholas said harshly, biting out each word. "Did Jacqueline seduce you? Tell me!''

Cyril's head snapped up. "I am just as m-much a m-man as you, N-Nicholas. Wh-why is it all right for y-you and n-not for me?''

Nicholas covered his eyes with his hand for a moment, trying to bring himself under control. "Sit down," he said very softly, but the words held an undertone of danger, and Cyril instantly complied, although he looked very surly.

"Start at the beginning, and I want the entire truth. When did this happen? Was it when I came home?"

"Your arrogance knows n-no bounds, c-cousin. You are very wr-wrong. We have been l-lovers for almost t-two years."

Nicholas slowly clenched his hand. "Damn the bitch," he spat. "Damn her to eternity." He pressed his fist hard against his mouth and tasted blood where his teeth cut into his lip.

"P-perhaps you are j-jealous. C-could that b-be the cause of your distress?"

"Jealous?" he said, dropping his hand. "Sweet Jesus, Cyril, but how you misread me! I am angry, very angry, and I am sickened, and above all, I think perhaps I am furious with myself for having let this happen."

"It is n-nothing to d-do with you. M-must you always see everything in t-terms of yourself?"

"Coming from you that's a sweet irony, but we'll let it go for the moment. And to answer your question, no. I am not jealous. Jealousy is about the farthest thing from what I'm feeling. Now, start at the beginning."

"Why should I?" he answered sulkily. "It's m-my private b-business."

"You'll damned well tell me, Cyril, or I'll wring it out of you!" Nicholas said, exploding, and Cyril cringed back in the chair. "You may take this lightly, my boy, but believe me, it is no laughing matter."

"She was l-lonely," he said sulkily, "and she had no one else to t-turn to but me. My f-father was useless in b-bed, even before his s-stroke. So she c-came to m-me for comfort. I know how to s-satisfy her. I m-make her h-happy. So there. N-now you know."

Nicholas swallowed against the violent anger that pulsed through him with every heartbeat. "Now I know? Listen to me, and listen to me well, for there will most surely be an end to this. If you have been acting as Jacqueline's lover, then you are man enough to hear what I have to say to you now."

"Why should I? Why should I l-listen to anything you have t-to say?"

"Because I'm the only person who can help you."

"What m-makes you think I w-want your h-help? Anyway, y-you're in no p-position to d-do anything for anyone. You are totally r-ruined."

"And that will change. But that is not the point. My God, Cyril, not only have you been duped, you've been used in an unholy manner. This is going to be terribly painful to hear, but it has to be said. I have been telling you the truth, Cyril, I swear it to you. I was more fortunate than you, for I was older than you when she came to me, and more experienced, and I wasn't under her control. At least I managed to escape her abuse, if not her accusations. But hatred can do terrible things to people, cause them to act in unconscionable ways. It is beyond belief and unforgivable that she would use you to her own ends, and I want you to know that I do not put you on trial in this matter, only Jacqueline. I do not know what she did to manipulate you into becoming her lover, although I can guess at it. No doubt it was the first time she had paid you any attention at all, wasn't it?"

Cyril hunched a shoulder. "She s-said she had n-never thought of me as a s-son anyway. And that one d-day she had l-looked at m-me and r-realized I had b-become a m-man. And as I had n-never thought of her as a m-mother, it wasn't incest. She wanted m-me."

"Yes, perhaps she did, but can you not see what was behind it? Cyril," he said very, very gently, "try to understand. Look in the mirror."

Cyril shook his head violently. "No," he said. "N-no. It's not true. It's n-not. It was m-me she w-wanted. M-me, n-not you! She l-loves me!"

"She does not know how to love. She only knows how to take, how to destroy."

Cyril was silent for a long moment, and then he looked up at Nicholas uncertainly. "You are s-saying that the only reason she t-took me as her l-lover is because I remind her of y-you?" he said tonelessly. "You are t-trying to t-tell me that she has been using me to g-get back at you b-because you would n-not s-sleep with her?"

"Yes. That is what I am saying. I'm very sorry, Cyril. But I believe it must be true. I cannot see any other reason for her to do such a thing. She knew it was morally wrong to take you to her bed. She was doing it out of vengeance and perverted lust.''

Cyril gave a low, keening cry and put his head in his hands, his body rocking back and forth. "N-no. N-no,'' he said over and over, and Nicholas put his hand on Cyril's back.

"I'm sorry. I'm so very sorry, Cyril. I will do what I can to make it up to you. It is not your fault, you know. You mustn't blame yourself. Jacqueline is entirely responsible. My God, but the woman is evil. Seventeen years older than yourself, married to your father, and you an innocent boy—surely you must see how she manipulated you?''

"I knew she was t-taking other l-lovers,'' he said miserably. "I f-found out.''

"I have always suspected as much, Cyril, after what happened to me. But the one thing that must never be known is that you have been one of her lovers. I will certainly do my best to see that no one ever hears of it. You have a full and I hope a happy life ahead of you, and I will not see Jacqueline ruin it for you. I cannot express my rage to you enough. I really cannot.''

"You are n-not angry with me? You are n-not?''

"Oh, Cyril, for the love of God, how could I be? How could I be?'' Nicholas knelt down and took his shoulders, looking him in the face. "You are my cousin. I have loved you since the time you were born. You were truly like a younger brother to me. You have no idea how much your mother and your father anticipated your birth, after years of waiting for a child, and I was as excited as they were, for I had been with them four years by that time. It was a great tragedy when your mother died, but then to see Jacqueline step in—I felt desperate, Cyril. And when she did what she did to me, and I was cast off, I cannot describe to you how it felt. Now—to learn what she has done to you, and you an innocent victim . . . I am very, very angry.''

"I am s-sorry about your h-house,'' he said in a small voice. "I have always f-felt b-bad about it. Jacqueline t-took out her h-hatred for you on it, and I c-couldn't d-do anything to s-stop her.''

"I know, Cyril. I know.''

He bowed his head. "We would c-come here, you know. M-most times. To b-be secretive."

Nicholas nodded. "Did you? I suppose I'm not surprised. Jacqueline most likely wanted to desecrate me a little more. It wasn't quite enough to let the house fall to bits."

"I'm sorry about the c-cat too. I was . . . I was angry. I know y-you r-realized. I r-received your m-message."

"It wasn't too difficult to work out. Was that the room you and Jacqueline used? Is that why you put the cat in Georgia's bed?"

He nodded miserably. "And to m-make her s-sorry for b-being m-mean to m-me. And then the shipwreck h-happened, and I s-saw how she h-helped all those p-people, and I f-felt ashamed. And then there was P-Pascal, and I helped him to l-live, and it changed everything. I c-can't explain it. But everything s-seemed d-different after the shipwreck. And when I l-looked at you, and you were so b-broken and ill, it was hard to h-hate you. Jacqueline had m-made me b-believe it was all t-true about you, and I was s-so angry that y-you had gone away and l-left me, that you were n-not the p-person I had l-loved. There was no one l-left after that."

"I know, Cyril, and I'm sorry too. I wish I had been here to protect you from her."

He raised tear-filled eyes. "I was a f-fool. I d-didn't s-send her away. I was shocked at f-first, and f-frightened, b-but then I w-wanted it. God help m-me, I w-wanted it. I felt so g-guilty, b-but then the next t-time I would w-want it just as m-much. I would d-do anything for it. I thought she loved m-me. I s-swear to you, Nicholas, I thought she d-did. And no one else c-cared."

"Not even your father?"

"He ignored me in f-favor of her. M-maybe I reminded h-him of you too. I d-don't know." The tears fell over and ran down his cheeks. "I feel so wicked, s-so s-stupid. The last few w-weeks, for the f-first time I felt important, as if what I d-did counted for s-something."

"It did, Cyril. Believe me, it did."

"I felt as if I m-mattered to someone. I suppose n-now that you know, you'll c-cast me off. I'd d-deserve it." He put his head on his arm and started to cry brokenly.

Nicholas placed his hand on the top of Cyril's head, the hair so uncannily the dark shade of his own, the curl at the nape exactly the same.

"No. I would never cast you off. I told you that I would help you, and I will."

"B-but how? How? She is v-very p-powerful."

"Not for much longer. Listen to me, Cyril. I plan to go to London. Jacqueline is stirring up all the old stories and adding some new ones, and now they involve Georgia. I'm going to put a stop to this. I'm certainly going to put a stop to what she's been doing to you. You're not helpless anymore, Cyril, nor powerless. You have me, and you have Georgia. We love you, you must believe that."

"I have t-treated you v-very b-badly."

"Never mind, that's all over now. And let us not forget Pascal, who thinks you are very wonderful."

"He thinks you m-more w-wonderful than m-me," Cyril said, wiping his eyes. "It s-seems everyone c-compares m-me to you, for g-good or b-bad."

"I imagine it's been very difficult for you. I am sure I wouldn't like it myself. But I don't think Pascal compares us at all. He treats you like an adored elder brother and me like a doddering old man who has to be humored along."

"Oh, n-no. You d-did not see him when you were ill, Nicholas. He has g-great admiration for you, g-great respect. He only treats you g-gently b-because he wants to be certain of your r-recovery. You will see. When he s-sees you are c-completely well, he will be j-jumping all over you."

"Ah," said Nicholas. "How reassuring."

"B-but what is Pascal to d-do while you are gone?" Cyril asked. "Shall I have him at R-Ravenswalk?"

"There's no need. We'll take him with us. You are more than welcome to come along if you like. However, you might want to think about it. I would not damage your own name by linking it with mine, and there is no guarantee that I will be able to recover my reputation. It is your decision."

"I will c-come."

"All right, then. But can you face seeing Jacqueline, now that you know the truth about her?"

"I think s-so. G-God, I hate her, N-Nicholas."

"That's not surprising. I'm none too fond of her myself, and Georgia is ready to take a knife to her throat."

Cyril managed a small smile. "Georgia has a t-temper on her. But I d-don't think she could hurt a f-fly."

"Georgia? No. She could blister its ears, though, if she thought it would move it along."

"You l-love her, d-don't you?"

"Yes, Cyril, I do. I love her very much. I'm a damnably lucky man, and I hope one day you'll be as lucky yourself."

Cyril only shrugged. Then he said, "We shall s-see. For n-now, we go to L-London."

"Be ready to leave in two hours," Nicholas said, "for this isn't going to wait."

Cyril nodded, then walked out of the room without another word.

Nicholas stood there for a long moment, unmoving. And then he grabbed up a candlestick from the table and threw it against the wall with all of his strength, bringing down a shower of plaster dust. "You will pay for your sins, Jacqueline," he said through gritted teeth. "This I swear on my life." He picked the candlestick up off the floor and looked at it, then carefully set it back on the table. "Oh, yes," he said softly. "You will pay."

16

Nicholas strode into the kitchen like a man bent on a mission. "Georgia!" he shouted. "Where in blazes are you?"

Binkley poked his head out of the pantry. "Mrs. Daventry is with Lady Clarke off the buttery, sir. Young Pascal is with them. He has informed me, sir, in a most energetic fashion, that we are to repair to London in two weeks' time. Is he correct, or is his imagination also energetic?"

"Neither, Binkley. We go to London, but we leave as soon as you can organize it. Right now would do nicely."

"I see, sir. Would it be correct to assume that Mrs. Daventry has been enlightened?"

"Mrs. Daventry," Nicholas replied shortly, "has been enlightened as to a great many things. As have I. Hence our immediate departure: there is no time to waste. The house will be open and staffed?"

"It will be open, sir, although the staff is at a minimum. That will pose no trouble, as I will be able to raise a full complement with alacrity. May I ask the reason for our haste, sir?"

"I plan to trounce Jacqueline de Give, Binkley, in no short order."

"Very good, sir. It is a most reassuring thought and an act long past due."

"You have no idea how true that is."

"If I may say so, sir, it is bad enough to poison minds and reputations, but poisoning one's husband does seem a bit extreme."

"You are as remarkably well-informed as ever, Binkley."

"I could not help but hearing as I passed through the buttery, sir," Binkley replied equitably.

"Yes. Well, you have heard nothing yet."

"Indeed. I will begin preparations immediately, sir. Shall we leave tonight?"

"It would be preferable. We can put up at one of the inns on the way. I should like to reach London by tomorrow evening."

"Very good, sir. I shall pack a picnic to avoid stopping for luncheon tomorrow. And will Lily be accompanying Mrs. Daventry?"

"No. We'll need Lily and Martin to oversee the Close. We'll have to find someone in London to attend to Georgia, someone who is properly trained. However, Pascal and Cyril will be coming along with us."

"Very good, sir." Binkley began to bustle about, and Nicholas, his insides still churning with suppressed fury, went to find Georgia and inform her of the change of plan.

Georgia shook out her dress, deeply preoccupied, for Nicholas had been like a silent, self-contained bomb ever since he had told her they were leaving. She hadn't had time to think, rushed into a whirlwind of activity, seeing to packing for herself and Pascal, not that there was much to trouble with. Marguerite had taken the herbs for Lord Raven and departed, saying she would look forward to seeing them in London as soon as they were settled. They'd had a late supper at the inn, and Nicholas had been quiet throughout. Cyril, too, had been silent, and it had been left to Pascal and herself to provide the conversation.

"Come to bed, sweetheart," Nicholas said, pulling the covers back and sliding under them. "We have a long day ahead tomorrow." He rested his head on his arm, his back turned away from her.

"Nicholas," she said, climbing in next to him, "this is no good at all. I can feel your upset, your anger. I think you should tell me what is bothering you, for it is not good to hold things inside yourself. You've only just come out of your illness, and I worry."

"I'm quite sane," he said shortly. "You needn't worry in the least."

Georgia sat up and pulled her knees up to her chest. "This has to do with Cyril, hasn't it? You had that long talk in the library, and then you decided we had to go up to London immediately, and this when you had been so reluctant to go at all only an hour before. What happened?"

"I'd really rather not say."

She reached out and touched him, running her hand over his hair. "It must have been very upsetting."

"It was. Georgia, please. Let's go to sleep. I don't want to think about it anymore."

"I don't think you're going to sleep, not when you're this upset. I know I won't, worrying about it. Why don't you talk it through? I do not think you can have fought with each other, for Cyril didn't seem the least bit hostile toward you, just quiet—and upset himself."

He rolled onto his back and put his arm around her waist, pulling her down to him. "I don't mean to exclude you, sweetheart, but I think this is a thing best left untouched. I don't want you upset any more than you already have been."

"Nicholas, you're protecting me again. If you expect me to deal with the situation, then I should know everything."

"Not this, you shouldn't. Not this."

Georgia thought. "It's not about the cat he put in my bed, is it?"

Nicholas looked at her in considerable surprise. "How did you know Cyril was responsible?"

"Simple deduction, once I'd had a chance to think it through. I remembered that Cyril has a strange fascination for blood."

"What do you mean?" Nicholas asked, for the first time his attention truly on her.

"Oh, the first time I met him, it was in the woods and he was intently tearing up a piece of cloth. It was badly bloodstained. He shoved it away as soon as he saw me, as if I'd caught him doing something he shouldn't have been. Later that afternoon I found a rabbit shoved beneath a bush. It had been gutted, and at the time I thought

it must have been poachers, although I couldn't understand what purpose they would have. And then another
time he cut his hand, and he kept squeezing the bandage
and looking at the stain. It was rather strange—there were
all sorts of little things he did and said that made me
wonder about him. So the way in which he killed the poor
cat made perfect sense.''

"Yes . . . I see what you mean. That's interesting.''
Nicholas sat up and leaned forward, resting his elbow on
his knees. "And he confessed to it today. He said he'd
been angry. But wouldn't you agree that it would have to
have been extreme anger that would drive him to kill,
and in such a violent fashion?''

"Yes, I would think so.''

"I suppose it does make sense. If Cyril is as angry as
I think he is, and has felt as helpless as I believe he has,
then all of that helplessness and anger has to go somewhere, doesn't it? I know what I did with my own. I kept
it buried so deeply inside that it nearly ended up destroy-
ing me. But Cyril, he's been going about slashing cats'
throats and gutting rabbits and God only knows what
else.''

"But he's been so much better of late, almost happy,
calmer.''

"Perhaps, and he did indicate that he felt better about
things since the shipwreck.''

"He saw a great many shocking things that night,
Nicholas. I think it gave him a new respect for life, which
caring for Pascal has only encouraged.''

"And that's a blessing, because Cyril had very little to
live for before that point. No father to speak of, a vilely
wicked stepmother, a debauched cousin, and precious
little else but an enormous house to rattle around in.''

"But now he has you back, and Pascal, and the Close
to come to. It's what you wanted for him when you first
brought him here.''

"Yes, but look at him—he's still such a mess of nerves
he can barely get a sentence out without stumbling all
over his words. He's an entirely different boy from the
one I left. I still love him, Georgia, I do, although I
hardly know him anymore. He's been badly injured, and

I don't have the faintest idea of how to go about repairing him, save to remove Jacqueline from his life."

"What happened, Nicholas? What happened this afternoon?"

Nicholas pushed both hands through his hair. "What happened? I suppose I learned the world was an uglier place than I had ever imagined and that Jacqueline is one of the most corrupt people on the face of the earth. That is what happened."

"I see," Georgia said quite calmly. "It sounds to me as if Jacqueline has done something very terrible to Cyril."

"Yes . . . yes, she has." His eyes had gone distant, and he appeared lost in thought.

Georgia chewed on her bottom lip. What could Nicholas be so reluctant to tell her? It drew her mind back to their earlier conversation regarding himself and Jacqueline and his reluctance to speak of what had happened. She could well understand why, and it more than explained his violent dislike for Jacqueline. It was the sort of thing that would be burned on one's soul for all time. He must have felt not only betrayed but also horribly violated. How corrupt could a person be? And as Nicholas had feared, because of the resemblance, she had obviously been taking out her malice on Cyril.

Georgia sat up very straight, her blood suddenly running cold. "Oh, Nicholas . . . Dear heaven. She didn't. Did she? Not that. Of all things, not that."

Nicholas gave her an incisive look, and then, seeing that she had grasped the truth of the matter, he sighed in resignation. "Your brain is unfortunately quick. I hope to God the rest of the world never makes the connection."

"Oh, how dreadful! Poor, poor Cyril—no wonder you're so upset! She ought to be shot!"

He looked over at her. "Tried, sentenced, and hanged by the neck until dead, if I had my way. But as her crime can never—never—be allowed to become public, I will have to find another way."

Georgia wrapped her arms around herself. "I can't begin to imagine how this has affected him."

"I think you've seen," Nicholas said bitterly. "I should

296

have fought her. I should have stayed to protect him. But never, never did I ever imagine that she would go so far. Never.''

"Who would have? It is not your fault. It is not your fault, Nicholas. He was what—only seven when you left? You had no way of knowing that he would grow up to resemble you so strongly, or that the situation would be so twisted, or Jacqueline so corrupt. How can it be your fault?"

"No . . . the honors go to Jacqueline, I suppose. It's been going on for two years. Two *years,* Georgia. He was only just fifteen. Fifteen years old, and she was having him. Her stepson. How the hell am I supposed to find a way to accept that? How the hell is Cyril ever supposed to come to terms with it, once he fully realizes what she has done to him? And he must hate his father for not having prevented it, and now, of course, for being helpless to stop it. How else is the boy supposed to feel but angry and betrayed and abandoned?"

"I don't know," she said honestly. "I really don't know. It's quite terrible."

"He knows he wasn't her only lover. He knows he was just in the background, used at her convenience. And yet she was all he had, or so he thought. She pulled him in, Georgia, somehow she pulled him in and convinced him it was all perfectly acceptable. Damn her!"

Georgia drew Nicholas to her. "You can take Jacqueline on this time. You can see to it that she doesn't hurt again—or at least not anyone in your family."

"I'll most certainly do my best. And now you know what a viper you have to face."

"Knowing what she's done to Cyril makes it even easier to face her, Nicholas. I am so furious that I will not let myself be cowed."

Nicholas managed to smile. "I've never once seen you cowed. I find it impossible to imagine."

"But I was very easily cowed until you came along and showed me there was no need to be. Look at what I let Mrs. Provost do, and Jacqueline. They ran roughshod all over me. And in between there were Madame La-Salle, who was a proper tyrant, and Lady Herton, although she was not so bad, only stupid. And—"

"Enough," said Nicholas, laughing and silencing her with a kiss. "I believe you. But you were helpless to protest, weren't you? And now you're not. Now you can protest as long and loudly as you like. You may take on all of London if you wish."

"But I am still an imposter, Nicholas," she said quietly, "and everyone will know it, even if I am now your wife. I know enough about your world to know that one can have fine clothes and fine jewels, but a servant is always a servant, and people don't forget. I am happy to stand at your side, but do not expect anything more than for people to see I am not a gutter-bred harlot with stringy hair and blackened teeth."

Nicholas grinned, wrapping one soft golden curl around his finger. "God, I would love to hire one just like that for the evening and walk into Almack's with her on my arm, just for the reaction I would get. Actually, I would think the picture Jacqueline has tried to create is more one of a brittle, overpainted woman of low moral standards and crass manners. But soon enough all of society will see what a brilliant choice of wife I have made. Now, come here, wife, and do wifely things."

He kissed her, and kissed her again, and then, suddenly aroused, he slipped her nightdress up over her hips, running his hands over her skin and cupping her breasts, bending his mouth to them. He felt the sweet stirring of her response, her nipples hardening, her arms coming around him, her head arching back to accept his caresses. He impatiently pulled her nightdress over her head and bent his head to pleasuring her. The sheets tangled around them and a pillow fell to the floor as Georgia answered him, her body moving more urgently, her excitement growing, her caresses becoming more needy. And when he pushed against her hot, swollen, ready flesh and felt her give, felt her take him into her and enfold him, heard her breathless little cries of pleasure, saw her eyes close and her brow furrow, he knew that there really might be hope after all.

He lost himself in her, in her heat, her softness, her passionate response to his thrusts. He pushed her knees up and plunged more deeply, and she gave a low moan of pleasure. He hungrily pulled at her breasts, suckling them as his hands pressed and shaped her buttocks, tilting her hips even further up against him. Georgia responded by wrapping her legs around him, her excitement building to a fevered pitch. He caught his breath as he felt his entire gut gathering toward an explosive climax.

"Nicholas!" she cried, her body suddenly tightening, and he drove harder, then stayed as she convulsed around him. It was more than he could bear. He groaned as his body emptied itself into hers, her tight muscles fiercely milking him with her pleasure until he gasped with surprise and drove into her again, wondering if he was going to survive a second climax. Georgia's survival was just as much in question, for she was sobbing with renewed pleasure, her response as violent as his own. It seemed to go on forever—there was no time, there was nothing at all but the joining of their bodies, the heat of their flesh, the pounding of their hearts, and the love that bound them and made sense of it all.

"I think I'm dead," Nicholas finally said when he could speak at all. "I must be dead."

She kissed him with soft, warm lips, her arms resting about his neck, her thighs still enclosing him. "Your heart beats. Your lungs are taking in air. I think you might still be alive, Nicholas."

"No, it is not possible. Not possible. No man can survive such pleasure. It's not natural." He rested his forehead on hers. "When I explained about passion, I was misrepresenting it. It wasn't deliberate misrepresentation, mind you. I didn't know myself that it could be quite so life-threatening."

"Mrs. Provost didn't know it either. She was under the impression that it was more like having a tooth pulled."

Nicholas raised himself up on his forearms and looked down at her. "Mrs. Provost didn't know a damned thing about anything."

"I am beginning to think you are absolutely right."

"Naturally I'm right. Am I not always right?"

"Not always, but very often," she conceded.

"A minor victory. I must make love to you more often. It makes you so compliant."

Georgia smothered a laugh against his shoulder. "I love you, Nicholas Daventry," she said.

"And I love you, Georgia Daventry." He smoothed the hair off her forehead. "More than I can say. Now, sleep, sweet wife, and do not worry another moment about anything." He slipped out of her and turned her against him so that her back rested against his chest and her hips were cradled securely in the hollow of his own. Her breathing gradually slowed until he knew she was asleep. Nicholas lay awake for some time, thinking about the woman in his arms, his seed in her body, her love in his heart, and despite everything else, he couldn't help but count his blessings.

Georgia looked up from her conversation with Pascal. Nicholas had been quiet and distracted all day, and she more than understood. The river Thames had just appeared, and she could well imagine the direction of his thoughts. Cyril's thoughts were not so easy to divine. He sat silent, looking out the window of the carriage. His face was as unreadable as his older cousin's. Her heart went out to him, but there was nothing she could say or do to ease his misery, for she knew he would not welcome the realization that she knew of his situation.

"It is a very exciting journey, is it not, monsieur?" Pascal said with enthusiasm, and Nicholas tore himself away from his thoughts.

"I am sure it is a very exciting journey, Pascal, for one who has never made it before."

"Ah, yes, it must be your business that makes you so solemn. It weighs heavily, the business, my father always said."

"My business? Oh, yes. I suppose it is just that, Pascal."

"But you cannot do your business all of the time, monsieur. Perhaps you will come to the gardens with us. Madame and I have just been having a very satisfying discussion about botany. We shall see many new plants and decide which ones to buy and bring home. I cannot say I am happy to be leaving our own garden exactly in this moment, but Martin and Lily will look after things, and who cannot be happy about seeing London! You are happy, are you not, Cyril? You have been monstrous quiet."

"Monstrous quiet? Where did you learn that expression, Pascal?" Cyril asked. "You sound like a fop."

Pascal looked extremely pleased with himself, and Nicholas shook his head with a small smile.

"I learned it from the man at the posting inn this morning, the one with the coat with the very, very many capes. He said the inn was monstrous full. And what is this fop?"

"A man who wears too many capes on his cloak," Nicholas said.

"Ah, it is not good, this, not fashionable?"

"It is perhaps slightly too fashionable. Clothes are meant to be useful, not to deck a man out like a peacock."

"Ah," Pascal said. "It is best to be simple. Yes, this I can see. You and madame, you are very simple."

Georgia gave Nicholas an amused glance. "I'm not so sure, Pascal," she said. "You have a few surprises in store for you, I think."

"But I like surprises very much," Pascal said, pressing his nose against the window as the carriage rattled through the busy streets. "This is not like Paris, not at all. I was born in Paris, monsieur, did you know?"

"Yes, I did."

"My English, it is monstrous good, is it not? My mother was English and she made me learn to speak her tongue."

"And she would have been horrified to hear you speak so. Your English is excellent, Pascal, and will remain so, if you please. I would appreciate your not picking up any vulgarisms in the name of questionable fashion."

"Whatever you wish, monsieur," Pascal said, crushed. "I did not mean to offend."

"You do not offend, Pascal. And I mean only to instruct, so you must not take my words so much to heart. Now, pay careful attention, and I shall point out to you some of the interesting sights of the city. . . ."

The house was magnificent. It was built of white stone and was situated on Upper Brook Street, overlooking Hyde Park. Georgia drew in a sharp breath of surprise as Binkley stopped the carriage in front of it and jumped down, going to the front door and inserting a key in the door.

"*This* is your house?" Georgia said faintly.

"I bought it at the same time that I purchased our marriage license, although one was considerably more expensive than the other. Do you like it?"

"I don't quite know yet," she said, her hands crossed at her throat. "It's . . . it's very grand."

Cyril gave his cousin an extremely interested look. "You own this? It is a p-prime p-piece of p-property."

"It is, isn't it? I wanted to impress Georgia. But then she insisted I be poor, so I couldn't really bring her to it without offending her sensibilities."

Georgia looked over at Pascal, whose mouth was hanging open in wonderment, and then she looked at Nicholas, who appeared extremely pleased with himself. "You are outrageous," she said.

"Only rich as a nabob," he teased. "Actually it's a good investment, and I purchased it at an extremely low price. But say the word, my love, and I shall trade it for a shack."

"I think I can make do," she said, swallowing. "It is far grander than Lord Herton's house, Nicholas, and that's the grandest I've ever been in, next to Ravenswalk."

"Good. Here comes Binkley. I am sure he would be very gratified if we all behaved as if we were completely unimpressed." He climbed out and offered Georgia his hand, then lifted Pascal down.

Cyril was the last out. "F-full of surprises, aren't you, Nichol," he said, looking the house over with approval.

"And ever surprised," Nicholas said. "You haven't called me that for ten years. It's astonishingly nice to hear it again. Come, coz, let us go in and see how things have progressed. The house came furnished, but I had some changes made and I'm curious to see how they came out."

He offered Georgia his arm, took Pascal's hand firmly in his own, and walked up the steps like a man who belonged.

* * *

"It is quite perfect," Marguerite declared the next afternoon, sitting down in the drawing room, having made a thorough inspection of Number Two, Upper Brook Street. "It will make exactly the right impression. Not too opulent, beautifully situated, everything done in the finest of taste. Now, to you, my dear. We must launch into our plans. It is just as well Nicholas has gone out for the day, for we shall be at this for hours, and we would bore him to tears."

Georgia had not yet adjusted to any of this change of fortune, and she found it a little bewildering. Footmen and chambermaids and scullery maids she was accustomed to, as she had been one of their number. But to have them deferring to her was a strange sensation. It was a good thing she'd had Binkley, and even Lily, over the last few months or she should have been overwhelmed. Nicholas had been extremely amused by her shocked reaction that morning, when she had come down for breakfast only to see a sideboard laden with dishes of fish, eggs, meats, bread, and a variety of other foods, when they had been accustomed to such simplicity. Nicholas had laughingly told her that Binkley felt he had a great deal to make up for, and it was only fair to give him his head until he had worked his indignation out of his system.

Georgia had to suppress a laugh as Binkley appeared in the drawing room with a laden tray. "Tea, madam," Binkley said, placing the tray down. "You dine at a late hour this evening, and so I took the liberty of bringing you nourishment."

"Thank you, Binkley," Georgia said solemnly. "You are most thoughtful."

"Would her ladyship prefer ratafia?"

"No, thank you, Binkley," Marguerite said, equally seriously. "A cup of tea will be most refreshing."

Binkley bowed and discreetly disappeared again.

"He is a marvel of good taste," Marguerite said with wry amusement, and Georgia soon had her in stitches as she described how Binkley had acquired Nicholas in India.

"And not only did Binkley take Nicholas in hand and see to it that he behaved himself as Binkley saw fit," Georgia added, "but Binkley has also been training me for months to be a suitable wife for Nicholas. I wonder if he thinks I haven't noticed. A proper lady does not interfere in the kitchen. A proper lady does not sit on the floor, even if there is no chair available. A proper lady does not view her husband in an undressed state. I am not sure about behind the bedroom door. He has never addressed the point, or at least I don't think he has. Binkley is also a marvel of subtlety.''

"Oh,'' Marguerite gasped. "It is too good to be true.''

"I am truly very grateful to him, for there are hundreds of small things that I should never have known. Did you know that a proper lady never—but never—sits at the same table with the servants? She certainly does not attempt to wash the dinner dishes. I told him that more hands make lighter work, and I thought he was going to have the vapors. He told me that a lady's hands were meant for other things. What do you suppose he meant by that?''

Marguerite wiped tears of laughter from her eyes. "I cannot begin to imagine, my dear.''

"Well, neither could I. But really, he has been most gracious about accepting me. After all, Nicholas might have married a proper lady and spared him all that trouble.''

"I doubt very much that Binkley regrets his master's marriage in any way.'' She started to laugh again. "Oh, I do wish I could have been a fly on the wall over the last months. Having seen how you and Nicholas have been living, Binkley must have been thwarted at every turn.''

"Well, I don't know if he was thwarted, exactly. Binkley puts me in mind of a soldier on a battlefield: he does what needs doing, regardless of personal sacrifice, and he obeys his superior officer in all matters, while gently guiding him to the correct decisions. Above all, he is the guardian of rules and regulations.''

"I think you have it exactly. But if we are to complete the image Binkley has worked so hard to create, then we must turn our heads to business. Otherwise, I shall laugh the rest of the afternoon away.'' Marguerite accepted the cup Georgia handed her. "You will need a complete wardrobe, of course, and there simply isn't time to have one made. So, as I have far more clothes than I can possibly use, all made by the superb Madame Girondaise, I have assembled a selection that I think will suit you. It is a good thing we are much of a size, although I am slightly taller, I believe. Between your skill with a needle and my own, we will have you seen to in no time. I have asked the footmen to carry a trunk up to your dressing room. When we are finished with our tea, we will go up and inspect its contents.''

"But I couldn't possibly accept!" Georgia said, her hand stopping in midair.

"Naturally you will accept, my dear. If I am to take you under my wing, then you have to bow to my judgment. As I said, there is no time to demur. I have given the situation a great deal of thought, and we must move quickly if we are to forestall Jacqueline. Soon enough word will be out that you have come to town, and I wish to make the first move.''

"But what sort of move?''

"I have spoken to my husband, and he agrees with me on all points. We cannot ignore Jacqueline's actions anymore. He also agrees that we must offer you our full patronage and scotch these foolish stories. We are giving a ball next week, and I think it would be the perfect time to introduce you. All the *ton* will see that you and Nicholas have our unqualified approval. What can Jacqueline do?''

"She will be there?''

"She will indeed be there. We must keep you out of sight until that time, of course, for forewarned is forearmed.''

"I did promise Pascal I would take him out to see various things . . .'' Georgia said, worrying her lip with her teeth.

"But that is easy. It is only places that Jacqueline might frequent that you must avoid, social engagements which would alert her to your presence. But as for going about with Pascal, no one would know you anyway.''

"That is true. And as I am in no hurry to begin making social calls, I do not feel in the least deprived. Preparing for a ball is quite enough to worry about.''

"I understand. But perhaps you and Nicholas would dine with us next Wednesday? Our evenings are filled until then, but I should so like for you to meet my husband, and I know it would give Nicholas very great pleasure to see George again, and George is naturally very anxious to see Nicholas. And now, let us go up to your chambers and see to a dress for the ball, for I have included one that I think will be perfect. I never managed to wear it last season, and it is still *le dernier cri*.''

"You are far too good," Georgia said, overwhelmed by Marguerite's kindness. "I do not know what to say. Here, on Nicholas' behalf, you have taken me on when you know me not at all, when I am nothing in your world.''

"But, Georgia," Marguerite said gently, "you do not give yourself enough credit. You may have married above your touch, but no less so than I did when I married my husband. I was poor, I had nothing. I, too, was employed in the household. It is easy enough to understand how you feel, although at least I had the benefit of having been born to the aristocracy. And I also did not have to face rumors, for Jacqueline was not going to muddy her own family name, as much as she tried to eliminate any trace of her accent.'' Marguerite gave a most unladylike snort. "She did not want people remembering she was a poor émigrée, only that she was born a de Give.''

Georgia shook her head. "It is a sad thing, what happened to your sister.''

"Yes, it is a sad thing, although I think she must have been born with a fatal flaw of character, for I experienced the same set of circumstances, yet did not emerge with a desire to poison my husband or slander his relatives. As I told Nicholas, I never believed a word of Jacqueline's story, although I never could understand why she would invent such a thing. And I cannot see what purpose it now serves her to drag you down as well.''

"I believe I understand her reason," Georgia said slowly.

"And what is that? Annoyance that she lost her clever seamstress to Nicholas?''

"That I took what she wanted and couldn't have.''

Marguerite went very still. "I see," she finally said. "So that's how it was. Jacqueline always was rather vindictive when she couldn't have something she desired. Poor Nicholas.''

''Can you understand why Nicholas did not publicly defend himself? His uncle would have looked like a fool, and Nicholas loved his uncle too much to expose him to ridicule. So he left the country instead. At least, that is what I believe happened. Nicholas has not said as much, but then, he wouldn't.''

''You are very wise, my dear. Very wise indeed, and I believe you must be correct. George once suggested the same, but I found it difficult to believe that Jacqueline would go quite so far. And so now she goes about calling you ill-gotten and loose-moraled, implying that you were the only woman Nicholas could convince to marry him. It is jealousy if ever I heard it.''

''I should be flattered, I know,'' Georgia said with a pained smile, ''but I cannot like being called a whore. And as for being old Lord Herton's whore, forgive me, but that is really too much, for I practically had to beat him off with his own stick!''

Marguerite laughed. ''Yes. And that reminds me—I paid a most productive social call this morning to Lady Herton and managed to discover how it was that Jacqueline convinced her to let you go. It was quite underhanded of her, but clever. Lady Herton breathlessly described to me how Jacqueline had come to her and told her she had heard of your loose ways, and Jacqueline was very much afraid that rumor had it young Robert was beginning to pay more serious attention to you than was good for anyone. She implied that you were a fortune hunter, and said that if Lady Herton did not want you in the family, she would be well-advised to dismiss you.''

Georgia's mouth opened, and then she closed it again, for there was nothing to say.

''Jacqueline then offered, although it was at great inconvenience to herself, to take you off Lady Herton's hands.''

''I don't believe it! But why? Why would Jacqueline do such a thing? She loathed me once she met me.''

''No doubt she had admired your talents and wanted them for herself. She knew Lady Herton would not let you go easily. Really, it is quite amusing if you think of what elaborate measures Jacqueline took in order to steal you away. She must have thought about it for the longest time."

"And I suppose she buried me in the country so that someone else could not do the same thing to her as she'd done to Lady Herton. Honestly, she really is the most devious woman. And now she is using her own planted story to try to ruin me. All I can say is thank God I have Nicholas, or I really would be ruined and out in the cold— although I hope Nicholas' name has not been further damaged because of me."

Marguerite became serious. "I do not know the details of your upbringing, my dear, but you are most certainly none of the things my sister has implied. You are a fine woman, a good woman who cares about her husband's welfare and not about what she can take from him. You say you are not a lady, but from what I have observed, you are far more of a lady than many who go by the title. You look after those in need—I heard about what you did that terrible night on the coast, never mind what you later did for Nicholas. And taking Pascal into your home, that is yet another example of your generosity."

"You make me out to be a saint, ma'am, when I am nothing of the sort. I have a soft spot for orphans, having been one myself. And as for the other, it is only what my mother taught me to do."

"And bless her for it, for it is my experience that more mothers than not teach their children all the wrong things, if they bother to teach them all. Furthermore, it seems she taught you gentleness of nature and sweetness of manner, despite what you might think your shortcomings are. It cannot all be Binkley's doing, for I do not think that he can have taught you innate grace and a style that is all your own. I look forward to presenting you. As I have said before, you will be an instant success."

"You are kind, but overly optimistic, I fear," Georgia replied ruefully.

Marguerite put down her cup. "Nicholas is a very fine man. I mightily doubt that he would have chosen to marry a woman of whom he was ashamed in any way. He most certainly wouldn't have fallen head over heels in love with you if you were anything less than what he needs. And that he is head over heels is more than obvious. It gives me a positive *frisson* to see the way he looks at you. The room could be in flames and I don't think he would notice for his own fire."

Georgia blushed furiously and Marguerite burst into delicious laughter. "You must forgive me," she said. "It is my French blood—I blame all of my faults on my blood; it is so convenient. But *l'amour,* the grand passion, that is my greatest weakness."

"You think it is because of your blood?" Georgia asked, astonished.

"Oh, I think the English are capable of great passion too, or so has been my experience," Marguerite replied with a mischievous smile. "I have been very fortunate in my marriage. I don't know what I would have done if George had been as quiet in the bedroom as he is out of it." Marguerite started to laugh again. "Have I shocked you, my dear? I know it is most improper to speak of such things, but I feel uncommonly comfortable with you, and after all, it appears you have an equally happy marriage, or you would never look at Nicholas as you do. You are just as lost as he. It is a delight to see."

"It is?"

"But naturally. I would have despaired if Nicholas had married a cold fish, for he would have been miserable."

Georgia was infinitely relieved. It seemed that Nicholas was absolutely correct and the pleasures of matrimony were meant to be fully enjoyed. It also seemed that she should bless her hot blood rather than be ashamed of it. "I feel so foolish," Georgia said. "I thought I was being most unladylike."

Marguerite collapsed. "No, no, Georgia. There is something you must understand. The bedroom is the last place you want to be ladylike. That is where you must let all your unbridled passion out. And then, when you are sitting in Lady Herton's drawing room, bored to death with her stupid, vapid chatter, and behaving the perfect lady on the outside, you can remember every delicious unladylike thing you did the evening before and amuse yourself vastly."

Georgia, highly entertained by this image, said, "I doubt very much I will ever find myself sitting in Lady

Herton's drawing room, but I cannot imagine thinking about such things without starting to squirm and blush and behaving altogether as if I had a bad case of fleas!''

"Discipline," Marguerite said, pulling out her handkerchief again and mopping at her eyes. "Discipline, you see, is the hallmark of being a lady."

Georgia gave a hiccup of laughter. "Discipline and a highly active imagination. I am so pleased I have you to instruct me, Marguerite, for Binkley would never have thought to inform me of such important matters." She pulled a stern face. " 'In cases of severe *ennui*, madam, you need only to imagine Mr. Daventry in an inflamed state.' "

They both doubled over.

"Oh, Georgia," Marguerite finally said, "I don't think I've laughed so much in years. I really don't. I am so looking forward to showing the world what a fine woman Nicholas married. I am going to instruct you in every particular you might need to know. It is not that you are lacking in any way, it is more a matter of your confidence. Confidence is a very powerful tool. And I cannot wait to see you come up against Jacqueline, you on Nicholas' arm, his eyes on you with that heated look in them."

Georgia grinned. "I fear that a heated look might only confirm everyone's suspicions of both our moral characters."

"Good heavens, no. They'll be dripping with envy. There is nothing more powerful, nor more obvious to the interested observer, than the sort of love that you and Nicholas are fortunate enough to share. You also make a most striking couple, and that is all to the good. And so let Jacqueline eat her words in front of the polite world. I must confess I feel positively wicked taking such enjoyment in the prospect, but I suppose that for years I have secretly been longing for an excuse to challenge my sister. And to know that she will be thwarted in her attempt to destroy Nicholas is a particular pleasure. She has injured too many people as it is, my own family included."

"But will thwarting her be enough?" Georgia asked

with a worried frown. "Surely she will look to take her revenge elsewhere?"

"Where else, once she realizes it would only compound her troubles? Try not to worry, my dear Georgia. It will all work out for the best. We cannot sit by and do nothing. We shall make a beginning and see where it leads. And I must say, Nicholas is even more of an honorable man than I had realized, and Raven is a fool for ever thinking otherwise. But I suppose the poor man has been punished enough for his lack of judgment. We can only hope he recovers. So let us turn our attention to your wardrobe and our strategy to besting Jacqueline in this venture. She has played long enough. It is long past time she is given exactly what she deserves."

17

"It was the grandest thing ever, monsieur," Pascal said sleepily, securely tucked in the shelter of Nicholas' arm as the carriage made its way back to the house. "I have never seen such a sight as the men flying through the air, or the man who put the sword straight down his throat. Did it not hurt him, monsieur?"

"He p-probably eats swords for breakfast," Cyril said.

"No, he does not. I am sure he eats a very normal breakfast. He only puts swords in his throat to make money. Isn't that right, monsieur?"

Nicholas ruffled Pascal's hair. "I am sure he practices very hard with his swords so as not to hurt himself."

"And the lady who stood on the horses? She must have fallen off many times before she learned this trick. But she was very splendid."

"It is just like y-you, little monkey. It takes a little t-time to learn to stay on your h-horse."

"I am riding much better, though, am I not, Cyril? Cyril, he is an excellent horseman. Will you come one morning to see, when you are not busy with your business, monsieur?"

"Indeed I will, Pascal, for I should like to see how you've come along. Binkley says you are coming in only twice as dirty as you went out, and that sounds like improvement to me."

Pascal snuggled closer. "I only fall now two or three times in a lesson," he said, yawning. "It is not bad. Cyril is very patient, although he becomes annoyed when I do not remember to keep the reins, for then he must go chasing after my horse. But it is not the horse's fault. He is a very nice horse you have bought. Thank you, monsieur. . . ."

"My pleasure, Pascal." But his words went unheeded, for Pascal had fallen fast asleep.

Nicholas smiled to himself. The visit to Astley's Amphitheatre had taken its toll in excitement. The entire week had been filled with such things—an excursion to Vauxhall, a tour of Work's Mechanical Museum, which had particularly impressed Pascal, and even a visit to the Tower. Pascal had been more interested in the elephant in the menagerie than in the history, and Nicholas was not particularly surprised. Nor, sadly, was he surprised by Cyril's fascination with Tower Green, the site of many a beheading. Pascal had been disgusted and had given Cyril a sound telling-off for concentrating more on the dead than the living. Nicholas had stayed out of the ensuing argument, but he began to see what Georgia meant by the special relationship that existed between the two, and he thanked God for it. At least Cyril had one healthy, uncomplicated relationship to fall back on. Not only that, but Pascal had an extraordinarily optimistic view of life, and it seemed to counteract Cyril's understandable pessimism.

Nicholas found he had grown astonishingly fond of Pascal. It would have been near impossible not to have done, for the child was quixotic and bright, and sometimes blinding in his simple wisdom. And who could not like being treated like a combination of father, hero, and the pope? Cyril's attitude could not have been more different. Even now he kept his distance, despite the fact that the truth was out between them. Nicholas had tried to spend as much time as possible with him, to show him that he cared about him and that he did not blame him for what had happened. He really didn't know what else to do to reach him. It seemed that Pascal was the only one who could humor him out of his dark moods, and it appeared he was having one now, for he was staring out of the window, his brow drawn into a slight frown.

"Is everything all right?" Nicholas asked.

Cyril started and turned his his head. "F-fine. Why d-do you ask?"

"With everything that has been going on, I haven't had any private time with you. I only wanted to make sure you were not worrying overmuch about what is yet to come.''

Cyril's eyes flickered, and he looked away. "Why should I w-worry?''

"Because no matter how well things go, it is bound to be distressing one way or another. To tell you the truth, I'm frightened out of my mind at the idea of confronting Jacqueline in front of half of London.''

"Are you?'' Cyril said, looking at his cousin as if he might be human after all.

"Christ, Cyril, I've already been badly scalded by her. I don't look forward to putting myself directly back in her path. However Pascal might choose to look at me, I'm no hero. I'm just a coward when it comes down to it. I'd rather climb back into that broom closet than have to face Jacqueline's venom. But I can't. There's too much at stake.''

"I . . . I'm frightened t-too,'' Cyril admitted reluctantly.

"Good. That's two of us. And Georgia, despite the brave face she puts on, is frightened out of her wits. With every day that goes by I can see her dread growing.''

"I thought she w-wanted to be p-part of all this.'' Cyril waved his hand at the window.

"Are you mad? Georgia would be just as happy to climb into the broom closet with me and live happily ever after. You have to remember that she's never had any exposure to this kind of life, and she certainly never asked for it.''

"Then why d-did she m-marry you?''

"Quite honestly, I think she felt sorry for me. And Jacqueline was making her life hell on earth. If you think she married me for social cachet, you are sorely mistaken. I am sure that is what Jacqueline led you to believe, but it is very far from the truth. Surely you can see that at the moment I'm more harm to her than I am good?''

Cyril was silent, mulling this over.

"You will have to learn to trust me, Cyril. I am not in the habit of lying, nor of misleading. When I tell you I am terrified, you can believe me.''

Cyril managed a half-smile. "That m-much I will b-believe."

"All right. Let the rest follow. Will you be joining us tomorrow night for dinner with Lord and Lady Clarke? They have extended you an invitation. And as I think it would be a good idea to set you up in university, Lord Clarke is just the man to speak with. He has strong connections with Oxford and will no doubt be able to help. He can probably also recommend a decent tutor to bring you up to snuff. There is no point sending you away to public school at this late date."

"Are you attempting a m-misguided p-play at f-fatherhood, Nicholas?" Cyril said, his voice suddenly cold.

"Certainly not. I have my hands full with Pascal. I am merely trying to see to a way of getting you out into the world and away from the confines of Ravenswalk. You will enjoy university mightily. I did. It's the perfect blend of wine, women, and study."

Cyril shifted uncomfortably on the seat. "I find it d-difficult to imagine."

"Yes, but you will soon see for yourself."

"I am n-not so sure. And I d-don't like being m-managed."

"Just give it some thought," Nicholas said as patiently as he could. "That's all I ask."

"I h-have responsibilities at R-Ravenswalk," Cyril said. "If you are g-going to g-get r-rid of Jacqueline, then I will have to t-take over." He looked out the window again.

"Possibly. But there is a good chance that your father will recover."

Cyril's eyes shot to Nicholas. "What do you m-mean?" he asked, and there was a note of real panic in his voice.

"Jacqueline has been up to some mischief there too. I think she liked having your father incapacitated, and she decided to see to it that he stayed that way."

Cyril swallowed hard. "What do you m-mean?" he said again.

"She's been dosing him with something. But Georgia thinks she's found an antidote. We'll have to wait and see, but Georgia has high hope that he will improve, and

315

I trust her skill. You might well have a father again, Cyril."

Cyril had gone ghostly white. "When?"

"As I said, we'll have to wait and see. But it will certainly free you to have a life of your own."

"The only l-life I want is R-Ravenswalk," he muttered.

"Because it's the only life you've known. You cannot spend all of your life closed up there. There is a whole world waiting for you, Cyril."

There was no reply, and Nicholas gave up. The carriage turned off Park Lane and stopped in front of the house. The minute the footman let down the steps, Cyril was out, and he went quickly into the house without another word. Nicholas scooped Pascal up into his arms and carried him in, stopping only to kiss Georgia, who had waited up for them.

"I'll be with you in a moment," he whispered, then went up the stairs with his small burden. He managed to wake Pascal long enough to undress him and put him in a nightshirt, and then he deposited him in bed and pulled the covers up over him.

"Bon nuit, cher monsieur," Pascal murmured, burrowing more deeply under the blankets. "Whatever you might say, you are a hero. And do not worry about Cyril. He will work his troubles out."

Nicholas gave Pascal an incisive look, wondering just how much he had heard. "I hope so, Pascal, I truly do. He deserves some happiness."

"But for Cyril it is a struggle to be happy, monsieur. He battles the darkness."

"You are an insightful one, aren't you?" Nicholas said, rubbing Pascal's cheek. "But now it is time to sleep, little man. Sleep and have happy dreams."

"Thank you, monsieur. You have happy dreams too." Pascal's eyes fluttered heavily and then closed, and after a moment Nicholas went out, softly shutting the door behind him.

"Georgia, Nicholas! You have arrived!" Marguerite hurried toward them with outstretched hands. "But where is Cyril?"

"He became indisposed at the last minute," Nicholas said. "He sends his apologies."

"It is of no importance. Come, here is George. George, at last you meet Nicholas' wife."

Georgia, who was in a state of nerves, still managed to curiously regard Marguerite's husband as he made his bow to her. And finally, with a warm smile, he shook Nicholas' hand.

"It has been far too long, Daventry. I cannot express to you how happy I am that you have returned."

"Thank you," Nicholas said. "Your support means a very great deal. I assume Marguerite has told you everything?"

"Most likely more than you realize," George said, smiling. "May I offer you a sherry? We have a great deal of catching up to do."

The conversation drifted easily enough, but Georgia thought she might snap with tension. Yet it was no one's fault but her own. George was as relaxed as his wife, and very obviously pleased to see Nicholas, and Marguerite's bubbling laughter bound them all together. But by the time they sat down for dinner Georgia had lost her normally healthy appetite. If anything, she felt sick. What if she picked up the wrong fork, forgetting all of the instruction she'd been given? Or suppose she knocked over her glass and stained the beautiful rose crepe dress Marguerite had so generously given her and which she had so painstakingly altered? Or suppose she opened her mouth and absolutely the wrong thing came out, as it so often did. She could not count how many times she had humiliated herself at the vicarage and had been sent from the table. It was a miracle that Nicholas put up with her at all. And as for Marguerite, who was the height of elegance and who had been so extraordinarily kind—Georgia couldn't bear the idea of embarrassing her at her own table.

Georgia took a large swallow of wine and then a sip of soup. All of her life she had made up fairy tales, putting herself in just such a situation. But it had not once occurred to her through the fog of fantasy that there were other things involved. Everyone at the table with the exception of herself knew inherently which fork, which knife, which glass, to use. It was as natural as breathing to them. She wondered if Cinderella had been faced with the same problem when she'd married her prince and had been thrown into life at the palace. Or perhaps life had been simpler back then. Maybe there had been only one set of silverware in Cinderella's time. Surely they had used one goblet over and over instead of three different glasses all at the same time?

Georgia started, suddenly realizing she was being addressed by Lord Clarke, who sat at her left at the head of the table. "I beg your pardon?" she asked, clearing her throat as her soup plate was whisked away and another plate put in front of her.

"I was asking whether you were interested in reading, Mrs. Daventry."

"Oh, yes, I enjoy reading very much. And please, won't you call me Georgia? Everyone else does. Nicholas has a fine library at the Close, although it suffered some damage. But the selection is excellent, and there is a particularly fine edition of *Candide*. I was very excited to discover it, as I'd only ever read it in English and had always longed for the original. It is one of my favorite stories. Especially the end, in which Candide decides after all his trouble that the best thing in the world is to cultivate one's own garden. It makes perfect sense, does it not?"

"It does indeed," George said, amused. "You speak French, then?"

"Well, yes, although I haven't very much since my mother died. I'd speak it to Pascal—he's our French child—but I think it is best for him to perfect his English since he will be living in this country." She stopped abruptly. "I beg your pardon. I fear I am babbling. I find I am desperately nervous."

George's face broke into a slow smile. "You are not babbling in the least, and I quite understand your nervousness, although there is no need, I assure you. My wife has described you as unusually delightful, and I must confess that I concur. I hope I do not embarrass you by telling you so."

"Well," Georgia said, coloring, "I think I should be very pleased, for Marguerite keeps going on about con-

318

fidence, and if you find me not too terribly *gauche,* then I think there might be hope. I know I have babbled, Lord Clarke. It is no good your denying it. I always babble when I am nervous. Either that or I can find nothing to say at all. But I promise you, I shall keep my lips firmly buttoned at your ball. I am sure the *ton* does not want to hear about the cultivation of gardens or buying people out of slavery. Oh!'' she said, covering her mouth. ''I was referring to *Candide,* not myself, you understand.''

George gave a great crack of laughter, which caused Nicholas and Marguerite to interrupt their conversation and look over at them. ''Please excuse me,'' George said, exchanging a quick glance of amusement with his wife. ''Georgia and I have been having a most interesting discussion about . . . about gardening.''

''Georgia is an extraordinary gardener,'' Nicholas said, giving them both a speculative look. ''She has worked miracles with the gardens at Raven's Close, and I had thought them ruined beyond repair.''

''Oh, no,'' Georgia said. ''I told you, Nicholas, it was only a matter of caring.''

''I agree with Georgia,'' Marguerite said. ''My own mother always said that whispering to the plants could make miracles happen. It was the same with people who were sick. It was never enough just to give them medicines, you had to make them believe they were growing better. And then nine times out of ten they would.''

''Exactly!'' Georgia said with delight. ''Exactly so.''

''It must be the French in you both that produces this whimsy,'' George said dryly. ''I cannot imagine finding myself whispering sweet nothings to a poppy seed.''

''You would be most unsuited to such a thing, George. Save your sweet nothings for elsewhere,'' Marguerite said with a light laugh. ''But what is this about your having French blood?'' she asked Georgia, still smiling. ''I am intrigued. You said nothing when we were discussing it the other day. Perhaps it explains a great deal.'' Her eyes danced with mischief.

Georgia's lips trembled with laughter. ''But I am only half French,'' she said. ''You have to take into account my Scots blood too, which explains my terrible compulsion to pinch pennies.''

"Oh, that's right," Nicholas said with a grin. "I'd forgotten your father came from the Highlands. It does explain some things, doesn't it? But I hadn't realized your mother was French. George is right—that must have been where you acquired your fancifulness . . . I beg your pardon, but am I missing something here?" He looked at George and Marguerite, who were staring at his wife.

"What was your maiden name?" Marguerite asked Georgia, her face having lost its animation, now very still and pale.

"Cameron," Georgia said, looking up, and it was her turn to stare as Marguerite's fork fell from her hand and clattered to her plate.

"It can't be," Marguerite said, her voice barely a whisper.

Georgia met Nicholas' eyes in question, but Nicholas only shrugged, as baffled as she was. "What can't be?" he asked into the silence. "There is obviously some significance here, and I'd very much like to know why you are both looking at my wife as if she'd suddenly grown two heads."

"And your mother's maiden name?" George asked very quietly.

"I don't know. She never spoke of her family. Please— what has upset you so? Is it something I said?"

Nicholas leaned forward as if to press the point, but George made a small checking movement with his hand, and Nicholas sat back again. He looked back and forth between the two of them, his brow drawn into a frown.

"I believe I see Jacqueline's hand at work here," George said quite calmly. "Do you not agree, darling?"

Marguerite pressed a shaking hand to her cheek. "Of course. Jacqueline must be behind this! Oh, George, you must be right! It does make sense. . . ."

"For the love of God, what makes sense?" Nicholas said impatiently.

"Just a moment, Nicholas. It will all become clear." Marguerite drew in a deep breath, then turned to Georgia. "Georgia, my dear. Listen to me carefully. Do you remember how I told you that Jacqueline hated our older sister, would torment her every chance she had?"

Georgia nodded, by now thoroughly bewildered.

"Jacqueline fabricated a story about her out of jealousy, for she had fallen in love with a handsome young man from a good family. Jacqueline created a situation to make it appear as if our sister had behaved very improperly. My father had no choice but to ask her to leave home. And the young man's family disowned him. He was disgraced, forced to leave his regiment. His name was Charles Cameron."

Georgia's lips went bloodless, and Nicholas reached over and took her hand. "That . . . that was my father's name," she said, her body starting to shake all over.

"Yes," Marguerite said gently. "I thought so. And your mother's name was Eugenie, was it not?"

Georgia just nodded.

"Her maiden name was de Give. She was my sister."

Georgia sat completely still. She concentrated on breathing, for she thought her heart might stop with shock. She was only dimly aware of Nicholas coming over to her and kneeling down beside her, only dimly aware of the tears that rolled down her cheeks, only dimly aware that Marguerite, too, was crying.

"I . . . I don't understand," she whispered. "I don't understand."

Nicholas stood and rested his hands on her shoulders. "This is one hell of a turn of events," he said. "Would someone mind explaining to me just how we ended up here?"

"I don't know why I didn't see it sooner," Marguerite said, wiping her cheeks. "It seems so obvious now."

"*Obvious*?" Nicholas said. "That is the last word I'd use for this situation. And Georgia is clearly just as confused as I am."

Georgia looked over at Marguerite. "Please . . ." she said tightly. "Please, will you explain? It makes no sense to me. Are you sure there isn't another explanation?"

"But how, my dear?" Marguerite said gently. "Your mother, a Frenchwoman named Eugenie, was married to a Scotsman named Charles Cameron. They lived in anonymity and near poverty because neither family would acknowledge them. I understand your shock, for I feel it myself. But it cannot be a coincidence."

"No, I suppose not," Georgia said uncertainly, still sure that a mistake had been made somewhere.

"And there are other things," Marguerite said, smiling at her. "My mother supported us by dressmaking. You are very clever with a needle. But more important, my mother was renowned in France for her healing abilities and her knowledge of herbs and other plants. She taught us all, but Eugenie followed most closely in her footsteps—as you have followed in Eugenie's."

Marguerite rose and went over to Georgia, taking her hands. "I cannot quite believe it, but it is the most wonderful thing in the world, don't you think?"

"I . . . Yes," Georgia said, blinking back her tears. "I have missed having a family."

"Oh, my sweet girl," Marguerite said with a little laugh, "you do indeed have a family—and it is a very fine one. Not only are you the granddaughter of the Comte and Comtesse de Give, but your own grandfather is Ewan Cameron. He is a Highland chief."

"Good God," Nicholas murmured. "*Those* Camerons?"

"Indeed. Those Camerons. And here you were worrying all this time that you were not a lady. My dear, your bloodlines are impeccable. You have not a thing to fear from the *ton*, for they shall be falling all over themselves to meet you."

"Dear heaven, I've gone and married an aristocrat," Nicholas said dryly. "Whatever happened to my simple farmer's wife?"

Georgia put her face in her hands, and her shoulders began to shake.

"Sweetheart?" Nicholas gently touched her hair. "Have I upset you? I was only teasing, you must know that."

Georgia dropped her hands and looked up at him, tears pouring down her face. She was laughing so hard she could barely speak. "I can't . . . I can't . . ." she gasped. "I'm sorry—it's the shock." She put her head on her arms and lost herself in hysterics, and Nicholas grinned and looked over at Marguerite.

"Sorry," he said. "I realize it's a momentous occasion, but Georgia does this sometimes."

Marguerite started to laugh. "She is more like her mother than you know. Eugenie had an irrepressible sense of humor, no matter what the circumstances. Oh, Nicholas. The entire thing is quite unbelievable, but all I can think of is that in a most extraordinary way Eugenie has been returned to me. My heart never ceased to break over her sudden departure, and then—not another word. And I loved her so."

Georgia lifted her head, having finally managed to collect herself. She was a mass of conflicting emotions: disbelief battled with the extraordinary realization that she had a family of her own, that she belonged somewhere, that she had a history. "You are my aunt," she said in wonderment. "I have an aunt."

"I am sorry to say that you have two aunts," Marguerite replied. "I am only one of them."

"Oh, my God—Jacqueline." Georgia's hand went to her mouth, and she looked up at Nicholas. "What must you think of me?"

"Think of *you*?" he asked incredulously. "What the devil is that supposed to mean? You cannot think that I in any way equate you with Jacqueline? Georgia, I love you. You are your own person. You have suffered at the hands of Jacqueline just as it seems your mother did— which brings me to another question. What happened to Eugenie? What charge did Jacqueline bring against her, Marguerite?"

"It was rather vile. You have to understand that Jacqueline was unbearably jealous when Eugenie met Charles. He was such a dashing guardsman, and Eugenie was so beautiful, so much in love with him. It was a great secret, their romance, for Eugenie was only sixteen. They were waiting until such time as she was of marriageable age, but Jacqueline managed to find out. She was eleven, and I think she couldn't bear the idea that Eugenie might be happy—worse, that she might leave and Jacqueline would have to take on her work load. Eugenie and Charles used to send letters back and forth—delivering them was my job, and at the tender age of six, I thought it unbearably romantic. And then Jacqueline discovered where Eugenie hid her letters, and she took them to my father along with her story."

"I can't see what could have created such an uproar," Nicholas said. "What story could an eleven-year-old girl possibly have fabricated?"

"I'm afraid that Jacqueline was rather advanced for her years and very clever when it came to knowing just what would incriminate both Eugenie and Charles."

"And?" Nicholas demanded. "What did she come up with?"

Marguerite blushed and George answered for her. "She said that Eugenie had been meeting with Charles in the bedroom that she and Eugenie shared. Forgive me for my indelicacy, but she told the Comte de Give that she could bear it no longer, listening to them night after night while she waited outside on the roof. And she also told him that she had heard Eugenie tell Charles she was with child."

"Oh, poor *maman*," Georgia whispered.

"And the man *believed* Jacqueline?" Nicholas said angrily. "What, does everyone believe every foul lie that woman produces without ever questioning her?"

"He believed her because he could not credit that Jacqueline would know about such things," Marguerite said. "Jacqueline had lied, naturally. But she had interspersed just enough truth to make it sound credible. And when my father questioned me, as much as I tried in my childish fashion to defend Eugenie, I could not deny carrying the notes. So she was banished. The biggest sin was not the child she was supposedly carrying, but the behavior to which they had exposed Jacqueline. That was unforgivable in my father's eyes. It broke his heart to do it, but he sent her away and told her she was never to attempt to communicate with the family in any fashion. It was not unlike what Jacqueline caused your uncle to do to you, Nicholas. Perhaps now you understand better why I never doubted you."

"Jesus Christ," Nicholas said. "I don't quite believe any of this. What are we dealing with here? The woman must have been spawned by the devil himself." He pulled out his chair and sank into it, rubbing his forehead.

"I did not really understand what had happened, as I was so young, only that my beloved sister left in disgrace and I would never see her again," Marguerite said, also returning to her seat. "But years later, when I was old enough to understand what it was Eugenie had been accused of, I was sure that Jacqueline must have lied. And poor Charles, who was only twenty at the time, to have his reputation destroyed in such a fashion—ah, it doesn't bear thinking about. But I am as sure as I can be that he would never have compromised Eugenie. Tell me, Georgia, just to satisfy my own curiosity. When were you born?"

"August 4, in the year 1797."

"You see—there! Didn't I tell you? Eugenie left in July of ninety-six! She could not possibly have been with child, not if Georgia was born a year later. And did she have no other children?"

"Just myself. I . . . I am sorry. I am finding this a bit difficult to absorb."

"Naturally you are." Marguerite's face glowed with happiness. "You have no idea how much you are like your mother, Georgia. Not so much in looks, for you have your father's fair coloring, although you did inherit Eugenie's curls—and her humor, and her gentle nature, and . . . Oh! So many things! This really is too wonderful. And yet it saddens me to think how Eugenie's life must have been."

"It was not so bad," Georgia said earnestly. "She and my father loved each other very much, and there was always laughter in the house. They had each other, even if they had lost their families."

"And they had you, my dear Georgia," Marguerite added. "You must have given them great happiness despite everything else they might have lost because of Jacqueline. Tell me, if it is not too painful to speak of it. How did my sister die?"

"She contracted typhoid from one of her patients. I nursed her for three weeks, but in the end there was nothing I could do."

"Oh, poor Eugenie," Marguerite said, tears glistening in her eyes. And Charles? What became of him?"

"He had died five years before." Georgia briefly described those early years, trying hard to make them sound as glowing as possible, for she could see Marguerite's distress. But she didn't miss the incisive look Nicholas gave her, and she colored, for he knew just how much she was embellishing the situation.

"Oh, it is such a sad story," Marguerite said, wiping her eyes. "My poor dear sister, forced to suffer so. And no doubt Charles's health was broken by it all. What a terrible shame, when they might have had the blessing of their families to marry, once Eugenie had come of age."

They were all silent for a few minutes, and then Nicholas sighed. "Well," he said, "it seems clear that Eugenie and Charles were very badly used by Jacqueline. And it also seems clear that Jacqueline knew exactly who Georgia was from the start. It cannot be coincidence that she brought Georgia to Ravenswalk and proceeded to lock her away."

"It is not standard treatment of one's modiste, no," Marguerite said with a twitch of her lips.

"It does explain why I felt she hated me from the first," Georgia said. "I couldn't understand it at the time, but it was as if she were trying to punish me for something."

"Being Eugenie's daughter would be quite enough reason," Marguerite said, "never mind being Charles's daughter as well. Do you know, I have always wondered if Jacqueline hadn't had a secret passion for Charles herself."

"Oh, Marguerite, you are a hopeless romantic," George said with exasperation. "As you've said yourself, the girl was only eleven!"

"You'd be surprised what girls think about when they are eleven," Marguerite said. "And Jacqueline probably more than most."

"So," Nicholas asked, exchanging a quick look with Georgia, "you think she felt rejected by Charles Cameron and doubly sought revenge?"

"It's possible," Marguerite replied.

"Yes. It's very possible. And that is why she would treat Georgia as she did. It makes sense, for she's repeated the pattern since. It also makes sense of why she was so very furious over Georgia's marriage to me, aside from the obvious. Hmm . . . how long do you reckon she's known that Georgia is Eugenie's daughter?"

"How can we know?" Marguerite said helplessly. "I

cannot think it was before Georgia came to London, for how could she have known where to find her, or even that Georgia existed at all? She must have recognized something about her, although I cannot think how she even met her."

"I think I saw her one day when I was collecting material for Lady Herton," Georgia said, straining to remember when it had been. "I did not know who she was at the time. But it would have been at Madame LaSalle's, for I always bought material from her. Madame knew a number of things about me, as I'd lived with her for over a year. It is possible that Jacqueline might have asked questions."

"Yes," Marguerite said. "Jacqueline might have started by asking questions out of curiosity, and then put the pieces together. Oh, she is dreadful!"

"But I do believe we have her cornered," Nicholas said with satisfaction. "It puts the finishing touch on this ball of yours, for now you can introduce Georgia as your niece. What can Jacqueline do? She will look a fool."

"She will look a fool indeed. And I shall play my cards very close to my chest," Marguerite said happily. "Oh, it will be perfect!"

"My wife was born to intrigue," George said wryly. "Nothing could make her happier. Look at what a tender age she started, running messages for her sister."

Marguerite shot her husband a look of high amusement. "At least when I intrigue," she said, "I do it for the good of others. Why, only last year I had a great success."

"If you speak of Edward and Eliza Seaton, my darling, I feel quite sure they would have managed very well on their own, both being eminently sensible people."

"My dear George, you understand very little about the art of romance. It has absolutely nothing to do with being sensible: affairs of the heart cannot be run like affairs of state. However, since this latest intrigue involves my very sly sister, then I shall listen to your advice most carefully."

"Yes," said George, "and I think I have a plan. It will require timing and some luck, but I think it might just do the trick. The key lies with Hermione Horsley. . . ."

"Do you have any idea how happy Binkley is going to be to hear of your blue blood?" Nicholas said in the carriage on the way home. "He will positively perspire with suppressed delight and no doubt say he knew it all along."

"I still cannot believe it," Georgia replied, snuggling up against him. "It felt so wonderful to be hugged and kissed and welcomed so. I have missed having a family, Nicholas."

"Yes. I know how that feels. I am happy for you, sweetheart, for not only is it nice to know that you have blood relatives, but I also know how much it has troubled you to believe you married above yourself. I am trying to work out if it is I who have married above myself. I believe I must have done. Shall I now grovel before you and hope you will continue to love me out of the goodness of your elevated heart?"

Georgia burst into laughter. "I do not think you would grovel very well, Nicholas. And I assure you, I am no better than I was two hours ago, and just as ignorant. But oh, it is like a dream come true—save for the part about Jacqueline. I cannot like sharing blood with her, but I like it most excessively when it comes to Marguerite. And I hate Jacqueline more than ever, for she is truly evil. She has destroyed so many lives. My mother's, my father's, yours, your uncle's, Cyril's—"

"Do not forget yourself, love. Do not forget yourself. You have every right to be very, very angry."

"I would rather be angry for you and Cyril right now, for it is a waste of time to lament the past. And I most likely would never have met you if Jacqueline had not thrown me into her turret. So some good has come out of it. I told you I believe in magic."

"You are ever whimsical. And I must say, this latest development is straight out of one of your fairy tales. Cinderella trades her sackcloth for satin, or something like that, not that I ever thought of you as Cinderella for a moment."

"Cinderella actually had very respectable blood, Nicholas. It was only her wicked stepmother who put her in sackcloth in the first place."

"My point exactly," Nicholas said with satisfaction. "Jacqueline is perfect in the part, isn't she?"

"And so are you, for I shall go to the ball and dance with the prince."

"Please, sweetheart, I thought we had established my role in this piece. You shall go to the ball and dance with your reprobate husband."

"It sounds very inviting," Georgia said, moving against him. "I am particularly fond of that side of you."

"Really? How encouraging you are. Do let me oblige you." Nicholas reached over and pulled the curtains across the windows, then gathered her into his arms and kissed her, at the same time deftly sliding his hands under her skirts.

"Nicholas?" she gasped as his fingers found her soft feminine flesh and moved over it. "Here? Are you sure it is proper? Oh . . ."

He muffled a laugh against her throat and slid his fingers inside her. She shuddered and her legs eased open to give him easier access, and her head fell back against the squabs as he bent his head to her breasts, impatiently pulling down the material of her bodice with his free hand. He ran his tongue over a blue vein and pulled her hard little nipple into his mouth, moving his fingers at the same time, and she moaned and thrust up against his hand.

"Georgia, wait a moment," he whispered raggedly, his own urgent need growing. He quickly undid his trouser buttons with a fumbling hand and freed himself. He took her by the hips and with a quick lift sat her on his lap. With another lift he sheathed himself in her hot, swollen flesh, his breath coming in hard pants.

"Cinderella was never so sensual," he said, choking as the carriage hit a hole in the road and threw them up and then down again, driving her down on him with full force. Nicholas groaned and grabbed for a handhold to keep from toppling over, and Georgia gurgled with laughter.

"What do you know about Cinderella?" she said, looking down at him with half-closed eyes. "I'm sure she liked it every bit as much as I do. I only hope her prince was as accomplished at pleasing her."

She shifted on him slightly and his heart lurched halfway into his throat. She was every bit the seductress, her skirts bunched up around her naked hips, a smile on her lips, her ripe naked breasts quivering with the movement of the carriage. Every last inch of her emanated sensuality. *Circe,* he thought hazily as she leaned down and ran her tongue over his mouth, then lightly over his ear. *I'm married to Circe.* Her hands came to rest on his chest and she shifted her weight, resting on her knees. Nicholas closed his eyes and prayed for control and smoothly paved streets as Georgia began to move, riding him high and shallowly until he wanted to scream with frustration. It was everything he could do not to take her by the hips and pull her down hard on him. But he restrained himself and clenched his teeth, surrendering to her will. And then, just when he thought he might lose his mind, she deepened her thrusts.

"Oh, Jesus, Georgia!" he cried as she moved up and down his aching length and his insides clenched. He was about to explode, he could feel it coming. And just as he reached the point of no return, she pushed down on him hard and drew him into her deepest recesses, her body contracting on his. He pulled her against him, smothering her high keen of release in his shoulder, and it was everything he could do not to cry out himself as his own release overwhelmed him.

He suddenly realized that the carriage was making a left turn, and he knew it had to be into Upper Brook Street. "Georgia, love," he said with a combination of a laugh and a groan.

"Oh, I do love you. I love you, Nicholas."

"Yes, I know, sweetheart, but we can discuss it later. We are about to be discovered *in flagrante delicto.* Quickly, now."

She moved off him like a shot, pulling her skirts into place and adjusting her bodice. He managed to get his trousers buttoned and his coat pulled on, and when the door opened, he and Georgia looked as if they had been sitting just so since leaving Lord and Lady Clarke's. Nicholas chose to ignore the fact that his hair was damp and disheveled and Georgia's face was very flushed, and he hoped the footmen would have the good sense to ignore it as well.

18

Georgia took one last long look at herself, her stomach tied up in knots every bit as tight as the ribbons on her bodice. She scarcely recognized her own image. The maid, Florentine, had woven a garland of roses through her hair, colored to match her dress, a robe of white lace over a slip of pale pink satin. The hem was trimmed with pearls and silk roses, and a small bouquet of silk roses nestled on one shoulder. Nicholas had given her a double strand of pearls, and earrings to match. She did look a little like a lady, she decided. And she really wasn't an impostor—not really, not with her mother's blood and her father's, too, running in her veins.

But what was that really, when measured against half a lifetime of servitude? Surely that would be what showed, her gaucheness, her lack of the confidence Marguerite had tried so hard to instill? She marveled that any of them had confidence in her at all.

She drew a deep breath and practiced an experimental curtsy, wondering what would happen if she overbalanced and fell on her backside.

"Beautifully executed," Nicholas said from the doorway, and she quickly turned, blushing at her foolishness.

"Georgia . . ." he said on a note of awe, taking in her appearance. "My God. I never imagined . . . I scarce know what to say."

"Say I look presentable," she said, "for I need reassurance most dreadfully."

Nicholas walked over to her and kissed her lightly. "You look not only presentable but also look incredibly, gloriously beautiful." He ran his finger down the side of her throat. "I almost look forward to the evening, if only to see the stunned reaction when people lay their eyes on you."

"They will indeed be stunned," she said with a rueful smile. "But for quite a different reason."

"I doubt it. I am stunned, and I have known you for nearly half a year, in clothes and out of them. I've never doubted your beauty. But tonight, dressed like this, you are . . . I don't know. There is something about you that is extraordinary. I cannot say it any better than that. I am overwhelmed."

"Nicholas, you are silly."

"So you constantly tell me. But who knows, perhaps it's a saving grace. It would be truly overwhelming to take everything too seriously, or so I have discovered. If anything, I have learned that lesson from you."

"You have?"

"I have. Do you know, when I think of the months we've spent at the Close, I don't think of the hardships. I think of the laughter more than anything else, and the companionship, and how it felt to fall in love with you. I am so damned grateful for that, Georgia. You will never know how much."

"I think I might," she said, resting her hands on his chest and looking up at him with a smile. "I am grateful too. I gather it is permissible to use the word again?"

"I think we have moved beyond that particular obstacle." He bent his head and gently kissed her. "I wouldn't trade these past months for a moment. Ever. Not for anything. But now it's time to move ahead, and I cannot help but worry."

"I think you worry too much, Nicholas. What is it now?"

"I worry about you, sweetheart. Not about how you will be received—I think that is virtually assured after the revelations of last night. But if I do not manage to salvage my name, my reputation, then where does that leave you?"

"At your side," she said. "Where I want to be. Where else?"

"Georgia, you deserve a great deal more than a life in exile. I want to give you a great deal more. I always have.

But now that I know the truth of your background, it matters more than ever."

"Why?" she asked. "I am the same person. I am the same Georgia you married, the same Georgia with whom you've lived all this time. What is different about me now?"

Nicholas took her hands in his. "Nothing is different to me. But we both know that you have been denied your rightful place for all of your life. I understand how that is, how that feels, because it was taken from me also. But the difference is that you never knew it was yours to begin with. You were led to believe you were somehow unworthy, and you grew up without a sense of your own history. You have been robbed of a very essential part of yourself. I abhor snobbery, you know that, but this is something that goes far beyond. I believe very deeply in family, in blood, and I think you must have known somewhere deep in yourself that you were not where you belonged. But tonight you will be. It may not seem so at first, but it will be true."

"Nicholas, just because we know some of the details of my background does not change the manner in which I grew up. These people will know that. It is the same as trying to dress Lily up and expecting her to be accepted."

Nicholas laughed. "I don't think it is quite the same, my love. For one, your parents may not have told you anything about your background, but they did see to it that you were properly educated, at least while they were alive. Did it ever occur to you to wonder why it is that you do not speak like a village girl from Cumberland, why you speak exactly as I do, as anyone born to the aristocracy speaks?"

"No . . . I suppose I never thought about it."

"No. You wouldn't. And to tell you the truth, I didn't really think much about it either, although I probably should have done if I'd had any sense. There are quite a few things about you that I should have put together."

"What?" she asked, puzzled.

"Oh, little things, really. I remember your being enthralled over *Candide*, but it was only this morning that I realized that the only edition at the Close is in French.

Village girls are not generally fluent in the language. Most of them cannot read or write, for that matter. There were also your innate grace, your quickness of mind, and your quiet strength, all things that set you apart from the average.'' He took her by the shoulders and turned her to face the mirror. ''Look, Georgia. Try to see what I see.''

''But what do you see?''

''I see my wife, who has worked beside me, nursed me when I was ill, chastised, encouraged, and supported me through everything, never once complaining. I see my lover, who excites me as I have never been excited before. I see Georgia the brave, the stubborn, the generous, and the woman I love to distraction. But tonight I see yet another side of you. I see the person who was born to assume position and responsibility. I see the translucent skin and delicate bone structure of a woman of noble birth. It is that Georgia I want you to see. It is no accident that you bear yourself the way you do, that you behave the way you do. You cannot help yourself. It is stamped on every fiber of your being, put there by generations of noble breeding.''

Georgia met his eyes in the mirror. ''In truth, Nicholas?''

''In truth, my love. In this I would not humor you.''

She nodded. ''I know you would not. And I believe you because I believe the same thing is true of you.''

Nicholas shook his head. ''How is it that you are always able to turn the conversation around?''

''It must be all those generations of practice,'' she said with a mischievous smile. ''And, Nicholas?'' She ran her eyes over his black tailcoat and black breeches, his white clocked stockings and black kid pumps. His only jewelry was the signet ring that he always wore. The stark simplicity of his costume only emphasized his powerful figure.

''Yes?''

''You look extremely elegant. You are also a fine example of your breeding.''

''I wonder if I ought not to throttle you for that remark,'' he said with an amused smile. ''Do you think to tease me now, wife?''

''But I meant every word, truly I did. You are extremely dark and handsome, and you look very fine in evening clothes.''

"I don't know about that, but Binkley professed himself satisfied." He touched his cravat. "The Oriental, no less. We left behind an enormous pile of crumpled linen, but Binkley is a perfectionist. He was just seeing to Cyril's final touches when I left. But come, sweetheart. We should go down. Are you ready?"

Georgia picked up her white kid gloves and slid them on. "I don't know if one could ever be ready for a thing like this, but there's no point putting off the inevitable."

"Brave girl—braver than I. Had you said no, I should have been content to sit up here all night with you."

"I don't believe you for a minute," Georgia said. "You just have pre-battle nerves. Remember what Harry said at Agincourt."

" 'Stiffen the sinews, summon up the blood, disguise fair nature with hard-favor'd rage'?" He sighed. "I will do my best, for I would never think to disappoint you. But Harry was a king."

"A king outnumbered five to one. And look what he did."

Nicholas tucked her hand into the crook of his arm. "You keep forgetting I am an ordinary man."

Georgia gave him a sidelong smile. "So you keep trying to tell me. But as far as I am concerned, you are every bit as much a king in heart as Harry ever was. And tonight your detractors will know it for themselves. You have been very brave, carrying the burden Jacqueline placed on you for all these years. It is the last battle, Nicholas. Tonight shall see an end to it."

Nicholas muttered something unintelligible, then pulled her out of the room and led her downstairs.

"Madame, monsieur!" Pascal said with a little gasp of delight as they appeared. "Oh, you are truly magnificent! It is just like the pictures in a storybook, the king and the queen going to the ball!"

Georgia gave a smothered laugh. "You see?" she said to Nicholas. "There is no escaping it."

Binkley, who had been waiting with Pascal, drew himself up. "If I may be permitted to say so, madam, young Pascal is very close to the mark. You look regal indeed.

I am quite sure you will make a very fine impression. No one could doubt your fine breeding, not for a moment."

"Thank you, Binkley. I will try very hard not to let you down."

Binkley allowed himself a small smile. "I have no concerns, madam. Lord Brabourne is waiting in the carriage, sir. He is a trifle nervous, but well-turned-out."

"Thank you, Binkley. We are all a trifle nervous. However, Georgia believes it will be a repeat of Agincourt. Unfortunately, she has me pegged as Harry himself."

"Most apt, madam. I have full confidence that you shall emerge victorious, just as his majesty did."

"I hope so, Binkley," Nicholas said. "I do hope so. Pascal, it's long past your bedtime."

"Oh, but, monsieur, may I at least watch from the window as the carriage goes away? It is all so grand and exciting."

"Very well, little man, but then to bed with you and to sleep. We'll tell you all about it tomorrow." He accepted a hug and waited while Pascal kissed Georgia. "Let us go to our fate, sweetheart," he said, holding out his hand to her.

Binkley saw them out the door and into the carriage, and he, too, watched as the carriage drove off into the night. And then when it was out of sight he turned and walked back up the steps with a satisfied smile on his face.

" 'Cry "God for Harry! England and Saint George!" ' " he said, and shut the door behind him.

Georgia swallowed nervously, her heart knocking against her rib cage as they entered the Clarkes' house. They were all three of them very, very tense, and had barely exchanged a word in the carriage. Her heart went out to Cyril, for he had something quite different to face than either of them. She wished she could have offered him reassuring words, but she knew there was nothing to be said. She could only pray that this night he would be strong enough to confront his own demons and put them away for all time.

She glanced over at him. His face was pale, his eyes nervously darting around, no doubt for a sign of Jacqueline. Nicholas, on the other hand, looked surprisingly cool and collected as he waited for the footman to take her wrap. And then he tucked her hand back in his elbow, curling his fingers around hers.

"Quite the crush, is it not, my love?" he said to her, leading her through the entrance hall to the ballroom. "Marguerite will be so pleased. Cyril, you must go into the gallery at some point. Lord Clarke has an important collection. There is a particularly fine Van Dyck, not dissimilar to the one at Ravenswalk. Your father and Lord Clarke's father were great friends and avid collectors. I spent many an hour listening to them discuss art."

A head turned as he spoke, and then another, and suddenly there was a stir. Nicholas ignored it, continuing to chat, but Georgia felt the reassuring pressure of his fingers on hers. They crossed over the threshold of the ballroom, and as more heads turned to see who the new arrivals were, an almost perceptible hush came over the huge glittering room.

Georgia had a fair idea of what they must be thinking: Nicholas the debaucher next to his young cousin, so strikingly similar in looks and no doubt in nature. And herself, the whore of Babylon as Jacqueline had made her out to be, having the gall to appear in their rarefied company. She was surprised that a shriek didn't go up.

"Perhaps I should have blackened my teeth after all," she murmured.

Nicholas looked down at her, considering. "I rather like your teeth as they are. They're so . . . so French."

"French?" she said, unable to resist smiling. Nicholas had always had an uncanny ability to lighten her mood.

"I think we have c-created a s-sensation," Cyril said, looking about uncomfortably.

"We certainly have their attention," Nicholas replied quietly. "Buck up, coz. Honor is on our side, after all. It will all come out right in the end. Just look as if you're enjoying yourself vastly. You might as well confuse them."

A path had parted around them and an excited whispering had begun. It might have been the Red Sea parting, so wide was the sudden gulf. Marguerite realized instantly that they had arrived. She turned from her conversation and smiled broadly, excusing herself.

"How marvelous to see all three of you!" she said, going straight to them through the cleared path, and had a pin dropped, it would have echoed into the sudden silence. "I was wondering when you would arrive; I have been watching for you." She held out her hands and kissed their cheeks. "Georgia, *ma belle,* you are absolutely enchanting this evening. How the color pink suits you. And what a lovely set of pearls Nicholas has given you! I knew he was intent on spoiling you." She dropped her voice. "Your timing is perfect. Jacqueline is in the other room. It will give us a few extra minutes to set the stage. Come," she said, raising her voice again. "I mustn't stand here monopolizing you. It has been an age since you've been in London, Nicholas. No doubt there are many people you wish to speak with. And it is your first time up from Ravenswalk, is it not, Cyril? How handsome you have grown since last I saw you. I must find some young ladies for you to dance with. Georgia, dearest, there are so many people I must introduce you to—we shall be at it all night!"

Georgia managed to produce what she hoped was a glowing smile, although she felt as if her lips might crack. "Thank you, Marguerite. I should very much like to meet your friends." What she really wanted was to drop straight through the floor, never to be seen again, but she knew it was not to be.

"There are enough of them here, are there not?" Marguerite said, gesturing around her. "I am sure you will find them very amusing. The evening will not be dull, I promise you. Nicholas, do bring your wife along. And, Cyril, give me your arm, won't you? Ah, good, there is George. I know he will want to welcome you."

George was indeed welcoming. He could not have been more affable. Within a matter of moments he had managed to give the impression of great friendship with Nicholas, affection and respect toward Georgia, and polite interest in Cyril, whom he took off to introduce to some people closer to Cyril's own age. Marguerite quickly took them off in the opposite direction, and Georgia felt as if she were in a dream, for she knew such a thing could not really be happening to her. Where was the Georgia who had been married to Baggie Wells, the Georgia who had slaved in the vicarage, the Georgia who had spent long hours toiling over other women's wardrobes in cold, solitary rooms under the eaves? She felt almost a stranger to herself in this bright room filled with the cream of society. Had Nicholas likened her to Cinderella? If that were the case, she had better warn the coachman that he had less than an hour before he found himself transformed into a rat and the footmen into lizards. And that thought made her smile.

"What amuses you so, sweetheart?" Nicholas asked under his breath, glancing down at her. "Could it be the looks of polite horror we are receiving as we pass?"

"Oh, no," she answered blithely. "Polite horror is the least of it, although it is amusing to see the fans go up and the faces disappear behind them. Such a colorful sight. I was merely thinking of how it would be to ride off in a hollowed-out pumpkin."

"Fairly damp and drafty, I should think," Nicholas replied, looking straight ahead.

"Actually, I was more concerned about the seeds. They'd get everywhere."

"Yes, seeds would definitely be a consideration. And then there is also the odor to be considered. I should think you would find it quite musty."

"What are you two going on about?" Marguerite asked, having overheard this last exchange. "What would be musty?"

"We were discussing the drawbacks of a pumpkin as a method of transportation," Nicholas replied.

"In a hypothetical situation, of course," Georgia added.

"Ah, but of course," Marguerite said, smiling at them both. "I am pleased that you can see the humor in the situation."

"How could one fail to?" Nicholas said. "It is not every day Georgia and I have the opportunity to shock a good portion of the polite world. I'm finding it quite stimulating, aren't you, sweetheart?" He bowed his head at someone in passing, and the poor woman looked about to swoon.

Georgia had to resist an overwhelming urge to laugh, for Nicholas was a devil, without doubt. "Oh, yes," she said, "I quite agree. I adore stimulation. I cannot think what I ever did without it."

Nicholas gave a snort of laughter and squeezed her waist.

"Georgia!" Marguerite said with mock horror, but her eyes danced. "You must control these French impulses to which you are prone!"

"Must she?" Nicholas said sadly. "What a pity. I'm rather fond of Georgia's impulses."

Marguerite tapped him on the shoulder with her fan. "As well you should be, wicked man. But careful now. We approach our objective. Fortunately our progress has been without incident."

"No, the commotion is yet to come," Nicholas answered tightly, his amusement gone. "Let's get on with it, Marguerite."

Georgia found herself standing in front of a stout elderly woman bedecked in garnets, who was sitting comfortably in a corner, watching the proceedings with a sharp eye.

"Lady Horsley, you remember Nicholas Daventry, do you not?" Marguerite said.

"How in heaven's name would you expect me to forget, may I ask?" she said as Nicholas bowed over her hand. "Good evening, Mr. Daventry. I have watched your progression across the room with some interest. You have a great deal of spleen, showing your face in this crowd. You are either very stupid or very courageous. Marguerite, what are you and George up to? You have the entire place in a flap. I cannot believe you would invite Daventry here unless you had a very good reason. I assume you know something the rest of the world does not?"

"George and I wish to correct a number of past wrongs, Lady Horsley, and as you are one of the fairest people I have ever known, and also one of the most influential, I thought you might be pleased to help. May I introduce Nicholas' wife, Georgia?"

Georgia sank into a curtsy. "It is a pleasure to meet you, Lady Horsley." She prayed her curtsy had not been lopsided. It was hard to tell with her knees feeling so weak. She had never been so nervous, nor so terrified, in her life.

"Humph," said Lady Horsley, examining Georgia through her lorgnette. "You don't look in the least like a cheap hussy to me, my girl."

Nicholas' face broke into a sudden unexpected grin. "You have very keen eyesight, Lady Horsley."

"There's never been a thing wrong with my eyesight, young man, and what I see in your wife is good bones and refinement. The girl's got a familiar look about her. So what's all this nonsense that's going about? From the way I've been hearing it, you're still as depraved as they come, and your wife's no better than a harlot."

"My wife, Lady Horsley, is anything but a harlot. And as for my own depravity, I would say that is a matter of interpretation. I cannot claim complete purity, but I do at least attempt good manners."

Georgia's hand slipped to her chest at this audaciousness on Nicholas' part. She risked a quick look at Marguerite, who seemed amused, and Lady Horsley seemed amused also, for she gave a bark of laughter. "It's no more than any of us can do," Lady Horsley said. "So, boy, your step-aunt said she had to leave Ravenswalk once you came home, she was so upset by your return. How do you explain that?"

"I would not attempt to explain anything my step-aunt says or does," Nicholas said calmly. "However, I would say that there has been a certain amount of misrepresentation."

"Then here is your chance to have the truth out, with most of London to witness it and only me to hear. You have engineered the situation beautifully, Marguerite. My compliments. You always were a clever girl." She gestured behind them with her lorgnette.

Georgia turned around, only to see Jacqueline. She was standing a few feet away, staring as if she could not believe her eyes. Her face was as white as chalk and her dark eyes blazed with a violent fury. She started toward them. Georgia recognized the dress she was wearing, for it was one she herself had sewn, and it brought back everything with a great sick rush. Nicholas put his arm around her waist and she was grateful for it, for her legs truly felt as if they wouldn't hold her.

"Why, good evening, Jacqueline," Nicholas said. "How interesting to see you again."

"Jacqueline, just the person," Marguerite said in a good imitation of nonchalance. "I was wondering where you'd gone to. Look who is here!"

"I am not blind. What is the meaning of this, Marguerite?" Jacqueline hissed in a voice worthy of any viper. "Why have they not been removed?"

"But we invited Nicholas and Georgia most particularly. Why would I have them removed?"

"No," she said, truly shocked. "You *invited* them? I do not believe it!"

"But it is quite true," Marguerite said. "Why would I lie to you?"

Jacqueline's hand fluttered at her breast. "Marguerite! How . . . how could you insult me so?" she gasped in tones of hurt indignation.

"I certainly did not meant to insult you," Marguerite said quietly. "I intend only to set matters straight."

"Set matters . . . Marguerite, you have always been a feather-brain," Jacqueline spat furiously, dropping her injured tone in sheer surprise. "But now I do believe you have taken complete leave of your senses!"

"I find that a bit harsh, Jacqueline, seeing that this is my house and I am giving this ball. It seems to me that I may invite whomever I please, even if my choice does not meet with your approval."

Jacqueline paused for one astonished moment, then doubly renewed her assault. "You would dare to fly in my face so? I warn you, Marguerite—"

"You warn me of what?" Marguerite asked, as if she could have cared less about her sister's threats.

Jacqueline twitched her skirt into place. "I tell you now that if you will not have them removed, then I shall leave myself."

"Oh, please, not on our account," Nicholas said. "It would be such a loss." He examined the back of his hand as he spoke, looking extremely bored.

Jacqueline shot Nicholas a look of true venom, her lips compressed, then turned back to her sister. "I would have a word with you in private, Marguerite. I am sure you do not wish to be embarrassed in front of your guests.''

"Please, don't mind me in the least," Lady Horsley said. "I am spellbound. I haven't enjoyed myself so much in ages."

Jacqueline, her bosom heaving with a display of injured indignation, nodded curtly. "Very well. If you will not even give me the courtesy of a private audience, Marguerite, then I shall indeed leave. And do not think that it will go unnoticed. Furthermore, don't think I won't have something to say about this later."

"I would not doubt it," Marguerite said.

"I can ruin you, don't think I won't," Jacqueline said into her sister's ear, but her words carried nevertheless.

"I don't doubt that you would attempt that either," Marguerite replied. "However, I do doubt your success in this particular attempt."

"I agree," Nicholas said lazily. "And I must say, you have developed an unpleasant habit, Jacqueline. It really is getting to be tiresome, this unceasing effort to ruin your relatives."

"You filthy animal!" she spat, then spun around on her heel, only to find her exit blocked by George, who had come up behind her.

"Ah, Jacqueline," he said. "I see you have been welcoming our guests."

"Welcoming? *Welcoming*? Are you mad? I would have thought at least you would have had some sense, George, but instead you allow this . . . this degenerate into your house, knowing I will be faced with him, knowing how I feel? And further, you allow him to bring her?" She pointed a shaking finger at Georgia. "I am sickened. Sickened. How could you?"

"But it is a family gathering, Jacqueline," George said. "Naturally Nicholas and Georgia should be here. Cyril is here also."

Jacqueline took a small step backward. "Cyril?" she repeated. "Where?"

"Somewhere in the house," George said, gesturing about him. "I left him with a group of young bucks."

"You . . . you had no right to take him from Ravenswalk without my permission. He is my stepson, under my authority."

"Is that what you would call it?" Nicholas asked coolly. "I would use a different word. Actually, it was my decision. I felt it was time for Cyril to have a normal life, to be with people his own age, to meet appropriate young women. I am sure you would not object to such a natural pursuit, Jacqueline? I know he seems young, but he is very advanced for his age in many ways."

Jacqueline's hand jerked almost imperceptibly, but Nicholas did not miss it and he did not hesitate to press his advantage. "Surely you must agree, Jacqueline, that Cyril needs a strong male influence in his life. I am quite happy to provide it."

"You? You think to provide any kind of influence over an impressionable boy?"

Nicholas gave her a cold smile. "My point exactly."

Jacqueline did not move a muscle. "You have no point," she said. "Nor have you any right to interfere."

"Oh, but I think I do. As Cyril's father is so unfortunately ill, I am the only blood relative Cyril has left to him. I intend to take his father's place until such time as he is recovered. But I do think that we really must clear up past misunderstandings, for there is no need for Cyril to pay for the mistakes of others."

"What do you mean by that?" she asked, her eyes narrowing.

"It is quite simple. I am well aware of your version of events, Jacqueline, but I have explained to your sister and her husband what really happened ten years ago."

Jacqueline stared at her sister, one hand creeping to her throat. "And you *believed* him? You believed his word over mine? He is a liar! A liar, I say! He would make up anything! Oh, Marguerite, how could you turn on me in such a manner?"

"But I don't turn on you in the least!" Marguerite replied. "Jacqueline, do not be foolish. Do you think George or I would have welcomed Nicholas back if we thought he had harmed you in any way? But when Nicholas told us what had happened, we realized what a terrible mistake had been made."

"I do not know what he could possibly have explained," she said nervously, looking from one to th other of them.

"I explained that nightmares are terrible things, Jacqueline, and can seem extremely real," Nicholas said easily enough, but his tone made it clear that he meant not a word of what he said. "Sometimes it is almost impossible to distinguish a nightmare from reality."

"A—a nightmare? What sort of nightmare do you mean?"

"As I told you then, when I went to your room that night, it was because you were crying out in fright. I was concerned that something might be wrong. Obviously you were dreaming that you were being assaulted, and in the process of my waking you, you confused me with your dream. Do you really not remember even now, Jacqueline? Of course, at the time I know you believed the story yourself, and it spread so quickly that I had no means of defending myself against it. But do you truly not remember how it really happened?"

Jacqueline was silent. Her eyes flickered around the room as if searching for a means of escape, but all that met her was the concentrated collective gaze of a crowded roomful of very interested guests. Her eyes dropped to the floor.

"I am sure that, if pressed, I could jog your memory, Jacqueline." Nicholas crossed his arms over his chest.

Jacqueline finally passed a hand over her face. "No, that won't be necessary. I . . . Perhaps I was mistaken after all. I was so panicked that it never occurred to me I might have been dreaming. I thought you were only trying to excuse yourself. But if you are quite sure, then I am prepared to accept your explanation. For Cyril's sake."

"That is very generous of you," Nicholas said, his voice dripping with irony. "And does that mean that you are also prepared to accept my wife?"

"Do not push me, Nicholas," Jacqueline said coldly. "There are certain standards which you might have ignored, but the polite world will not."

Nicholas looked at her with thinly veiled disgust. "Really? You might be surprised. What is it you cavil at the most? The fact that Georgia was in your employ? Or is it that you believe she has no breeding?"

"I refuse to go into this with you," Jacqueline said with annoyance. "You may have no judgment as to how to behave, but I have, and I am sure Lady Horsley would agree with me. We have said quite enough. Let us leave it alone, if you please. You cannot want to embarrass your wife any further."

"You are quite right. I think Georgia has been embarrassed enough. I only wish to set the record straight, for my wife has every bit as much right to be in this room as you have."

"What do you mean?" Jacqueline said sharply. "Just what do you mean by that?"

"Jacqueline. Can you not see it?" Marguerite said, taking her shoulders none too gently and turning her to face Georgia, whose eyes she'd avoided during the entire conversation.

Georgia met Jacqueline's eyes evenly enough, but as she did, she thought of what this woman had done to all the people she loved and she felt her insides twist. It was almost impossible for her to believe that another human being was capable of such deliberate cruelty. The thought helped her to steel herself against the enmity in Jacqueline's eyes.

"What is it I am supposed to see?" Jacqueline said, shrugging off her sister's hands. "I see my dressmaker, who had the impudence to run off with Raven's nephew without giving any warning. I see an upstart who has no place here. I see—"

"Our sister Eugenie," Marguerite interrupted. "You are looking at her daughter. That is what you see, Jacqueline. You see your own niece, Eugenie's daughter, standing before you. I wonder how that makes you feel."

"No. I don't believe it. She's lying." Jacqueline sounded almost panicked. "She was in my household long enough to learn all sorts of things about our family! And now she thinks to make herself respectable with this absurd claim? It is ludicrous! I cannot credit that you believe it, Marguerite!"

"Oh, I believe it, Jacqueline. It would be impossible not to. I discovered quite by chance that the woman before you was born in August 1797 and named Georgina Eugenie Cameron. I am sure you are delighted to hear of it.''

"Good God!" Lady Horsley exclaimed with shock, her lorgnette flashing to her eyes as she reexamined Georgia. "Not dear Charles's daughter? Tell me, child—is this true?"

"It is true. Charles Cameron was my father," Georgia said, her throat suddenly tight with unexpected tears.

"Oh, my dear . . . oh, my dear child, I can scarcely believe it! That's what's been pricking at me—I knew there was a resemblance! If it isn't the most extraordinary thing! Charlie's daughter. Oh, those were tragic times. Near broke my heart, it did, and his parents' too."

"It broke my parents' hearts as well, Lady Horsley," Marguerite said. "But my father felt he had no choice but to believe the story, given the source. You'll be happy to know all of it was untrue, as Georgia's birthdate will confirm. Charles and Eugenie were quite innocent of any wrongdoing."

"Well, of course they were. Of course they were. Charlie was a good boy. The allegations were ridiculous. Can't think how these sorts of things get started, although I do seem to remember where this story came from quite well." Her eyes went straight to Jacqueline, who stiffened but said nothing, pretending complete disinterest.

"Humph," Lady Horsley said with disgust. "It just goes to show that some people never change. But never mind, it's all water under the bridge now and can't be helped. Old Ewan will be overjoyed to know he has a granddaughter at last, and one born on the right side of the blanket. It is a pity Georgina didn't live to mark this day, for she would have been terribly happy. Goodness, I feel quite like crying, and I haven't indulged in tears in years. My dear Georgia, allow a sentimental old woman to bestow a kiss upon you, for I find I am truly over-whelmed."

Georgia, blushing fiercely, but terribly touched, moved over to Lady Horsley and bent down. But it was she who kissed the woman's wrinkled cheek, and she who wiped the tears from it afterward. "Thank you, Lady Horsley," she said quietly, her own voice choked with emotion. "Thank you."

"For what, dear child? For what? It is I who should thank you for reminding me of my dear godson. It was one of the saddest moments of my life when that gentle boy was so maligned, his life destroyed almost before it had begun. And here you are with his eyes, and such a look of your grandmother. No wonder Charlie named you after her. Well, if this isn't a fine day indeed. So, what say you now, Jacqueline? Are you going to continue to slander your own niece? I believe you called her no better than a harlot, with manners to match?"

Jacqueline's eyes flickered back and forth between them. "I . . . I don't know what to say," she said, passing her tongue over her lips. "I had no idea. How was I supposed to know? I thought she was something quite different."

"It is no longer of importance," Marguerite said. "It is quite clear that Georgia is Charles's and Eugenie's daughter. You must be terribly pleased."

"I . . . Yes, of course. I am only surprised. Overwhelmed." It was Jacqueline who now looked ill.

"Yes, I can scarce imagine your emotion," Nicholas said caustically. "I know how strong Georgia's emotion was to learn of her relationship to you. And my own, naturally, not to mention your sister's. You must feel quite bad about having maligned Georgia in such a way, now that you know the truth of the matter. I am certain you have every regret. Haven't you, Jacqueline?"

"Yes . . . yes, of course."

"Yes, naturally you do. It appears you have made a number of errors of judgment. I am delighted to have had them corrected this evening. I have discovered, you see, that it is rather difficult laboring under a cloud of undeserved disgrace, and I certainly did not want my wife to have to undergo the same experience. Ah, well," he said, turning his back on her, "there's no point dwelling on the past. If you'll excuse us, Lady Horsley, I hear the waltz striking up. I think I shall ask my wife for a dance. Jacqueline clearly needs time to recover herself."

"No . . . wait," Jacqueline said, aware of every eye upon them. "I feel I should . . . Not having known, of

348

course, that you were my niece . . . Well . . . It is most awkward, naturally, but I feel I must welcome you to the family, Georgia.'' She moved toward her, and Georgia could not help recoiling.

"Thank you, Lady Raven,'' she said, dropping a low curtsy, thereby avoiding Jacqueline's attempt to kiss her cheek, for the gesture went directly over her head.

Lady Horsley snorted with laughter. "Very prettily done, my dear,'' she said. "Now, off you go with your husband, but don't you forget to come back and sit with me later. There is much I wish to discover.'' She turned her attention to Jacqueline. "Well, I must say, I have never thought much of you or your tactics, but you've gone and made a real hash of it this time. I truly wonder how you think you are going to recover the situation. I doubt very much it will be possible. And I must say, it gives me great satisfaction to see you finally about to receive your just desserts. Believe me, I will do all I can to help it along. If I were you, my dear Lady Raven, I would make myself scarce. There is not a thing left you can say without making yourself appear a bigger fool than you already have.''

Jacqueline took one deep shuddering breath, then spun on her heel and marched off, her head held high.

Lady Horsley nodded. "Very clever,'' she said to Marguerite and George. "Very clever indeed. A stroke of genius, in fact. I can hear the lot of you cooking this one up. And I must say, I would love to know the true story, for I do believe Daventry was offering a very sanitized version of events.''

"Nicholas has told the true story to no one save his wife,'' Marguerite said. "But you can be sure that he was not the villain of the piece.''

"That much I do believe. There was a look on his face that told me as much. It is a pity he did not defend himself in the first place.''

"Apparently his uncle's honor meant more to him than his own,'' George said. "But I doubt we'll ever know. Nicholas would have the story he told tonight stand.''

"A wise decision,'' Lady Horsley said, pushing herself to her feet with a grunt. "A very wise decision. Now, rejoin your guests, and I'll start doing my job. I'm going to see to it that Charlie's daughter is received with every bit of approbation she deserves, and her fine husband along with her, for Daventry has suffered far too long under your sister's slings and arrows. Oh, this is going to be a very great pleasure indeed.'' She stumped off, chuckling to herself, and George exchanged a quiet look of satisfaction with his wife, then took her hand and led her into the crowd that was waiting agog for enlightenment.

''Come here,'' Nicholas said, pulling Georgia into his arms and moving her into the waltz. ''That was exhausting but quite gratifying. How are you, sweetheart? You managed beautifully.''

''I didn't do a thing—I just stood there like a sack of flour, Nicholas!''

''I don't think you in any way resembled a sack of flour. You very wisely held your peace. I am sure the temptation to box Jacqueline's ears must have been great.''

''Actually, I was concentrating more on staying upright. There is something about the sight of that woman that makes me want to run and hide under a bed.''

''I know the feeling,'' Nicholas said with amusement. ''I have been pushed to hiding from her myself. But all in all, I think things went quite well. Lady Horsley certainly seemed prepared to believe the story.''

''Nicholas, you were brilliant! Jacqueline did not have a chance against you! I have never before seen you so . . . so *menacing*. I've always thought of you as such a gentle man, but I had been faced with your contained anger tonight, I should have gone flying from the room in terror.''

He grinned down at her. ''You told me to emulate Harry, and so I did. I routed the French, did I not?''

''You did, my darling, you did, and without a drop of blood shed. I am very proud of you.''

''I think it went quite well. It was a good plan. Now all we have to do is see how Jacqueline reacts after the fact.''

''And everyone else,'' Georgia said, glancing around, then quickly bringing her attention back to the waltz, for she had practiced it for only a week and was not completely sure of herself.

"Oh, I wouldn't worry," Nicholas said, leading her easily, not the least concerned with her lack of skill. "The biggest obstacle was Lady Horsley, and if you look over toward the door, you will see that she is very busy putting the word in the right ears. What a stroke of luck that she was your father's godmother. By the by, if I'm correct, your grandmother must have been Georgina Savile, the younger daughter of the Earl of Hargrove and a renowned beauty, so there's another aristocrat to add to your list. When the dance finishes, we will no doubt be besieged by various interested factions claiming kinship. Enjoy your last few minutes of privacy. I think you have had a grand success without even having to open your mouth. I wonder if you feel blessed or cursed."

"Only blessed, and that because of you. Nicholas, I think you are very wonderful."

"Do you, sweetheart?" he said, looking down at her with a tender smile. "You do have a tendency to glorify me, but I must say it feels rather wonderful to have my reputation restored. Well, maybe restored."

"Absolutely restored."

"We'll see. The *ton* are a fickle lot. Your acceptance is guaranteed. Mine is still slightly questionable. I did manage to frighten the hell out of Jacqueline, though. Did you see the expression on her face when she thought I'd told the entire story to her sister?"

"Oh, yes, and when you brought up Cyril too. That was a fine moment, for I could see she couldn't tell how much you knew, but she was worried."

"Witch," Nicholas said succinctly. "She puts me in mind of Morgause. Her morals are about on a par. But let us forget about Jacqueline for a few minutes, anyway. It seems we've thought of nothing else for the last fortnight, and it's still far from over. I want to concentrate on nothing more complicated than holding you in my arms and relishing the feel of your toes upon mine."

That remark caused Georgia to burst into laughter. She did not notice in the least the heads that began to turn toward them in fascination as the story started to make its appointed rounds, nor Jacqueline's flight from the room as she realized the tide had suddenly and irrevocably turned against her.

Cyril watched Nicholas and Georgia through the veranda window, just as he had watched the confrontation with Jacqueline. He had slipped out of the house the first chance he'd had, finding that he was acutely uncomfortable with the people Lord Clarke had made such an effort to introduce him to. He had nothing in common with them. Nothing. He probably never would. He far preferred being alone in the dark.

He sighed and leaned back against the wall, something inside of him sad and heavy. He wasn't sure what it was, although he knew it was all tied up with the stain on his soul. It almost hurt sometimes to see the happiness that Nicholas had found with Georgia. It wasn't that he begrudged Nicholas his happiness, for if anyone deserved it, Nicholas did. It was just that he knew it was something that he would never have himself.

He often thought about killing himself, but that would probably only compound his sins. Not that he thought God even existed: he hadn't believed in God for some time now. What it really came down to was that he was far too much of a coward. But there were times such as now when he didn't know what to do with the terrible, bleak melancholy that ate away at him like a great weeping canker in his soul.

He wondered if it was apparent to anyone else. Sometimes he thought Pascal guessed at it. But Pascal was uncanny when it came to guessing at what was inside of people. And there had been a time or two recently when he had wondered just how much Nicholas understood. Funny how he had hated him for so long, so deeply, and now all he could feel was a strange detachment. He knew Nicholas was trying his best. But there were so many things Nicholas did not know, things Cyril could never tell him. Maybe that was the worst of all—the darkest secrets he could never speak. As hard as he had tried to run away from them, they were always there, waiting.

"So there you are."

Cyril spun around and stumbled with his shock. "J-Jacqueline. . . . Oh, G-God. You s-scared me."

"Did you think to hide from me out here? You should know better, Cyril. And what have you been up to, I wonder? Just what do you think you are doing in London with your cousin? Have you suddenly changed camps, Cyril? Do you really think I would allow that?"

He raised his chin. "It is n-not any l-longer a question of what y-you w-will allow."

"So. Have you been corrupted by your cousin? I never would have thought it possible, but I can see that you must have been."

"S-strange for you t-to use a w-word like 'c-corrupt,' " he countered, "g-given that you have b-been p-poisoning my f-father."

"This is a fine time for you to start objecting," she spat. "Do you really want him back? Do you want him remembering, Cyril? Surely you haven't forgotten what made him fall ill in the first place?"

"I'm n-not likely to f-forget," Cyril said furiously. "And d-don't think I w-won't have to l-live with the l-look on his f-face for all eternity. B-but he would have b-been b-better off d-dead than the way you've k-kept him."

Jacqueline was silent, staring off into the distance. "Yes," she said. "Maybe it is time for that. You are growing up, Cyril, I can see it now. You have become much stronger. Maybe it is time for you to take charge, and with me behind you, we can make Ravenswalk even greater."

"T-tell me," Cyril asked, "what would you d-do if my father r-recovered? How would you explain m-matters? Would you explain them as you explained them to m-me? Would you t-tell him how you l-loved m-me, how you p-preferred my attentions to his?"

"What is this nonsense, Cyril? He will never wake. I promised you that. It is a moot point. I can see I have left you alone too long, and you are feeling neglected. But truly, Cyril, I could not bear being in the same vicinity as your cousin. I really could not. I had hoped by this time he would have given up on trying to restore the Close and left. Imagine my shock and dismay to find him here tonight, spreading his lies. And to bring his whore— it is beyond belief! But what I cannot understand is your presence here. Have you been keeping an eye on his activities, perhaps, playing along with him? Of course that must be it. I knew you would not betray me, my sweet one.''

Cyril said nothing. He felt thoroughly sick and weary. He wanted nothing more than for Jacqueline to vanish into thin air, never to be seen again. He wouldn't have minded vanishing himself.

"Cyril? Why are you so silent?" She put her hand out and touched his chest, her fingers moving sensually on him.

"You are a f-fool," Cyril said, taking her hand and violently moving it away. "D-do you want p-people to s-see?"

"You are quite right. How masterful you have become. I find it most attractive in you, Cyril. Do you know, I find I have missed you. Why don't we leave for Ravenswalk tonight? We could be together again. Wouldn't that be nice?''

"N-not p-particularly," Cyril said. "As a m-matter of f-fact, I can think of n-nothing more d-distasteful."

He turned abruptly and walked down the stairs into the garden, leaving her standing alone.

The minute he was out of sight, he was violently sick.

19

Pascal listened with rapt attention as Nicholas described the ball over breakfast the next morning, detailing for him the food, the music, the lights, the bright colors. Nicholas was amused to see that Binkley was also listening with rapt attention from his post by the sideboard, where he was taking rather longer than usual with the teapot.

"And then what happened, monsieur? Did people stand back with great admiration and watch you dancing?" Pascal's hand still held the untouched piece of toast he had picked up five minutes before and forgotten.

"No, they were far too busy admiring themselves and each other. Those who weren't dancing were very busy gossiping. But once the music had finished, all sorts of people were very eager to be introduced to Georgia, for they thought her very beautiful and fine."

"But of course. And did they think you very beautiful and fine too?"

"They most certainly did not, although there didn't seem to be any objection to my presence. Binkley, do you think I might have that tea now?"

"Certainly, sir." Binkley brought the pot over and poured.

"And what of Cyril?" Pascal asked. "Did he dance many dances and flirt with all the ladies?"

"Actually, I didn't see Cyril at all, not until just before we left. He must have been playing cards."

"Yes. He likes to play cards very much, although he does not like it when he loses. And the wicked *belle-mère* of Cyril's? What happened to her?"

"Who told you she was wicked?" Nicholas asked with exasperation.

"Cyril did. And I have heard you and madame talking, of course. She is wicked, is she not?"

"Yes, Pascal, she is. Very wicked indeed, although I do hope you have not picked up Cyril's habit of listening in on other people's conversations."

"Oh, no, monsieur. But one cannot help sometimes hearing. And what became of her?"

"She left early. She discovered quite quickly that the tide of public opinion had turned against her, for she had told some nasty stories about Georgia and me that were not at all true. The *ton* is so fickle. In any case, I expect she is feeling rather cross with me this morning. As a matter of fact, I expect her to appear on the doorstep sometime today."

"Why would she do that if she is cross with you? When I am cross with someone, I do not want to see them at all."

"Very understandable," Nicholas said, stirring a spoonful of sugar, an almost forgotten luxury, into his tea. "But Lady Raven is not like normal people. She likes to make trouble in any way she can. And you see, I want her to come to visit me, for I have a great many things to say to her. So I shall wait for her."

Pascal's smooth brow puckered slightly. "You will be careful of her, monsieur? I think she sounds very evil, this Lady Raven."

"I will be careful, Pascal. But I cannot let her continue to hurt people as she has been doing."

"Yes, I understand. It is only that I do not have a good feeling."

Nicholas smiled broadly. "I think you are overprotective of me, Pascal. I am not quite as feeble as you might think."

"You are not feeble in the least, monsieur!" Pascal said indignantly.

"Well, I try not to be. But I should like you to stay out of the way today, for it could become slightly complicated. I think it would be nice if you and Cyril spent the afternoon riding in the park."

"Very well, monsieur, although it is very dreary being sent away from the excitement, and I should very much like to see this wicked woman."

"I am quite sure you would, my little man, but you will simply have to bow to my dictates on this matter. And as I don't want Cyril anywhere near her, you can be the excuse for him to leave for a time."

"Ah, if it is for Cyril, then naturally I will ask him to take me away. The morning grows late, monsieur, and the wicked woman might come at any time. I will go and wake Cyril now and take him out of the house."

"Thank you, Pascal. You are most considerate."

Pascal threw down his uneaten toast and disappeared, and Nicholas looked over at Binkley. "That child," he said, "is quite beyond belief."

"Indeed, sir. More tea?"

"No, thank you, Binkley. I believe I will go up and have a word with Georgia. She was so tired last night when we came home that she was asleep before her head hit the pillow. Oh, and I expect we will have quite a few visitors this afternoon, Binkley; Georgia was a great success last night. Should Lady Raven be foolish enough to appear while anyone else is here, have her shown into my study. However, I do not look for her until later."

Binkley bowed. "May I express my delight, sir, that your campaign has been successful?"

"Let us not be premature, Binkley. My campaign will not be a success until Jacqueline de Give is out of the country, never to return. However, the situation looks favorable for such a thing. If my guess is correct, she will discover today that she is *persona non grata* among the very people whose acceptance she has so craved."

"It wouldn't be surprising, sir. People do not take well to being deceived."

"So it seems. But that is the least of her troubles, and so she will discover. Would you have Florentine take up a tray to my wife, Binkley? And you might want to take a tray to Cyril. He was looking very pale and worn last night and could probably use something to eat."

"As you say, sir." Binkley went back into the kitchen, and Nicholas started upstairs.

Georgia woke to find Nicholas pulling back the curtains and letting the light in. She pushed herself up in bed, rubbing her eyes.

"Good morning, sweetheart," Nicholas said, coming over to her and dropping a kiss on her head. "You are absolutely enchanting and I should like to take every advantage of you, but I shall have to restrain myself. The hour grows late and you have things to do."

"What a shame," she said, yawning and squinting at the window. "What time is it?"

"Coming up to eleven. I've never known you to be so lazy, woman, lying in bed till all hours, frittering away the day. There are cows to be milked, you know."

Georgia hit him with a pillow. "I am a very fine lady now, in case you haven't noticed. Very fine ladies not only do not milk cows, they are absolutely expected to wallow in their beds until all hours."

He sat down on the edge of the bed and kissed her hand. "Well, see here, my fine lady. Unless you plan to entertain the *ton* from your boudoir, you had better think about rising fairly shortly. You are going to be having a busy afternoon."

"Oh!" Georgia said with alarm. "Do you mean we must start this all over again? It seems we just went to bed."

"I'm afraid we must. Actually, it's all on your shoulders this afternoon. I am expected to stay well out of the way, which suits me very well indeed."

"It makes the Close seem more inviting than ever," Georgia said, yawning again. "I would far rather be putting my energies into gardening than entertaining a slew of curious women."

"A slew is exactly what you can expect. Now, up, my love, for if you are not out of this bed within a minute, you shall find me in it with you, and that could seriously delay matters. Your callers await."

He was right. There was a flood of callers that afternoon. Georgia knew they'd been motivated by curiosity more than anything else, but nevertheless she was gratified to see how readily they had decided to accept Nicholas and her. Lady Horsley had led the pack, and Georgia could see how very wise George and Marguerite had been in their decision to appeal to Lady Horsley's sense of justice. Once convinced of their innocence, she had spared no effort to bring other people of influence over to her side. And she had indeed gone after people of influence. Lady Sefton, Lady Cowper, and even Princess Esterhazy had been persuaded that Jacqueline had grossly misbehaved, and they had descended upon Number Two, Upper Brook Street in tandem and pronounced themselves satisfied that a terrible injustice had been done. Lady Jersey, not to be outdone, arrived shortly after.

It was all Georgia could do not to laugh. She felt not unlike an animal in a zoo. She knew well enough that this afternoon parade had more to do with a dislike of Jacqueline than it did with any admirable qualities on her part, but she was truly amazed at how quickly the story had spread. People must have been up and running about very early in the morning, for they seemed to know an uncanny amount about it all. And on one thing they agreed universally: Jacqueline had deliberately set out to destroy Nicholas' reputation.

Lady Horsley contended that Jacqueline had also deliberately set out to destroy her sister and Charles Cameron, and took great pleasure in the telling of that story.

Lady Sefton decided that Jacqueline must have known that Georgia was her niece and had done everything in her power to see that Georgia suffered ostracism.

Mrs. Drummond Burrell, sniffing, announced that Jacqueline would most certainly never be allowed inside the doors of Almack's again, and that she would be the first to offer Georgia and Nicholas vouchers. She also hailed Marguerite as a heroine for having had the courage to present Nicholas and Georgia at her own ball and the moral fortitude to denounce her own sister.

Marguerite had also been busy, for the story of Nicholas' heroism during the shipwreck had spread. He would be most annoyed, Georgia knew, but it only enhanced his good character in the eyes of society and so it was all for the best, one more piece of ammunition against Jacqueline.

By the afternoon's end it had become clear that it was Jacqueline's reputation that was in shreds. It almost seemed to Georgia as if people had been waiting for an excuse to turn their backs on Jacqueline, and she wasn't particularly surprised. Maybe the *ton* had better taste than she'd thought, although she could easily have done without some of their stuffiness. It made her even more thankful for Nicholas' easy manner.

She saw the last of the callers out, than wandered over to the window, looking out onto the street. London. How different it seemed to her now. Here she was standing in her very own drawing room, having just received a good portion of the aristocracy. Last night she had been to her first ball, had curtsied and danced and conversed as if she'd been doing it all of her life. At her side had been her husband, not only a magnificent figure of a man but also kind of heart and keen of wit, with a sense of humor to match.

Baggie flashed into her mind. She saw him lumbering into the kitchen, throwing himself down onto a chair and demanding his supper, wiping his greasy mouth on his sleeve when he had finished his meal. And then she saw him lumbering off again, this time to the tavern to play dice and drink himself half-senseless. She shuddered. That life sometimes seemed more real than the life she was living now. There were still times that she thought she might be dreaming and would wake up to find herself back there, if not in Baggie's kitchen, then in her turret at Ravenswalk.

"Georgia? Love? What are you dreaming about?"

She started, and turned around. Nicholas stood inside the door with a quizzical smile on his face. "Are you feeling pleased with yourself? Binkley is over the moon. I think he feels his life is back on course. He can now finally hold his head high and be proud of his charges."

"I can well imagine. Funny how we work so hard to please Binkley, isn't it, Nicholas?"

"But he deserves our every effort. Just think of the sacrifices he has made in the name of love, Georgia."

"Do you know, I felt his watchful eye on me all of the afternoon as he came in and out. I think I managed most of it correctly, though, for he never once cleared his throat."

Nicholas gave a short laugh. "A sure sign. So, What were you thinking when I came in? You seemed very far away."

"I was thinking that the very same blood thrums in
360

my veins as always has. It is only society's opinion of it that has changed."

"Hmm. I suppose that is true enough. But my opinion of your blood remains exactly the same as it has always been. It is very, very red. And I should know."

"Nicholas," Georgia said, laughing. "You have never seen a single drop of my blood. Not one!"

"That is what you think," he said. "What about the time that you jabbed your thumb with a needle when you were talking about the vicarage?"

"Oh, yes. Then."

"You see? And you think to doubt me." He took her in his arms. "All teasing aside, I am very proud of you. I know it has not been an easy time, but you have come through beautifully. I must confess, I never thought I would be married to a darling of society."

"I am no darling of society. I am merely the latest *on-dit* and a convenient way for some of these tabbies to get their own back on Jacqueline, who I suspect has needled them for years."

"Likely as not. God, it was satisfying seeing her face last night when she realized that she had made a few serious miscalculations. Today the full implications of the matter must be sinking in. I wonder what she is doing now."

"Walking up the front steps, by the look of it," Georgia said softly.

"Is she, by God? It took her long enough. I don't know that you want to stay for this, sweetheart, although you have every right."

"I think it is best if you handle her, Nicholas. I would only serve to distract."

"Yes, you are probably right," he said. "Better to give her only one target."

"Be careful, Nicholas," Georgia said, suddenly feeling anxious.

"Don't worry, my love. I have promised Pascal the same thing, for he seemed to think she might take me down with her. But she will not. This shouldn't take very long."

The door to the drawing room opened, and Binkley

appeared. "Lady Raven requests an audience, sir. Shall I show her in?"

"If you please, Binkley," Nicholas said in a very haughty voice, and Georgia had to smile.

"Good luck," she whispered, then kissed him and went out the door.

Jacqueline was standing in the hall, looking around her with a degree of incredulity, and Georgia gave her a brief glance. "Good afternoon, Lady Raven," she said, then started up the stairs.

"Do not think you will get away with this," she heard Jacqueline say, and she paused, then turned.

"Do you speak to me?" Georgia asked calmly, despite the churning of her stomach at the very sight of the woman. "I am surprised. And quite honestly I have no desire to speak with you at all, save to say one thing. To have accused my mother and my father in the manner you did is alone enough to see you cast off the face of the earth. But everything else you have done since then only indicates to me that you deserve to burn in hell for all eternity. Good day, Lady Raven."

She continued up the stairs, pleased to hear nothing but sputtering from behind her.

Nicholas closed the door behind Jacqueline. "Would you care to sit?" he asked.

"No, thank you," she said tightly. "What I have come to say is just as easily said standing."

"And what might that be, Jacqueline?" he asked. "I somehow doubt this is a social call."

"Do not think to play with me, Nicholas. You may have taken the first round, but you have by no means taken the match."

"Haven't I?" he said, folding his arms across his chest. "And how is that?"

"It is quite simple. You and your wife are in a very precarious position. You only made fools of yourself last night in your desperate ploy to attain respectability. Do you think anyone really will believe your absurd story about a nightmare?"

"No," he said. "I don't think anyone with an iota of intelligence will believe it. I am sure they will guess at the truth, as distasteful and unbelievable as it might seem. However, I am sure that with a little thought it will become obvious that I gave you a way out.''

"You are despicable," she said, her voice low. "Can you not forget a youthful indiscretion?''

Nicholas looked at her with disbelief. "A youthful indiscretion? Have you so quickly forgotten that your so-called 'youthful indiscretion' resulted in your accusation that I'd raped you? You attempted to destroy my life, Jacqueline. You would have very happily continued on that course had your sister not stepped forward. You also attempted to discredit my wife, your own niece, knowing full well who she was, and knowing she was ignorant of the fact.''

"You expected me to acknowledge a girl who grew up in a nasty little village? She is not fit to clean your boots, Nicholas. I don't know what she told you, but she was married to a pathetic drunken farmer. She doled out pig slops. She waded in manure. She hired out her services to any takers, you fool, in order to make enough money to survive.''

"And how do you know all of that, I wonder?'' Nicholas said slowly, wanting very much to put his hands around her neck and wring it. "One is not usually so well-versed in the background of one's modiste.''

"You really are a fool. Naturally I suspected Georgia's background. She's a true example of her disgraceful parents in looks and behavior. I discovered the name of her village from her previous employer and I went there to find out what I could. Go yourself. The vicar and his wife will confirm everything I have said. The girl is a slut, Nicholas. She inherited her mother's morals.''

"I see. You spoke with Mrs. Provost?''

Jacqueline hesitated. "You know of Mrs. Provost?'' she asked warily.

"Jacqueline, I know of everything. It might disappoint you terribly, but Georgia has been completely honest with me in all regards. I know all about Mrs. Provost's idiotic accusations. I know that she married Georgia off to Baggie Wells because her fool of a husband was chasing after a young innocent girl who had already been turned into a slave in their house. And I know that Georgia's life with Baggie was nothing but a nightmare. She most certainly did not hire out her 'services,' and I really ought to slit your throat for that insinuation."

"Oh?" Jacqueline said icily. "But did you know about Georgia trying to seduce poor Lord Herton, looking for favors from him? I cannot think she told you about that too."

Nicholas folded his arms across his chest. "Go on, Jacqueline. I am most interested."

"Ah, I see I have your attention now. It is quite true. I learned all about it from Lady Herton. And then when Georgia was sent away from London to Ravenswalk, she wasted no time, did she, Nicholas? She fooled you in a matter of days. I am sure she has convinced you she is a sweet innocent. The woman you have married, Nicholas, is a scheming fraud."

"Funny," Nicholas said, "that you should use such words. I wonder if you have examined yourself recently, for it seems that the motives you attribute to Georgia very closely resemble your own. It has been my observation that people very often have the tendency to throw off their own faults on those who threaten them the most. I suppose it is the only way they can justify their own actions and make themselves comfortable."

"And what is that supposed to mean?" Jacqueline asked with an air of boredom.

"It is not so complicated. Let me see if I can clarify for you: we are dealing here with greed, avariciousness, jealousy—certainly manipulation of circumstances to make matters appear very differently from what they are in fact."

"I do not understand you in the least," Jacqueline said.

"Do you not? Then I must add stupidity to the list. What a shame. I had thought that despite all of your other faults, at least you had inherited intelligence from the de Gives. You see, from my understanding, your sister Eugenie was a sweet, good person, not unlike her daughter. You have chosen to make them both out to be exactly like yourself. And if you think for one moment that you can malign Georgia in my eyes, you are very much mistaken. I know you and your techniques far too well, Jacqueline. Furthermore, I love my wife. No—that's not quite correct. I not only love my wife, I also respect her and I honor her, and I count myself damned fortunate to be married to her at all. That all came about without knowing anything about Georgia's early life. I could have cared less that she had been married to Baggie, or gathered manure, or whatever other absurd points you brought up. Georgia has more heart and more soul, not to mention true character in her smallest finger, than you will ever have in your entire body."

"You fool! How dare you compare me to that filthy, uneducated girl? You didn't know a thing about her, it is true, but you married her, didn't you, and only to spite me."

"I married Georgia, but not to spite you, Jacqueline. I married her because she struck a chord in me. Yes, at the time it might have been convenient, but I should never—but never—have taken a woman to be my wife if I hadn't felt a sense of kinship with her. Georgia and I, as you might have noticed, suit each other very well indeed, in every respect."

Jacqueline turned her back on him.

"Do you know, what amazes me is that it wasn't enough for you to destroy Eugenie, you had to go after her child as well. You had to see that she suffered, that she had a miserable life, even after knowing what a misery her life had already been. It is little wonder you were so damned upset when I married Georgia. I thought at the time that your reaction was a bit extreme for merely losing a servant. I knew that any woman I married would be met with extreme disapproval by you, and we both know why. But Georgia—that was a bit much, wasn't it, given the circumstances? You couldn't bear the fact that Georgia was welcome in my bed where you weren't and never will be. In a peculiar way, Eugenie won out over you after all, didn't she?"

She spun around. "That is enough! You make assumptions that are untenable! And now you think you can spread your gossip? I am telling you, no one will believe you!"

"No? It seems to me that virtually everyone believes us, if the number of visitors we had today is anything to go by. Not a one had anything but support to offer. I am sorry to have to point this out to you, but you are ruined, Jacqueline. You have ruined yourself with your lies, your insinuations, your hunger for revenge. It worked quite well for a number of years, but it is over.''

"It is not. It has only just begun. I will fight you. I will accuse you of things you haven't even dreamed of. And I will make them so convincing that there will be no hope for you. I came to make peace with you, to offer a truce, but I can see that there is nothing else than to take you down all the way. I will do it, Nicholas. Believe me, I will. I have influence in high places you have not even imagined.''

"Really?" Nicholas said mildly. "And what will happen when I tell the world what you have been doing to Cyril for the last two years?''

Jacqueline tensed. "What nonsense are you talking about now?'' she said, attempting to sound amused.

"I only wonder how all these influential people will feel when they hear that you have been seducing your young stepson. Cyril has been quite candid about the matter, Jacqueline.''

"You lie!'' she cried, her skin turning the color of chalk. "He would never say such a thing!''

"Because in doing so he would incriminate himself as well? But he has, Jacqueline. He has told me everything. He has told me how, and why, you first took him. He has told me how you used the Close for your sordid little encounters. He has told me all about it. And I don't think he would hesitate to tell the rest of the world if he had to, if that is what it would take to stop it from ever happening again.''

"And did your precious Cyril tell you why his father had an apoplectic stroke?'' she spat, seeing there was no use denying the truth. "When Cyril was telling you everything, did he bother to mention that his father went into his bedroom and found Cyril buried between my legs? Did he tell you how we laughed at the fool after he had staggered out the door? Can you picture it, Nicholas? Picture it, please do. It would give me such pleasure.''

Nicholas turned his back on her, feeling as if he had just been kicked in the gut. He could picture it far too well. And it explained far too much. "Dear God,'' he said, turning around again. "How evil you are. You are truly, truly evil. I think I understand now why you have been poisoning my uncle. Had he recovered, he would have seen you out of Ravenswalk so fast that you wouldn't have had time to draw breath. And naturally you wouldn't want him dead, for then Cyril would have thrown you out as soon as he realized you had no more control over him. A little pinch of monkshood every day was just perfect, wasn't it?"

She just stared at him.

"Oh, Jacqueline, there's no use in looking at me with such surprise. There are a number of things we know about your nasty activities. And one thing you don't know is that your dear husband is on the road to recovery. Your so-called medicinal tisanes have been stopped. Marguerite and Georgia have seen to that. Soon enough my uncle will be back to normal, and when he is, I do not think you will be welcome at Ravenswalk. I fear your dark reign is over, Jacqueline. There is only one course left to you."

"What is that?" she said shakily.

"Exile. Permanent exile, as you once wished on me. You seem fond of Italy. Will that do? Of course, you might need to go just a bit farther, once word spreads, which no doubt it will. However, I will make you one condition. If you leave England within twenty-four hours, then I will never speak a word against you beyond what I said last night. What Cyril might say, or your husband, or even what the *ton* might guess at, I cannot promise. I would imagine that neither Cyril nor your husband would ever want a word spoken. I know I would prefer not to have your disgraceful behavior come out. It is up to you, Jacqueline. Your call."

"I hate you, Nicholas Daventry!" she hissed. "I hate you! You have been nothing but a thorn in my side from the first!"

"I rather consider it the other way around. And remember that I never did a damned thing to provoke your unwelcome attention. Nor did Cyril. You have brought everything down on your own head. You slandered your own sister, Jacqueline, and you most probably murdered your first husband, poor devil, although sadly I'll never

367

have any proof of that. You poisoned your second husband, you've been sleeping with his son, never mind attempting to seduce me, and you've attempted to drag your own niece's name through the dirt. It's really not a very attractive picture. Twenty-four hours, Jacqueline. That should give you ample time to pack the things you need. Everything else I will see is sent after you. No doubt you have been siphoning money off my uncle for some time, but I am nevertheless prepared to offer you an income of five thousand pounds a year—provided you never set foot back in England. And you will sign this letter I have drawn up, relinquishing all claim to the Raven estates.'' Nicholas pulled a letter from his pocket and held it out to her.

Jacqueline snatched it out of his hand and quickly ran her eyes over it, her fingers shaking. ''Do you think I am a fool?'' she said with disgust. ''This document says this money comes from your own pocket. You have no money, everyone knows it.''

''You are quite wrong. But if you doubt me, do turn down my offer. You will receive no other offer from my family, of that I can assure you.''

''But how can I be sure that I will continue to receive this money? Suppose you should die before me?''

''My God, you are cold-blooded and calculating, aren't you? In fact, there is a provision in there. Read the last paragraph more carefully. It guarantees the income to you for life, regardless.''

Jacqueline snatched up a pen from the escritoire and signed it, blotting her signature. She threw the document down on the desk. ''There. Have it your own way. I find I no longer care. I have never liked the English climate anyway.''

''Then allow me to bid you farewell, Jacqueline. And take note. That document you have just signed also provides for the immediate cessation of monies should you ever again set foot upon British shores. The other condition, you'll have noticed, is that it never reach my ears that you have continued to slander any member of my family, or yours, in any fashion.''

She inclined her head in agreement.

''Good. As for your sudden departure, it occurs to me

that your health might be frail and you need a fortifying climate.''

"I can come up with my own reasons,'' Jacqueline snapped. "And I must say, I will be happy never to lay eyes on any of you Daventrys ever again. You are a pitiful lot. Not a one of you has any spine.''

She went to the door, and as she was turning the handle she paused and looked over her shoulder. "I will send you my forwarding address. Good riddance, Nicholas.''

"Good riddance, Jacqueline,'' he replied affably enough, but when the door had shut, he sank into a chair and buried his head in his hands.

Nicholas was very quiet that night and Georgia understood and did not press him. He had explained what had happened as briefly as possible. She knew he would elaborate if and when he chose to. If there was one thing she knew about Nicholas, it was that things ran very deeply with him. He bore his pain in his own way. She also trusted in his ability to deal with that pain, for he had already come through the fire and survived. Jacqueline was nothing next to that. Now that he had successfully banished her, she could never harm him again, but it was typical of him that he did not choose to gloat over that fact. Instead, Georgia suspected that he was experiencing a great deal of turmoil.

He was not the only one. Cyril had come in from his ride with Pascal, and Nicholas had called him directly into his study. They had been closeted away for some time, and then Cyril had emerged white-faced and gone upstairs to his bedroom. He had not been down since. Nicholas had not mentioned what they had discussed, but it was no doubt contributing to his silence. Georgia pushed the veal about on her plate, her appetite having fled. Jacqueline might have been banished, but her influence still touched them all. To see the unhappiness that pervaded the house on this night made her sad, for it was all because of one twisted woman.

Pascal came into the sitting room later that evening in his nightshirt.

"Monsieur,'' he said quietly, "I am concerned for

369

Cyril. I knocked on his door to say good night and he did not answer, but I heard him crying.''

''Yes, I know, Pascal. He has some difficult things he needs to work out. He needs to be alone just now. Tomorrow I hope he will be better.''

''It is his *belle-mère* who makes him cry, monsieur?''

''Indirectly, Pascal. But it is Cyril's business, no one else's. Sometimes people need to work out their pain in solitude. There are some burdens that cannot be shared and certain things for which one can answer only to God.''

''You are very wise, monsieur.''

''I only wish that were true, Pascal,'' Nicholas said wearily.

''But it is true, monsieur. I know that you see this great sadness inside of Cyril and you have tried your best to help him, but as you say, now it is between Cyril and God. I will say good night then, monsieur, and pray that God gives Cyril the answers he needs. And I will say a prayer for you, too, that God helps you with your own sadness.''

He picked up Nicholas' hand and pressed it to his mouth, then went out again.

Georgia rose to go tuck Pascal into bed. She saw the tears glistening in Nicholas' eyes, but she chose to say nothing, instead saying her own little prayer of thanks to God for having sent them Pascal.

When Nicholas finally came to bed that night Georgia was still awake, but she said nothing, not knowing whether Nicholas still needed his own solitude. And then his arms came around her.

''Georgia?''

''Yes?'' she answered, turning toward him. ''I'm here.''

''Sweetheart, I'm sorry,'' he said, stroking her arms. ''I know you must have been wondering and most probably worrying about what passed between Cyril and me.''

''You needn't tell me a thing, Nicholas. I understand. Whatever it is, if you want to speak of it, then I will listen. But you need never speak of it at all, not if it is private between you and Cyril.''

''Thank you for that. I wish I could tell you, for I can't

quite seem to come to terms with this . . .'' His voice caught, and he pulled her tightly against him.

Georgia wrapped her arms around him and held him close, feeling his distress. ''It will work out, Nicholas,'' she whispered. ''One way or another it will work out.''

After a few moments of silence he pulled slightly away from her. ''I wonder if it can,'' he said miserably. ''It's all rather dreadful for Cyril, worse than we'd ever imagined. I really don't know how he is going to find a way through. I cannot heal him, nor absolve him. It is not my place to do so. And I can see that he cannot give himself absolution, nor will he seek it elsewhere. The one person who might be able to help him is the person he fears the most.''

''Surely not Jacqueline?'' she said with dismay.

''No. Certainly not Jacqueline.''

''Oh . . .'' Georgia said with a sigh. ''I see.''

''Knowing you, you probably do see. God, I don't know what I can do for him, Georgia. And we thought we had trolls. The boy is so damned wounded that it hurts just thinking about it.''

''I know, Nicholas. I know. But perhaps time will help. Look at yourself—you came through the worst of battles and survived.''

''I also had you,'' he said simply. ''And Cyril's battle is with his conscience, a far more exacting beast than the one I was fighting. I think Cyril's salvation lies with God now. We can only pray that God is merciful.''

''He works in mysterious ways, Nicholas. Let us trust in that.''

''As you say, Georgia. As you say.'' He gathered her to him again, but he held her that night as if it were his own soul that needed safe harbor.

Cyril finally emerged from his room late the following day, and Nicholas looked up from his desk to see him standing in the doorway. ''Cyril,'' he said gently, putting down his pen. ''I am pleased to see you.'' He was indeed very pleased, for their conversation yesterday had been fairly brutal, and he had been worried for the boy.

''I have c-come to offer you an apology, N-Nicholas,'' he said. He sounded very tired.

"An apology? For what?"

"For the things I s-said to you yesterday. I was w-wrong to l-lash out at you. Y-you have d-done s-so many things for m-me, and I have shown you n-nothing b-but ingratitude. You have n-not once c-condemned me when you should have."

"Cyril, it is not my place to condemn you. I have done many foolish things in my time. As I told you yesterday, what is important is to have the full truth between us."

"You know it all n-now."

"That's good, for I shouldn't like to discover you have misled me. And although I imagine it will be very difficult for you, you must be completely honest with your father as well. I very much doubt that he will condemn you either. He has also been Jacqueline's victim."

"Even if you are c-correct, Nicholas, it d-doesn't excuse m-me, any of the things I d-did. I was r-responsible for his illness. And G-God help me, I didn't want him b-better."

"Cyril. Listen to me. Your conscience is your own, and you are the only person who can make an accounting of it. But do not be harder on yourself than you need be. You hold yourself in far harsher judgment than I do, that I promise you. I think it is time for you to make a new start, a clean beginning. Jacqueline is gone. We must all put her behind us."

"How, N-Nicholas? How c-can we put her behind us when she has r-ravaged our l-lives? How c-can we ever forget?"

"We may not ever forget, but we can pick ourselves up and go on. She will never return, Cyril. She would not dare."

"Jacqueline would d-dare anything if she thought it would g-get her something she wanted."

"Perhaps. I have good reason to doubt her mental stability. But in this case she knows that she has been defeated. She would not risk what little reputation she has left to salvage. So. Let us not dwell on all the misery she has caused. I think we need something to distract us. Why do you and I not go out together after dinner? We might as well enjoy London while we are here, for it will soon be time to go home. I've heard how much you enjoy billiards, and Pascal tells me you have some admirable shots. I am sure you will be able to teach me something, for although I've read White's book cover to cover, I am no hand.''

"Yes, all right, N-Nicholas," Cyril said with an attempt at a smile, but it did not reach his eyes. "After d-dinner."

He left, and Nicholas went back to his work, but he still felt troubled. He was not at all sure that the wounds Jacqueline had inflicted on Cyril would ever truly heal.

Jacqueline paced the floor of her study, the last of her papers packed away. Evening had drawn down and it was time to leave. She could not understand how everything had changed so quickly, not when she'd so carefully built her position over the years, not when she had worked so hard to regain her birthright and more. No one understood how important that had been to her—no one had understood her humiliation at living above a shop, forced to work. She had not forgotten the Château Tourlaville, not for one day, nor how fine life had been there, how she had been looked up to, respected.

And now Nicholas thought to take away not only her reputation but also Ravenswalk, and it was like a knife in her heart.

She slumped down at her desk and picked up the dagger with the pretty ivory handle that she used as a letter opener and regarded it for a long moment. Then she pressed it down on the blotter and cut a long, deep line, imagining it to be Nicholas' throat. He had stood there so smugly, challenging her, backing her into a corner from which she could see no escape.

The night of the ball had been a bad-enough shock when Georgia's identity had been disclosed: she had never thought it would ever come out about Eugenie's brat, but it had, and there was nothing to be done about it. Eugenie the pious, Charles the self-righteous—they had managed to pass it all on to their daughter. She even looked like him—that had been the biggest shock of all, the thing that had set the bells off in her head the day she had first seen Georgia in Madame LaSalle's dress shop. The eyes were unmistakable, that shade of cornflower his and his alone. And the fair hair, the color of spun gold. . . .

She winced, for the memory of Charles never failed to scald her in the deepest recesses of her soul. Charles—how he had laughed at her when she had made her earnest confession of love to him. But she had made him pay for that, hadn't she, and Eugenie too? Oh, yes, they had both paid, and paid dearly. Eugenie had probably spent the rest of her life regretting the harsh, unkind words she had spoken to her own sister. It served them both right. And if it hadn't been for their daughter marrying Nicholas, everything would have been perfect. What fluke had led them to make the connection to Eugenie? She supposed she would never know.

But if the truth about the girl wasn't bad enough, then there was Cyril's little revelation to deal with, for she knew that would never be acceptable.

"Oh, Cyril, you idiot," she muttered. His defiance had been a terrible shock, for she'd had him completely under her control. She still could not quite believe that the fool had told Nicholas about their sexual liaison—told Nicholas, of all people, the cousin he so hated. But Cyril was just one more person who had betrayed her. Why should she be surprised? People had been betraying her all of her life.

And Nicholas Daventry was the worst of the lot.

"Damn him!" she cried, throwing the dagger onto the ground. Its point caught in the Oriental carpet and stuck, the handle quivering. She looked at it for a long time, her brain working hard over her next course of action. She could think of no way out of her predicament. Nicholas had her trapped. And even if there were a way around Nicholas, now there was William to worry about. She thought she'd had that situation taken care of, but if he recovered, he would most likely threaten divorce. It would be better to take Nicholas' five thousand per year, not that she didn't have a nice fat sum she'd salted away just as Nicholas had guessed. Better to leave the country with it now, before anything else could happen.

What did she care? She was still Lady Raven, after all. She would go back to Italy, where she would be fêted and admired, where they would laugh off whatever stories

374

might come out of England. William would die soon enough, for surely the monkshood had permanently weakened his system? She could remarry, and perhaps another fortune would be hers.

And yet she did care. She cared terribly. She did not take kindly to humiliation, nor to being snubbed. She certainly did not like being bested by Nicholas Daventry, the arrogant bastard. He would pay for ruining her life. She would see to it that he paid, and his whore too.

But how? What could she do to them that would destroy their pathetic happiness?

Her eyes went back to the carpet and she smiled, a small, tight smile of satisfaction as she saw her answer.

Oh, yes, she would leave the country. But not before one last meeting. One last, very final meeting. She would have her revenge after all, and then they'd all be sorry for ever having crossed her.

She pulled the dagger out of the carpet and tucked it into her reticule. And then she went downstairs, calling for her cloak, and went out to the waiting carriage.

Nicholas ruffled Pascal's hair, kissed Georgia, and took his hat and cane from Binkley. "We'll walk, as the evening is so fine," he said. "Do not wait up, any of you. And that includes you, Binkley. Cyril and I are going to have a night on the town and will no doubt not return till dawn."

Cyril gave Pascal a pat on the shoulder. "G-good night, little m-monkey."

"Good night, Cyril," Pascal said, grinning up at him. "Do not take too much money off the good monsieur, or we shall be back to the bread and water."

"I shall be f-fair," Cyril said, waving away Binkley's offer of a coat. "C-come, N-Nicholas. You c-can kiss Georgia some other t-time. You've already k-kissed her t-twice already."

Cyril went out the door and waited at the top of the steps for Nicholas. He found he was impatient for the evening to begin, mostly because he was eager to show Nicholas his skill. And he very much wanted a distraction. He was thoroughly sick of himself and the thoughts that plagued him.

Nicholas came out to join him a moment later. "Look," Cyril said, pointing at the window, where Pascal's nose was pressed to the pane. "He is j-just like Raleigh when you l-leave."

"He is certainly as unswerving in his loyalty," Nicholas said, waving a finger at Pascal. "By the by, how did the riding lesson go yesterday afternoon? Has there been any improvement?" He started down the steps.

"Pascal is having a l-little trouble with d-discipline," Cyril said, following him. "He d-does not want to hurt the horse, and the horse is t-taking advantage of the f-fact."

Nicholas chuckled. "I can imagine. Maybe I should take the beast out myself and let him know who is master."

"I d-do not know if it would d-do any g-good. It is Pascal who m-must harden his heart. He does not like to k-kick or use the c-crop." As he spoke, Cyril vaguely noticed a woman who was moving toward them, her hooded cloak obscuring her face. But an ominous prickle moved down his spine. He suddenly stopped, his blood going cold as ice. She was nearly on them, and he knew without doubt that it was Jacqueline.

He saw her hands shift beneath her cloak and then a sudden flash of blue steel, and he knew what she intended.

"No!" he cried, and with all of his strength he shoved Nicholas to one side. He threw himself on Jacqueline as the blade came stabbing up with the swiftness of a striking snake, plunging past hard bone into soft flesh. Cyril clutched at his chest, feeling only a strange chill.

"Not you, you little fool!" she gasped, staggering back against his weight. "It wasn't meant for you!"

"And yet I welcome it," he said, choking on the blood that suddenly bubbled up into his throat. He took her by the shoulders. "And you will n-never . . . hurt . . . again."

With a last, almost superhuman show of strength, he pushed her away from him, flinging her across the sidewalk directly into the path of a passing carriage. The horses panicked and reared, their hooves coming down

376

on top of her, and he watched with satisfaction as she was trampled under them, her screams abruptly stopping.

"Jesus Christ!" he heard Nicholas shout. "Cyril!"

Cyril turned toward him, his hands going to the knife embedded in his chest. He met Nicholas' horrified eyes, then sank to his knees, suddenly unable to stand.

Cyril only just felt his cousin's arms come around him. He knew Nicholas was saying something to him, but he didn't really hear, nor did he feel any pain when Nicholas pulled the knife out. He knew only that he was very, very cold. And yet he felt as if an enormous burden had been taken from him. He closed his eyes as Nicholas lifted him, and he rested his head against Nicholas' shoulder. He was very nearly home at last.

"Madame!" Pascal cried. "Madame, something very terrible has happened! Come quickly!"

Georgia dropped the book she had selected for Pascal and came running out of the library. "What? What is it, Pascal?" she asked, alarmed by his white, distressed face.

She looked out the window to see a crowd gathered in the street, surrounding a woman's body. She quickly opened the door, prepared to go out to help. And then she gave a little cry as she saw Nicholas running toward her, Cyril's limp body in his arms.

"Nicholas . . . Oh, my God, what happened?"

"Jacqueline," he said, coming up the steps and moving past her. "She stabbed him." His voice was painfully tight.

"Cyril . . . oh, my poor Cyril," Pascal whispered. "Can you help him, madame?"

"Take him to the drawing room, Nicholas," she said. "Quickly, Pascal. Fetch Binkley. We need linens and water. And then fetch my medicine bag."

Pascal said not a word. He flew off, and Georgia ran after Nicholas. He gently placed Cyril on the sofa, stroking his brow.

"Is it Jacqueline in the street?" Georgia asked, ripping away Cyril's blood-soaked jacket and shirt, and she drew in a sharp breath as she saw where the knife had penetrated.

"She is dead," Nicholas said, looking down at Cyril anxiously. "I don't know how he did it with a knife in his chest, but he threw her in front of that carriage. Jesus, Georgia, he took that damned knife for me." He pushed a shaking hand through his hair. "Can you do anything for him?"

Georgia just shook her head.

Binkley hurried in and placed a bowl of water and a pile of linens on the table next to her. "Is there anything else you need, madam?"

She shook her head again as she made a pad, pressing it against Cyril's ribs, trying to see through the hot tears that clouded her eyes, for she knew her efforts were in vain. Cyril had very little time left.

"Madame?' Pascal said, coming in with her bag and looking down at Cyril's ashen face. "Is it very bad?"

"Shall I remove the child, madam?" Binkley asked.

"No, Binkley. I think Pascal needs to be here now." She looked up at Nicholas, and he nodded, the pain in his eyes acute, and she knew he understood.

"Cyril?" she said, touching his cold face. "Cyril, can you hear me? Pascal and Nicholas and Binkley, they are all here."

His eyes fluttered, then opened. "Nicholas," he whispered through dry lips.

"I am here," Nicholas said hoarsely, leaning over him and taking his limp hand. "Cyril, I'm so sorry. I wish to God I had seen her in time. I would never have let this happen to you. Never. I promised to keep you safe from her."

"And you did," he said, licking his lips with the tip of his tongue. "You did not throw me in front of her knife, Nicholas. I did it myself. Please, do not be sorry. You have always done your very best for me. And I do love you, even if I have not shown it very well."

"What you did tonight more than showed it," Nicholas said, his voice choked.

"It was justice," Cyril said faintly. "It was right. Now I can finally rest."

Pascal fell to his knees and touched Cyril's face. "Are you going to die now, Cyril?" he asked, tears streaming down his cheeks.

"I believe I am, little monkey," Cyril said, his blue lips turning up slightly at the corners. "But do not be too sad for me. I am happy."

"I understand," Pascal said, his voice catching on a sob. "You go to be with the angels now, where there is peace for you. This is what you and God decided on, perhaps?"

"Yes," he said with a shallow sigh. "I think it must be. Be happy, little monkey. Take good care of Nicholas and Georgia."

"I will, Cyril," Pascal said, wiping at his eyes.

"Nichol . . ." Cyril moved his head slightly.

Nicholas bent down to him, straining to hear. "What is it, coz?"

"Please," he said, his words now barely audible. "Tell my father that I loved him, and I am sorry. And tell him that I went in peace. It was for the best."

Nicholas squeezed his hand. "I will tell him all that."

Finally Cyril looked up at Georgia. "You taught me so much. Thank you. Will you send me now as you sent the sailor?"

Georgia sank down next to him, her heart breaking, hot tears blinding her eyes. She smoothed his brow, then kissed his forehead. "Go now, Cyril, and know that everything is finally all right. Go with God. Go with God and be happy."

"Thank you," he murmured. And then he sighed deeply and was still.

Epilogue

Pascal picked up the kicking, giggling little boy in his arms and tossed him over his shoulder. "You are a monstrous handful, Charlie," he said, running with him down the length of the garden, only causing the toddler to laugh more furiously and beat his small fists against Pascal's back. Charlie was a happy, uncomplicated child and they all adored him, including old Ewan Cameron, who had come down from the Highlands especially for the christening of his great-grandson and hadn't gone away again for three full months.

"If you would not mind," Binkley said with dignity, sidestepping as Pascal came barreling straight toward him, "I should like to deliver this tray unscathed."

"A million pardons, Monsieur Binkley." Pascal placed the child on the ground and grabbed his hand to keep him in place. "He was eating the roses, you see."

"Far better he should eat the gingersnaps," Binkley agreed, continuing on his regal progression. "Good afternoon, your lordship." He placed the tray down in front of Georgia. "Madam. Shall I pour?"

Georgia smiled, watching as young Charlie amused himself by climbing onto his adoring great-uncle's knee. "Please, Binkley," she said. "Pour away. Don't be shy, Uncle William. I can see you eyeing the gingersnaps. Help yourself and Charlie, too, for I can see he is wanting them every bit as much as you are."

"Thank you, my dear," Lord Raven said. "I believe we will help ourselves. Lily makes gingersnaps unequalled by none. Pascal? You cannot possibly be so self-contained."

"I am trying very hard to learn discipline, Lord Raven. Monsieur tells me it the secret to success."

Lord Raven nodded and moved his hands on Charlie's back. "I imagine he is correct."

"Monsieur is nearly always correct," Pascal said firmly, and Georgia shook her head with amusement. Pascal had not lost one shred of his adoration for Nicholas, but then, why should he? She only loved Nicholas more herself as every day went by.

Her hand went to her belly as she felt a vigorous kick. Nicholas would soon enough have another child to adore him, which was as it should be, for he made a wonderful father. Charlie's birth had gone a long way toward easing the pain that Cyril's death had caused, and she knew that this new child would only add to his happiness. She could not help but glance over at the tree they had planted two autumns before in Cyril's memory. It was a fine little maple, strong and fast-growing, and it did its job, keeping Cyril constantly in their thoughts. There were times when she felt he was still with them, or at least watching over them from what she was sure was a very fine position in heaven. It would have made him happy to know that they remembered him with love. It would also have made him happy to know that his father did not in any way hold him to blame for what had happened with Jacqueline. But Georgia couldn't help but wonder if Cyril had not been right: his death had been his only hope for peace.

Nicholas came out of the house to join them, his dark hair shifting in the spring breeze, Raleigh at his heel. Charlie wiggled off Lord Raven's knee with a shriek of delight and ran to embrace his father's leg.

"Hello, Uncle William," Nicholas said cheerfully. "You're becoming quite a regular for tea. Sorry I'm a bit late—business called. Thank you, Binkley." He balanced the cup Binkley had given him in one hand and ruffled Charlie's hair with the other.

"I cannot resist coming to sit in the garden, Nicholas. No doubt when you are an old man living at Ravenswalk you will find yourself making your way over to the Close to sit out here and amuse yourself with your grandchildren."

"I hope so," Nicholas said, putting his tea cup down and glancing up at the house, now fully restored to its former beauty. "It's the sort of place that needs to be filled with happiness."

"You have certainly succeeded in that," Lord Raven said. "I would never have thought that it could have been so again after so much time."

Nicholas rested his hand on Georgia's shoulder and she looked up at him. His face had gone dreamy with memory, and she knew just what he was thinking. She too remembered well how it had been. She remembered Nicholas the first time she had ever seen him, his eyes wet with tears of anguish over what had become of his beloved house. She remembered their wedding night in a cold, wet ruin, empty save for a few pieces of furniture. She remembered how bewildered she had felt to be married once again to a man who was a virtual stranger, and yet how Nicholas had made such an effort to make her feel comfortable, had told her stories and tried to fill the empty rooms with memories of a happier time.

Her gaze shifted to the statue of the young boy, a host of bright spring blossoms pushing around the base. A shaft of filtered sunlight touched gently upon the crimson bowl of a single peony, its petals slightly unfurled as if to stretch up to the benevolent warmth. The profile of the child was caught in the same beam, and he seemed to her almost to be smiling. He was no longer lost or alone, a stone child forgotten in a deserted garden. He was where he belonged, surrounded by love and laughter, part of a family . . . just like Nicholas. He too was finally back where he belonged and he was at peace.

She would never forget the night that everything had irrevocably changed, when Nicholas had been driven beyond his own ability to cope with his pain, nor his long and difficult battle homeward. She looked at him now, knowing him so well, his faults as well as his strengths. He was a man who had survived a descent into hell and returned, not unscathed, but whole. Whatever private battle Nicholas had fought, he was stronger for it, freed to live his life without fear of a nameless terror always at his back. In that private battle Nicholas had not only gained his freedom, he had also finally learned how to say goodbye.

Georgia's breath caught in her throat as she was overwhelmed by a sudden rush of love for the man standing beside her. It wasn't just his physical presence; Nicholas never failed to stir her with that, and she knew exactly how lucky she was to love him and to be loved by him. It was more a sense of incredible good fortune that they had stumbled upon one another, almost as if God had taken one deep, relenting breath and blown her toward Raven's Close and Nicholas as easily as if she had been a dandelion puff tossed in the wind.

God had truly smiled on her and she knew she was blessed.

Nicholas echoed her thoughts exactly. "Ah, well, uncle," he said, "all it really took to bring it back was a little magic and a push from God in the right direction. And here we are. Look around you. Was there ever a garden so fine?"

He dropped a kiss on her brow, scooped Charlie up into his arms, and went off with Pascal to investigate the apple blossoms.

About the Author

Katherine Kingsley was born in New York City and grew up there and in England. She is married to an Englishman and they live in the Colorado Mountains with their son.